LEAVE IT ALL BEHIND

MM PARANORMAL ROMANCE

N. A. MOORE

Copyright © 2023 by N. A. Moore

All rights reserved.

No part of this book may be reproduced in any form or by any electronic or mechanical means, including information storage and retrieval systems, without written permission from the author, except for the use of brief quotations in a book review.

This is a work of fiction. Names, characters, places, events, and incidents are products of the author's imagination. Any resemblance to actual persons, living or dead, or actual events is purely coincidental.

Cover design by The Awkward Bean LLC

www.theawkwardbean.com

ISBN: 9798844023859

ASIN: B0C9V9GP6K

LEAVE IT ALL BEHIND

N. A. MOORE

HEY THERE, READER!

So, you're about to dive into this novel, and I'm *genuinely* excited for you. But, heads up, it's not always a smooth ride. This story gets real and raw. We're talking scenes with gore, some heavy violence, a brief touch on child abuse, and slavery.

If any of that makes you go "nope", or brings up tough memories, please take care of yourself and consider if this is the right read for you. No judgment either way! Remember, books are about our individual journeys, and it's super important to make sure yours feels right.

The chapter *It's Okay to Let Go* ends with a scene some may find upsetting. I don't consider it suicide based on the circumstances, and there is nothing violent or graphic in this scene, but I understand that others may have a different perspective.

Here's to all the feels, twists, and turns you're about to experience. Enjoy!

Catch you on the flip side,
    N. A. Moore

BOOKS BY N. A. MOORE:

**Chronicles of Astoria
(MM+ Dark Fantasy Romance)**
The Consorts
The Black Curse (Coming 2024)

(MM Vampire Romance)
Leave it all Behind
Beauty and the Beast (Coming Soon)

(MM Non-Shifter Omegaverse)
Heat
Rut (Coming Soon)

(MM Psychological Suspense)
Sick & Twisted

For all the vampire lovers...just in time for spooky season.

PROLOGUE

Some say she's a goddess and I don't see how they could be wrong.

The moon seemed to glide over her dark skin with the intimacy reserved just for lovers. A part of me was jealous.

Fucking jealous of the moon.

A laugh bubbled out of me, breaking the silence.

Lilith turned, red eyes bright with mirth. Even after all these centuries, my stomach still twisted in knots at the sight of her. The urge to crawl to her, *please* her, vibrated through every fiber of my being.

"It won't always be like this," she declared, voice light despite the edge of warning.

I frowned and joined her on the balcony, leaning against the railing while we gazed at the night sky.

"Meaning?" Being cryptic was her favorite pastime. Who knew if I'd get an answer, much less a clear one?

"You and I," she hummed. She held out her wrist and with one pointed nail, cut deep into her skin until it blossomed with the dark red blood that had given life to so many. The scent was rich and potent, evoking both the familiarity of home and the adventure of places yet explored in one oxymoronic aroma.

Transfixed, I watched as the precious blood spilled out of her wound and dripped down her arm, until a single drop fell into the pool of water below.

It disappeared into the blackness, a small ripple of disturbance, invisible even to me as it inevitably bloomed and dispersed.

"Sterling," she called.

My head darted back up to her, feeling uneasy, but also... excited, like something big was coming.

Something transformative.

"He's waiting for you."

"Who?"

She simply smiled in that unnerving way she does. Just as I opened my mouth to pester her with more questions, my phone buzzed.

Stasia's name flashed on the screen as I pulled it out of my pocket. A resigned sigh left my lips as I begrudgingly answered.

"What?" I growled.

"Another ring, New Orleans." *Click.*

Before I could hiss a curse, my phone buzzed again. They had sent the location. I groaned and put the phone back in my pocket before fixing my attention back on Lilith.

Except, she was gone.

STAGE ONE

1

MY NAME IS BEAU

Rising from a deep and wistful sleep, with a thick, cloying haze begging for me to close my eyes once more, was disorientating enough. To wake unaware of my surroundings with no knowledge of how I had gotten there and no clothes on my body made the experience infinitely worse.

And yet, *panic* wasn't my first reaction.

As my vision began to focus and fatigue loosened its grip, I took in my surroundings. The room was dark, but I had no trouble making out the surrounding shapes, like the large sultan bed covered in deep red satin that I laid in on a platform overlooking the lavish decor. A little ostentatious, if I was honest, but hey, who was I to judge?

I sat up to get a better view.

Across from the bed were towering bookshelves that reached from floor to ceiling, stuffed to the brim with old leather-bound books, practically falling off the shelves. Every librarian's dream.

Hmm, so we had ourselves a reader...They could be completely harmless, or they could be utterly unhinged and know exactly how to kill me and where to hide the body.

The structures sat on either side of an unlit fireplace with red velvet chaises and couches before it. Velvet. Actual velvet.

As if it couldn't get anymore pretentious, to the left were thick velvet curtains trimmed in gold that partially blocked what looked like an office space, though that wording didn't quite seem to fit the time period of the decor.

To the right was an ornately carved armoire, chest, and vanity with expensive looking colognes and powders. Something right out of a historical film, honest to God.

Where was *I*?

I tried to think back, desperate for any clues as to how I got here, but drew a blank. It was like trying to grasp at clouds, nothing was tangible. Ice traveled through my veins as the reality of my predicament hit home.

Did I get kidnapped? Or...was this *my* home?

Surely I would remember if it was, right? Was I the pretentious asshole with a museum for a bedroom?

I shivered, tugging the sheets closer to my chest. A slight throbbing in my head made me wonder if I had been struck. I felt around for any wounds and froze when I came across the thick, neatly wrapped bandage around my left wrist.

There was no pain, but the edges of the white bandage were crisp and fresh, which meant it hadn't been that long since it was wrapped. There was even a faint darkness seeping through, which probably meant I was still bleeding.

I couldn't remember getting injured or being treated for it. Yet something tugged at the back of my mind. There was something about this wound that seemed...familiar.

The more I tried to remember, the further it disappeared into the recesses of my subconscious and the throbbing in my temples intensified.

Damn it!

I couldn't just *sit* there and wait for someone to come. I

needed answers. Well...what I really needed was clothes and *then* answers.

Pulling the sheets back, I swung my legs over the edge of the bed until my bare soles hit the cool planks of the dark wood floor. I shivered again, feeling my nipples harden and skin tingle, oddly sensitive.

I ignored the sensation and padded over to the armoire, trying not to get distracted by the incredibly detailed gilded frame. Was that *real* gold?

Focus.

I pulled open the heavy doors and noticed it was filled with expensive looking tops. They were all large, meaning the owner had a massive frame, confirming it *definitely* wasn't my room.

Part of me was relieved, for the simple fact that I did not have such a garish taste in decor.

I picked a gray cotton button down that smelled heavily of citrus and clove, rolling the sleeves a couple times, so my hands weren't drowning in fabric. I didn't bother looking for pants because if the size of the shirts were any indication, I would never even *dream* of fitting them. I *did*, however, find a pair of boots by the vanity, but after trying them on, they proved to be more of a hindrance to shuffle around in, so I put them back.

Now, there were three doors that could possibly lead me to answers...or danger. My gut felt oddly settled though, so I didn't think it was the latter. Even so, it's always better to be safe than sorry.

I couldn't find much in terms of weapons, but was able to snag a small letter opener from the desk. It could do a little damage at least, if used right anyway.

With my weapon at the ready, I opened the first door. My nose was assaulted with that intoxicating scent of citrus and clove again.

Inhaling deeply, I let the smell consume my senses. I

couldn't tell if it was a cologne or a natural musk, but it was... *divine*. I couldn't get enough of it. Made sense when the door revealed a walk-in closet full of more clothes fit for a giant.

Slowly, I shut the door and moved on to the next one which happened to be a luxurious en suite.

The last door led to a dark hall.

Bingo.

A few candles sat in wall sconces, enveloping the space with a gentle light, though it seemed more for decoration than illumination. There were no doors lining the hall except for the one at the very end. Carefully, afraid someone would magically appear and attack, I made my way down the hall. There was light seeping from underneath the door. Pressing my ear against the wood, I strained to hear any activity on the other side.

There were some soft noises, possibly voices, but I couldn't be sure. I could deduce that it was likely there were people beyond the door. I had nowhere else to go which made it clear I had no choice but to move forward.

My heart hammered in my chest. This was either a really dumb move or a smart one. Even worse, it was my *only* one. Sitting in that room, waiting to be found was *not* an option.

Taking a deep, shuddering breath, I pushed the door open—happy that it was unlocked—and peeked around. The room was vast and dimly lit. Octagonal in shape, the space was framed by thick wooden pillars. To the left were some couches occupied with a few people. To the right were even more. In the center sat what looked like a throne atop a pedestal.

I crept forward, surprised that no one stopped me. No one even seemed to notice my presence at all. It only took me a second to realize why.

To my left, there were four men. Two sat on one couch, side by side. They each had another man straddling their laps. One had hair of spun gold waving to his shoulders while the other's was a rich bronze. Their hips undulated in sync, each ebb and flow perfectly timed.

Transfixed, I stood frozen, eyes never leaving their writhing forms flushed with ecstasy. There was a grace in their movements, every push and pull of their bodies a part of some fluid dance that made my heart race and breath quicken.

I should have looked away. I *wanted* to, but every fiber of my being refused to follow my will, intoxicated by my inane desire.

The one with golden waves tossed his head back, spine arching into a perfect bow, drawn tight by the lover who impaled him so passionately.

Like a plucked string, the man's body jerked and mine along with it, tasting the orgasm that had claimed the couple. It was only then, breathless and wanting, that I found the strength to look away, stumbling forward.

Still, no one noticed me, or even spared me a glance. I wasn't sure if I should have been grateful or not.

There were people everywhere, yet it wasn't a crowd. Talking, laughing, kissing, fucking. They stood, they lounged. To the left. To the right.

I tried to take them all in, but their faces seemed to blur like light trails on a highway, amplified by some drug-induced high. There were halls in the octagonal room and so many doors, but it was too chaotic to see where they might lead. The lights were dim, only cast by the few candles posted along the walls and tall pillars. The decor matched the room I had awoken in, full of deep rich colors, lavish gilding, expensive fabrics, and dripping grandiosity.

My world tilted as I stumbled forward, feeling a dull tug in my chest. Breathless and unsettled, I came across the raised platform where the golden pedestal sat. And on top of the pedestal was a loveseat, if one could really call it that, it more resembled a throne. It was covered in deep purple pillows with a high back, golden foliage chiseled into the edges, and gold clawed feet. The piece was stunning, but not as much as the couple upon it.

After what I had previously witnessed, I should not have been surprised by yet another couple openly engaging in lewd behavior, yet it still startled me.

A woman sat on the throne, a wicked grin splitting her full blood red painted lips. The smooth brown skin of her throat was bare for all to gaze upon as she leaned back into the lush pillows behind her. She wore a thin slip of dress hiked up around her waist. One long lean leg was resting comfortably on the broad shoulder of the man on his knees before her, head buried between her thighs. His face was completely obscured as he worked to pleasure her. The only thing visible was his light gray hair.

I didn't remember moving, but as if tugged by a leash getting shorter and shorter, I drew near them, filled with awe and longing.

The woman opened her eyes, revealing glowing red irises. Her gaze landed on me, smile widening. Something about it was unnerving. It urged me to be afraid, but I was not.

Why wasn't I afraid? My sense of self preservation was nowhere to be found. Instead, I grew eager...*needy*.

"Ah, he's finally awake," the woman mused. Her voice was deep and smooth and nothing like I imagined it would be. It did not match her somewhat dainty features. Instead, it curled around me, clouding my mind, increasing my desire.

The gray-haired man pulled back, sensuous lips glistening with fluids as he turned to look at me.

A pulse jolted through my body as the man's bright green eyes met mine. Overcome by the sensation, I fell to my knees, hardly registering the pain. Not when my attention was wholly consumed by him.

"Sterling, bring your fledgling to me," the woman

commanded, forcing a shudder down my spine. The man gazed at me intently before uttering one word.

"*Come.*"

Fuck, I should have been embarrassed, but I couldn't muster the strength. I crawled to them.

Actually *crawled*.

My limbs were shaky and eager, the need to please the ones before me enveloped my entire being. Heart pumping, body shaking, eyes watering, I couldn't fight *any* of it.

When I finally reached the lower ledge of the golden platform, I cautiously raised my gaze, unsure if I should be so bold.

"It is alright, my child," the woman cooed. With her allowance, I raised my head and met her stare full on.

She was ethereal in her beauty, with long raven black braids woven into a crown high on her head. Her features were round, small, intense...and her eyes, they were huge and majestic, framed with long black lashes, like a deer.

My bottom lip trembled as she smiled at me.

"*Beau.*"

I didn't know how or why, but I knew it was me. This woman had given me a precious gift.

She gave me a name.

I didn't know how I knew this, I just...did. I couldn't even remember what my name had been before. I didn't know who I was.

Did I even exist before or was I born anew?

Who was I? Who *am* I?

Beau.

That's right. I'm Beau.

"Come here, Beau," the man, Sterling, commanded.

The urge to crawl overcame me again, but I refused to succumb to the desire. I would walk, damn it. Enough with the humiliation already.

But...I couldn't. My limbs were too heavy, nearly impossible to even drag myself to my feet. I struggled, desperate.

"Don't fight the desire, Beau. Come," Sterling's voice held no inflection, no emotion, but there was power in it. And I yielded. Immediately falling back on my hands and knees, I dragged myself to him.

The closer I got, the more I smelled it.

Citrus and clove.

It was him. It *had* to be.

He opened his arms to me and I did not hesitate to climb into them, straddling his waist. I wrapped my legs around his hips and my arms around his neck, pressing my face into the expanse of his massive chest.

Oh my god. What am I doing? Why can't I stop?

"Don't fight it," he whispered, breath tickling my ear. I shivered, pressing myself closer to him, squeezing my eyes shut so I could immerse myself in him.

Master. Master. Master.

His arm came around me, holding me close.

"Bring him back after he's properly fed," the woman instructed.

"Yes, High Priestess."

Sterling rose in one swift movement and my body barely jostled. One hand cupped my bare ass while the other crossed my back, holding me like I was a child. I certainly *felt* like I was compared to his ridiculously colossal form.

Time ceased to exist in his arms. One second he was lifting me up, another, he was laying me down. We were back in the room I had woken in. This time, the fireplace was lit, illuminating the once dark space. Sterling's body hovered over mine, eyes boring down into my own.

Looking at him, I could see nothing else. From the slick gray hair to his surprisingly young face. He had to be in his late twenties, early thirties. His eyes were narrow, hooded, a little fleshy beneath the lower lids. His nose was long, but small in comparison to the rest of his face, with a narrow bridge and slightly upturned base. His lips looked soft, plush, the top one thin and bow shaped while the bottom was thick. He had a slight cleft in his chin, just barely visible underneath the dusting of a beard trying to make itself known. His jawline was intense and square, and his body...well, it was incredible. Those long limbs were wrapped in thick, prominent muscles, that broad chest and narrow waist only accentuated his form. Superman would be jealous.

Maybe he wasn't beautiful by typical standards. Not everyone found intensity attractive...but to me? He was *everything*, and for the life of me, I couldn't figure out why. Who the hell *was* he?

I wanted to ask, but I couldn't find my voice. I could only stare up into those amazing green eyes of his. Silent. Choking.

"Sleep well?" Sterling asked. His voice was deep, smooth, and assured. Someone who didn't need to raise their voice to command a room.

"Yes," I whispered without meaning to. The words just forced themselves out. He asked, and I *needed* to answer.

What was *wrong* with me?

Sterling tilted his head, a knowing look on his face. "It's alright. I understand what you are feeling. I know how I make you feel. I will explain in time, but for now, I don't want you to fight it. Fighting it only makes the feeling worse."

Fighting it *had* made it worse. Frighteningly so.

"I will not hurt you. I will protect you. I will make you full again."

How did he know? How did he so accurately describe this clawing emptiness inside me? I didn't know who I was, *what* I was, how I got here, who *they* were. I didn't know anything. It was *terrifying*. But I felt the sincerity in his words. I felt safe and comfortable as he hovered above me, easily keeping me from feeling his weight.

Sterling shifted, eyes never leaving mine, and gripped my bandaged wrist lightly. He inspected it, running his nose along the soft material.

"Still bleeding," he murmured with a frown. Then his intensity increased. "Does it hurt?"

"No," I mumbled.

There was relief in his eyes, but it was a slight, subtle shift in his pupil dilation that gave any indication.

With a swift and precise movement, Sterling brought his finger to his neck and sliced it open. Crimson bloomed from the cut immediately. He tilted his head and offered it to me.

I yelped, jumping back, trying to scurry away from him, but he kept his hold firm. Absolute. In a quick, graceful move, he pulled me over so I lay atop him and his hand landed on the back of my head, pushing me down. My face grew closer and closer to the wound on his neck, spilling steady rivulets of blood.

"Don't fight. You're thirsty. Drink."

"No! No, no, no," I protested, trying and failing to turn my head away.

"Don't fight it. It will seem strange now, but after your first taste, you will understand."

When Sterling commanded it, I could not fight it. I tried and tried, but as he said, it only got worse.

So I acquiesced.

The first touch of my tongue against his skin was sublime. I didn't immediately taste the blood, just the smooth expanse of skin on his neck. As my tongue swiped up, the flavor exploded. Sweet, tangy, with a bit of a bite.

It was *delicious*.

Euphoric.
Orgasmic.

I held him closer, latching my lips to his skin, sucking in as much as I could. My body was flush against his, eager, needing to be closer. Sterling's hips rose to meet mine. I couldn't see his face, but I could feel him. The hardness poking my inner thigh was all the proof I needed that he was experiencing this much the same way I was.

We rocked against each other, hips grinding, cocks stiffening, climax approaching. All that could be heard was the rustling of clothes, the suckling of skin, low grunts of pleasure, and the crackling of the fire.

My head went light at the sensation of it all. When I pulled back to breathe, Sterling's breath hitched and hips jerked one last time. Like a punch in the gut, my peak smashed into me. It stained the shirt I wore and a bit painted Sterling's chest.

Breathless, I collapsed onto him, smearing the mess between our bodies. I could hear Sterling's heart beating furiously in his chest as he panted. After a few moments, his breathing settled and silence overtook the room. Nothing but the fire now.

Lips brushed my ear. "Sleep, Beau."

And this time…I didn't fight his command.

2

I EXIST TO PLEASE YOU

Waking up this time was less jarring. There was no disorientation or darkness...and I wasn't alone.

Sterling sat on the couch in front of the raging fire, with a leather-bound book in his hands. He wore a black button down and black dress pants. His feet were bare, long and narrow. Something about it seemed almost...sensual.

Did I have a foot fetish?

Without lifting his gaze, his voice pierced the silence. "Come here, Beau."

I sat up, slid off the bed, and walked to him–walked this time, not crawled–naked as the day I was born.

He looked up at me as I stood before him, feeling the warmth of the fire caress my back. He patted the seat next to him. I sat.

Sterling closed his book, but not before I got a glimpse of the passage he was reading. I didn't paint him for a spicy romance reader, but I guess you really couldn't judge a book by its cover. This mysterious man grew more interesting by the minute.

He pulled one of my legs over his and braced his hand on my

inner thigh. My cock twitched once, but didn't show further interest.

"Show me your wrist," he commanded softly.

Without needing an explanation, I showed him my bandaged wrist. He brought it to his nose, closed his eyes, and inhaled lightly.

"Stopped bleeding," he murmured, then unraveled it. When he pulled away the rest, he inspected the skin. On my wrist was a puckered line of scar tissue. But for something that was bleeding only a few hours ago, it should not have healed this much.

Sterling brought my wrist to his lips and placed a gentle kiss to my skin. It tingled.

"This mark...it means that you are mine. Mine to protect and mine to mentor. Do you understand what you are now, Beau?"

"Vampire," I whispered shakily.

Because for what other reason would I need to drink his blood? And *like it*, no less.

Sterling smiled, revealing two sharp fangs. "Not quite, but almost."

I frowned. "What am I then?"

"A fledgling. You have begun the Change."

That sounded familiar. I didn't know how, but I knew Vampires were fledglings for the first few years after the blood exchange. It seemed like all the knowledge *about* Vampires, from an extremely watered down perspective, had transferred. I knew that humans were aware of Vampires and lived in a somewhat awkward but generally peaceful coexistence. And yet, nothing else about myself had translated.

"Why me?" I asked him.

Sterling looked away from me. His gaze fixed on the fire. "When you first accept the Change, you lose all of what you once were. You are born anew. As your mentor, I cannot let you sink into what you are no longer. Why you? I cannot answer that. It no longer matters. But who you are has never changed, you've simply forgotten how you came to be."

"You knew me as a human," I concluded. There was a slight downturn of his lips, but it was gone as soon as it appeared. "Was I not a good person? Is this punishment?"

Sterling fixed his gaze on me again. "Do you think it is?"

"I don't know," I answered honestly.

Sterling released a breath and went back to staring at the fire. "Neither do I."

We sat in silence. I didn't want to disturb him when it seemed like he was lost in his thoughts. Besides, I was still reeling from the new information. I was becoming a Vampire.

I would no longer walk in the daylight. I wouldn't go to work, buy a house, marry, have children...*die*. Because those were the things I was supposed to do, right? The beaten path every human was expected to follow. Sure, some veered off that path, but it was always the expectation.

Where did that leave me?

Why me?

"No," Sterling said suddenly. I startled, looking over at him. He was still looking at the fire.

"No?" I repeated, confused.

"No, you were not a bad person," he said, then rose. "Come, you need to eat."

I frowned. "I thought I just...?"

Sterling smiled and that one thing transformed his entire face. It was small and like a foreign concept, but conveyed all that it needed to. "Fledglings cannot survive on blood alone. Not yet at least."

He helped me up and brought me past the curtains into the office area I spied before. What I didn't notice was the other door next to yet another bookshelf. The man *really* liked his books.

Sterling pulled the door open and revealed a large closet. He walked inside and I followed.

Well this would have been helpful to find, the clothes in here were much smaller.

They were *my size*.

No way, this couldn't have been here before, I would have noticed.

Sterling pulled out a white button down and cream pants. He handed it to me with a few other underclothes and shoes.

"This...wasn't here before," I pointed out.

Sterling stopped. He looked around the closet before laying his hand on the dark wood of the doorframe. "Sometimes this place moves. Creates. Shifts. We don't have any control over it really, but it always seems to anticipate our needs."

Very much confused, I waited for him to elaborate. He didn't. He just slipped out of the room.

So the place was a sentient being...wonderful.

I shoved on my new clothes and shoes before following him.

He led me out, down the hall, and back to the common space I had discovered earlier. Only this time, there was no one there. The couples having sex had disappeared, the woman on the throne was gone, and all of the other people lounging about had cleared.

I glanced around curiously, while keeping up with Sterling. He led me out of the common area and down one of the many halls to a dining space. There was one pair there, sitting at one of the many small bistro style tables. One man had food in front of him, while the other watched him eat. I tried to get a better look at them, but Sterling steered me toward a secluded corner away from them.

"Sit," he ordered, before walking away. I did as I was told. A few seconds later, he came back with a plate of spaghetti, a side salad, and a glass of water. He set them in front of me and took the seat opposite. "Eat."

I obeyed.

The silence was not suffocating or uncomfortable and for that, I was grateful. I wasn't even weirded out by him just watching me. Though my curiosity did get the better of me.

"Since I'm a fledgling, I have to eat food. Do you?" I asked him.

"I don't have to at my age. But I can, yes."

I frowned. "And exactly how old are you?"

Sterling smirked, but did not answer. Instead, he jerked his chin at my plate. "Finish that up. You'll need to feed again soon after."

I swallowed hard. "Feed? Like...on blood?"

Sterling nodded.

"On *your* blood?" I asked, feeling my heartbeat speed up.

Sterling nodded again.

I cleared my throat uncomfortably. "Um, will it...will it be like last time? Will I–will you–" I couldn't finish my question, but I hoped he understood my meaning. I mean, it was pretty obvious considering my face was sure to be beet red even with my dark skin.

Sterling's eyes sparkled.

"Are you asking if it will be sexual?"

I gulped and nodded.

Sterling's lip twitched and he gave a single nod. I cleared my throat again, shifting awkwardly in my seat. "So um...you're like...bi or something?"

Sterling barked out a laugh. It startled me so much, I jumped in my seat, nearly knocking over my water.

"What a human thing to ask. That doesn't exist here."

"What do you mean?"

Sterling leaned closer. "We are not like humans. We do not

label or limit. We are creatures of sensation and gratification. We are open in our lust. It is a part of us, a necessity. I'm not bisexual and neither are you."

I didn't know how to respond, or if I even should, so I concentrated on my food. The cheesy spaghetti didn't seem as appetizing once I considered the fact that I'd be tasting blood again soon. The thought of what I had consumed a few hours ago made me feel a little sick. Though I couldn't know if I'd ever heard of blood-drinking before, my initial instinct had told me it was wrong. To not drink it.

Alternatively... I was now aware of how bland food tasted compared to what flowed in Sterling's veins. Despite my brain's insistence that this was the food I should eat, I knew it could never taste as heavenly as blood.

Following a period of internal procrastination, during which my food grew cold, the Vampire deduced I had finished my meal. Sterling sighed a little, then took my plate to the kitchen, while I followed behind like a lost puppy. The notion of this powerful and sophisticated man doing such a menial task as cleaning up after me horrified me. Inside, I battled the sense of obligation that it was my duty to clean up and serve him, not the other way around.

However, when I volunteered to do it in his place, he simply shook his head once and remained quiet until he escorted me back to the bedroom.

"Will I get my own room?" I asked him.

"No."

Oh.

"My own bed?"

"No."

Huh. So was I supposed to share with him?

When he opened the door, I walked over to the couches. The fire was starting to go out. I used the poker to shift the wood around and threw another log in to keep it going. When I turned back around, Sterling was sitting on the couch watching me. He patted the spot beside him.

I joined him and we sat in companionable silence.

"What are you to me?" I asked him.

"I am your everything," he answered simply. "I am your mentor, your friend, your protector, your father, your brother, your lover, your creator. I am everything to you."

His words, as audacious as they were, held so much truth in them. There was no malice or ill intent, it was a simple matter of fact. He *was* all of those things. And I wasn't quite sure how to feel about it.

"Come, Beau. Drink," Sterling said.

I scooched a little closer, feeling a bit unsure. Would he cut his neck again? Would he make *me* do it? Was I supposed to just *go* for it? I don't think my nails are sharp enough to cut through his skin like he did and I don't have any fangs yet.

He seemed to notice my uncertainty and raised his wrist to his mouth, biting down, before offering it to me. The wound gushed with blood and while I would have been alarmed before, I was now fixated. I needed it in my mouth. I needed to taste it again.

Not needing any encouragement, I feasted, grabbing his arm with both my hands and greedily latched on to his offering.

It didn't make sense why I was so thirsty again. I mean, I literally *just* drank his blood *and* had a meal full of carbs. Yet here I was, drinking like I was starved, like it was the first time.

Sterling groaned, his head rested on the back of the couch while his eyes closed in ecstasy. I could see the bulge in his pants, but he left it hard and untouched. As if he needed no further stimulation than my lips on his wrist.

It was strange really, to be so intimate with someone and know nothing about them. Granted, this entire turn of events has been nothing *but* strange. Though, I had to acknowledge that...I was comfortable. Maybe it was because having his blood inside me changed the very foundation of my being, but this man could tell me to slit my own throat right here and now and I would do it without a second's hesitation.

Having that sort of control should have terrified me. Honestly, he could very well have asked me to do anything, and I'd do it all. Without a single question or moment of hesitation. Knowing that should have made me distrust him. It should have made me hesitant to listen to a single word that fell from those beautifully sculpted lips. However, that lack of trust was not present. For whatever reason, I trusted him and would continue to do so.

No matter what.

How fucked up was that?

"Enough, Beau," Sterling said quietly.

Immediately, I raised my head and licked my blood stained lips greedily. I hadn't even realized I had been drinking long enough that the fire had long since died or that both of us had shared an orgasm. I looked down at my soiled pants.

"Maybe...in the future...we should...um...take our clothes off first?" I suggested.

Sterling laughed as he held his bleeding wrist. "That'll come much sooner than you think."

My laughter died off as I stopped to stare at him. "What do you mean?"

Sterling smirked and it dripped with mischief. With a casual grace, he crossed his ankles and threw his arm along the back of the couch. His wound was no longer bleeding.

"Well, after the initial exchange of blood, the fledgling undergoes seven days of Stage One. Day one, the fledgling sleeps. Day two, the fledgling feeds three times from their

Creator. Days three through seven, the fledgling endures the Frenzy."

The Frenzy? Why did that sound so ominous?

"What's the Frenzy?" I asked, a little cautiously.

Sterling was quiet for a moment, contemplating.

Was he not going to tell me? Was it something...*bad?*

Seeming to read my thoughts through my expression, he smiled. "It's nothing bad. It's just, considering your history of trying to fight our forming bond, I am not sure it is something you will like."

My eyes narrowed. "What is it?"

Sterling scratched the stubble along his jaw, not looking at me. "How do I describe it? It's been so long since I've experienced it."

He cleared his throat. "Well, I should start by saying all your human blood must be purged from your body."

"Wasn't it already when you first took my blood to change me? Isn't that how it works? You take my blood, I take your blood?"

Sterling bobbed his head side to side as if debating. "Yes and no. I didn't take all of your blood. I am not physically able. I only needed to take an ounce of your blood and give you an ounce of mine to trigger the change. The full transition takes multiple feedings."

"So, I still have mostly human blood?" I asked.

"Yes, it is why you cannot heal as fast. That will change once you get more Vampire blood. Then as you feed again three more times, you'll carry at least six liters of blood in your body."

I frowned, looking skeptical. "The human body only has five liters of blood. How is that possible?"

"It's not. And that's why you will soon feel hot and stiff. You might start bleeding from your nose or your eyes and ears. You might even start throwing up the blood or expelling it from any other orifice. That will happen once the Vampire blood and human blood separate. Like oil and water. Human bodies are... intricate, complicated machines."

I grimaced. That sounded downright awful. I didn't want to go through that, especially since I never signed up for any of this. I don't think I did, anyway... it was still so hard to remember the details and apparently I never would, if Sterling's vague explanation was to be trusted.

"Is there any way to prevent that?" I asked.

"I will do my part as your creator."

"And what exactly does that entail?"

"I will drain your human blood from you. As I take from you, it will give the new blood you receive somewhere to go. What starts in your stomach will find its way into your veins."

Oh.

I thought about all the times I'd fed from him so far and how euphoric it had been. A part of me grew eager at the thought of feeding him. My Creator. Giving him every part of myself. Needing it. Needing *him*.

A soft groan left my lips before I could stop it.

Sterling grinned wickedly.

"Whatever you are thinking...it will be *much* better."

I shivered at the promise.

"But with that being said, it brings me back to my earlier statement," Sterling continued. "Your body already recognizes me as its creator. It craves me. And earlier, after you had first awoken and come to find me, you were drawn to my being. The bond was forming. During the Frenzy, it will happen again and the call will be much stronger. You will need to be close to me, touch me and be touched by me, feed me, please me. You will submit to me in every way. You won't be able to help it. And despite my telling you to let it happen, you continue to fight it. I fear that you will fight it again and it will make the experience more painful for you."

The heated air cooled almost instantly. That fiery desire that raged within me still kindled, but it was dull in the face of this new information.

I remembered that feeling. I remembered crawling to him, pressing myself against him, needing to touch him, needing to be one with him. I had fought and lost that battle, miserably and immediately. I didn't think I could handle feeling that pull any stronger than before.

Was there anything about this new life that wasn't completely terrifying?

"I've told you before, I will not harm you. I will protect you. I know it will take time for trust between us. But in this, you need to let your instincts guide you." His words held a bit of a warning.

"Or what?" I asked, sensing that was the real question. The *important* one.

"Or there might be some irreparable damage."

Ominous indeed.

"What do you mean?"

"I do not want to frighten you, but in the best way to describe it...your mind will turn against you."

"What does that mean?" I insisted with a bit of fear in my voice.

Sterling looked at me then, swallowing me whole with those deep green eyes of his. "I will not say more, because I will not let it happen. My job as your creator is to take care of you, so believe me when I say, you will be fine. You have nothing to fear. The feelings you have...they won't last forever. Hang on to that."

It wouldn't last forever. I mean, that was comforting, but I was still hung up on the "mind turning against me" or "irreparable damage" thing. I could almost taste the truth in his words—a very weird feeling, by the way—but I could tell there was more to it. He was hiding something, and it was never good when someone who kept secrets wanted you to trust them implicitly with your life.

But what choice did I have?

No matter what, I was completely at his mercy.

"So when will this Frenzy start?" I asked.

"Probably soon after your third feeding."

I'd just had my second feeding, so that gave me a little bit more time, I supposed. I couldn't tell if that was a good thing or not. Part of me just wanted to get it over with. If I waited, then I would stress out about it.

"Who was that woman earlier?" I asked, remembering that it was not just Sterling I was pulled to, but her as well. And it was she who named me.

"Lilith. She is our High Priestess and the Mother of all Vampires," Sterling answered. There was something in his voice, sort of like awe, and I could see it in his eyes. When he said her name, there was a flash of flame deep within them.

"Who is she to you?" I asked. I mean, clearly she was someone important if that reaction was anything to go by. I also met him when he was...um...well very *intimate* with her.

"She is *my* mentor and *my* creator."

"So, you feel for her what I feel for you?" I asked.

He nodded.

"Is that why I feel a pull toward her as well?"

Sterling paused and thought a moment before answering. "Partly, I suppose. But Lilith is our supreme creator. She is the *first* Vampire. None came before her. We are all her children, including you. She is also the High Priestess of this Coven, which also plays a part in the pull you feel. She is the strongest Vampire in the world and has power that we cannot even comprehend. I am her first son. Not her first made, but the first she chose to mentor. After me is Marcelle, then after her is Stasia. We are Lilith's chosen three and the Elders of Athens Coven."

"Athens?" I knew that covens were usually named after locations. This was the first clue about where I was, but there were many Athens in the world.

"Athens, Georgia. That is where we are," Sterling told me. "When you are well enough to leave the Coven House, I will show you around."

I nodded in thanks. It was nice to know I wasn't a prisoner here. That I could leave. But I imagine I wouldn't be able to go without either Sterling by my side or his permission.

"So...the other Elders...do they have fledglings too?"

"Yes, you will meet them all soon enough. Marcelle's fledgling is Julia. Stasia's fledglings are Asher and Cadence."

I cocked my head in interest. "This Stasia...has two fledglings?"

Sterling nodded. "They are twins. Vampires with more than one fledgling at a time would have to be exceptionally powerful. Stasia is very...special."

"You're powerful. I can taste it in your blood. Do *you* have another fledgling?" The words felt bitter on my tongue. I didn't like it. The thought of having to share him...Sterling was *mine* and mine *alone*.

Sterling laughed, obviously sensing my jealousy.

"I have turned another, but I was not their mentor. It's just you, Beau."

The heat in my veins cooled. I was content with that bit of information, even if a warning bell went off in my head, it was easily ignored.

"When will I meet them?"

"When you are properly fed."

"Which is after the Frenzy?"

Sterling nodded.

"And after Stage One...then what? What am I supposed to do for the rest of my *immortal* life?"

"Well first, we're not immortal. Though we can live for many millennia, our cycle ends eventually. We are also not invincible. We can be killed in a number of ways; fire, beheading, starvation, direct sun exposure, and silver to the heart. It's best if you avoid those things," he said with morbid mirth in his voice. "You will join one of the five factions: Scholars, Shamans, Knights, Artisans, or Elites. Once chosen, you'll know what to do."

"You sound very sure about that."

"Because I am," he said. "I know it is strange for you, waking up to this new life. But I promise you, that you will find your comfort in it. This place and the people in it will become your home and your family. You are not alone in this. There are others going through the same thing you are in this very building. After the Frenzy, you will meet the other fledglings. Perhaps you will even make some friends to share this journey with."

I remembered the four men on the couch. Were they fledglings? How long had they been fledglings?

"Sterling?"

Sterling raised his brow. "Hm?"

"Exactly how long will I *be* a fledgling?"

He let out a slow breath. "I don't know. It varies by person. Some take two years, others take six. The most common time span is four years, but it is still unclear if that will be the case for you."

Four years...that seemed like such a long time. But that was a human way of thinking, wasn't it? I mean, if I am going to be living for hundreds of years, I should start getting used to being alive for a long time. Time won't have the same meaning anymore. Four years is probably nothing in comparison to the rest of my Vampire life.

Do I even *want* to live forever?

Fingers brushed my cheek. I tried not to startle from the touch, but Sterling noticed me jump anyway. He smiled gently at me, thumb swiping tenderly underneath my eye.

He was so *warm*.

"Don't think too hard about it. Things will start to make sense soon. Trust me on that."

I nodded slowly, transfixed by those beautiful eyes. This close, I could see the small flecks of gold and light green surrounding his pupil and the dark ring that lined his outer iris. They were truly stunning.

I studied the rest of his face, from his soft looking pink lips, to the tiny scar at the tip of his left brow. His brows that were thick and...dark. How had I not noticed the sharp contrast? Even his stubble was dark, but his hair...it was pure gray. And I could see the roots, the color was seamless.

"Your hair...did you dye it?" I asked, resisting the urge to run my fingers through the silky gray tresses.

The corner of his lips quirked.

"No."

"Then why...?" I let the question trail off, still staring in wonderment, trying to figure it out.

"When you change, sometimes your human doesn't fully translate to your Vampire."

I frowned in confusion. His fingers trailed up my cheek to smooth out my furrowed brow, his lips still quirked in amusement.

"Come, let us clean up. We've sat in our spend long enough," he said, standing. I grimaced, completely forgetting the now flaky remnants of my feeding. I stood with him.

Bathing together should have been embarrassing, but I did not feel embarrassed or modest in the least. My nudity was just another thing that belonged to Sterling. It wasn't sexual, even though it easily could have been from my body's natural reactions to him. But Sterling kept it platonic. We dried and dressed for bed.

"Don't I have to feed again?" I asked as he lifted the satin sheets and slipped underneath, then held them open for me to join him. I slid beside him, sucking in his radiating heat.

I always thought Vampires were cold. Sterling was anything but, and he smelled so damn *good*.

Sterling pulled me close until my face was inches from his t-shirt clad chest. I tried to look up at his face, but could only manage to see his chin before he tilted his head exposing his throat. With deliberate slowness, he brought a finger to his neck and sliced a small delicate line across his skin. The blood was slow to bloom. My guess was to keep it a neat and short feeding.

"Just a few sips," he said.

I leaned close, licking the first drop with the tip of my tongue, closing my eyes to savor the unique flavor before latching my lips to his skin. I sucked and pulled, trying to drag out as much blood as I could but it was like he had control over the flow because no matter how hard I tried, I could only get a few drops.

"Enough, Beau. Sleep."

And with that one command, my body went limp and I was met with darkness.

3

THE FRENZY

There are things in my human life that I thought I could remember. My mother's smile, my father's laugh...a brother? Maybe? Their faces were too bright, like a photo exposed early in development, wiping their features clean.

As a Vampire, would I truly even exist?

Would those whose faces I could not see, could not remember, miss me?

Did they miss me now?

Beau.

My body jerked awake, a loud gasp leaving my lips.

"Easy, easy now. Relax, Beau, I've got you," a low, husky voice whispered close to my ear. I tried to move my head to see Sterling's face, but my body would not do my bidding. I felt stiff, like my limbs were swollen, and hot...feverish even.

I opened my mouth to speak, but could only groan. My tongue was thick and dry, chafing along my mouth, sticking and tugging painfully to the walls.

Sterling's large, cool hand cupped my cheek and turned my

head to him. I knew I had to be running a fever if he felt cold to me.

His green eyes were blazing as he stared down at me, still slightly hooded from sleep.

"I'll make you feel better," Sterling whispered.

He tilted my head further back, exposing the expanse of my neck.

I knew what this was the moment I felt it. He warned me beforehand. But I did not know it would feel so horrible. He should have told me I'd feel like death. Like something old and bloating, left to rot in a deep crevasse somewhere.

I couldn't speak. I couldn't move. I just laid there like some fat sausage waiting to explode.

"Breathe," Sterling whispered. I inhaled deeply and in my exhale, Sterling struck. His fangs cut deep into my neck, piercing the flesh in a quick, precise movement. It didn't feel like the tiny sting of a mosquito bite, or even the sharp uncomfortableness from a needle shot. No, his fangs were too thick for that. It hurt like being impaled with a pencil or getting stabbed with scissors.

Fuck!

Helpless groans tried to escape, but the sound couldn't find its way around my engorged tongue.

I felt his fangs retract, leaving gaping bloody holes in their wake, spilling my life's essence all over the pillow. I couldn't move. I couldn't *move*.

Sterling started to suck.

It was light at first, but after the first smooth drag and gentle caress of his tongue against my wound, it changed. It was like a switch had been flipped, and everything was suddenly different–that's the only way I could describe it, as a shift. Shift in sensation, shift in time, shift in mentality. But it was no longer me and him. It was just him.

Master.

I needed him. I needed to be closer. To touch him, smell him, give him everything. Every single last drop of blood in my veins was his. Take it all.

"Mas...ter," I managed to whisper, feeling my tongue deflate. My lips felt raw, as if we had spent hours kissing, but his lips hadn't touched mine.

Sterling's pulls became stronger and with it, my need for him grew. My need to please him in any way I knew how.

My body pushed and strained, trying to move despite its current condition. I sought every inch of Sterling's cool body to press against. It soothed my fever, the cure for everything.

"Master," I whispered again, my voice hoarse.

He didn't respond, only pulled me close, tipping my head back further, taking more of my blood into him.

Take it all, Master. Take every single drop. Drain me. Let me give you everything.

Sterling pulled away, his head tilted back and bloody fangs glistening in the glow of the roaring fire.

When did he light it?

Sterling closed his eyes and his tongue darted past his lips to lick the remnants of my blood from them. He inhaled as if savoring the taste.

Did my blood please him?

"Master...good?" I choked, trying to talk past the swelling.

When Master opened his eyes again, they were red. Red like the satin caressing my skin, red like the velvet on the couch before the fire, red like our Mother's eyes.

Master was *beautiful.*

He lowered his head, so close to mine that I could taste the sweetness on his breath.

"You are perfect, Beau," he whispered.

I whimpered, wrapping my arms around his neck, pulling

him close and urging him to take more. He needed no further encouragement, falling between my legs and sealing his lips on my neck. We thrusted and moaned, gyrated and panted. Anything to get closer. Again and again, in and out of consciousness. I could no longer discern life from Master.

He was *everything*.

After hours of on and off feeding, waking up and passing out, the heat eased and I could move freely again. But I was so tired, I curled up in the bed, swaddled in sheets, inhaling Master's scent.

Master rose from the bed. His movements were graceful, energized, as if he hadn't just spent the last forty-eight hours in the throes of passion.

His hair was damp with sweat, clinging to his skin and looking much darker than his typical light gray.

There were stains of blood on his face, chest, hands, and all the way down to his stomach. My blood and his. It was beautiful.

"Master?" I asked, wondering why he was getting out of the bed.

He turned to me, but the expression on his face was pained. His eyes glistened and his frame was stiff.

"What's wrong?" I questioned, growing more concerned. What happened? Why was he upset? What could I do? What could I do to fix this? I needed him to be happy. His happiness meant everything.

"Beau, listen closely," Sterling said, eyes meeting mine and never wavering. I scrambled out of my cocoon and crawled to him, desperate to touch, but he pushed me down onto my back. "I am with you always."

I frowned, not understanding.

"Always," he repeated, still holding my gaze. We watched each other unblinkingly until I heard a metallic click. I glanced and saw the thick titanium shackle fastened around my wrist.

"Master, what are you...?"

Sterling hovered above me, reaching to the other side of the bed before pulling out another shackle and fastening it to my other wrist. Both were connected to thick chains that disappeared over the side of the bed.

Sterling slid over me, his eyes shining, before he leaned close and pressed his lips to mine in a chaste kiss. "I am with you always," he said again. And then...

He left.

"Sterling?" I called out in building panic. I tugged the wrist shackles, but they were too strong to break. It kept me chained to the bed, unable to do anything but writhe. "Master! Master! Master!"

He was leaving me. Why was he leaving me? I needed him. I couldn't be apart from Master. *Must touch Master. Must please Master. Must be with Master, always.*

But Master left me. Master doesn't want me. Master is unhappy with me. I displeased Master.

I displeased Master. I have to be punished. I have to die for Master.

Die.

Die.

Die.

I kicked and writhed, desperate to do anything to right my wrongs. I had to make it right again.

"Master is angry with me. Master doesn't want me," I whispered, staring up at the dark ceiling. Tears made the planks of woods blur into one big mass of darkness.

"Master, please! I'll be better! Master!" I begged into the darkness, hoping that he would hear me.

Please come back.

I'll be better.
I'll do better.
I'll please you.

But he didn't come back. I waited and waited and waited. At first I begged and pleaded. Then I waited in silence, not making a sound or moving an inch. Then I lost myself to the screams. Screaming again and again, louder and louder until my throat strained. And then I sobbed. I just wanted to please Master.

And then I heard a familiar voice.

"He's almost as bad as you were."

My head snapped around, trying to locate the voice, but I was alone in the room. Just me and the flames.

I wish I could submerge myself in them, wipe myself from existence.

"As his Creator, you feel his pain, but you know that this is necessary. It's what's best for him."

There were more words, more voices, but I still couldn't tell where they were coming from. And so I let myself drift into nothingness.

4

THIS IS MY LIFE NOW

I awoke with a start.
I didn't remember going to sleep, but when I opened my eyes, the room was completely dark. The fire had long since died.

Sterling lay with me, face inches from mine, sharing my pillow while he ran his fingers through the short coils of my hair.

He was curled around me almost protectively, but there was a sadness in his eyes that stole all of my attention.

"How are you feeling?" he asked, breaking the silence.

I cleared my throat a few times, but it only flared up in pain. Sterling noticed immediately and moved to fetch a glass of water he must have had on standby. Like a child, he cupped my head and helped me drink. The room temperature liquid helped soothe the pain a bit, but my voice still came out scratchy and rough.

"What happened?" I asked after the water was gone, and Sterling put the glass back down.

"The Frenzy," he said.

Huh? It was over already? How long had it been?

"You look sad," I commented, reaching up to touch his face. He looked away, almost appearing guilty. And that's when I realized my wrists were free.

"I hope you can understand why I had to keep leaving. I didn't want to, but it's dangerous during the Frenzy. Our bond grows stronger and if I didn't force separation, you never would have been able to function without my touch. That horrible sense of dread and hopelessness would overcome you the moment we stopped touching."

"Why didn't you just tell me beforehand?"

"It was useless to do so. If anything, it might have exacerbated the problem. The thought of losing control and having the mind work against oneself is a terrifying notion. When I was a fledgling, Lilith told me and I spent hours in fear and anxiety, just anticipating it. I didn't want that for you."

"Shouldn't that have been something that I decided on my own? What I can and can't handle? Or *how* I handle things?" I asked, feeling a little upset.

Sterling gave me a serious look before uttering, "No."

I flinched incredulously. "No?"

Sterling's gaze was unwavering. "No."

And I couldn't argue it.

I tried to roll away from him, but he yanked me back until I practically slammed into his chest.

"Don't be upset. It's over now and you'll never have to go through it again. Things will get better, I promise."

I wanted to believe him, but there was this odd sense of foreboding that I couldn't quite shake. There was still so much about this world and my new life that I knew nothing about. They had given me small snippets of information, but nothing of actual substance. What were they keeping from me? Were they afraid of scaring me away?

I mean, it's not like I could go anywhere, so what was the point?

"Sterling?"

"Yes?"

"Why me? Why did you choose me?"

I knew I had asked him this before and didn't really get an answer. I'd been hoping that maybe things would be different now? I officially had all of his blood in my veins. I "belonged" to him. Maybe that counted for something.

Sterling sighed. Given his tendency to give ambiguous responses, I didn't think he would answer. To be honest, he might as well have been silent most of the time. But he shocked me by saying, "Because you asked me to".

"I *asked* you to?"

Who *was* I as a human? Someone with an obsession with Vampires? Someone with a terrible life? Someone running from something?

I hated not being able to remember.

What was my name? My purpose? Who *am* I?

Beau.

No.

I am not Beau. Beau is a lie.

"Let it go, Beau. It doesn't change what your future is. You will be a Vampire. Your name is Beau and you are my fledgling. This is your world now–accept and embrace it, because you have no other choice."

With that, Sterling rose from the bed and headed into the bathroom.

I laid there for a few minutes, just trying to comprehend all that has happened.

This was all so fucked up.

I sighed and rose from the bed. I ached *everywhere*, like I had done a full body workout then was run down by an eighteen wheeler. My skin felt dirty, covered in dried blood, sweat, and semen, even though Sterling must have wiped the majority off while I was unconscious. I tried not to think about it as I staggered to the bathroom where Sterling already had the bath going.

He was sitting on the ledge, hair sticking up in every direction with a focused expression creasing his brows. One large hand was submerged under the faucet that spouted hot water. Slowly, the tub filled.

When it was about three quarters full, Sterling turned off the faucet and stood. He peeled off his cotton pants in one swift movement, not giving me a chance to ogle him before he slipped into the water.

Nudity between us had become normal, so I slipped off my pajama pants and joined him in the bath. We sat across from each other, that familiar silence filling the air between us again.

Sterling had wiped all emotions from his face, but it was strange. I could still tell what he was feeling.

Apprehension. Sadness. Guilt. A little anger. And...affection. That last one was for me. There was no question in my mind about that.

"This connection we share...will it ever fade?" I asked him.

A part of me hoped he would say yes, but a bigger part of me enjoyed it, though I wouldn't say it out loud. Admitting it felt like a weakness. We both knew he had absolute power over me, but I liked to keep the illusion–if even just to lie to myself–that I had a little control.

I *did* like the connection, the bond that grew between us. It was intimate. Something to cherish. At least, that's what my mind tried to convince me. I couldn't tell where I ended, and he began anymore. Which thoughts belonged to Sterling, and which were mine?

But I supposed that was the point of a Creator and fledgling–my thoughts would never be my own again.

"No. Not if it is nurtured properly," Sterling said and his eyes grew sharp. "And I don't plan on ever diminishing our bond."

"What if I displease you?" I asked, not meaning to let the bitterness slip into my tone.

The corner of Sterling's lips quirked. And that only irked me more.

"Are you planning to?" he mused, a humorous glint melting away the severity of his earlier expression.

"I can't be sure of what the future brings. I also don't know you. Maybe you'll set me up to fail, or maybe you'll get angry and take it out on me. Maybe we'll even grow to hate each other."

Sterling frowned.

"It is true that you don't know me all that well, but you can feel me. My blood runs through your veins. I can feel you just as I know you can feel me. You'd *know* if I was the kind of person to do that or if I ever have ill intentions."

"I can't even tell if anything is real anymore," I sighed, no longer feeling angry. Just tired. Exhausted, really. From all that I had gone through these past few days, to thinking about what the future held, and just from existing. My existence alone was exhausting. Maybe I shouldn't have been so quick to make enemies. Sterling had shown no signs of ill will...yet. He had taken care of me from the moment I awakened. If this was to be my life, it was better to just accept it and make the best of the situation.

This is my life now. What a scary thought.

"I'm sorry. I don't mean to antagonize you; you have been nothing but kind to me. I'm just...confused and tired," I said, sinking deeper into the heated water.

"I understand. More than you know," Sterling said quietly.

After that, we didn't speak another word. Just bathed in silence. When we were both clean, we stepped out of the bath, grabbing separate towels to dry ourselves. Sterling drained the tub while I wandered back into the bedroom, then over to the office where my closet was.

Except the door wasn't there anymore. I frowned, pausing in toweling my hair.

Looking around, I couldn't locate the door anywhere. It had disappeared just as mysteriously as it had come.

"Over here," Sterling called. I walked out of his office area to where his armoire and closet door was. When he opened his closet, the room had doubled in size. One half adorning the clothes that had been there originally, the other half holding my new clothes.

"Is it going to keep changing? Because that will get old, very fast," I grumbled.

Sterling laughed. "I don't think so. But like I said, these walls have a mind of their own. If it messes with you, I won't be able to help."

I shot him a dirty look and slipped past him to where my pajamas were. I slipped on some gray cotton pants, a white t-shirt, and a satin headscarf. Sterling wore something similar–sans the headwrap. Together, we changed the sheets on the bed before settling in.

There was distance between us and it felt...wrong. I scooted a little closer, hoping he didn't notice. But of course he did, because my body was then tugged flush against his as he cradled me in his arms. His breath tickled the back of my neck and his hands gripped my waist tightly.

Just that simple touch made everything feel right. I felt whole again. I wanted to hate it–truly; I did–but I just couldn't.

It felt way too damn good.

5

OWNERSHIP

When we woke, which I assumed was the next day, though I did not know what hour, there was a noticeable eagerness in Sterling that I had not witnessed before. It was subtle in the hurriedness of his dressing and the care he took with his clothing.

"What is it?" I asked, pulling on my trousers and adjusting my fitted vest. The closet had decided I was to wear this today, as it took away any other option of clothing when I opened it earlier.

Sterling raised a brow at me in question.

Really? Are we feigning innocence here?

I gestured to his clothes. "Something special happening?"

Sterling tilted his head and the barest hint of a smile ghosted his lips, but bled out in his clear green eyes. "We are seeing Mother."

Mother...the High Priestess, Sterling's Creator and mentor. Okay, the eagerness made sense now. It honestly amazed me that he could be away from her for so long if he felt for her what I felt for him, but it also relieved me. I'd get to that point...*eventually*.

When I finished dressing, Sterling was quick to lead us out of the room. As we made our way, quite a few people greeted him as we passed, but not nearly as many as I had seen when I first arrived.

We turned down several halls until we reached two massive wooden doors embedded with jewels and gold. The sight was impressive to say the least, but I couldn't enjoy the view as Sterling nearly yanked them off their hinges and rushed inside.

Giant pillars stretched up to the high ceiling, making the room appear even larger. My breath caught as I stared at the center of the room where the ground receded, exploding with lush green grass and a tiny pond filled with clear water. Trees towered around the space, reaching far past the ceiling and disappearing into this strange light that illuminated the water. It was a tiny oasis that could only be brought about by magic. I didn't even notice the woman–Lilith–sitting on a root at the base of one of the trees, cradling a naked man.

His hair was white, long, and curly, glued to his back as the water clung to it. His skin was golden, and he had the kindest, most beautiful face I had ever laid eyes on. Sterling excluded, of course.

The pair created a beautiful sight. With Lilith's smooth dark skin and feminine curves against his lighter brown and hard angles, it was a contrast that exuded balance and completion.

Sterling bowed deeply as we approached the edge of the grass.

"High Priestess, High Consort."

"My sweets, look at the gift my dear child has brought us."

Lilith's bright red eyes fell upon me and was soon joined by a pair of deep blue ones. I cowered under their gazes, feeling unworthy of the attention.

"Beau, come greet your Mother," Lilith called. I stiffened, looking up at Sterling desperately. He wasn't looking at me though, his eyes were trained on Lilith. A look of utter devotion and awe there.

Tentatively, I took one step toward her. Then another and another, until I was a couple of feet away. Not liking that I was above her, I dropped to my knees and crawled until I was next to her thigh, just out of the water. I didn't look up, choosing to wait, unsure of what I was supposed to do. Sterling was no help.

Warm hands gripped my cheeks, and I shivered at the touch. Red filled my vision as Lilith gazed down at me, a smile curving her lips.

"You'll be a powerful one. I can feel it," she whispered, then placed a soft kiss on my lips. I melted at the contact, eager to feel more of her on me. My thighs trembled as my erection strained against my pants.

"Stunning," a soft, but deep voice murmured, just as a wet hand gently traced a line up my thigh, soaking through to my skin. Trembles raked through my body at the slight whisper of feeling. It was warm and gentle, but evoked such a carnal response.

Lilith's lips trailed down my chin to the expanse of my neck, forcing my head back. Small whimpers escaped my lips, eager for more.

"Not far from Stage Two. I wonder what affinity he will have," the High Consort murmured.

"I can feel Sterling's fire in him," Lilith sighed, sweet, warm breath fanning over my skin. She pulled back until I could see nothing but the red depths of her eyes, endless and churning like glistening rubies, clouded skies, and flickering flames all at once. There was such raw and endless *power* in that gaze.

"My sweet child, you will be strong in your Father's gaze. You will endure the four stages of transformation and you will be a powerful Vampire."

"Four stages?" I managed to choke out, surprised that I could find my way back to my body after falling into that omnipotent stare.

"First stage, the Frenzy," Sterling said, his voice deceptively void yet commanding. So similar to when I first heard him speak. "Second stage, developing an affinity with one or more of the four elements: earth, air, fire, and water. Third stage, blood lust. And finally, the fourth stage, complete transformation."

I looked at Sterling, and finally he stared back. Deep in his eyes, I could see something twisting and writhing. Fire.

My skin warmed from that look alone.

They hadn't needed to tell me what his affinity was. It was obvious.

"I will...have fire? Like Master?" I asked, voice just barely a whisper, still caught by that emerald flame.

"Most likely, as unusual as that is," the High Consort purred. I glanced at him, noticing how close his voice was. He had climbed out of the water, perched on the edge next to Lilith, gently leaning on her shoulder. His eyes, they were so big and kind and welcoming.

"Nexus, my sweet, show him," Lilith said.

The High Consort, Nexus, dropped his head in obedience before turning his gaze to the pool of water. Slowly, drops of water rose, dancing in the air on an invisible current, washing over my heated skin until it glistened with dew.

"Every day you will learn, and you will grow strong, then you will find your place in this Coven," Lilith said to me before turning her gaze to Sterling. "Send for Executioner, my child."

Sterling bowed his head before standing and pulling me up and into his arms. Like a bucket of cold water, whatever entrancement I had been under had abruptly vanished. Without even allowing me another glance at Lilith and Nexus, Sterling guided me out of the room.

The common area, which I overheard someone call the

salon, was filled with people again. I studied them, trying to decipher who was a fledgling and who was a Vampire. It was strange, but I kind of got this *feeling* whenever I was around a Vampire. I could just *sense* it. *Must be a perk of the change.*

Sterling set me down before leading me through the space, nodding at those who bowed their heads as we passed to show their respect to the First Elder. I guessed I was lucky my mentor was a big shot in the Coven. Though that probably meant that there would be higher expectations of me as his progeny.

Just what I needed: the fear of disappointing a bunch of people.

Sterling had brought us to a set of loungers, close to his—er—*our* room. And there sat four men. Two I didn't recognize, but the other two...I'd know those copper curls and golden locks anywhere. I'd seen *way* too much of them before.

The blonde one was young, maybe even a few years younger than my twenty-six, with a stocky build.

Funny how I can remember my age and not my name...

His features were square, full of hard lines and sharp edges. They didn't match the softness in his brown eyes and the gentle curve of his wide uni-lip. With sun-kissed skin and wavy golden, chin length hair, he looked like he belonged on a beach somewhere in California.

I could still remember the eager way his body moved as he rode the other man. What a first impression.

The man beside him was huge. Built like a linebacker with powerful wide shoulders, big bones, wide torso, tree trunks for legs, and thick arms wrapped with bulging muscles. He clearly spent some *serious* time in the gym.

His hair was a curly summer brown that matched the hazel in his eyes. Eyes that were big yet severe, with heavy hoods and a strong brow. His nose was aquiline and lips thin, but despite his hawkish appearance, he was still attractive. Confidence oozed off him in waves as if he were the best looking guy in the room. It was that confidence alone that made him striking.

"Beau, this is Hale and his fledgling Kyle," Sterling introduced. Hale was the big guy, Kyle being the blonde. They both gave easy grins and small waves. I'd bet a million dollars that it was Hale that Kyle rode with wanton abandon on my first night here.

Beside them sat another couple.

One with shaggy, curly black hair and olive skin. He had a dark beard, hiding heart-shaped lips. The bridge of his nose was long and narrow, leading to a sloping base. His eyes were enormous, round, and light brown. He had an average build, and from the slim fitting shirt he wore, I could see the curls from his chest hair peeking up from the deep neckline.

Sitting on his lap was a smaller man with a head of short copper curls and skin so pale I was actually relieved he would never see the sun again because I could only imagine how easily he would burn. His skin was sprinkled with freckles. His eyes were small and blue. They matched his button nose and very pink bow-shaped lips. And yet, even with his youthful features, I saw the lines and creases around his eyes and mouth. Though he appeared near adolescent, I'd put him somewhere around late twenties, early thirties.

"And this is Joel and his fledgling Alexander."

The dark-haired one, Joel, nodded his head in greeting while Alexander, the red head grinned widely.

"Hello," I mumbled. Not that I felt shy, it was just strange. They were going through what I was. Yet they seemed...so happy. Did *they* know anything about their human lives? Did they ask to be changed like I apparently did?

Sterling took a seat on the couch opposite the men and I followed suit, sitting next to him, but with a respectable distance. My shoulders were back and my legs were crossed casually, the picture of nonchalance. I wanted to show that I was still my own person. I still had power over myself. But I wanted to curl into Sterling's side like a kitten, basking in his warmth and scent. I wish we had the relationship that Alexander and Joel seemed to have, where I could sit comfortably perched on Sterling's lap.

But we didn't. So instead, I pretended to be perfectly content with the distance between us. Ignoring every instinct that urged me to glue myself to his side.

"So, Beau, how does it feel to be bonded to the most powerful man in this Coven?" Hale asked with an amused grin.

Sterling rolled his eyes. "I'll just bet Nexus would love to hear you say that."

Hale shrugged. "We all know the hierarchy of power."

I frowned and looked at Sterling. He was more powerful than Nexus?

I remembered those shimmering blue eyes and that gentle smile. Nexus did seem soft compared to Lilith's raw grace, but he held this unbelievable aura, *and* he was the Consort to the Mother of Vampires. It made little sense for Sterling to be the stronger of the two.

And yet, I knew it to be true. I had tasted his blood, like ripened berries and full of citrus and spices. I could feel it in every step he took, every breath he took. Sterling was a beautiful monster behind that handsome face. A predator. Power incarnate. Though it seemed illogical, it was undeniably the case.

"I don't know," I answered, a bit delayed. "I still don't know much about him or *anything* for that matter."

"Well, you're in excellent hands," Joel said cheerfully. As he spoke, I picked up the bare hint of an accent. Something rich and deep, with soft exhales and a rolling tongue. I'd place my bet somewhere in the Middle East.

"Alexander and Kyle will take over showing you around the Coven House once Blake arrives," Sterling told me.

"Blake?" I asked.

"Executioner's fledgling," Alexander answered softly. There was a forced calmness in his voice that made me study his face and the looks shared between him and Kyle. It was too blank, too practiced.

"Executioner?" I asked, even more confused. But before anyone could answer, two men approached. The air felt thick the moment they entered the area. The fledglings drew quiet. Even their mentors had strained expressions. The only one that seemed completely at ease was Sterling.

He smiled as they approached. "Blake, it's good to see you again. Executioner, I hope the Frenzy wasn't too taxing. Mother is looking for you, you'll be assigned another job."

Everyone stiffened.

He was called the Executioner—though they used it as more of a name than a title—it wasn't difficult to figure out what that 'job' was. I expected to be afraid, but I felt strangely at ease. I couldn't be when the man attached to that name radiated waves of such sadness and despair. My throat felt tight and eyes watered as I studied him.

His hair was a deep black with a slight wave at the end, coming down to his muscular yet sloped shoulders. His skin was pale with warm undertones, with thin yet intensely sculpted bow-shaped lips. And that was as much as I could tell about what he looked like, because he wore a stunning white mask with a jagged stripe of silver across the left cheek. I couldn't see his eyes, an opaque white film covered them. It amazed me that he could see, but I could feel that gaze, the solemn attention.

Executioner. Was that the name Lilith had given him?

Why?

Beside him, at a much more average height, was a young

man. Younger than Kyle even, with short dark brown hair, tawny skin, and soft brown eyes. He was smiling wide with adorable dimples in his cheeks and it seemed to radiate from his pores like he was filled with sunlight. It melted away any tension from the group.

"Hi, Sterling! It's nice to see you again, too," Blake greeted. He offered his hand to everyone as we all exchanged names. He was warm and bright and full of life. It was refreshing.

And strange.

No one else seemed to notice the space between mentor and fledgling. They didn't notice how Blake avoided touching, let alone looking, at Executioner. As if he did not exist. No one picked up on how Executioner hung back, not a part of the group, but some dark shadow trailing it. How the Vampire was so impossibly tall and yet, one could easily overlook him in a crowd. Even with his unique style of dress.

He did not move, did not speak, did not integrate himself in the conversation that had struck up between all the lounging men. He was alone...just *standing* there.

Until Sterling looked at him. They stared at each other for a few moments as if having some private conversation before Executioner gave a near imperceptible nod and disappeared. He did not spare a word or glance for his fledgling.

Blake noticed. I saw those brown eyes briefly dart toward the Vampire's retreating form. His smile faltered, but it was so swift the change would not have been noticeable to anyone who wasn't watching for it.

Like I was.

Blake sat beside me and gave me a warm smile. "Looks like we're the newest additions," he said.

I raised a brow in question.

"I'm only a few days into the change, like you. I was going

through the Frenzy when you first arrived," he said by way of explanation.

"You seem to be taking it all well," I commented.

Blake shrugged. "Nothing I can do about it. Besides, all the fledglings I've met seem happy."

He was right about that. Alexander and Kyle were prime examples. But coming from him, the words seemed wrong. Not after what I had just witnessed.

"You don't find this whole thing strange?" I asked. Wondering if there was someone that might feel as unsure about it as I did. If even just a little bit of doubt. There was no way that everyone could just accept this all blindly without giving the possibility of it being ominous any thought. Lost memories or not.

Blake's expression became pensive as he contemplated his answer. "Strange? I suppose so. But I figured it didn't hurt to be cautious while still keeping an open mind. With everything that we are wiped clean, you can only trust your gut, right?"

I sighed and shook my head, but not really in response to him. How could he not see that if our minds are compromised, so might our instincts be?

Hale and Joel stood. Joel planted a soft kiss on Alexander's temple while Hale brushed Kyle's cheek affectionately.

"We'll be back," Joel announced.

When Sterling made a move to stand, I couldn't control the impulse and moved quicker than I thought I possibly could, latching both hands around his wrist.

I frowned at my hands gripping him, and hurried to let go. "I'm sorry, I don't know why I did that," I mumbled, feeling my cheeks heat.

Sterling smiled at me, caressing the side of my neck with one large hand. "It's alright, it's just part of the forming bond. I'll come find you once I'm done."

I didn't look at him, but gave a small nod.

When he left, I felt like half of me had gone with him. That clawing emptiness threatened to come back.

Master.

No. No, get a hold of yourself, I scolded internally. I couldn't keep pining after him like this. It was embarrassing. Especially in front of the others, who were all watching me. Alexander and Kyle both had identical knowing smiles.

"Does this ever go away?" I asked them, clutching my chest as if to keep my heart from leaping out and chasing after him.

"No," they said in unison.

Alexander sat beside me, his crystalline blue eyes warm and kind. "But it does get easier to manage. He'll come back to you. He will *always* come back to you. And once that sinks in, it becomes bearable."

I winced. Dealing with this forever is just another downside to this entire situation. I turned to Blake.

"Shouldn't you feel it just as strongly with your mentor? It didn't seem to affect you when he left," I asked and immediately regretted it. Blake's light dimmed and a sort of sadness emanated from his aura.

"I feel it. Trust me," he said softly and didn't offer any more information on the matter. I didn't pry. It was clearly something that was difficult for him.

Maybe I was being selfish. Here I was, with a pretty decent mentor—at least from what I could tell so far—and I was trying to find something wrong with it when I could be in a pairing like Blake, which was clearly broken.

My chest ached horribly. I rubbed it through the soft cotton of my button down. Nothing eased the pain. The only thing that could make it go away had just left.

"It's *horrible*," I murmured.

"I used to think so, too. But that was before I understood

what this connection was; it's a gift," Kyle started. "Give it time to make sense. And in the meantime, trust your mentor, obey your innate desires."

I nodded numbly, but only because I didn't want to talk about it anymore. Just because they went through the same thing I did, didn't make them my best friends. It didn't mean I could trust them. Who knows? They could have been brainwashed.

Stop it, Beau. Make up your mind. Are you for this or against it? Do you really think poorly of Sterling?

No.

No, Sterling was perfect.

"Fuck!" I hissed, hating the conflicting thoughts and feelings.

"Let's take a walk. It might distract you," Alexander suggested as my breath quickened and sweat gathered on my brow. I nodded, though we both knew there was only one reprieve from this feeling.

Alexander helped me stand. Blake and Kyle followed behind us as we made our way out of the salon.

"This is the library. You can literally find everything on anything here. Marcelle and Julia make sure that it's updated regularly to include all the latest information. What you can't find a book on, you can most likely search it up in the database. It's important when we begin to develop our affinities," Alexander said, gesturing to the large wooden double doors with foliage carved along the brass handles and outer trims.

Inside, the room was vast with rows and rows of floor to ceiling bookcases. There were tables and computer stations in every aisle. Everything was light wood with detailed etchings. Some depicted battles past fought while others were more abstract in their messages, resembling Hieroglyphics. There were few people milling about inside. We didn't enter.

Moving along, they pointed out the different facilities that were open to us and when they would become relevant in the timeline of our change. I wasn't sure if it was impolite to ask them what stages they were currently in. I'd already made Blake uncomfortable with my probing questions. It'd do well to make friends, not enemies.

When we made our way around and then back to the salon, the tightness in my chest eased. I didn't need to look to know Sterling was nearby. He appeared at my side, falling into step with us.

He thanked Alexander and Kyle for their time and bid farewell to Blake, who did not have a mentor to come greet him like the others did. I watched his strained smile as he waved and turned to walk down the hall to his own room...alone.

Where was his mentor?

As we separated and headed to our own rooms, I decided to ask. "How come Executioner and Blake don't seem as close as the rest of us? They don't even talk to each other."

Sterling sighed.

"Their relationship is a complicated one. It would do them both well to get over their differences and make an effort to step outside their comfort zones, but that is much easier said than done. Especially since the nature of their powers and purpose are so different. Opposites even."

"Purpose?" I questioned, pulling off my shoes the moment we made it back to the room.

"They both have an affinity for Earth, but in two very different ways. It hasn't manifested yet in Blake, but we suspect —"

"We?" I interrupted, hating the jealous note in my voice.

Sterling grinned.

"Lilith and I suspect that Blake's powers might be tied closer to life than death. You can imagine how that would make for an odd companion of the Executioner."

Yes, it most certainly would.

"But I thought fledglings take after their mentors when it comes to affinities?" I asked him. Though Nexus had mentioned it was unusual that I would have fire, like Sterling, so maybe that wasn't the case.

Sterling's brow twitched, but that was the only indication that I got that he heard me. He didn't answer, only pulled off his boots and headed to his office.

"I have some work I have to do. You don't have to stay in here, but I figured you'd want to after being apart all day," he said, completely changing the subject.

Yeah, that won't work on me. "Sterling, the more you try to hide something from me, the more curious I become and I *will* continue to pester you about it," I told him, sauntering over to his desk where he sat.

The corner of Sterling's lips pulled up in a half smile as he stared up at me. I leaned against his desk, just out of reach.

"You're going to be a thorn in my side, aren't you?" he said with a joking lilt in his voice. I grinned broadly.

"Of course! Now answer the question."

"Since when do new fledglings give orders?" he asked, still stalling.

"Sterling," I said with every ounce of warning I could muster. He was right in that I was rebelling against my instincts. Playful banter or not, my mind and body wanted to submit. I wasn't supposed to challenge him in anything. I was supposed to do what he told me immediately with no questions asked. But as he had once told me, who I was had not disappeared. I just didn't remember *why* I was that way. And apparently, I was stubborn as hell.

Sterling sighed, hand brushing his throat while he leaned his head back and closed his eyes. The smile was gone.

"It's not my story to tell. I will respect Executioner and his secrets, even if my precious fledgling wants answers."

Well when he put it that way, I felt bad.

I decided not to push anymore, but I wouldn't forget. No, I stored that information in the back of my mind to revisit at a later date.

"What are you doing now?" I asked, glancing at the piles of documents on his desk. He opened the lid of his laptop, powering on the device before answering. The bright cool glow was harsh against his face. It countered the softness of the fire's illumination.

"Answering correspondence from a few of the neighboring Covens. With the upcoming Mabon and Samhain festivals, they'll be visiting our Coven House for the latter. Many plans need to be put in place before they step foot in our territory. Especially near our Mother," Sterling replied mildly. His eyes never left the screen, most likely scanning emails. It made me realize that they have electricity and technology yet there doesn't seem to be a damn light in the entire facility. Everything was lit by candles or fire and even those did little. It was more of an aesthetic statement.

"Why aren't there any lights?" I asked.

"Because we don't need light to see, they hurt our eyes. Creatures of the night, remember?"

It was valid. It still seemed strange, though. Especially with the old furniture and decorations. The candles made it seem like we were stuck in the 1800s. Not that I would be walking around free if we were.

"How old are you?" I asked bluntly.

Sterling stopped reading to look up at me. A dark brow raised.

"Older than you."

I rolled my eyes. "You keep avoiding that question. Fifty? A hundred?" I pushed, studying him. He sighed and looked back at his screen, typing something.

"I fought in the battle of Auray against the English forces," he murmured, distracted, though his words were nothing to glaze over.

I remembered little from European history—amazing how that transferred over during the change and not my own name—but I did remember enough about the Hundred Years' War to know that it was nearly seven hundred years ago.

"Oh my god, you're *ancient*," I gasped, slightly horrified.

Sterling grinned without looking at me. "And Lilith is even older."

He must have seen so much in his lifetime. I wondered what it was like to live through so many different changes and advancements. Was it difficult to adjust or did he just mold himself to fit in with every era?

With history that far back, he must have lived through the colonization of America. As that registered, my eyes narrowed.

"Did you own slaves?" I asked him sharply, though it was foolish to expect an answer seeing as he would likely not remember if he had.

"You're not blind," he replied simply.

"What?"

He stopped typing and looked at me, eyes solemn.

"Look at my master, my *Mother* with skin darker than yours. Then ask me again if I owned slaves," he said icily.

"Not all slaves were African so skin color doesn't mean anything. If my lessons in history were correct, Christians brought Muslim slaves to France in the thirteenth century. Besides, you weren't always a Vampire. You changed when you were well into adulthood. Who knows what life you might have lived before then."

Sterling scoffed. "A 'life' isn't something I would call it. Besides, I was much too poor to even *think* about owning a slave."

But if he had the money, would that answer change? Would he have *owned* another person like they were a painting on the wall? A link on his cuff? An *object* with no freedom or will of their own?

Was that not similar to what we are now?

A master and his slave. His to do with as he pleased. No will or mind of my own, existing only for him.

I tried not to grow angry. Not to let it show because I wasn't sure of the words that might escape. And it would be foolish to damage the relationship with the single link I had to this new and frightening world.

So I stood, about to walk away and leave him to his work when it struck. I whirled on him.

"You *remember!*"

Sterling didn't react, didn't even move.

"I remember some things from my human life, but not much. It may happen to you, it may not. But any bit that I did remember, was not much to piece together on my own. It was Lilith who explained to me the things I saw. But we had learned that it was best that our human lives remained in the past. Forgotten. They cause unnecessary grief."

His voice had taken on a somber timber. And it was clear to me that there was some unpleasant history behind those words.

Was my human life something that was best forgotten? Was it something horrible?

"Why did you change me?" I asked him.

It was the third time. The third time I tried to pry this answer from him. Again and again he evaded, but I would get this answer from him. I would push him until he snapped and everything—good or bad—came tumbling out. Until I could make the decision on my own whether or not becoming a Vampire was my salvation rather than my eternal punishment.

"Beau—" Sterling groaned, annoyance clouding those mossy eyes.

I hardened my gaze, "Tell me, Sterling. Because you and I both know, I won't stop asking."

Sterling's jaw ticked.

"I already told you. You *asked* me to. You do not need to *know* anything else. Your life now is better than it was before. *Will* be better. So just let it go, Beau," he snapped.

"No! Because that's not up to you to determine. Only *I* can decide if my life is better now. And in order to do that, I need to know what my life was *like* as a human."

Sterling growled.

Actually *growled*. Low and dangerous in warning. Something that should not have come from a throat that looked so human.

But Sterling was not human. He was a Vampire. An ancient one at that.

A creature more deadly, more *powerful* than I could even imagine. Yet there I was, challenging him.

He wouldn't hurt me though.

I knew that with every fiber of my being. He was wholly dedicated to protecting me from everything. Even myself.

"Maybe not now, but in the future, can you please tell me? Trust me, like your Master trusted you? I don't think I'm as fragile as you seem to believe. And if my life was something truly horrific, then I know now that it is no longer a life I am forced to live," I responded gently.

The ice in Sterling's expression melted. His eyes softened to something more sorrowful. Heavy. As if the mere knowledge of who I was weighed down on his being. He gave one small nod before turning back to his computer.

I decided to leave him alone, stubbornly fighting the ache to stay by his side, and venture around the House on my own. Maybe I could learn a bit more about what my life would be like.

Since getting information is like pulling teeth around here...

I walked across the salon, noting the few groups of people around. They were all Vampires. Something about approaching them made me feel like a child trying to talk to the adults. I didn't really want to be near them unless I was with Sterling or they had their fledglings with them. Fledglings seemed safe enough. I wouldn't embarrass myself too much in front of them.

Strolling through the darkened halls that seemed to breathe with every step I took and passing door after high arching door, I found myself back at the library. It was strange though, I had looked for different things, turned down several halls, but it was like a maze was created and all paths led to the library. The House itself was leading me there.

There weren't as many people in the library as earlier, which if I admitted it to myself, made me feel a lot better.

I wandered through the aisles, scanning the shelves filled with books of all shapes, sizes, and topics. Academic textbooks, cook books, romance novels, travel guides, art books, dictionaries, journals...everything lined these massive shelves.

The tightness in my chest was near unbearable. It longed to be near him, to be by his side, to touch him.

I can't keep going like this. I have to push past it...

Brushing my fingers over the spines of a few books, I hadn't noticed the aisle was not empty.

"Japanese erotica. My favorite," a voice mused.

Startled, I turned to my left and saw a petite Korean female smiling at me. Her eyes darted to the book I was touching then back to me, grin widening. I followed her gaze and realized I was indeed stroking *Shunga: The Essence of Japanese Pillow-Book Eroticism.*

Jerking back, I smoothly shoved my hand in my pants pocket and turned to face her. Ever the picture of grace, I leaned against the shelves and smiled at her.

"I could play that off, but I doubt anything I say would make you believe me," I told her. She laughed. It was a pleasant sound, light and cheery.

"You'd certainly be right about that," she answered. We were quiet for a moment, appraising one another. I felt her odd gray-blue eyes trail up and down my form. And while she studied me, I did the same to her.

She was small, maybe five feet even. Her features were tiny, with a button nose, pointed chin, and small pillow lips. Her brows were thick and arched, matching her sleek black bob that moved with such smoothness, it could've been made of ink.

She wore a short white shawl with a high neck trimmed with gold. The piece was fastened together with a pendant. A loose white tunic was tucked into flowing white pants, cinched at the waist and clamped with a gold belt. Her shoes disappeared under the long white cloth of her pants.

"Done with your perusal?"

My head snapped back up to her smirking face.

"I'm Julia," she greeted.

Ah, so this was the Second Elder's fledgling.

"Beau," I offered.

"Oh, I know. You've been big news these past few days."

I frowned.

"That sounds ominous."

Julia snorted. "I mean, it's to be expected when one of the Elders takes a fledgling. Especially the *first* Elder. You'll have to get used to the attention. It won't go away."

"Sounds like that's the case with a lot of things," I muttered unhappily.

Julia quirked a brow, never losing her grin. "Trouble in paradise already? It's only been like, what...four days? Five?"

I sighed. "You're an Elder's fledgling, you should know."

Julia snorted, "I suspect my experience with Marcelle was a lot different than your experience with the First Elder."

"I suspect so too. Was it difficult getting information out of the Second Elder?" I asked, hoping that maybe this was a normal part of the process. That *eventually* I'd come to know all that my new life seemed to hide.

Julia pursed her lips before casting her gaze downward. Not a promising sign.

When she opened her mouth again, I perked up, hoping that I would finally get some answers, only to be disappointed when the next words actually left her lips.

"You don't trust your Master much, do you?"

My chest throbbed. I clutched at it reflexively, but knew what the pain was. I could stubbornly fight the desire all I wanted but it wouldn't go away.

I wanted to yell *of course not! Who in their right mind would?* But that would be a lie. Because I did trust him. Not that there was even a choice in the matter seeing as he quite literally owned me

He *owned* me.

When did that become such a comfortable phrase? So *normal* yet anything but. My ancestors are probably *screaming* right now.

"Listen, I'll be honest. At first I was skeptical, maybe it was the shock of my change or entering into this new world, but the moment I felt that connection snap into place? When I was given a name and Marcelle called me to her? I just knew it was going to be alright. And that feeling was right, I've been more than alright for years now."

I frowned. "How many years?"

Julia gave a small smile, "Thirty-five."

At first, I thought I heard her wrong and nodded about to ask another question until it hit me. *Thirty-five?* Sterling never said it could take that long.

"I can tell by the look on your face you want to ask. I am a special case. I can change any day now, but not even our High Priestess knows when."

"But what about–" the words caught in my throat that was too dry and scratchy to continue producing sound. I had been ignoring my physical discomforts for too long, I hadn't realized it had grown this intense.

"Go back to him, Beau. You'll need to feed soon," she said before giving a small wave and sauntering off down the aisles before I could even question her more.

I wanted to know more, learn more, but the ache in my chest grew. I was uncomfortable. I *needed* him. Damn it!

The pain was overwhelming, thick and heavy, locking my limbs until I could barely even stumble.

Could I make it back?

Sterling.

"Beau," he hissed, my name coming from his lips like a curse but full of worry and concern. It was so close, I could almost feel his breath against my ear, but I could tell he was still far away. My back slid against the shelves and my vision faltered as I went down.

Sterling.

Sterling, please.

As my head finally hit the floor, the world went black.

When I awoke, it was to the soft crackling of a fire. My nose was filled with that familiar citrus scent highlighted with the earthiness of cloves. As I struggled to open my eyes, I felt a weight shift beside me and a gentle breath fan over my face.

"Julia came to get me. Said your withdrawals were getting worse," Sterling murmured in my ear. The weight of my eyelids were much too heavy for me to lift, so I lay in the darkness, relying on my other senses to paint a picture. "Drink," he commanded.

A warm wrist was pressed to my mouth and that delicious sweetness dripped on my tongue, waking a beast of ravenous hunger. With burning force, my eyes tore open, stinging and tearing, but I didn't care. I gripped Sterling's wrist and sucked as hard as I could, greedily devouring mouthfuls of his essence like it would be snatched from me.

This feeling of utter contentment could only exist with Sterling's blood pouring down my throat. Nothing else would do. I *lived* for it.

"That's enough," Sterling whispered, pulling his wrist away. Despite wanting to latch on tighter, my body obeyed, releasing him from my grip and leaning back.

My eyes continued to burn, but the blurriness began to fade, the moment I swallowed that first gulp of blood. A soft groan left my lips as I squirmed, feeling my erection rub against the soft fabric of the sheets bunched around my waist. *When* I lost my clothes, I didn't know. It wasn't important.

"I want more," I croaked.

"You will get more later, but for now you need rest."

"Don't want to rest..."

I felt like I had been sleeping for ages. Sleep and feed. Since waking as a fledgling, those were the only two things I ended up doing. When there is so much more to discover about this new world, or even this Coven House, how could I continue to confine myself to this room and rest?

Because Sterling told me to.

Fuck this.

I sat up, forcing myself to disobey the clawing in my gut and the primal instincts that urged me to submit. I wouldn't. Fledgling or not, I would not succumb to his ownership.

I was no one's slave.

"You are so very stubborn," Sterling sighed. "I wonder if it is my blood that made you so."

I snarled at him, "Don't take ownership of *my* strength!"

Sterling blinked once, shock clear in his eyes. Cold dread filled my veins.

Obey Master. Apologize to Master. Apologize. Apologize!

"I-I'm sorry," I whispered, trying to breathe past the heaviness in my chest.

Too far. I had taken it too far. Baring my teeth at Master was too much. Raising my voice...*challenging* him, it was all too much. I never meant to go that far. Now I...

"Easy, Beau. You are fine. I am not upset with you. Take deep breaths." Sterling's voice was low and even, but his words did not comfort me because I read the coolness in his tone. He was angry. I *made* him angry with my aggression, my *disobedience.*

Small whimpers bubbled up from my lips as the heaviness threatened to crush me.

Submit to Master.

"I'm sorry, Master. I'm sorry. I'm sorry."

The words were so difficult to utter when my entire being felt like it was caving in on itself.

"Beau, it's okay. You are okay. I am not angry with you." There was a slight shift in Sterling's tone that instantly relieved the weight on my chest and allowed me to take in deep gulps of air. I clutched my chest, rubbing away the lingering traces of pain.

"I'm sorry," I whispered one more time, coughing as words still proved troublesome to formulate.

Sterling didn't say anything, just gently ran his fingers over the tight coils on my head. We sat in silence for I don't know how long, listening to the crackling of the fire and easy exhales of breath, alternating from one second to the next.

"Sleep, Beau."

And this time, I did.

6

WHEN WATER BURNS

Sterling was irritable today.

At first, I thought it was because of what happened the other night, but after observing him this morning, I deduced that the cause was related to the phone call and not anything I had done. I could still remember the quiet fury in his hushed whispers. The words he spoke were much too low for me to pick up, even with my sensitive hearing.

I tried to keep as much distance from him as I could, but even the thought had my chest aching and the task proved to be next to impossible. Not after last night.

The ache has proven difficult to deal with on a regular basis, but something about last night...the defiance, it triggered a response in me that begged for his approval. While before I could stand to be in a different room than him for a little, now, if I wasn't within touching distance I had a damn heart attack. It was awful. I fought it the best I could, settling for always keeping him in my sight, but it wasn't enough.

Fuck it all to hell.

"You're hissing," Blake whispered. I blinked, looking over at him, startled. My gaze shifted to others for confirmation. Both Kyle and Alexander wore identical expressions of concern.

"Something happen?" Kyle asked, brown eyes wide and all consuming. There was a gentleness in his tone that allowed for my retreat, but I figured who better to go to for help than them?

"Have you ever...disobeyed Hale?"

Kyle and Alexander shared a look of immediate understanding.

"Of course," he answered.

I frowned, not expecting that answer. "Really?"

"Not often, but yeah. The repercussions though...they can be a little unbearable." And by that, I knew he didn't mean that Hale punished him. Our instincts did well enough on that front.

"I didn't mean to. I mean, it wasn't even really disobeying, but I raised my voice...and I felt like-"

"You were suffocating?" Alexander finished.

I nodded.

"I just needed him to forgive me. I don't even think he was mad, but...I just *had* to beg for forgiveness. And now, I can't stand to be away from him. I feel like...I need to touch him, be near him, *please* him. It's fucking horrifying."

Blake placed his hand on mine and squeezed gently. Fledgling bonding. Sterling mentioned that some fledglings could find comfort in others.

"It's intense, but it will pass. Sex helps," Kyle offered.

I choked on my spit. "What?"

Kyle and Alexander frowned. "You mean you haven't had sex with him yet?"

"What do you mean by *yet*? Of course not! I don't think of him that way...really."

Well I mean, there were those few times that we...and he did say that we'd...

"Well no wonder your bond is so fragile. Sex is a necessary

part of Vampirism. We aren't human anymore so there is no stigma attached. We have sex whenever, wherever, and with whomever we want," Alexander said matter of factly.

Considering the first time I ever saw them and what they were doing, I shouldn't have been surprised by that response.

"Executioner and I never..." Blake said quietly. He was looking down at his lap, wringing his hands uncomfortably.

It was the first time I heard him speak about Executioner. Usually he avoided talking about him or even being near the male. This time I offered a squeeze of comfort.

"We know how strange this is and how much of you is still human, but you both need to understand that things are very different here. You are not restricted by the same things, but there are still rules. One of which is bonding with your mentors. Believe me when I say, your lives and transitions will be so much easier because of it. Embrace this new life and embrace your Master."

I heard them. I understood them. But I just couldn't follow. It went against everything I am...*was*...but I didn't even know what that meant anymore.

Sterling and I had taken baths together, slept together, and even found pleasure with each other, but sex? Actual penetrative sex? That was taking it to a level I wasn't sure I was willing to go. My uncertainty of this new world and the circumstances that brought me here might've been the reason for my reluctance, but it didn't change anything. There was no way I could put that level of trust in him. Not with the peak of intimacy.

"I can't stomach the thought of touching someone so close to death," Blake whispered.

Neither Kyle nor Alexander had anything to say to that. They could say whatever they wanted, but Blake's situation was unique. Sterling might think that the issues in their relationship are due to mindset but there was a lot more to it than that.

I couldn't blame Blake. No one could. But it only made me question the way everyone so blindly followed their Masters. What if it was a mistake that Blake and Executioner were paired? And if that's the case, what else could they have been mistaken about?

The uncertainty of it all, the smoke and mirrors, it made me uneasy. That's why this all had been so difficult. And the fact that I couldn't stand the thought of Sterling being more than twenty feet from me was just icing on the cake.

Fuck, my chest hurt.

I gently rubbed the ache as if that physical motion would really soothe the psychologically inflicted pain.

Because he could probably sense it, Sterling was at my side, gently brushing my cheek and immediately the pain dissipated. Well, the pain in my chest did at least; it did nothing for the raging headache that pounded behind my eyes.

Blake shrank into himself. At first, I thought it was because of Sterling's gesture, but then realized it was Executioner, silently approaching.

"Blake," Executioner said softly. His voice was so deep, slight, it was like a whisper in the wind. Blake went rigid. As Executioner reached to touch him, Blake flinched away before jumping up and shoving past, muttering, "I know!" and disappearing from the salon. Executioner stared after him for a moment, his blank mask more telling than a thousand words, before following after him.

When both were gone I found myself whispering, "I worry for him."

"Blake will be fine," Alexander reassured.

"Not Blake."

Alexander and Kyle's eyes widened.

"Such a quick study," Sterling murmured, brushing his fingers along my jaw, approval heavy in his tone.

My toes curled at the praise. I leaned in to his touch, no longer caring that the others saw.

"We have to get moving soon," Sterling said. I stood and said my goodbyes to the others before following behind Sterling. All my previous grievances and worries forgotten.

Strange how he could do that.

"Where are we going?" I asked when I realized he was taking me to a wing that was much different than the others I had explored. There were Vampires everywhere, with the occasional fledgling, all dressed in long black coats with large hoods that obscured their faces.

"Out of the Coven House. There are some things that I must see to."

"I get to come with you?" I asked, a bit shocked. Was I finally going to see Athens? I thought this would happen when I was more...stable.

"I can't leave you in your current state," he said matter of factly.

Even though he was right and I'd just thought the same thing, it still made me bristle. *Excuse me for being such a burden.*

He grabbed a coat, similar to those everyone else was wearing, from a hall closet and handed me one.

I slipped it on without having to be told, pulling the hood over my head.

"Stay close to me at all times. It's nearing twilight so you should be fine but if you feel even the slightest burn, tell me immediately. I won't have you going up in flames before you've even learned to control them."

I frowned, but didn't respond.

Sterling received bows from everyone as he moved through the halls, purpose in every long and powerful stride he took. I tried to maintain some grace, but it was difficult to keep up. The man was a giant.

When we reached two large black doors, guards on either side, Sterling finally turned to me, green eyes blazing with some unspoken promise.

"Where we are going is going to be unpleasant. I will not let any harm come to you, no matter what happens. Do you understand?"

I nodded slowly, unease beginning to fester in my gut like a rotting wound. Should I have been afraid? What had Sterling so worried? And if he was on edge, I definitely felt like I should've been too.

"Sterling..." The fear was evident in my tone as I stared at the large doors.

His hand brushed along my cheek and down my neck until finally reaching down to brush the puckered wound on my wrist. The one that started it all.

"I'm with you. Always," he swore, and then the doors opened.

I'm not sure what I was expecting, really. It wasn't as if I was swept away to another magical dimension. It was Georgia. And when we crossed that threshold...it *looked* like Georgia. I think the only strange thing really was that we were wearing coats in eighty degree weather.

Heat was a thick wall despite being autumn as we pushed through on to a sidewalk that led through what looked like a park. It was so *normal* that I was actually uncomfortable. Talk about strange.

Sterling moved quickly down the path, passing trees and benches as the early moon's light followed us in the crevices of the leaves. When we reached a black wrought iron gate, it parted, and a sleek black car waited for us on the street.

Without hesitation, Sterling pulled open the black doors and gestured for me to get inside. I slid into the cool interior, marveling over the leather and silver trims. I didn't have to know cars well to know that this was *expensive*.

Too busy marveling over the luxury, I didn't notice the man sitting in the far end of the car. The back of the SUV had U-shaped seats lining the edges like a limo, but smaller, more intimate. The stranger sat with his back against the driver's divider, in a cloak similar to ours with the hood pulled up, casting a shadow over his features.

I froze, staring at him uneasily until Sterling slid in beside me and gently patted my thigh. The moment he was seated, the car began to move and the male pulled back his hood, bowing his head in respect.

"Elder Sterling," he greeted. His voice was low and raspy, as if he hadn't used it in a while. When his head rose, I met the most piercing gray eyes I had ever seen. His hair was a mass of thick black curls, framing surprisingly tanned skin and a chiseled jaw. He was giving me Marlon Texiera vibes, for sure. His jaw was covered in a thin beard that framed plush pink lips.

"Judas. You've been well, I hope?" Sterling said, voice smooth, full of authority but lacking emotion. Similar to how he was when I first met him. Aside from Executioner, the High Priestess, and myself, he spoke with little familiarity to anyone. Even with Hale and Joel he was reserved, and from what I knew, they were his friends.

"Yes, Elder," Judas replied softly, his eyes brightening from that small acknowledgement. It was strange. I knew Sterling was important, but this was next level. I guess being holed up in Sterling's room and the limited amount of interactions I had with the other Vampires kept me from really grasping that.

Suddenly those gray eyes slid to me, yanking me from my thoughts.

"Judas, this is my fledgling, Beau," Sterling introduced.

"Hi," I rasped uncomfortably.

His gaze never wavered, he didn't even blink. "Hello."

Clearing my throat, I shifted ever so slightly closer to Sterling. Judas's eyes followed the movement and the corner of his lips twitched downward.

Sterling, obviously sensing my discomfort, gently brushed his fingers over my neck and then against the puckered wound on my wrist that marked our bond, as if staking his claim even though he did not need to. I appreciated the gesture, even if my mind screamed against it.

Judas's eyes darted toward my wrist, then back to my face, eyes glinting. It only served to make me more uncomfortable.

"Report," Sterling commanded, fingers still brushing gently against my skin. His thumb was blistering with heat. One would think the scalding temperature would be unpleasant or even painful, yet it was anything but. I wanted to roll in the flames like a feline in catnip.

I don't know if I'll ever get used to these strange cravings.

"This is the fourth ring we've found in the past month. It was smaller than the others. Sixteen slaves were found alive, but there are about twenty-one separate remains still intact. Ashes were found in the lower levels. We assume they tried burning the others so it is unlikely we will have a true body count."

"Any masters around?" Sterling questioned.

"Three. Beni and Leilia are with them now, awaiting you."

"The press?"

"Waiting outside the facility. The police have blocked them off the best they could, but it seems to only be garnering more attention."

Sterling sighed. Unease curled in my gut, not liking how unhappy the sound was. I shifted closer, running my own hand down his side. This urge to comfort–to pet him–was all consuming.

The car stopped and Sterling slid out, then turned to offer

me a hand as if I couldn't manage climbing out on my own. I was tempted to ignore it, defiantly claim my independence, but I could already see how poorly that would play out. I felt I'd learned my lesson on that subject, and it was not one I was keen on receiving again.

We pulled up to a side alley. A few people, dressed in cloaks similar to ours, were waiting by the door. They bowed as Sterling approached, opening the sole door they guarded. I followed after him as Judas closed in on our rear.

Inside was dark and eerie. The building had clearly been abandoned from the amount of debris and dust covering the ground. It looked like it might have been a restaurant or an event hall? But it was hard to tell. Something was vaguely familiar about it.

There was another door by the back with even more cloaked figures guarding the entrance. Sterling headed that way and as I made a move to follow him, he turned and stopped me.

"Stay here, Beau."

Anxiety rushed through me. "Alone?"

"I'll be right back. Don't move from this room. Do you understand?"

"M-master?" I hated how easily that title slipped out, but just the thought of him leaving had me in physical pain.

"What did I say to you before?" Sterling said softly, looking down at me with those glimmering green eyes of his, passionate and gentle once again. "I'm with you always. I will not let *anything* happen to you."

"I don't like this place," my voice was barely a whisper. Sterling's eyes widened a small fraction before falling back into place. It was such a swift change that even staring at him, it was easy to miss. He was silent for a moment too long.

"I'll be back soon. Stay here," Sterling said finally, then disappeared with Judas and the others.

Alone, it was even more creepy. I also couldn't shake the vague feeling of familiarity. The old musty smell, the thick atmosphere, the dread that seemed built into the very foundation of the walls. It was so familiar. My head throbbed. The ache came back full force.

Don't close your eyes or it will be all over.

I jumped, whipping around to find the source of the voice that brushed along my ear. It was soft, almost childlike. After scanning the room, it was clearly empty.

Fuck. I really don't like this place.

With every creak and smell, there was a warning to get out and get very far away.

Taking a few deep breaths, I didn't let it shake me. Sterling said he wouldn't let anything happen to me. I could trust him with that much. I was important for some reason. Maybe it was just because I was his fledgling, but my gut and the way Lilith looked at me said it was more.

Deep breaths, Beau. Just keep taking deep breaths.

Don't run, you'll make it worse for the rest of us.

"What the fuck?" My eyes continued to scan the room. With my slightly heightened senses, I didn't have any difficulty seeing in the dark. I walked around, peeking behind every fallen table and toppled chair.

Someone had to be messing with me.

Run.

"Shut up!"

Run!

"Fuck this!" I spun on my heel and headed for the door Sterling disappeared behind, consequences be damned. Sterling shouldn't have brought me if he was just going to leave me. Besides, he'd better get used to me disobeying. I wasn't going to roll over just because he changed me.

Okay, so maybe I would.

But not when he wasn't around to guilt me into it.

The hall was long and decrepit. It was a wonder the building was even standing. I checked every door I passed but the rooms were empty.

Damn it, Sterling. Where are you?

A quiet murmur of voices caught my attention. I drifted closer, but remained light on my feet, choosing to eavesdrop instead of making my presence known.

"Lilith hasn't made an appearance in several months. They aren't going to just let this go," an unfamiliar voice hissed.

"She sent me. That should suffice."

Sterling. *Finally*.

"You know it won't. The more bodies they find, the angrier they'll get. She is the face of all Vampires, it's her head they'll put on a spike as long as these rings keep turning up."

"Watch your tongue as you speak of my maker," Sterling growled and the sound was utterly predatory.

Silence ensued. As it stretched, I contemplated coming forward, but the voice spoke again. "Please, Elder. Give me *something*. I cannot keep them at bay for long."

Sterling sighed, "No."

"What should we do with the slaves then?"

"Assign them to Covens. They will be turned as soon as they reach maturity," Sterling commanded. It left my veins cold. They mentioned slaves before, but I was so focused on myself, I didn't even process the information.

Slave rings. Bodies. Children.

What kind of fucked up shit was Sterling involved with?

I could piece enough of the information together to know there was someone out there enslaving children. Making them do what?

Fight. Keep fighting. If you let your eyes close, you'll never open them again.

"Sterling, what's going—" I stepped into the room, scanning the hooded figures, searching for Sterling. The room was large and spacious. Most of it was falling apart with more overturned tables and cracking drywall littering the floors. There were about seven unknown Vampires in cloaks. Some were huddled in one corner while the others were circling a group on the floor.

Sterling was with them, looking down at three figures, bound and forced to their knees. Once I saw Sterling, I headed toward him until my eyes settled on one figure bound on the ground. Dark hair, blue eyes, and crooked nose.

That face. I knew that face.

I knew those fangs, intimately, as they tore into my neck. Over and over again. I couldn't get enough air. Never enough air.

If you let your eyes close, you'll never open them again.

Rage and fear erupted from me like cold flames. It was all consuming, empowering yet frightening. There was no controlling the flame, the force, the sheer power of it all. It raced, relentless and angry. Vengeful. I felt so hot, but freezing, like a bitter frost had sunk into my bones.

He'd hurt me.

This man had hurt me.

The fangs. The *fangs.*

Darkness edged my vision, threatening to tear away the bright blinding blue.

"If I let my eyes close, I'll never open them again," I whispered, not sure where the words came from, but it was important. I lived by them.

Don't let them close.

I forced my eyes wide, past the blazing blue until everything cleared, like water had swept it all away. All the fog, the confusion, the rage. Until I was cold, numb, and dripping wet.

"It's okay, Beau. You're okay. I'm here. Nothing will happen to you. I'm here."

It took a few moments to process the words and the voice. A couple more to realize I was on my knees and Sterling was wrapped around me, protectively. We were soaked.

I blinked past the few droplets of water that skated down my face. The whole room was wet, like a tidal wave had drowned us all.

"They're dead," someone said, shock in their tone.

A cloaked figure looked down at dark grayish brown sludge smeared along the ground. Right where that man used to be.

I knew him. Somehow, I knew him. But I couldn't remember from where or when. I just knew that he'd hurt me. He bit me over and over again.

I remembered flashes of pain and terror, but nothing concrete. The images slid around my brain, rolling and folding into each other. It blurred and dissipated until I had nothing but the aching numbness that started it all.

"I need to get him out of here. Judas, you handle the rest," Sterling said, but he sounded far away.

"Sterling…" I croaked. The weight of my eyelids was a force I was too weak to fight. I wouldn't last much longer.

"I'm right here, Beau. Right here."

Sorry.

I let my eyes close.

STAGE TWO

7
WELCOME TO STAGE TWO

My head throbbed so painfully I didn't want to try opening my eyes, but there was this nagging feeling that urged me to do it anyway.

"Beau?" Sterling's voice was soft, gentle, close to me. I stirred, trying to find the will to open my eyes. I was *exhausted*, completely drained. Like I had run a marathon and hadn't stopped to breathe.

"Open your eyes for me," he pushed.

And just like always, I was powerless to disobey. Blinking past the pain and confusion, I stared up at the blurry image of my maker. His hair was wet, making it look a much darker gray instead of his usual light shade. His eyes gleamed and it seemed way too bright. I shielded myself from them, wincing at the movement and the pain that had burned their way into my corneas.

"Hurts," I garbled, unable to make any more of a comprehensive sound than that. Sterling seemed to understand.

"Drink," he commanded, tugging my arm away from my face until a few drops of warm, sweet blood splattered on my lips. I lunged, feeding like I had been starved for years. So warm, so safe. I didn't want to let go. I didn't want to stop. I could stay like this, wrapped up in him, *forever*.

"Stop," the command broke the spell and immediately I unlatched myself from him. The pains that covered my body and raged through my head dissipated. Enough that I braved opening my eyes again and looked at his face. His eyes, they were still that brilliant green, but it didn't hurt anymore. "Better?" he asked.

I nodded then shifted my gaze around. We were in the car, but it didn't seem to be moving.

"What's going on?" I asked, licking my lips, trying to get the last bits of his blood on my tongue.

"You've reached Stage Two."

Stage Two...that's when I was supposed to develop my affinity. Fire. Like Sterling. But something about that didn't seem right. I didn't remember anything, just that voice. And running. And needing Sterling.

He left me.

"You *left* me," I accused, pulling back from him. Something sharp and unforgiving as it twisted in my gut. It soured the blood that still coated my tongue, tasting like betrayal.

Sterling frowned, eyes concerned. "What are you talking about?"

"You left me in that place alone! And those voices..." I remembered them. The warning in them, the fear it instilled in my bones. Familiar and yet...unknown. I still couldn't figure it out. Who *was* that? Where did the voice come from? Why did it feel like I *knew* them?

And that male...that Vampire with cold blue eyes.

"What voices, Beau? What did you hear?" Sterling asked, his voice careful and soft, as if trying to comfort me.

"'If I let my eyes close, I'd never open them again'," my voice sounded hollow as I recalled the warning. The mantra. It played in my head over and over again until I could hear nothing else. "He *hurt* me. You *let* him hurt me."

The accusations were irrational, but I couldn't stop them. Not with that voice still reverberating in my head.

"I'm sorry, Beau. I'm so sorry," Sterling said, pulling me into his lap and cradling me tight. It was just like when I first met him, the way he held me so close, nothing would come between us. "You're still here, Beau."

I blinked, confused. "What?"

"The voice told you that if you closed your eyes, you wouldn't open them again. But you're still here. Your eyes are open."

I blinked. Then blinked again. I saw only the skin of Sterling's neck, but it was true. I could see.

I'm not hurting anymore.

"I'm going to take you back to the Coven House. We won't leave again, not until you've changed. I'm sorry, Beau. I didn't mean to trigger any bad memories. It won't happen again–I won't leave you again."

I nodded and squeezed him tighter. He wasn't going to leave me even if he wanted to. He'd have to pry me off, limb by limb, because this is the only place I felt safe and I wasn't going to let it go.

But, those eyes. Their memory haunted me, mocked me, with cold odium.

"Who was he?" I asked. Sterling knew, I didn't need to clarify.

"Someone who will never hurt you again."

That wasn't an answer, but it was so typically Sterling. I don't know why I'd expected anything different.

"Yeah, because he's dead," I muttered, remembering the pile of wet mush on the ground where the male was once kneeled. I wouldn't have known that's what happened if one of the cloaked Vampires hadn't mentioned it.

Before Sterling could respond, the door to the car opened, letting in a small wave of thick southern heat. Judas climbed into the backseat. His eyes remained downcast but there was an energy surrounding him. Like the air itself was charged. It felt *aggressive*. Like a predator stalking its prey, ready to strike.

I curled around Sterling tighter, as if his presence alone could shield me from it. Sterling's arms tightened around me as his nose skimmed the top of my head. A comforting, soothing gesture that instantly calmed me. I couldn't be sure it was the gesture or something intangible that caused the sudden relaxation. Yet another thing this bond took from me.

"Judas," the name came out sharp and warning. I was startled at the sudden change in atmosphere. Sterling sounded angry. "Control yourself."

"They're all dead now because he couldn't keep his *shit* together. We have no one to question now. These rings are going to keep popping up. We could've gotten some answers, but now?" Judas's voice was a hiss, frustration clear in his tone.

I didn't mean to kill anyone. I didn't even...I didn't know what was happening. I *still* didn't really know what happened.

Sterling moved, it was quick and sharp. My head jerked up at the movement. His arm darted out and he held Judas by the throat. There was nothing but empty boredom in those cold green eyes as he casually strangled the Vampire.

"You forget yourself and I have no patience for ignorance," Sterling said. Commanding without any effort. He didn't raise his voice, bore no inflection in tone, just simply spoke. He spoke and all were compelled to listen. Listen and *obey*.

"Sterling," I murmured, looking at the unnatural shade Judas's skin became as the circulation of blood and air stopped flowing.

Sterling held him there for a few moments longer before releasing him. His arm resumed its place around my waist, gently stroking my sides as if to comfort a frightened child.

Judas didn't make a sound as the color returned to his face, didn't even look up from his lap. Just lightly massaged the skin around his throat before returning his hands to his lap and not uttering a word for the rest of the ride.

Sterling didn't say anything either, making the trip very long and very quiet. Only the sounds of the car and our soft breathing could be heard. I was grateful when the car stopped, nearly tripping over myself to get out of the vehicle, but Sterling didn't let me go far, pulling me back to his side. I had to beg him not to carry me inside. He settled for tucking me close and glaring at anyone who dared step within five feet of us as we entered the Coven House again.

Judas did not follow us inside.

Instead, he stayed in the car and closed the door behind us before the car sped away.

Where did he stay if it wasn't the Coven House? Was he not a part of our Coven? What was his role? What was his relationship with Sterling?

The questions cycled in my head endlessly, I hadn't realized we had reached the salon, standing before Lilith's dais. It wasn't the High Priestess in the seat this time, instead the High Consort occupied the purple velvet throne, eyes closed, humming to himself quietly. He stopped at our approach, opening his eyes and welcoming us with a kind and gentle smile.

"My children," he greeted.

"High Consort Nexus, is Mother unwell?" Sterling asked, concern heavy in his tone.

Nexus's eyes clouded with sadness before giving a small nod. "She has been lethargic as of late. I am sure it is nothing to worry about. What ails you?"

"Beau has presented."

The words fell in the air ominously, refusing to fade into the background noise around us. Nexus's eyes widened with happiness.

"Lilith will be pleased to hear it. What is your affinity, my child?" He asked, voice eager and welcoming.

"I don't-" I hesitated, looking up at Sterling in panic. I mean, I thought I knew, but I didn't want to be wrong. Not in front of the High Consort. I didn't know much about the affinities and how they worked other than what they had briefly explained to me. Besides, my memories of the events prior were a bit fuzzy and clouded over with this intense blue haze, it was hard to determine what had actually happened. The shakes still hadn't left me. A fine tremor raked my body though I fought hard to hide it.

"Fire and water," Sterling answered.

Nexus's eyes widened even further, a bright smile enveloping his mouth. "This is wondrous news! A double affinity!"

Sterling gave a pleased nod. His expression was fairly blank, but there was clearly pride showing in his eyes.

Despite them speaking about me, I felt disconnected from the conversation, as if they were discussing another person entirely.

I imagined some big change when they spoke of Stage Two. I thought there would be some kind of ceremony or event. But if I was honest, it didn't feel as if I had an affinity for anything. I felt no more of a special connection to fire and water than I did before. I thought maybe they were mistaken, but this was Sterling. I couldn't imagine him ever being wrong. Not about this at least.

How easily my tune has changed.

Did Sterling have two affinities? I knew fire to be one of them, but was there another I was not aware of? If it was only one, then why did I have two if I was his fledgling? What–or who–decided who got what affinity or how many? It wasn't Lilith, despite being our Originator. Could it truly be up to chance?

"We will return when Mother is well enough for visitors to share the news," Sterling said before giving a slight nod in farewell and pulling me away.

I noticed that he didn't give the same amount of respect to Nexus as he did to Lilith. Was this a rank thing? Was the High Consort not a higher rank than the First Elder? Or was it simply a lack of respect for Nexus? With Sterling, so cool and guarded, I couldn't tell. It was nearly impossible to read him.

Yet another thing to ruminate on later.

I was grateful when the familiar hall and door came into view. One would think I'd be sick of it after spending so much time in the same room, but it brought me comfort. Stability when everything was otherwise in the air. I no longer had a grasp on my own body. I had only just started to adjust to this new change and now I was going through another one. It was terrifying.

Would I even recognize myself in the mirror anymore?

The room was dark for a moment before the fire in the fireplace came roaring to life. I blinked at it. Then at Sterling. He was staring into the flames with a faraway look in his eyes. It was unlike him to be so lost in thought. I couldn't help but worry there was something bigger happening with my newly developed affinities. And if the conversation with Nexus was any indication, something was definitely up.

Like Lilith being sick. It didn't seem to be common knowledge. I hadn't even thought it was a possibility, but everything that was said in that old building about Lilith not showing up in front of the press or making any public appearances, it was starting to all make sense. It would show weakness if our leader was sick. This was a secret best kept for the safety of not only the coven, but Vampires everywhere.

I thought the bigger issue though, is that Lilith *was* sick. How? And with what? I didn't even know it was possible for Vampires, let alone the Mother of All, to *get* sick. Somewhere in the deep crevices of my memory, I had some knowledge of Vampires and a common fact was that Vampires were impervious to all human ailments.

Which could only mean that what Lilith had wasn't something a human could have. Right?

The confusion of it all made my head spin. I stumbled, feeling the weakness seep into my limbs, making me feel cold and numb. Not even Sterling's blood was enough to shake this.

"How are you feeling?" He asked, voice a soft murmur. When I glanced over at him, he was still gazing into the flames. As if sensing my stare, he shifted his head to look at me. But there was something in his expression. Like wonder. He studied me like he was seeing a new person. It was strange. Was this because of the affinities?

"Strange," I answered, though it was mental rather than physical. My voice was a little hoarse, throat tingling like I had been screaming. I suppose I had been…earlier. I met Sterling's intense stare. "Do you have more than one affinity?"

Sterling's lips quirked. Raising one elegant hand and wiggling a few of his long and slender fingers, a trickle of water began to dance around him.

So I was like him.

"Do fledglings typically take after their Mentors?"

Sterling's soft expression hardened, just a little. "No. On the contrary, it is very rare for a fledgling to have the same affinity as their Mentors. It keeps things balanced or so I was told."

"But don't Executioner and Blake have the same affinity?" I asked with a frown.

"Blake hasn't entered Stage Two yet, but it is what we suspect, yes. And that in itself is rare. The difference between them is, while their affinity might be for the Earth, their power is inherently different. Not like you and I. Ours is...the same in every way."

The way he said that last bit was ominous. As if it wasn't a good thing. Like it was something to be cautious of.

"Is there something wrong with that?" I asked.

"I don't know," Sterling sighed, then ran a hand through his hair, tousling the silky gray locks, still damp from earlier. "I don't know," he repeated. Then his gaze fell on me again, wide and mesmerized.

"Why do you keep looking at me like that?"

Sterling didn't answer, just turned and went into the bathroom.

Anger and anxiety getting the best of me, I followed him inside. "What aren't you telling me?" I demanded in a tone that probably wasn't very demanding to begin with. My instincts still warned me to be cautious. Be respectful. Not to anger Master.

He ignored me, bending over the tub to turn on the water. A rush of it came tumbling out, drowning the air with its rushing symphony.

"Sterling!"

Sterling was quick, behind me faster than my eye could capture. His broad chest pressed firmly against my back, his lips just a whisper along my neck, and his hand, just one, digging into my jaw as he forced me to look in the mirror.

I noticed the difference immediately.

There were still many similarities from before. Still had the short brown coils, a bit of a mess without the proper pick and products to maintain it. My skin was still smooth and a deep brown with reddish undertones. Nose was still straight, my lips still full. A light beard had formed, different, but nothing crazy.

Not like my eyes. Eyes that had once been a deep dark brown, big and wide, framed with dark long lashes.

Now, they were green. The brilliant green that mirrored the ones peering at me over my shoulder. Like glowing jewels, they dominated my entire face.

Sterling's lips pressed small kisses up my neck and jaw until he reached my ear. His lips were hot against my ear and his breath was a gentle caress. "Sometimes all of our human doesn't quite transfer to our Vampire."

"Were your eyes always green?" I asked, but too stunned to look away from my reflection. I was nearly unrecognizable now. How could such a simple shift change everything?

Sterling didn't reply. I wanted to be angry at him for keeping me in the dark again, refusing to answer a simple question, but when I saw his expression, I knew he hadn't really heard me.

He was staring, but it was so intense, so heated, I stiffened, distracted by it. By him.

He...*wanted* me.

There was no sugar coating it. No hiding from it. That look in his eyes was pure, unadulterated lust. Vibrating and potent, it sang in my blood like a siren's call.

"Sterling," I breathed, my voice a little shaky, hesitant as I watched him. Apprehension was tight in my gut, warning me of the inevitable.

With gentle, expert fingers, Sterling slowly began to unbutton my shirt, still slightly damp from earlier, clinging to my skin. Doing nothing to stop him, I tracked each movement, watching as the fabric began to part, revealing more of my skin, until it eventually fell away.

A slight tremble racked my frame with this new exposure. I had been naked in front of Sterling enough times that modesty was no longer a thought. But something was different about this moment. I actually felt *bare* before him. Like that final tether of control slipped from my grip and I was wholly his. No doubts. No reservations. Just...his.

No longer fighting it, I leaned back against him, relishing in the simple whispers of his fingers along my chest, gliding over the skin and leaving a tingling sensation in his trail.

My eyes fluttered, almost shut, but I couldn't stop watching. I was compelled to engrain this moment in my vision forever. It was something to play back again and again.

"Sterling," I breathed, voice still low. There was something predatory in his stare, his focus. As if one wrong more could trigger him to strike. In what way? *That*, I was still trying to figure out.

Everything was too intense. As much as I wanted him, especially with that look in his eyes that *screamed* just how much he wanted me, there was a part of me that grew weary.

Is this the moment I forget everything I stood for? Is this the moment I *really* let him in?

Could I trust him? Could I give up my freedom?

You never really had freedom to begin with. You're a slave, *Beau. Always have been,* always will be.

The darker crest of my thoughts surfaced. Each unspoken fear, tentative scenario that I had been squashing down with Sterling's promises were rearing up and fighting their way out. I was drowning in them.

What if this was the plan all along? Get me comfortable, make me let my guard down, then take what little of myself that I had left?

I thought I could trust Sterling. I really did. I had accepted my role as a fledgling. That I belonged to him. That my autonomy was his. That he *owned* me. But why?

Why had I let myself believe that this was okay? Because my *Master* wasn't a total prick? It didn't *matter* that Sterling was kind to me. It didn't *matter* that life for the most part seemed fine.

The fucking principle of it all was fucked to hell. It's *not* okay to own someone. Ever.

My chest felt tight as the feelings warred within me. It expanded, filling until I could hear nothing but my heart drumming in my ears.

I can't breathe.

"Beau, what's wrong?" Sterling asked, concern bleeding into the lust that even now, under these circumstances, wouldn't fully dissipate.

"I can't–I'm not–I," I gulped. I couldn't get the words out. I couldn't get any air in.

You're a slave.

"I'm not," I choked.

Sterling frowned.

"Not what?"

"I'm not a *slave!* I'm not your slave, Sterling. I can't sit here and *pretend* that this is okay. I want to trust you, but I just–."

"Hey, it's okay," he cooed. Like I needed it. Like I was a child throwing a tantrum.

He didn't respect me. Not really. Because slaves aren't given respect.

When he tried to touch me again, I flinched away from him. He didn't seem upset or shocked by the action. Just calm. Understanding.

How could he *possibly* understand? There was no way someone like him would.

"I know this is hard. I know that there are certain aspects of our pairing that make it difficult. I know that no matter how hard I try to empathize, I will not be able to understand. I know that coming from my position, I *can't* understand. I know that this isn't just about me being your Master, or your past as a human. I know this isn't just about my being a white man and you a black one. I know that it's everything combined and more.

I can only promise you that I will never stop trying to make sure that our bond doesn't encroach on your free will."

With every word my shoulders hunched, trying to shield myself from the truths I never spoke aloud but burned in my chest and filled my head at every moment of every day. That plagued my dreams when I had hoped the world of the unconscious would grant me respite. No matter what he said, the mere existence of the bond already did.

"You're not a slave, Beau. Not anymore. And I am not going to chain you, I promise. You are my partner. My equal. I belong to you just as much as you belong to me," he continued.

He guided my face back to the mirror, where our eyes said everything. Though identical in color and shade, they were different. Sterling's were cool, but gentle. Wise. Intelligent. They spoke of several songs unsung. They spoke of regret and lost time. But there was compassion, curiosity, and ambition.

Mine were big, vibrant, and burning. They screamed defiance. Independence. *Freedom.*

So alike, but so different.

I am not a slave.

"I won't ask you to let me in. Not yet. But...I want to let you in, if that's alright?"

He kissed my shoulder and this time I didn't flinch. The air in my chest deflated. The beat in my ears still banged and demanded the attention I could no longer afford to give it, but I could think past it.

When I was calmed enough to let myself return to the feelings of want, without the guilt or anger, Sterling led me out of the bathroom and into the bedroom, our bath forgotten. He walked me to the edge of the bed, but sat down first so he no longer towered over me.

There were few times I was able to look down at him like this.

"You are in control," he whispered.

I am in control. Sterling did nothing to let me think otherwise.

Cupping his cheek, I savored the rough brush of stubble. His eyelids lowered, but didn't close. He reminded me of a cat that was getting some really good scritches.

I smiled at the thought. This large man of mine, being compared to a house cat.

My thumb swiped across his soft lips. Furthering my cat analogy, his tongue dipped past his lips to lick my thumb. I shuddered.

I am not a slave.

My body moved fast, wrapping my arms around his neck as I pressed my lips to his. Soft. Yielding. Sweet. He did not force my mouth open even as passion rode our bodies, taking control of our movements. He still let me take the lead.

I guided him, my tongue brushing against his. My fingers dug into the silky tresses of his gray hair. His hands wrapped around my waist, as *I* climbed on his lap.

Needing to feel more, needing to feel the heat of him against me, the bareness of his flesh against mine, I tugged away any remaining obstacles until nothing came between us. I touched, explored, *ravished* his body until there was comfort and familiarity that only came with this level of intimacy.

Every once in a while, between kisses, as we fought to catch our breath, I'd ask him if this was still okay. I knew he gave me control because he knew I wasn't ready to trust him with all of myself, but that didn't mean I automatically had free reign on his body. He said he belonged to me just as much as I belonged to him, which meant we both respected the other to grant choice in everything.

Not once did he tell me to stop.

Every kiss became easier, every touch grew needier, until the ache in our cocks was too much to bear.

When he pulled a small bottle of lube from the underside compartment along the bed. I froze.

"I've never–" I started. Intimidation began creeping in. I didn't know the first thing about sex with a man.

Sterling smiled at me. "I'll show you."

He leaned back on the bed, crawling out from under me. I sat back on my heels watching as he spread his legs. The dark hair around his cock trailed down his thighs, along his heavy balls, and dusted around his pink pucker.

Utterly enraptured by the display, I watched as he oiled his fingers and gently worked one inside himself. He didn't break eye contact with me. Watching. Gauging my reactions, my expressions.

I'm not sure what was displayed on my face, but it was enough to fuel him on. One finger became two. He thrusted and curled until his toes scrunched and his head fell back in the sheets.

I fisted my cock. I couldn't help it. He was stunning. Even as sweat dripped down his brow and the fire in the hearth raged higher, brighter, hotter, I was completely mesmerized.

I pumped myself, watching him with an intense focus that couldn't have been all that attractive, but I didn't care.

"Fuck!" I hissed, shutting my eyes and squeezing so hard it edged toward the side of pain. But I needed it, or else I would have blown my load right then and there.

As he pulled his fingers loose, it was one look that had me scrambling over to him, eager.

I positioned myself between his thigh, meeting his gaze. He smiled up at me. That rare gentle smile and I pushed inside.

He was everything and more.

We moaned in chorus as the slow descent of my cock in his

ass overwhelmed us with sensations neither of us had felt before.

I didn't know if I was a virgin before this, but I knew Sterling wasn't. That look on his face though, said it all. As if he discovered a whole new world. It hadn't been like this before.

I found his hand, buried in the sheets, and threaded my fingers through his. It was as if there were tiny threads braiding themselves, becoming thicker, stronger, binding us together.

His emotions flooded me, coming so clearly it was hard to distinguish them from my own.

I felt the love, the trust, the honor he felt. The happiness and hope that maybe this long existence wouldn't be so bad. Not if we were together.

Thrusting forward, I drove myself deeper into the warmth of him. He moaned, squeezing my hand tighter.

Faster, deeper, I pushed, thrusted, grunted. Took, gave, started, ended. All with him.

As this invisible rope between us solidified, my pleasure burst through me. I couldn't even warn him as my orgasm overwhelmed me.

"Fuck! Sterling!" I cried, falling against him, still rutting, still desperate to take him over the edge, even as my dick emptied itself.

He squeezed my hand so tight, I hissed in pain. With my free hand, I gripped his throbbing cock until he erupted, spilling over my hand and splattering on his chest. We panted.

There was a silence as we caught our breath. But the moment our eyes met, everything changed.

∽

I WOKE WITH ANOTHER HEADACHE.

The dreams had been getting more intense. A kaleidoscope

of what felt like memories but moved too fast for me to tell. If I even could.

I kept hearing a name over and over again.

Anthony.

But no matter how hard I racked my brain, I couldn't remember. None of the faces were defined enough to help me recollect them. Well, there was one.

Lilith.

With all that was going on, it made me wonder if it was somehow linked to my past.

I wanted to ask Sterling, but I knew I wouldn't get an answer from him. The Vampire was annoyingly tight-lipped. So much for being my *Mentor*. That title was only that...a title.

But I didn't fault Sterling. I knew his reasoning...kind of. I mean, if what happened was any indication of what my past was like, it seemed best forgotten. I didn't want to forget and I didn't think I should, but I was starting to see why he would want to keep that hidden. It was his way of protecting me.

Not sure what I needed protection from, my only option seemed to be to go with it for now.

But was that something I wanted? My doubts, as much as they'd decreased, still hadn't completely disappeared. I was still wary of this new life I had been forced into, especially after what happened earlier.

That male was tied to my human past somehow. That much I could figure. And he was linked to the "slave rings" I had heard about. It was safe to assume that that's where I was from, right? Sterling rescued me from a slave ring. It was the only thing that made sense, given my cryptic background.

But *why me?*

That was a question I still couldn't piece together. Why was I special? What made the First Elder, direct child of Lilith,

Mother of all Vampires, choose me to be his only fledgling after over six hundred years of none?

"Get out of your head, Beau," Sterling chuckled, bumping me on the forehead lightly. I jerked out of my thoughts and frowned at him, rubbing the spot even though it didn't hurt. His finger drew light circles along my exposed hip, illuminated only by the fire that never seemed to die.

"If only it were that easy," I murmured, not really to him, but more to myself. I wanted to understand, but the more information I gained, the more questions I had. I needed to know. There was something large and glaring, pushing me to a revelation that felt just out of reach. It was aggravating. And this bond stopped me from asking the questions I wanted. The headaches that persisted any time something that *should* concern me, or raise questions, stopped any sort of progress I could have hoped to make.

Then when I did manage to fight past it, Sterling shut me down. I felt like I was floating, in a dream. Living in this world yet not allowed to make sense of it. I was only left with my interpretations.

A frustrated groan escaped me as I turned to my side, burying my face in the pillow, hating how the scent of clove and lemon scattered my brain like some drug induced high. *That's* what made this so difficult. His scent was literally a drug. *He* was a drug.

And I was a full blown, goddamn junkie.

Fuck *me*.

"I can feel your apprehension, your frustration. Talk to me, Beau," Sterling demanded, leaning in to plant soft kisses along my shoulder and the nape of my neck.

My toes curled as I enjoyed the attention.

"I can't think, not if you keep doing that," I groaned, this time with lust.

Sterling chuckled before flopping on his back. "After sex, the bond has grown stronger. Our emotions will touch each other much more frequently now. It'll be harder to part until you begin to wean off my blood and regular food."

"That's Stage Three?" I asked.

"Mhm," he hummed.

I turned to look at him. His eyes were closed and there was a small smile on his sculpted lips. It was strange. He didn't really smile, but seeing him like this, carefree, it made him seem almost...happy.

Was he *happy* I was with him? Was he actually happy that I was his fledgling, despite all the trouble I've caused?

Content curled in my gut and I snuggled close to his side.

"You're not getting out of answering the question. What's on your mind, Beau?" he asked, not opening his eyes.

I sighed, moment ruined. "What's the point in asking if you won't tell me?"

Sterling's brows twitched. "Well you won't know that unless you actually ask."

I have. Multiple times. But after what happened earlier... maybe he actually would tell me this time, if I worded the questions differently.

"Did you find me in a slave ring? When I was human?"

Sterling let out a soft breath while I held mine.

"Yes," he answered after a long pause.

"Why did you pick me to change?" I asked again, for the millionth time.

"You were...the only one left. The only one we could save in time."

The breath I'd been holding rushed out of me, leaving me lightheaded. I knew, but to have it confirmed made me feel a bit nauseous.

Did that even make me special?

Or the most pitiful?

Gulping, I pushed on, needing to know more. More of this forbidden information of my human existence. I remembered the blurred faces and happy laughter in my dreams.

"Did I have a family?"

Sterling remained quiet and my gut clenched painfully. I needed to know. I couldn't continue on like this without knowing.

"Sterling, *please*," I begged, lower lip quivering as I held back the onslaught of emotions that threatened to overwhelm me.

"You...*did*. But not anymore. Your parents were murdered when you and your brother were taken...and your brother did not survive the ring."

My chest was heaving. Shaky, shuddering breaths rattled in my chest. I clutched at my heart as if I could reach inside and keep it together.

I had a brother and I couldn't even remember his face. No name. Nothing.

"Sterling, I need to remember," I sobbed, scratching at my chest, willing it to stay together, keep me together.

Sterling immediately sat up, pulling me close and locking me against him. "This is what I was trying to avoid. I didn't want you to go through this. It's best if you don't know more. You don't *need* to know more."

"That voice I keep hearing, it's his. It has to be," I whimpered, unable to see past the tear soaking my cheeks.

"I don't know," Sterling sighed. "I'm sorry."

I cried and cried for a life I had no recollection of. For a brother I couldn't remember. For parents who I would never know again. I cried for the horrible life I must have lived.

I cried until the tears were no longer clear, instead they were stained with blood. I tried to wipe it away, seeing the mess on Sterling's pale chest, but the more I wiped, the more it flowed.

"I'm bleeding," I hiccuped, too numb to really panic.

"No, it's a Vampire thing. The further along in your change, the more it will happen."

Crying blood, that's a new one.

When I could finally get a hold of my breathing, and my blood wasn't rushing in my ears anymore–or out of my eyes for that matter, I found the strength to ask one last question.

"What was my name?"

My voice fell just above a whisper, but he heard me.

There was a very slim chance that he'd tell me, but it was worth asking. I *had* to ask.

"Jamal...Jamal Noah Du Bois."

Jamal.

I heard it. Processed it. But...

I felt nothing for it.

I sighed. "Thank you."

Sterling hugged me tighter. "I wouldn't have changed you if I didn't feel the pull, the connection with you. And even then, I asked you. I wanted you to have that choice. You and I both knew that even if I were to set you free in human society, you wouldn't be able to adapt properly. You saw too much, *did* too much. You were there for too many years. So I offered and you accepted."

I felt the truth in his words despite not knowing any of this.

"Has it truly been that bad, being here with me?" Sterling asked. I was surprised to hear a tiny hint of insecurity in his tone, but this was a moment of vulnerability. He helped me through mine, it was only fair that I helped him through his own.

"No. Not at all. I just...I needed closure."

"And do you have it?" he asked.

The numbness prevented me from answering either way. "I don't know."

Sterling didn't press further after that. We just sat there, wrapped up in each other's arms and warmth, soaking in each other's scents, and finally accepting that we were no longer alone.

At the root of it all, I think this was what it was all about.

Sterling had nothing for thousands of years. Sure, he was the child of Lilith, but Lilith is the Mother of All, she didn't have time to give special treatment. Marcelle and Stasia had their fledglings, but Sterling was still alone. There was that one, he said he made, but he was not their Mentor.

As for me, I lost everything and everyone.

Now we had each other.

8

FOREBODING

Something had changed. Not just between us, but in me. A beacon or something placed on me because the knowing looks I received as we walked down the halls told me they knew. Every secretive glance, quiet chuckle, not-so-subtle wink aimed at us only made my skin heat.

Sterling didn't seem bothered at all. As if nothing had changed from any other trip down the halls.

Fledglings and Vampires alike obviously knew of our secret proclivities. Could they smell it, or was I just that bad at hiding it?

Was I even *trying* to hide it? It's not like I had anything to be embarrassed about, considering how often and how publicly everyone here copulated.

Sterling would say I was thinking like a human. Maybe I was. Maybe there was a part of me that still remained human. Maybe there was something *wrong* with the transformation.

Maybe there was something wrong with *me*.

Or maybe it would just take a little longer to get used to.

After getting something to eat, I thought Sterling would bring us back to our room, but we ended up in a vast room I had passed but never entered before, near the library. There were large glass domes all around. Some were occupied with fledglings and their Mentors. I watched as they moved and conjured up the elements. Some grew plants from a single mound of dirt, others created droplets of water that cascaded down the walls of the glass. There were all kinds of miracles at play, and it all utterly mesmerized me.

Sterling led us to an unoccupied dome, sliding open a hidden door I hadn't noticed from our original distance.

"What is this place?" I asked, still distracted by the others. I practically had my face pressed on the glass like a child in a toy store window.

"A safe space to explore our affinities," Sterling answered, slight amusement in his voice as he watched me with arms folded across his broad chest. I watched him back, heat in my gaze.

He chuckled, coming closer to lean down in my ear, "Later."

I shivered in anticipation.

"Using your affinities isn't very difficult. It takes minimal concentration and very little effort. You think of something you want it to do, chances are, it will happen. What makes having an affinity difficult is knowing your limits. You go too far, use too much, and you'll be drained of your life force."

Ominous.

"No fledgling is allowed in here by themselves. For the most part, a Vampire will be on standby," he continued, gesturing to a figure leaning against the far wall that I hadn't noticed earlier. He was large with big beefy arms folded across his chest, lazily gazing at all the domes. "If there isn't a Vampire free to watch, the room will be locked."

I nodded.

"We'll go over a few basics before turning in. It's been a pretty eventful night."

I couldn't agree more.

The lessons were as easy as Sterling said they'd be. It made me wonder if that was the reason I didn't feel any different. It all came so naturally.

And I could see how that also made it dangerous. Feeling the limits proved difficult. There were times I thought I could keep going, easy, but Sterling warned me I was using too much, getting too close to the limit. That's when it became clear the need for practice was essential.

"Start small, then work your way up. New fledglings tend to put too much power into the smallest of tasks. Once you can master the correct ratio, you'll be able to wield it effectively."

"How does a Vampire replenish their reserves?" I asked as we made our way out of the training room and down the familiar series of halls.

Sterling grinned, "How else? Blood."

Right. Duh.

"Blood from your Master is the most potent. Some Vampires keep a vial of it on hand when they know they'll need it, or for emergencies. It helps accelerate healing as well." Sterling pulled out a tiny glass filled with dark red blood from his cloak before returning it to its hiding spot.

When we made it to the salon, I saw Blake laughing with the others on the couches. A little off to the side, hidden in the shadows, was Executioner. Watching.

Sterling immediately veered off to greet the others. Instead of following, I drifted off to the side, toward Executioner.

The Vampire was massive, even taller than Sterling who was a giant in his own right. He wore a thin white shirt and black pants tucked into calf-length boots that had seen better days. His mask obscured the top half of his face, including his eyes, but I could still feel his stare. I knew he watched me. Curiosity maybe? Or wariness? Probably both.

"Hello," I greeted with a warm smile.

The male dipped his head in greeting, not uttering a word, causing the silky tresses of his ink black hair to fall forward.

"I don't think we've properly been introduced. I'm Beau," I offered my hand.

Executioner was impossibly still, I didn't even know if he was breathing. After a long moment, his head slightly moved, as if he was looking down at my outstretched hand before tentatively. He reached out and grasped it.

His grip was light, unthreatening, even covered in thick leather gloves. It made me wonder how someone so gentle could be the Executioner. The others avoided him like the plague. Fear in their eyes.

I didn't understand how anyone could fear someone so sad? Being this close, I was practically drowning in it.

Executioner released my hand quickly.

"Are you happy to be back from your mission?" I asked. Poor choice for small talk, but what else was I supposed to say? I couldn't ask him outright why he was sad. Why he didn't talk to Blake. Why he didn't talk to *anyone* but Sterling. If he was lonely.

He gave a slight nod.

"That's good. I'm glad you're back unharmed." Though I was unsure what his mission entailed so it might not have been dangerous. Then again, he was the Executioner so it had to be dangerous, right?

His head jerked, as if surprised by my words. I smiled at him again.

"We should have dinner together," I offered, really just curious to see what he'd be like in that setting. It was hardly necessary since he only consumed blood.

He shook his head. I frowned at the rejection, but nodded, respecting his decision. Just before I turned to head back to Sterling, I heard a low, soft voice.

"But maybe...someday."

Surprised that he answered, I whipped back around. He was gone.

Despite the abrupt departure, I took that as a win. He agreed. That was more than I expected.

If he socialized a little more, if everyone didn't ostracize him, maybe he wouldn't be so sad.

Maybe.

When I reached the others, they were all giving me weird looks. Well, everyone but Sterling. I expected that, though.

Blake's stare was the most intense.

"Did he speak to you?" He asked, voice quiet. I couldn't tell if there was a hint of irritation or if I was just being paranoid.

"Sort of? I invited him to dinner with us next time. You should come too," I offered, giving Blake the same smile I had offered Executioner.

"Like I'd want to have dinner with that monster," Blake spat.

The skin around Sterling's eyes tightened.

"Enough of that," I said evenly, leveling Blake's stare with one of my own. "That's your Master."

Blake let out a humorless laugh. "That's rich, coming from you. You were the main one against all of this! What? You got a bit of cock and now you're gung-ho for him?"

I don't remember moving. One second I was next to Sterling, the other, I was across the space, in Blake's face, baring fangs I hadn't developed yet.

"Watch yourself when you speak of *my* Master," I hissed. The tone was dark, low, ugly, and full of promises.

Blake is my friend, my fledgling brother...*and he's hurting.*

I took a deep breath, calming myself. Leaning out of Blake's space, I stared down at him. "It's because I was so against it before that I'm telling you now, the more you fight against it, the harder it will be for the *both* of you. Put some *effort* into developing a relationship with him. He's hurting, and he's lonely. Is that not what you were when you first got here? Is that not how you *still* feel, despite all the smiles and warmth you've shown to us?"

Blake glared at his lap but didn't reply, so I pushed on.

"You only have each other, Blake. I know you may not understand what he does or why. But give him the chance to explain it to you. Give *him* a chance."

"He won't speak to me," Blake whispered. It was quiet but wet, like there were tears just beyond the surface.

"Maybe if he felt like you'd listen, he would open up. He's just as wary of you as you are of him," I suggested, then squeezed his shoulder for reassurance.

"Your fledgling seems to have adapted well, Sterling," a low, smooth, unfamiliar voice cut across the space, drawing everyone's attention.

Standing behind the group was a Vampire dressed in a dark red satin shirt, black leather pants, with matching boots, under a dark-colored cloak. It still wasn't enough to cover their pale, almost translucent skin. Their face was a delicate triangle, framed by impossibly white straight hair that seemed finer than even Sterling's. Their eyes were large and light gray, framed by long white lashes. If it weren't for the thick black rings around their irises and the darkness of their pupils, I'd almost mistake them for blind.

But that attentive, searching, unyielding gaze saw everything. I was sure of it.

"Stasia," Sterling greeted with a slight dip of the chin, but was otherwise uncaring. He was back to the cold, no nonsense first Elder.

So this was the third Elder?

Something about them was not sure if it was an aura or just a vibe, but it screamed danger. I stepped closer to Sterling, my eyes never leaving the newcomer. Their gaze never left me either. They tracked the movement with a tiny quirk of their lips.

"Beau, this is the third Elder, Stasia. And their fledglings, Asher and Cadence," Sterling introduced with the same bored tone.

Fledglings?

Stepping from behind Stasia's back was a young man and woman. The man was tall, broad, roped with muscles. His dark head was buzzed low and skin was pale but not nearly as much as Stasia. He had strong features, square, full of hard edges, and sharp planes. Where the man was large and harsh, the woman was petite and soft. She had the same dark hair, pulled back in one braid. Her frame was thin, tiny, delicate looking, but that stare was anything but.

They had to be the twins. From their pale skin to their dark brown hair and ice-blue eyes. They were different, but identical. It was strange to look at. The same long noses and flat bridges, the same wide mouths, the same deep set light blue eyes.

I looked at them, then back to Stasia who still watched me.

Two. This Vampire had *two* fledglings. Aside from Lilith, I hadn't seen anyone here with more than one.

Just how powerful was Stasia?

"Hello," I said, with a slight dip of my head, mirroring Sterling.

Stasia raised a brow, and their lips quirked again before they turned on their heels. Just as they were about to walk away, they spoke. "Shame about the fire. Could have found some valuable clues there." Then they walked off.

Sterling's eyes tightened briefly before the smooth mask of casualness was firmly in place. When Stasia and their fledglings were well out of earshot, it was Alexander who broke the silence.

"I never liked them," he said with a huff.

"Why?" I asked. I needed to know more about Sterling's reaction and, more so, my own gut feeling. They were no good, that much was clear.

"They like to play rough, and by no one's rules but their own. Nasty attitudes too," Kyle said, with a sour look on his own face. "I'm surprised they're back after–"

"Beau," Sterling said, standing abruptly. His face was stony.

Shooting the others an apologetic look for the sudden departure. I hurried to his side, struggling to match his pace when he began a brisk walk.

"What's wrong?" I whispered, not sure where we were going. It certainly wasn't back to our rooms.

"Things just got a lot more complicated."

9

THE NEW MOTHER

I didn't have enough time to press Sterling for more information. All of my concentration was focused on not getting left behind.

Fledglings and Vampires alike took one look at Sterling and nearly leaped out of the way. He looked like a vengeful god on a mission. I couldn't blame them for their hasty retreats, and with this new bond in place, I could almost taste the frustration and anxiety that curled around him, yet didn't leak into his aura. There was no one else that could feel this from him. No one else but Lilith.

And it took me half a second to realize that's exactly who we were going to see. She was ill, I remembered Nexus saying that.

Should we really be disturbing her? What was so important that it had Sterling this riled up?

And what the hell did Stasia do to get this sort of reaction?

When we reached the familiar ornate doors, Sterling didn't knock or even hesitate before them. Instead, he pushed them open with a force that nearly knocked them off their hinges. I winced.

No one was in the main area, near the shallow pool where I

had seen her last. Not even Nexus, but that didn't deter Sterling. He continued off to the left where I saw another hall framed by a high golden arch. His stride never faltered as he headed in that direction. I followed close behind, trying to see past his billowing cloak.

After a few more twists and turns, we finally made it to a small dark room with a single window, bathing the walls with the moon's light. There was a large bed to one side that looked a bit rumpled, clearly slept in, and a low bench right beneath the open window, with a clear view of the waning moon.

Sitting on the bench was Lilith, dressed in a thin white gown, elegant braids free, snaking down to the floor with their impressive length. She held someone in her arms, her beautiful face illuminated by the moonlight as she murmured into the person's black hair. Her eyes were soft, pained.

But the man in her arms, he was contorted in anguish. Dark bloody tears streaked his pale cheeks. His expression alone nearly brought tears to my own eyes. And those *sobs*...they were gut wrenching, low, and filled with agony.

He was of Asian descent, southeast. Myanmar, if I were to guess. His face was made up of sculpted lips, high cheekbones, dark brown eyes, and thick dark brows. He was large, that much was clear. It was strange to see such a large man be cradled by such a tiny woman.

Lilith cooed to the crying Vampire, stroking his disheveled black locks. She didn't look up at our approach, didn't stop her cooing. We would wait until she was able to settle him down, that was the unspoken command.

I looked up to Sterling, to gauge how he felt about waiting when he was so anxious before, but I was surprised to see a look of anguish on his own face as he stared at the man.

"What happened, Obi?" Sterling asked, his voice taking the same soft tone that I thought had been reserved for me.

The man's shoulder's trembled. He didn't speak. Couldn't. Not with the sobs still consuming him.

"He can't keep doing it, Mother. It's breaking him," Sterling pleaded, rushing to the man and pulling him from Lilith's arms to cradle his head to his own chest. The man clung to Sterling, shaking.

Lilith sighed. "It's his nature, Sterling. There is no fighting that."

"There has to be another way," Sterling growled. I flinched. He'd never been so disrespectful to Lilith before. I didn't understand how he could even manage if what he felt for her was the same as what I felt for him.

"There is a way. Through his fledgling," she said sadly. Then her gaze landed on me, where I stood awkwardly, unsure of what to do, or even what was happening.

She smiled at me. I offered one back before casting my eyes downward, not wanting to be disrespectful. And there, at her feet, I saw something white lying on the ground. A *mask*.

My head jerked up to the man, with wide eyes.

Was that...*Executioner?*

With his mask gone, it was like the floodgates had opened and all the sadness, all the pain that he kept bottled up came tumbling out. I couldn't tell if the feelings alone were coming from him or if it was Sterling's, feeding through the bond. I staggered under the crushing weight of it all.

"We're here, Obediah. We're here," Sterling cooed to him, stroking his head as Lilith had done. I watched, frozen to that spot.

I shouldn't have been shocked. We had gone over this several times, but seeing it again after the connection we shared was... different.

Through the bloody tears, Sterling tilted Executio–er–*Obediah's* head up and kissed him. It was tender, but a promise. A promise that it would lead to something more, and the way Obi clung to him, pushed into him, desperate in deepening the kiss as if starved of connection, of contact, told me that their *connection* was all but assured.

A part of me was jealous. I couldn't help it. I didn't *want* to share Sterling. But knowing Obi's situation, that was selfish of me. Our nature didn't view sex or intimacy in the same way. I had to break out of those human habits.

So I watched. Tracked each slide of their hands, gently peeling away clothes. I listened to every whimper, every beg, and watched as they became one.

Lilith was smiling softly at them, then at me. She held her arms out for me. I joined her on the bench, right across from them.

She curled around me, tucking me close against her chest, resting her chin on the top of my head, and wrapping her arms around my waist. It was the embrace of a small child on their mother's lap.

Strange. All of this. How right it felt. How calm her embrace was. How okay I was with what happened not even two feet away.

I studied Sterling's face, glistening with sweat as he thrust into Obi, whose own face was a mix of rapture and pain, blood still smeared on his cheeks.

No human would understand this. None would feel the current of desire–not sexual–and comfort that flowed through the four of us.

"Obediah was the first Sterling turned, but he remained *my* fledgling," Lilith explained. "They are connected, but not in the same way you are connected. More than brothers, sure, but not too far off."

"Why? Why didn't Obi stay as Sterling's fledgling?" I asked, wondering if Lilith would answer where Sterling would not.

"Because neither of them felt the call. It was on my orders that Obediah was changed, but that alone."

"Was Obi ordered to change Blake?"

Lilith hummed, the rasp in her voice one of contemplation.

"No. He felt the call. It's his own mind, his own affinities, that he fights against. That is the cause of his pain. But their bond is inevitable."

As Sterling gave a final grunt, I focused my attention back on him. He was panting, but still whispering softly to Obi. Still comforting and stroking.

After a few more calming touches and soft words, they both dressed, not caring about the sweat and other fluids still clinging to their skin.

"What's the importance of the call?" I asked Lilith, still watching the two men, who were now dressed. Sterling was murmuring to Obi while helping him fasten his mask back into place.

"Not all humans survive the change into a Vampire. That's because the Vampire blood they had taken in was not compatible with their body. The call ensures compatibility. I do not allow changes to be made without the call. It's an unnecessary loss of life."

"Then why did you have Sterling change Exec–*Obi* if they didn't feel the call?"

"Because Obediah is special," she answered with a smile in her tone, though I could not see her face. I waited for more of an explanation. She didn't give one.

Typical Vampire.

Obi turned to us, with his mask firmly in place, looking as he always did. Large, still, and forlorn. He bowed at the waist to Lilith, who dipped her head in acknowledgement, before he nodded at Sterling–and even me.

When he left, Sterling watched him go. His dark brows

scrunched in concern before slowly fading back to neutrality when returning his gaze to us.

"You must never reveal his name, his identity, or anything about him," Sterling said to me. His tone brokered no argument and no room for slip ups.

"Yes, Master," I answered automatically. Sitting up and alert.

There was still a part of me–though much smaller than before–that hated calling him that.

"Are you feeling any better, Mother? Nexus said you weren't well," Sterling asked, the concern back in his eyes.

Lilith sighed. "There is much I must tell you, but first," Lilith's eyes traveled to mine. Her red eyes darted back and forth between my now emerald green ones. "You have entered Stage Two."

I nodded, then looked at Sterling.

"He has an affinity for water and fire," Sterling supplied.

Lilith didn't seem surprised, even though this was supposed to be a rare occurrence. Did she already know, being the first and the Mother of us all?

"And his control?"

I winced, remembering the manifestation of my affinities. How I *murdered* people. It didn't matter if they were awful, it wasn't my right to take their lives.

"He has potential," Sterling said, surprising me. "He took to his lessons quickly. Aside from his initial manifestation, he hasn't burnt out."

Lilith hummed in approval. My chest warmed happily.

"Then I think it's time to bring him into the mission."

Sterling frowned, "Lilith, he's only just entered Stage Two. He's not even fully–" Lilith held up her hand to stop him mid speech, which he did immediately.

"He is not like the others and you know it. His change will be swift. I have seen it and you have felt it. He's ready. Besides, we can no longer wait."

Lilith's tone was solemn, brokering no room for argument. Sterling didn't protest further, though the slight downturn of his lips said he certainly did not agree with the decision. He remained silent, waiting for more information. I just stared at them, confused and unable to pick up on the context clues.

This had to do with the sickness or the slave rings? What could I hope to contribute? I barely knew anything about our culture–our society yet. I was a newborn fawn just getting his legs under him. If anything, I'd be a hindrance to any investigation or mission. Judas made sure I knew that much.

"I am with child."

The air was sucked out of the room with those four simple words. My reaction was more of a residual effect of the bond with Sterling. His panic, shock, and unease blasted through me with full force despite his expression remaining calm and collected. It was incredible how unshakeable he was. Outwardly. That kind of control could only have been mastered in the six hundred plus years he's been alive.

"And this is the end of my cycle," Lilith continued.

Sterling lost his control, face crumpling. The gut wrenching despair was bitter in the bond. More intense than that of even Obediah.

"What does that mean?" I asked, unsure of Sterling's reaction.

"It means, my child, that my reign has come to an end."

I frowned. "But aren't you immortal?"

Lilith laughed, deep and throaty. "We all like to think so, but everything comes to an end eventually." She released a slow breath, her gaze traveling down to her flat stomach. Her hand gently caressed it, a small smile tugging at her blood red lips. "When she is born, she will be your new Mother."

She looked up at us both then, "And it will be your job to protect her until she comes of age."

Sterling's jaw clenched as he looked up toward the ceiling. His throat moved, Adam's apple bobbing as he fought past any emotions that were trying to overwhelm him.

I'm not sure if it was due to our recent connection through sex or if this was just an inherent instinct for fledgling and Vampire, but as his darker emotions grew, I sucked them out of him. It was like I was some sort of vacuum. All the rage, the sadness, the helplessness, it bled into me. The more I took, the calmer Sterling became.

I trembled, hunching over as salty, copper, tears stung my eyes and irritated the skin on my cheeks. Gasps left my lips in powerful bursts.

Calm down, Beau. It's not your emotions.

They aren't yours.

But everything that was Sterling's was mine. That's simply how the bond went.

"Calm yourself Sterling if you don't want your fledgling to go feral," Lilith commanded. Her tone was sharp with disappointment.

The overwhelming emotions tapered until there was nothing left to pull. Sterling was calm and so was I.

I wiped my face, frowning at the blood. That was going to take some getting used to. I'd cried more times in the past week than I had in my entire life...I think. Well actually, who knew, I could've been a total crybaby when I was human.

Sterling's expression was smooth, but his green eyes were dull. He may have stopped me from siphoning his grief, but that didn't mean it went away. "How long?" he asked Lilith.

"I likely won't survive her birth," Lilith answered. She was so matter of fact about it. Like we weren't discussing the end of her life. She'd lived for thousands of years...I guessed. How could someone live that long and then be okay with all of it suddenly ending? Didn't she want to be there for her daughter? To raise the new Mother?

Then again, living that long must've been exhausting.

"You've known this whole time, haven't you?" Sterling asked flatly.

Lilith didn't answer, just smiled. That only seemed to anger Sterling more. While I could see it behind his eyes, I could not feel it within our bond.

Was he blocking me somehow? Was that even possible?

I didn't like it. I mean, I knew it's necessary, but the block felt...unnatural. I was supposed to be connected to Sterling. Instead of the warm tendrils that usually hummed between us, I felt nothing but artificial docility. It was cold, unfeeling, and I hated it.

"And who is to raise her? This new Mother? Surely you don't expect the responsibility to fall solely on Nexus?" Sterling's eyes narrowed as a brief silence ensued. "Is Nexus aware of your condition?"

"No. And you are not to tell him. It would worry him unnecessarily and I need him to focus on the other Coven Houses."

"So that's why Stasia's back? After what they did you're just going to-" Sterling's angry hysterics died off as Lilith's expression changed. It wasn't really her face but her energy that made the blank stare more solemn.

"Has something changed?" Sterling asked, his gaze intense again.

Lilith pursed her lips, looking down at her stomach rather than Sterling. "High Priest Carlisle and High Priestess Ninetta are stirring up some of the more...*radical* of my children. They do not appreciate my methods of handling the humans. There have been a few groups taking matters into their own hands."

If Sterling's jaw clenched any tighter the bone might shatter.

My gaze worriedly flickered between the both of them, hoping for some sort of context.

"And who is to say they aren't behind the rings themselves? It's the perfect excuse to undermine your authority. To take *over*. We all know that's been their plan all along. And after that stunt the twins pulled, who knows where Stasia's loyalty lies," Sterling growled.

"You and I both know that we cannot assume and I will not have a feud start between my children, no matter how they feel towards me."

"Mother-"

"My word is final. No drastic moves. Not without concrete proof. Things will go badly if this is not handled with the utmost care. And you will be civil with Stasia. They are blood."

Sterling let out a small frustrated breath, but his agitation didn't so much as leak into the bond. There was still that artificial wall of calmness between us.

"We can't keep letting things slide. Someone has been leaking information to the other Covens. And any leads we have end up dead," Sterling told her, a hint of exasperation in his voice. "How long are we supposed to keep taking these hits?"

"As long as we need to. With the new Mother, there will be no mistake. Our power will shift. This is the time to build alliances not make more enemies. At the next Solstice, you are to welcome Ninetta and Carlisle as you would the others. Show all of the Covens that we are not intimidated by baseless rumors and small trials. Stability in times of hardship is important and shows strength. The others will see that. Not all, but the details do not matter. You need to build the foundation for the new Mother and this is how you begin."

Sterling kept his eyes downcast, but I could tell from the stiffness in his shoulders, he did not agree.

Lilith knew, there was no way she didn't, but she paid us no mind, just absently stroked her stomach, never losing that small secret smile.

"You will be good to her. I know it," Lilith murmured.

Unable to stand it anymore, Sterling turned on his heel and stormed out of the room. I followed close behind.

His strides were long and ate up distance that made it hard to keep up, but I didn't complain. Not when he was like this. I couldn't imagine how he must feel, to know that his creator, his mentor, was going to die. This bond between us was new, but I was just now starting to grasp its importance. The weight of what it means to be Mentor and fledgling. I understand a little bit more of what Hale and Alexander were trying to explain. Just a little.

When Sterling made it back to our room, I closed the door gently behind us, watching carefully as he ran his long fingers through his light gray hair. Again and again until the movement wasn't enough and he took to pacing.

Still, I felt nothing. Just that eerie artificial calm. The foreign sensation made me itch. I felt useless, just watching him pace back and forth, unable to ease his anxieties or do *anything* to help.

"It's okay, let me take it from you," I offered, taking one step toward him. It was the only thing I could think of. Who cares if I went feral? I could do this for him. I *would* do this for him.

Sterling stopped and spun toward me, his gaze looking haunted. I blinked, startled by the sudden change and attention.

"What?"

I sputtered, unable to find words as confusion settled in.

"Your emotions. I can take them, like before," I said. The words were choppy, unsure, and hesitant in delivery because I couldn't *read* him. I didn't know what he was feeling because of that damn block. Though his expression told me enough.

"You'd go feral, Beau," he stressed, as if that meant something.

I shrugged, not understanding.

Sterling frowned. "Feral means you lose all control of yourself. That you go rogue. Spurred into a feeding frenzy."

"I don't have much of myself to lose, remember?" I laughed, meaning it as a joke but the silence told me it did not land well.

He stared at me for a long moment. "You'd have to be put down if you went feral, Beau."

Maybe he was expecting that to be meaningful. Maybe he thought I was as desperate to live as I was when I asked him to turn me. I couldn't say I felt that way anymore. I mean, I belonged to him, right? My life included.

That's what the bond did to me.

"Beau..." Sterling's expression fell. He opened his mouth to speak again, but there was a knock on the door, interrupting the decidedly tense moment.

It was rare for anyone to disturb us. I mean, I'd only lived here for a few weeks, but not once had anyone come to visit.

Sterling went to the door, opening it a crack. When he glanced through, I didn't need to see his face to know it was twisted in a snarl. The animosity radiated off of him in waves, but the composed First Elder won out because he stood tall before stepping aside and letting the visitor in.

The Third Elder had a graceful gait. They moved like water with light and fluid gestures. Each movement was with purpose, intentional down to the tips of their fingers. The twins followed, sliding into the room with the same elegance as their Master. It was strange, considering how vastly different the three of them were built. It begged the question of whether or not all fledglings replicated their Mentor's movements. Did I, too, move with the cool indifference and undeniable command that Sterling did?

"You've got a lot of nerve, showing your face after what you did," Sterling broke the silence, an edge to his tone. Stasia looked down at their nails, completely unbothered. A small smile quirked at their thin lips before they continued on, perusing the room.

"Can you believe this is the first time I've ever been in here?" Stasia said calmly, conversational almost.

Anger twisted in me and it was all my own. How dare they come into *our* room, uninvited, and treat my Master with blatant disrespect?

Within mere moments, Stasia was in my face, grinning. My vision was filled with their gray eyes. Their lips were inches from mine, flat planes of their chest pressed against mine, and their slim thigh slid between mine. I didn't dare move, nor glance away. This was a spider's web if I'd ever seen one.

"You're hungry, aren't you?" Stasia whispered. Their lips a gentle caress. Sweetness filled my nostrils. I couldn't pinpoint one scent, it seemed like a blend of honeysuckle, gardenias, and thyme. Probably a couple of others too, but my nose and my knowledge were not that good.

"Practically *starving*," Stasia sang, then pressed their lips to mine. Too brief to be much of a kiss, but it was enough to push Sterling into action. I was yanked back and behind Sterling's massive back as he fixed his solemn gaze on Stasia.

"Done playing?"

"Never," Stasia hummed. They tilted their head to peek past Sterling at me. With a sly wink, they returned to the door. "I came to warn you."

"And?" Sterling drawled.

Stasia's gaze sharpened. "They're going to make a move at the Samhain celebration. It'd be best if you and your fledglings were not in the vicinity."

"How do you know?" Sterling demanded and even though

his voice was bored, I knew there was weight behind this question.

Stasia grinned and opened the door to leave. But before they disappeared, they tossed over their shoulder, "Feed your fledgling...or *I* will."

They were gone before Sterling could even react. Once the door was closed and it was the two of us again, I thought he would react...but nothing.

"What did they mean by that?" I asked when the stretch of silence became too uncomfortable to bear.

But in a typical Sterling fashion, he ignored the question. I would've pressed, if I hadn't seen his expression and the furious way his lips moved. Too quick for sound to make their way through. Running his fingers through his hair again, I watched as he began to pace.

"Can you please tell me what's going on? I'm extremely confused. About everything really."

Sterling stopped his pacing. I thought he was going to answer me when he finally opened his mouth, but once again there was a knock on the door.

Are you kidding me?

I went to answer it this time, but Sterling beat me to it. This time, it wasn't the Third Elder.

Hale.

Sterling let the Vampire slip inside then closed the door behind him. There was a look in Hale's hazel eyes that was far different than I was used to.

"What is it?" Sterling demanded.

Hale glanced at me, uncertainty clear in his expression.

"It's fine," Sterling told him.

"We found two more, just outside the Knoxville Coven House borders. They hadn't been reported. One of mine said they saw Ainsley on the site."

"Carlisle's newest fledgling," Sterling sighed. "They're getting bolder. Most likely under the assumption that if we haven't done anything by now, then we won't. But it's not enough."

"Still?" Hale asked helplessly.

"She's not budging. Have Judas tail them and keep an eye on your fledgling. I have a bad feeling."

"And the Third Elder?" Hale asked a bit hesitantly. My ears perked up.

"Be wary. They won't cause another scene, not like the last time at least. But that doesn't mean that they aren't up to something."

Hale nodded once.

"We have six days until Samhain. Have the Knights prepared," Sterling ordered before dismissing Hale. The Vampire gave one last glance in my direction before disappearing.

When we were alone again, I waited. My arms folded across my chest on my own. I was close to tapping my foot with impatience when Sterling finally spoke.

"Slave rings, like what you witnessed before, have been showing up more frequently in the last hundred years. They've always existed, but after the Moon War in 1614, Lilith made sure the practice was near extinction. The recent rings are not just growing in number, but whoever is running them, has been sloppy in covering their tracks. Humans and their media have gotten a hold of it and are holding Lilith responsible. The more they show up, the more enraged the humans grow and it has gotten to the brink of another war which we are fighting to avoid."

"What are slave rings?" I asked, knowing that it could have several meanings. And from my own scattered memories, I couldn't determine which definition applied.

"Vampires kidnap humans, children usually, and use them

as either blood bags, sex slaves, or to fight to the death in underground brawls for bids," Sterling's lip curled in disgust as he spoke.

"That's awful," I muttered. And to think that's where he found me. Was that how my brother died? Drained? Raped? Or murdered by another human as desperate to live as he was?

"It's monstrous," Sterling snarled. "And it's Lilith that's being blamed, when she has worked tirelessly for millennia to end them. Some of the other High Priests and Priestesses have been vocal about their distaste for humans and support of the slave rings, which only proves the narrative that Vampire kind is pushing for domination, instead of the peaceful coexistence that Lilith has worked so hard to maintain."

"You think they might be behind all of the rings showing up?" I asked.

"Someone is. And the others are being manipulated. We've been trying to figure out who's pulling the strings, but they have been meticulous in keeping themselves hidden. Using proxies in order to cover their tracks. It's proven very effective," he hissed that last part bitterly.

"And somehow Stasia is involved? What did they do that's made everyone so wary of them?"

"We don't know what role Stasia plays. Or their fledglings for that matter. After they publicly executed an entire slave ring including the human survivors on live television, we have been unsure of where their loyalties lie. They're dangerous. That's really all you need to know. And it's why it's imperative that we keep the new Mother and Lilith's condition to the chest."

"So why are fledglings in danger? What's going to happen on Samhain?"

"I don't know, but it would be foolish not to consider Stasia's warning. They've taken a liking to you which is why they even bothered to warn us at all."

Me? I'd only met them today. How could they have possibly known anything about me enough to even begin liking me?

"Don't bother trying to make sense of it; Stasia's reasons are all their own. It'd be futile to try and figure out why. Goddess knows I've tried," Sterling sighed.

I don't know how I feel about someone as dangerous and seemingly unhinged as Stasia liking me, but hell, if it helps us in the slightest, I can deal.

"So, what now?"

He had to have a plan. Sterling wasn't the type to leave things to chance. He was meticulous in all things, and if this has been a problem for as long as he'd mentioned, then he must've been prepared.

Though, how could someone really prepare for a new Mother of all Vampires?

I mean, we'd had to keep this huge secret while handling all of the slave rings that kept popping up, the human media who seemed to have it out for Lilith, and the rebellious coven leaders that may or may not have been planning something nefarious for the Samhain festival–which Lilith would not let us act upon.

And on top of all of that, Sterling had to deal with a stubborn fledgling who didn't know his own strength.

I sighed. *Reality really can be a son of bitch.*

Taking a deep breath and steeling my resolve, I made a decision. I didn't know who I was. I didn't know why Sterling felt the call with me. I didn't know what the future may have held, but I knew now that I was his and I would follow his lead. It was time to stop second guessing. He needed me, and clearly there were things much bigger than me happening. I couldn't continue to be selfish.

"I have eyes on the situation. We can't make a move until we know exactly what they are planning for Samhain, but I'm sure the slave rings and the rebellion are connected. If we can prove they're linked then we'll have permission to investigate, and I believe it will move quickly from there. But until then, we have to be careful. Lilith does not tolerate blatant disregard for her orders from her Elders."

It was interesting how punishment came to the Elders who disobeyed, but no one else. I guessed free will was a luxury. Perhaps I should be a bit more grateful that I was not tied in that way. Though I expected that being the first Elder's fledgling did prohibit some behaviors.

I should ask Sterling about that at a less dire time. Here's hoping he'll actually answer...

"What do you need me to do?" I asked.

Sterling seemed surprised, though I couldn't guess why. It's not like this was my first time expressing interest in what to do. Or was it?

"I just want you to focus on getting through the change. You've been progressing through the Stages rapidly. I suspect you'll reach Stage Three before the week is done."

Stage Three, blood lust. I'd be able to feed off of someone other than Sterling. Was that what Stasia was referring to? Could they sense the change in me? I wasn't sure how I felt about drinking from someone else. No one could've possibly tasted as good as Sterling.

No one. I was sure of it.

"You don't look very happy about that," Sterling commented, either sensing it from the bond or it was written all over my face. Maybe a little of both.

"I don't like the idea of feeding from anyone other than you," I answered honestly.

"I know. It'll be strange at first, but you'll quickly get used to it."

Doubtful.

After a few moments of silence, I finally asked, "Can you stop shielding?"

Sterling raised a brow.

"Your emotions. The blockage feels wrong."

Sterling chuckled and suddenly, he was there again. In my mind, in my soul, and in my heart. I could feel the small edges of worry, but it was shadowed by the pride that he felt for me. Don't know what I did to deserve it, pretty sure I didn't do anything, but I was happy that he was not as distraught as before.

"I wonder if that's why you were called to change me," I murmured.

"What's that?" Sterling asked.

"To give you something to live for now that Lilith's cycle is ending. I think. I mean, I'm not sure, but I know that if you were to die, I wouldn't want to keep living. I wouldn't have a reason to. So I figured it may be the same for you, if not more intense for how long you spent together. Perhaps, this is why it all happened."

Sterling pondered silently then murmured, "You might be right about that." Then he held his hand out to me.

I took it without hesitation. "Feeding?" I asked.

Sterling smiled and gave a nod before bringing his nails down on his wrist. Without having realized I moved, I caught Sterling's hand before he could split his wrist. Slowly, but with purpose, I brought his nails up to his neck. A silent plea in my eyes.

The corner of his lips lifted before he brought his nails down and sliced a deliberate line along his neck. Transfixed on the deep red blooming from the wound, I moved closer, mouth watering.

Sterling cupped my neck and gently guided me to the sweet source. Though it wasn't so much as guiding as it was caressing.

I didn't need any encouragement to take the meal offered, but there was something different about this feeding. Animalistic.

I pushed against Sterling forcefully, but with strength I hadn't previously possessed. He stumbled into the armoire, hitting the wood with a sharp *thwack*. Rutting against him, like a dog in heat, I thrusted and sucked, moaned and writhed. I needed it. A ravenous beast had taken control of me.

No reservations or uncertain thoughts clouded my judgment or halted my actions. I reached between his legs and cupped him roughly through his pants. Sterling groaned, tossing his head back and allowing me better access. His fingers dug into my sides, firm but hinging on untamed. Like there was a part of him still desperately clinging to control as his whole being begged him to let go.

Pulling back, blood dripped from my teeth, and danced along my tongue. I savored the taste. The connection between us hummed and burned. Panting, I opened my eyes, and he was staring at me. Pupils blown and nostrils flared, he watched me with a vivacious hunger.

"Do it," I whispered, desperate for him.

Sterling's fangs had descended, glistening with saliva, readying to strike. But it wasn't blood he wanted. I could tell. I knew it as well as I knew my own desires. He just needed to do it.

He leaned in close, breath brushing along the shell of my ear. A shiver traveled up my spine while my eyes closed involuntarily. *Do it.*

"Let me in," he whispered.

"Yes," I hummed, wrapping my arms around his neck. He grabbed me, lifted me by the hips, taking control of the moment. I let him. I *wanted* him to.

Was I finally letting go?

Was I *really* ready to let him in?

He thrusted once, grinding his cloth-covered cock against mine, through the fabrics, rubbing against my sensitive head. But that little flash of discomfort only fueled the need I had for him.

Could this be what they felt? Alexander and Kyle, that first night when I saw them writhing and riding like their lives depended on it. Right now, I wanted Sterling to take me and I didn't give a flying fuck who saw. No, I *wanted* someone–*everyone*–to see. He was mine. His blood was mine. His cock was mine.

They say fledglings belonged to their Masters, but my Master belonged to *me*.

Take control, Sterling. Let me have that raw untamed fire that rages inside you.

As if he could hear my command in the inner sanctuary of my mind, he spun me, throwing me down onto the bed, not letting my body bounce with the impact before he was there, covering me entirely. The space between us was nothing but an illusion. We were one in mind and very soon, body too. The anticipation heated my skin.

"Do it," I whispered again, tilting my head back to give him every part of me, even the blood that coursed through my veins. Because it was *my choice* to give it.

Originally, the thought of him owning all of me had infuriated me. But at that moment , I finally understood. The balance of power may not have been equal with all of the other fledgling and Vampire pairings, but ours? Ours was nothing like theirs, I made sure of it.

I may belong to Sterling in body and mind, but I was not his slave. The serpent that had wrapped around my neck was clasped just as tight around his. I had my own free will, even if it went against his direct order. I gave him my trust because *I* wanted to, not because I was compelled to.

For that reason alone, I was okay with this. For that reason only, I allowed him into the deepest parts of me and *allowed* him to take what he needed. Because at the end of the day, I could do the same.

"Drink me, Master," I purred and Sterling struck. His fangs were sharp and thin, but not even that was enough to dull the initial sting as they pierced the flesh. It hurt, only for a moment, but like some switch was flipped, all the pain dissolved into this unrelenting heat. It didn't trickle in with gentle calls and tiny licks. It was a ferocious monster that burned and devoured, like a concentrated dose of the strongest aphrodisiac. Maybe it was. I'm sure there's a study about it somewhere. Or maybe not. Maybe the secret of this was too well-kept. Because *shit,* it should be illegal to feel this good.

My fingers trembled as Sterling groaned, drinking deep and dragging the blood from my veins. It wasn't entirely necessary, considering my blood practically hopped, skipped, and jumped toward him.

And when Sterling held me, I didn't feel like I was in the arms of the First Elder, favored amongst all Elders, strongest Vampire, second only to the Mother of All. It felt like Sterling. Just the man with a stern face and a gentle smile. The man that read dirty romance books and secretly liked bubbles in his bath. The man that very few were allowed to see. He was tender, and careful, cradling me like I just might fade away.

I wouldn't though. This may not have begun as my choice, but it was now.

Sterling pulled back, head tossed in ecstasy, as my life's source glistened from his teeth. His eyes, like green fire, glowed and undulated.

"You may have to feed again. I think I took too much," Sterling panted. Because a sliver of him had lost control and I was all for it.

"Later," I whispered with a devious smirk. Lifting my hips, I rolled them, pushing our cocks against each other again. "I want something else right now."

Sterling's dark brow rose, but a smile spread across his lips. A look as if to say 'Oh?'.

"You sure you want me to?" The question trailed off, but I knew what he was asking. Last time he let me top because he knew the intricacies of my feelings. Bottoming required a level of trust that I wasn't willing to give at the time. Things were different now. I was ready.

Slowly, I pulled my pants and briefs off, awkwardly maneuvering so I didn't accidentally knee him where it mattered. I spread my legs and let him fall between them. Now that I was exposed, the friction was even more intense.

Sterling's wide eyes held all the shock and awe, he was literally rendered speechless. I chuckled before tugging at the waistband of his pants. That seemed to snap him out of it. He leaned back, sliding out of his own bottoms. I took that moment to yank my shirt over my head, just in time to catch him doing the same. A little more finesse on his end. I enjoyed the show.

I don't know if it was the years of combat and training, or if this was just simply how he was made, but this man was built like a brick house. Every muscle was tight, defined, and sexy as hell. It was the type of body that exercising simply wasn't enough. It made sense. When your body is a weapon, it was bound to look like one too. The dedication left its mark.

And mark it did. His chest, though I've seen it so many times, was littered with old scars. I hadn't really noticed them in the detail that I did now. Bullet wounds, blade scars, whip marks, burns. One day I wanted him to tell me the stories behind them. If he remembered. Because these scars wouldn't have stayed unless they were from his human life.

While I had been ogling him, he was taking his time,

perusing my own nude form. I wasn't built like him. It wasn't power I needed to survive, but stealth. If the little I did know about my life proved anything, it was that my body was forged from the need to be quick. To be quiet, to be still. I was toned, but lean. Muscles are hard to build when a person is too starved to fuel them. But this body of mine was scrappy. It could do what it had to in order to survive.

The both of us, warriors in our own right, were perfect for each other. I wouldn't believe anything less.

"Finished?" he mused.

I brought my hands up, caressing the skin on his chest. Warm, hard, *mine*. Sterling took one of my hands and kissed my knuckles before dragging my arm up so he could kiss the sensitive puckered skin of the bite that started this. My body trembled with anticipation.

There was something about the Maker's mark. Whenever the Maker touched it, it was like it triggered an instant calming effect.

Spreading my legs wider, I beckoned him. It didn't take much for him to trail those kisses along my body. Up my arms, along my jaw, down my chest, and my thighs. Teasing. Always teasing. Ignoring the one place I wanted his lips.

My cock jumped as he neared my hole. So close, yet still not close enough.

"Sterling," I groaned.

My Master didn't acknowledge my whining or demands for him to get on with it. He took his time, as if the frenzy of blood and lust did nothing to him. It was a lie though. I saw his length, hard and twitching. But his pace never hurried. He savored every lick of skin.

When he licked a stripe along my balls, I nearly lost it. This slow edging was torture. I wanted him hard. I wanted him fast. I wanted *us* to get so lost in each other, nothing else mattered.

Because nothing else did. Not when it came to us.

His wet warm tongue slid along my cock, deliberately and oh so deliciously. A soft sigh escaped my lips. Sterling licked me again and again until I was squirming and begging, only then did he slide the length of me down his throat, cupping my balls and squeezing.

Yes. Yes. I wanted more. Give me more, Sterling.

Each gasp that left me only fueled Sterling on, making him go faster until my toes curled and the tightness in my gut increased.

"Sterling, I'm gonna cum if you don't stop," I warned breathlessly, trying to tug his head away but his fingers only tightened around my hips, digging into my skin and keeping me in place while his mouth became a suction around my crown.

"Fuck! Fuck! Fuck!" I cried out, unable to hold back. One shot. Two shots. Three. My dick twitched as it emptied itself down Sterling's throat.

The final shocks of the orgasm trailed down my spine before I was finally able to calm my breathing. I melted into the sheets, feeling light and floaty. Giving Sterling a lazy smile, I watched as he wiped his mouth with the back of his hand.

"You weren't supposed to do that," I murmured. Sterling laughed, climbing up my body until his face was inches from mine, arms caging either side of my head.

"No?" he mused. "You saying you didn't like it?"

"Oh, I *definitely* liked it," I purred.

He chuckled, leaning to one side, head propped on one hand while the other...

"Need more time to recover," I protested, prepared to swat his hand away. But he didn't go for the dick. His hand traveled lower. "What are you–?"

Sterling's fingers brushed my hole and it quivered in response.

Oh.

All too soon, he pulled his hand away, messing with something I couldn't see. When I felt him return to my pucker, his digits were slick. He ran the lubricant along the outer ridges before dipping one finger inside. I was still blissed out from the orgasm, I couldn't even tense up.

Guess that was the plan all along. Sneaky bastard.

My body shuddered with each dip, his finger going deeper each time as he watched every change in my expression with an intensity that should have intimidated me. Feeling a little embarrassed with whatever was on my face, I tilted my head up, sloping my lips against his.

He never lost his rhythm as we kissed. Even as his tongue probed mine and we started a war that neither one of us was willing to lose.

I vaguely felt the pressure of a second finger. Then a third.

"Okay, that stings a bit," I huffed, unable to concentrate on kissing anymore. Sterling only kissed me harder, but his fingers did ease up. They searched and searched until he found it. My hips jerked upward on its own accord as I moaned into his mouth.

Sterling hummed in pleasure against my lips. I could feel him smiling. *Asshole.* No pun intended.

When he curled his fingers again, my cock finally decided it was time to make an appearance again. Thickening between us, the sensitive tip brushed the rocks of his abs with every undulation of my hips. It felt so good, my moans were all silent while my mouth was stretched wide. I gripped fistfuls of the sheets, trying desperately to keep myself from cumming again, because if I did, I'd be spent for the rest of the night.

No one wanted that...

But Sterling pulled away, removing his fingers and easing himself above me again. He pushed my legs up and apart before settling between them. His thick, red cock glistened with precum as he rubbed along my pucker, my balls, and my dick.

His eyes met mine with an intense stare. I knew what he was asking. Giving me the opportunity to stop this, asking if I had changed my mind.

I hadn't.

With an eager nod, I gripped his hips and waited. He didn't take long, sliding past the tight ring of muscle until he was partially sheathed inside me.

A shudder went down his spine as he nearly collapsed on top of me, catching himself at the last moment. His eyes were shut and jaw clenched. One might have thought he was in pain. But I knew that face.

That was his 'if I move I'm gonna cum' face. I had seen it only once before but it was engrained in my memory with such clarity I could pick out every detail. It was *my* face. I released one of his hips to cup his cheek.

"Give it to me hard, Master."

Sterling unleashed himself on me. Gone were the slow thrusts and careful caresses. At first, it hurt, but I didn't want him to stop. I knew he wouldn't do any real damage, I trusted him with the well-being of my body. So I decided to tap into his feelings, siphoning it through the bond and oh my Goddess...

It was glorious.

I could feel the heat of me wrapped around my own cock at the same time feeling the fullness of him inside me. All of the sensations were too fucking much.

Sterling's thrusts grew faster, sloppier. I screamed, clawing his back, digging my heels into his ass. Gripping, wanting, needing.

I struck his neck with my blunt teeth and bit down. Hard enough to make Sterling hiss in pain. Hard enough to draw blood, reopening the wound on his neck that had so easily healed before.

His blood.

His fucking blood.

It was *everything.*

I choked as I came again. My cum spurting between our stomachs.

Feeling boneless, I sucked lazily as he thrusted, enjoying the ride, floating with each euphoric sensation. So good. So fucking good.

Sterling's hips snapped up, rocking my whole body off the bed. Once. Twice. And then he came.

It was warm.

I could feel each pump of his cock, flooding me.

He panted, chest heaving. I released his neck and sighed, falling back into the sheets like a satisfied cat.

"Ooof!" I grunted as he collapsed on top of me. Heavy, but not crushing. Even as spent as he was, he kept me from feeling all of his weight.

"That was..." he started, still out of breath.

"Incredible," I finished for him, dreamily, licking the wound on his neck again.

He winced.

"You really took a bite out of me, huh."

I hummed happily. Sated and content.

It was just as Stasia said...I was starving.

STAGE THREE

10

I TOLD YOU SO

Blake was oddly quiet today.

I wasn't the only one who noticed. Alexander and Kyle kept glancing at him with concern in their eyes, but no one, not even *I* was brave enough to ask the question. We all knew it was related to Executioner.

As Samhain neared, the Coven house was a flurry of activity. There was excitement buzzing around, tinged with a bit of anxiety. Vampires and fledglings alike were flitting about, decorating, planning, and preparing for the celebration to come in three days' time.

Even *we* had our part to play, though Sterling didn't want me too involved. Whether or not he was planning to heed Stasia's warning and keep me away from the celebration was knowledge I *still* wasn't privy to. It didn't concern me as much as it probably would have in the past. I trusted Sterling and it was a relief to leave the decisions to him.

If only Blake felt the same as I did. Each day, I watched a little piece of him die inside. There was no longer any warmth in those hazel eyes. His fake smiles had long since made their exit and he no longer tried to hide it anymore.

I wondered if he knew. Executioner's real name, his face, his sadness? Did his fear prevent him from taking the steps to get to know him? The *real* him? Maybe if he knew, he'd understand that this was killing Obi the same, if not more than it was him. Blake wasn't the selfish type.

And it only grew worse when Blake entered Stage Two. Lilith and Sterling were right in their predictions. Blake had a double affinity like me. Earth and Air. But it was his Earth affinity that tied him to life the way Obi's tied him to death. That difference only proved to create a larger rift between the two.

With Blake refusing to feed, it was only a matter of time before the inevitable happened. His body would reject the Change.

It worried me just as much as it did Sterling. He could only comfort Obi but so many times before it would no longer be enough to keep him going. The Vampire had been teetering on the edge for such a long time and having a fledgling was supposed to help with that. Instead, it only served to make things worse.

If there was one thing I could do to help my Master, it would be this. I couldn't do much else. He wouldn't let me.

"Blake." The group fell silent as I did the thing that no one else would dare. I asked. "When's the last time you fed?"

With little enthusiasm, he lifted the quiche he'd barely nibbled at.

I raised an eyebrow at him. He sighed. He looked so exhausted. His normally brown skin was washed out and a little green. There were dark circles under his eyes and a hollowness in his gaze.

"About a week and a half," he mumbled. Kyle couldn't hide the sharp intake of breath. I shot him a warning look before grabbing Blake's hand and forcing the man to look at me.

"You're going to die and all of this would have been for nothing," I told him seriously, leveling him with a look that conveyed the gravity of the situation. There was no use sugarcoating it. Buttering up the truth wouldn't make it more palatable, he needed to know straight up.

"I know," he whispered.

There was something in his eyes, full of defeat. He'd all but given up.

Why? It was difficult to believe that he was so against being paired with Obi that he'd just give up on life. That wasn't who he was, who I'd grown to know these past few weeks. With every moment not spent with our Masters, we spent with each other. The four of us had bonded so closely, he could not hide from us.

I pulled him up. He stumbled to his feet with alarm. The others looked on curiously as I turned to them.

"We'll be back," I told them before tugging Blake along with me. We passed the table with Sterling and the others. Our gazes met briefly, before Sterling gave a slight nod. We left the dining room and headed for the library. Julia was putting away some books before she took one look at me, pulled out her key and handed it to me without another word. I took it from her gratefully before leading Blake to one of the back studies in the library. These rooms were usually reserved for Scholars, but Julia offered to let me use hers whenever I needed a private place to study. I had been doing quite a bit of research on not only Vampire society, but bonds between fledgling and Master.

The room was small, with books lining one of the walls, a small desk, tablet, and little figurines everywhere. And in one corner was a tiny loveseat with an equally small table in front of it. I led Blake to the couch where we sat side by side.

"I need you to help me understand. Tell me everything. What's going on? Because I refuse to let you give up."

Blake's shoulder's trembled. He looked so much smaller,

timid, everything he wasn't. It was hard to believe that only weeks ago, he was the warm charming young man who brightened the room with his smile. He was always so optimistic about our situation even when I was convinced that it had to be a punishment of some kind. There wasn't anything that could touch him in those moments and all I could wish for now was to bring him back.

I could do that for him. For him. For Obediah. For Sterling. And for myself. He was a brother to me in this and I had already lost so much, I refuse to lose anyone else again.

"Blake, talk to me," I pleaded.

The man took a deep steadying breath before speaking. His voice was so soft, I strained to hear it at first.

"I don't want it to be this way. I never did. I know…I know I let the rumors get to me at first. I'm not usually one to feed into gossip, but then I saw him and I was afraid. And I've *been* afraid. He barely stayed with me during the Frenzy, never spoke, always kept his distance. I thought he hated me. Any time I try to talk to him, he ignores me. When I touch him, he avoids it like I'm some sort of plague. He never lets me feed from him, instead just fills a glass for me to drink. I thought that if I stopped drinking it, he would notice. He would *say* something. *Care*. But he doesn't. It's like he can't stand the sight of me. I can't live like this, Beau. I'm trying but every time, he rejects me. And I *hate* that I need him so much. His approval, his acceptance, his touch, his *everything*, but he won't give it to me. I've begged him…" Blake was shaking so hard, the couch trembled. I put my hand in his and squeezed.

I hurt for him because I could not possibly imagine the pain of rejection from a Master.

"I *begged* him and he just left me there. Whenever he spoke, it was only ever to tell me he was leaving. And he's *always* leaving. One mission after the other. When he comes back, I can *feel* the death coming from him. Cold, harsh, bitter. It's awful and stifling. Yet, here I am, still wanting. I don't understand why I'm being punished this way. Why was I chosen to be his?"

"I think..." I started then paused, wondering how to word this in a way he'd understand and that wouldn't hurt him. "I think you are both the perfect match to one another."

Blake whirled on me, incredulously. His face a mask of betrayal and hurt. I rushed on, wanting him to understand. "You are both creatures of the Earth. That's apparent in your affinity for it. But the world is full of opposites because it's necessary to create balance. We used to worship the light as humans, but you can't have the light without darkness. You can't understand light without dark. They are two halves of a whole. One would not exist without the other and that is a simple fact. Words of others, *beliefs* of others may favor one above the other and sway the opinions in that direction, but it does not mean that the less favored has no value.

You both need each other. He needs the life you bring as much as you need the death he gives. It centers you, grounds you, and brings out the best in you. I know this is easier said than done, but I need you to have faith. I need you to fight for him. Demand from him what you need."

"But how? What more can I do that I haven't tried already?" There was a desperation in his eyes that I didn't realize existed. I grasped on to it, ingrained it in my brain so I wouldn't ever forget the stakes. I had to save him. I had to save them both.

"I will help you. If you can come to our room tomorrow evening, I'll help you bridge the gap and start the connection. But until then, drink. You will need your strength."

Blake frowned, but I saw that spark. That glimmer of hope that he hadn't let fade. As washed up and exhausted as it was, it existed. I could work with that.

I gave his hand another squeeze, imploring him with my eyes, "*Drink*."

He gave a small nod. I helped him to his feet, noticing how unsteady he seemed before walking him out of the study and library, back to his room, not stopping to greet anyone until he was safely at his destination. I'd never been in Obi and Blake's room, but from what I could see, it was bare, dark, cold, and lonely. From the doorway, I could see a small table where there was a single glass filled with a dark red liquid, I could only assume was blood, and...a single white rose.

Then the door closed and I saw nothing but the worn grain of wood it was made of. A rose, that didn't seem like a gift from someone who didn't care. And I knew it was from Obi. It radiated the same sadness as he did, even from this distance. But maybe, that was *his* hope.

They would get through this.

Feeling a bit more satisfied with my plan, I made my way back to the dining hall where I could feel the tug in my chest leading me. I needed to be back by his side.

Relief washed over me when I set my eyes on him. His green gaze met mine with an intensity saved only for Mentor and fledgling. As I approached the table, I noticed Marcelle sat with him. I bowed my head in respect to the dark haired woman who bore a striking resemblance to Julia Jones. The actress had to be a descendant because there was no way the two weren't related.

Sterling stood, "I must take my leave. Please consider it."

Marcelle smirked, brown eyes gleaming with mischief, but I could sense that behind that facade was actually a tendril of worry. Sterling must have warned her about what Stasia said.

I placed Julia's key on the table before Marcelle. The Elder gazed at it curiously, then slid it into her pocket.

As we turned to leave, I brushed my fingers along the seam

of Sterling's shirt, tugging the fabric enough to gently caress the skin on his side. I needed that contact, just as I needed blood.

Stage Three had come full force. Feedings had increased as did my sexual drive–things Sterling hadn't warned me about. Now, I understood why Kyle and Alexander had such a hard time not copulating in public. Sometimes the urge was too strong and I found myself rubbing against Sterling in ways I would not previously be comfortable doing in public.

When we made it back to the privacy of our room, I fought the desires churning within me. That could wait, I had to focus.

"Will you do something for me?" I asked.

Sterling raised a dark brow before he crossed his arms and leaned against the edge of the couch, eyes never leaving mine.

"What is it?"

"I need you to bring Obi here tomorrow evening and I need you to make him stay."

Sterling's brows furrowed, obviously not expecting this. "What are you planning?"

"I need them to see that they are asking for the same thing. They balance each other, but are too afraid of each other's differences to see that. I'm afraid it'll be that fear that kills them. They'd be perfect together if they could just get past this."

Sterling sighed. "I know how much you want to help but it isn't our place to–"

"Sterling, *please*. I don't want to lose another brother." Even if I couldn't remember the brother I had lost, the pain was still there. The knowledge of it was enough.

Sterling winced, closed his eyes and pinched the bridge of his nose. I watched and waited, anxious. He'd help me. I *knew* he would, he felt the same as I did. Obi is his brother too and as much as he hid his heart, I knew it would break if he lost him.

"I–"

"Sterling," I begged, stepping in close so I could stare

directly into my Master's eyes. So I could see into his glimmering soul that was hurting as I was. That was *scared*. That tugged on our bond like a lifeline that held him together, just as it did for me. "You don't want to lose him."

He exhaled, the sweetness washed over my face. The indecision was clear in his expression but eventually reason won out and he finally gave in.

"I cannot interfere with any mission the Mother gives him, but if he is not otherwise occupied, I will bring him here as you request and I will...*persuade* him to stay should he wish otherwise after seeing what you've planned. I cannot promise more than that."

"That's all I ask," I reassured, then stepped in for a brief kiss. His lips were cool, soft, and relaxed. He moved his mouth gently, coaxing me closer, deeper. The passion twisted in our bond and pulled me tighter into him.

He is warmth. He is power. He is completion.

Feeling lightheaded, I pulled away, gums tingling.

"Let me see," Sterling murmured, tilting my head up with a finger to my chin. I looked up at him and opened my mouth. The fangs were new. Sensitive. When my canines fell out, I nearly fainted after a full blown panic attack. Sterling reassured me it was normal before teaching me how to coax my fangs out. Once I was able to elongate them, they stayed in place. When I was hungry or emotions were running high, they'd extend past the line of my other teeth. I'd cut my lip more times than I'd like to admit.

They bit into the thickness of my lips, which I held away so it wouldn't cut them again. A look of approval was on Sterling's face as he examined them.

"Thirsty?" he asked, not releasing my chin.

I exhaled, squirming against him.

"For something," I murmured and Sterling laughed. A sound

that not many were privy to. It made me feel special that I was welcome to it on the rare occasions that it did happen.

"As much as I would like to sate your thirst, my child, there is something we must attend to."

"We?" I asked, stepping back so I could focus. He knew it was hard to think when he touched me. Especially now.

Sterling nodded, "With the Coven house welcoming new guests tomorrow, it is necessary to complete rounds with the factions as leader of the Elites and as the First Elder. As my fledgling, this duty will fall to you if I am otherwise occupied."

No pressure or anything.

"Don't be nervous," Sterling chuckled, reading my thoughts. "You will do fine. And it is imperative that you familiarize yourself with the different factions as you still haven't chosen which path you will continue on."

I sighed. It was something he started bringing up when I entered Stage Two but didn't start pressing until now. I understood the reason behind it. I was progressing through the stages much quicker than anticipated. Fledglings typically had years to figure these things out but in my situation, I had only days. Weeks would be too generous.

I still didn't know though. There were the Scholars, like Julia, that practically lived in the library and served as the intelligence for the Coven. They were all geniuses, and that was something I was very clearly not. Then you have the Shamans. They were spiritual healers that were more in tune with themselves and nature than I could even imagine, like Alexander. He always seemed the calmest, the most grounded and leveled. There was a lightness to him that I could never replicate. It was what I imagined Blake would be if he let himself.

The Artisans were the creatives of the Coven. The inventors, the dreamers. They were the abstract. The different. The outside of the box thinkers. This wasn't completely unfeasible for me. If anything, I could see myself fitting in here the most. But then again, there was a wall that separated me from the rest. I couldn't really create. I could only envision and the Artisans were very much so of both talents.

The Knights were the warriors. Something I absolutely was not. Kyle and Hale belonged to this faction and it fit with them. Both were strong, they were dauntless, courageous. They spoke their minds, yet embodied discipline. That type of commitment to authority and strength was not something that could ever attract me. My penchant for challenging authority made sure of that. I would obey Sterling...for the most part, but no one else.

And last but not least, the Elites. I'm fairly certain Sterling was secretly hoping I would choose this faction. I could be with him even more if I did. I wouldn't have to really worry about authority as it would be him.

The Elites were a little bit of everything, like the special agents of the Coven. They spent the most time outside of the Coven house on important missions commissioned by the High Priestess and Consort or the Elders.

I couldn't help but feel a bit inadequate, though. A part of me worried that I would only be there for Sterling, and that it wasn't really where I belonged. Picking a faction was about belonging. It was a battle within me. Was I doing it because that's what I was truly drawn to or was I doing it for Sterling? Because it's what's expected of me? It was clear from how everyone else acted that they already assumed I had chosen the Elites. Even Lilith hinted at it.

This had to be *my* choice though. I couldn't let others influence the decision. Which is why I haven't chosen anything yet.

I sighed. "Okay."

"Don't sound so enthusiastic," Sterling snarked with a hint of amusement. He knew my fears, but he didn't voice his thoughts because he knew this was my battle to fight. This was my decision to make and anything he might say would be counterproductive in that.

"What exactly do we have to do?"

"We'll speak to each of the heads and relay their orders for the celebration. The Knights are in charge of security. Checking everyone who enters, making sure nothing suspicious is afoot. Everything of that like. The Shamans are in charge of cleansing the Coven house and making the preparations for the rituals with the assistance of the Scholars. Scholars themselves, aside from helping the Shamans, are in charge of making sure everything is scheduled properly and runs smoothly. Their whole thing is organization. The Artisans are in charge of decor. And the Elites...well they have a few different tasks. Most have been split amongst the other factions in the guise of assisting, but really they will be executing their individual plans and smoking out anything that would be suspicious. They watch where the Knights cannot."

"Sounds complicated," I muttered.

Sterling shrugged. "Not really. This year will be a bit tense as I'm sure you already know. But once you do it enough times, you will get the hang of things and it will be like second nature."

We made our way to each of the factions and I watched as Sterling became the cool authoritarian that demanded respect with a simple look. It always amazed me that this was the man that everyone saw. The Sterling I knew was just for me. That kindness was saved for a few and I was one of them. And *this* man was not one I'd ever see. Our bond made sure of that.

I knew I should have been paying attention, but I couldn't be bothered. When we made it to the Scholars, Julia caught me zoning out and elbowed me in the gut.

"You should take this seriously, it's going to fall to you next year," she whispered. I shrugged, ignoring the anxiety that clenched in my stomach. Not because of taking over the task, but the uncertainty of where we'd actually be next year. Lilith said she wouldn't survive the pregnancy, how long would she be pregnant? Most likely less than a year. The New Mother will be too young to oversee the rituals. Then what? Who would take over? Would there even *be* a celebration or would everything dissolve into chaos?

After finishing our rounds, we headed back to our room. Only then did I dare ask. "What happens after Lilith gives birth? Will you be taking over the Coven until the New Mother is old enough?"

Sterling tensed then shook his head. "It'll most likely fall to Nexus."

"Does he know yet?" I asked.

"No. But he will soon. Lilith is due to give birth any day now. I don't know why she still won't tell him," Sterling sighed.

"Any day now? She's barely showing!"

Sterling tugged off his shirt as he spoke, making it quite difficult to focus on the conversation.

"That happens for human females sometimes, but it's rare. I'm not sure if it's because she is a Vampire or the first, or anything really. This is unknown territory here. It's one thing I don't think Stasia is lying about, though."

Pain lanced my chest, coming straight from the bond. It was the type of hurt that was easy to decipher. Lilith told Stasia about the pregnancy before Sterling.

I hugged him from behind, pressing my cheek to the strength of his back. "There is a reason, but it's not what you're thinking. She wouldn't have trusted you with the New Mother if that was the case."

To have your Master lose faith in you? That type of hurt leaves a scar.

He sighed, but brought my hand to his lips for a gentle kiss.

"I guess that's how she was able to keep it a secret from

Nexus, I can't imagine him not being able to tell when they are... intimate."

"I haven't been able to tell either," Sterling murmurs.

I expected to feel a pang of jealousy, but it wasn't there. I was fine.

Strange.

Was it because it was Mother? His Master?

For whatever reason, hearing about him being intimate with her or even witnessing him with Obi didn't bother me. But the thought of anyone else? Rage bubbled in my veins.

"Easy," Sterling warned, turning to look at me with concern in his eyes. I took a deep breath and cleared my head of the thought. No use getting upset over hypotheticals. "Come," he commanded gently, holding a hand out to me.

I grasped it without hesitation, feeling his warmth seep into me from just that small bit of contact. Stepping closer to him, I looked up. After being with him these past few weeks, I'd gotten used to how big he is. But this close, I was reminded just a bit. The man was a giant. I thought of my first night after waking. Searching for clothes and shoes and being shocked that everything was so huge. I chuckled.

"What's so funny?" Sterling purred, caressing the side of my face, eyes never leaving mine.

"Just remembered when I first woke up. As a fledgling. I was trying to find clothes and all I found were things literally fit for a giant."

Sterling tossed his head back and laughed, pulling me closer, hands wrapped around my waist. "I *do* remember. You came stumbling in there, looking *very* lost and confused, swallowed up in one of my shirts. It was kind of adorable."

"Adorable? Don't you mean ridiculous?" I laughed.

"No," Sterling said softly, sobering for a moment. "It was the moment my life changed." His eyes swallowed my vision.

Glowing green emeralds, shining, and passionate. "When you came to me...it changed *everything*," he whispered, leaning close, breath blowing on the skin of my neck.

"Everything?" I repeated, breathless.

"*Everything*," then his lips were on mine. Fast, hungry, furious. The grip on my waist grew tighter, with a near bruising grip. A soft gasp left my lips and Sterling swallowed it up. I shivered. The need in me grew. It wasn't just lust. It was *never* just lust. But now? With Stage Three?

I wrapped my arms around his neck and tugged him down. He tilted his head, just a fraction and that was all the invitation I needed to strike. I latched on, just lightly brushing his skin with my tongue before my new fangs descended and pierced it, flooding my mouth with his sweet blood. Citrusy, earthy, heavenly.

Sterling told me that at Stage Three, drinking from others would be a more common occurrence as I no longer could rely on food to sustain me. He even encouraged me to feed from one of the donors that came to the Coven house each week, if I didn't want to try feeding from my friends. The thought made me ill, but curiosity eventually won out and I tried it. Feeding from someone other than my Master felt wrong. It wasn't nearly as good and it didn't fill me. It was as if I were eating empty calories. Sterling's blood? Now that was a full course meal. And his touch? Well, that was just icing on the cake. A dessert that I couldn't possibly find anywhere else.

I gripped him tighter, drank deeper, rutted harder, until I could feel the bond that held us together, thrumming. The peak was just moments away for us both.

Pulling away before we could reach it, I licked my sensitive fangs, savoring every drop. When I tilted my own neck in return, Sterling struck. His fangs sank deep, pushing me over the edge. The bond pulled tight as our cocks emptied in our pants.

As an older Vampire, Sterling didn't need as much blood as I did, nor did he feed as often, but the few times he did? It was euphoric. It was also the reason we could feed from each other at the same time.

We sagged against each other, chests heaving and fangs retracting. Sterling gave the new bite mark on my neck a soft kiss before pulling me into the shower where we did it all over again.

11

BEAUTY AND THE BEAST

The next night–though sometimes I called it morning, since it technically was for us–Sterling told me he'd be in meetings for a while. Dealing with the ache of not being around him had gotten a bit better. I mean, it was *bearable*, unlike before. When I asked Alexander about it, he said it was because our bond had gotten stronger and I'd officially learned to *trust* that Sterling would return to me. No matter what.

"Sometimes, it's like this switch flips. All of sudden, you understand. It's what we tried to tell you in the beginning, but I know that if you haven't experienced it, it's hard to just take our word for it. I'm glad you two are doing so well. It's strange, really. I think your bond might be the strongest we've seen in quite a while."

"What makes you say that?" I asked, watching as he took a bite of his omelet. It was still odd to see them eat when I no longer had to. I found myself visiting the dining hall during feeding hours even though it was unnecessary now.

"Well, you've both got this aura and this sort of *glow* about you. Right, Kyle?" Alexander bumped the other fledgling, but

Kyle's eyes were glued to something over my shoulder, expression tight and focused.

I followed his gaze and saw a small table occupied by the twins. Most of the time, Asher and Cadence kept their own company if Stasia wasn't by their side, and they were rarely seen without each other.

They ate silently, nothing out of the ordinary, until I noticed the weird tapping they kept doing on the table. Asher wouldn't look at Cadence, but his hand would glide along the table's surface before his fingers would tap in quick succession. When he pulled his hand back to his side, Cadence would mimic the action. *Tap. Tap tap. Tap. Tap tap tap.*

I followed each movement, transfixed, before both twins' eyes shot up, staring directly at me. The ice blue gazes were fierce, intimidating, and something in that stare that had me on high alert.

I don't know how long I stared at them, but fingers snapped in my face, breaking my trance. I blinked, then looked back at Alexander who was frowning.

"What are you staring at?" he asked.

"The–" I looked back to point, but the table where the twins once sat was empty. "Nevermind. Sorry, you were saying?"

Alexander frowned again, but didn't push and continued to talk about things that if I'm honest, I did not care about. When I looked at Kyle, he was still looking at the empty table. *Had he seen what I had?*

His expression alone told me he definitely saw *something*, but I couldn't be certain what he knew. Rumors spread easily and oftentimes they were gross misconceptions that could completely defame someone's character. The twins had enough bad press, I wasn't going to participate in perpetuating it. They didn't do anything wrong. They were just...strange.

I trained my gaze back on Kyle who had that easygoing smile

plastered on his face as if it had been there the whole time. If I didn't know any better, I would've thought I imagined it. But I *did* know better. I'll have to remember to ask Sterling if Hale knew what was going on.

Falling back into conversation, I listened to their plans and what they were working on in preparation for Samhain.

"So what is the Samhain festival about?" I asked. Everyone talked about the food and decorations but no one ever mentioned what to expect. Why we celebrated. There wasn't an agenda or anything. Though I suppose Vampires who had been doing this for centuries didn't exactly need one.

"Right, this will be your first one as a fledgling. Well, I'm sure you know that most humans associate Samhain with Halloween, even though they don't always fall on the same date. They are actually two very different holidays. Halloween is dedicated to eating sweets, dressing up, and appreciating the occult. There are some humans who know that Samhain's purpose is to honor the dead. What they don't know is that it's actually to honor Vampires. It's the time of year that Vampires and fledglings are the strongest. We tap into the moon's power and then some progress through Stage Four to become full-fledged Vampires."

"Okay, but what do we actually do?"

"Well, it's a lot of mingling for the first half. Welcoming the neighboring Coven houses that come to visit. Then the High Priestess or Priest lead the ritual by lighting the points of the pentagram in order of the elements. Each Vampire and fledgling greets the High Priestess with ultimate submission, a kiss to their ankle and an offering of blood. Elders, other High Priestesses or High Priests, and a few chosen fledglings that are believed to transition into Vampires that night are allowed to take a brief sip from the presenting High Priestess or Priest. Then we all take a sip from the offering bowl before setting it on fire for the bonfire. It's supposed to cleanse our energy and welcome the new Vampires to this life. Then the mating ritual takes place to regulate the energy under the blessing of the moon."

"Mating?" I asked, hoping that did not mean what I thought it did.

Kyle and Alexander grinned at each other.

"You might want to get over your aversion to public sex and fast," Kyle laughed.

I groaned. "What is it with Vampires and their need to copulate in front of others? I don't get it!"

The pair laughed even louder as I sat pouting, not wanting to imagine what a massive orgy it was going to be.

My chest tugged and I looked up. Sterling approached our table flanked by Joel and Hale. His large hand caressed the side of my neck briefly before greeting the others. I was eager to get back to our room, wondering if Blake had arrived already.

A hand squeezed mine. I glanced up at Sterling, confused, unable to read him from the bond nor his expression, which usually was hidden behind a mask. One that everyone else saw. Hardly anyone knew the softness that I did.

"Alexander, there is an assignment that I would like you to work on. It will take you away from the Samhain celebration. It is of utmost importance, can I trust you with this?" Sterling said, leveling Alexander with the full weight of his powerful gaze.

There was no way he would reject a special assignment from an Elder, let alone the *first* Elder. But I saw the flash of shock, curiosity, and disappointment, before it was overshadowed by the excitement of being privy to a special assignment.

"Of course, Elder," Alexander finally responded after collecting himself from the initial reaction of the request. Though I saw him shoot Joel several glances, as if trying to gauge whether or not it was okay. I raised a brow, but didn't dare question Sterling in front of others.

"Your Master will be accompanying you, rest assured. You both will leave tomorrow."

And then it clicked. He was getting them to leave for their safety. Alexander seemed to be the most oblivious about what was going on, despite being the main source of information in the Coven house otherwise.

My heart ached for him. He had literally spent the last twenty minutes explaining the ritual and was clearly excited about it. And who knows what's going to happen after Lilith is gone. I can't imagine Nexus will step aside to let us raise the new Mother on our own to take care of continuing traditions.

It was to keep him safe and above all else, that was the most important.

"Beau," Sterling called softly. I stood, taking my place by his side and waving to the others while we made our way out of the dining hall, leaving them behind.

Blake was standing outside our door, shoulders hunched, still a bit pale, but there was a little life in his eyes and the faintest bit of blood in his cheeks which told me, he did feed. Good. That's progress.

"Hi, Blake," I greeted with a large smile. His answering one was weak, but I didn't take it personally. He was clearly going through so much, I was just happy he showed because that meant he was willing to put the work in to make a change. He didn't let his head block him from getting what he wanted. I could only hope that Executioner was just as willing.

"Blake," Sterling greeted softly. Then with a gentle push forward on my lower back, Sterling continued. "Why don't you both head inside first?"

I opened the door for Blake. He stepped inside, but I stayed in the doorway with question in my gaze. Sterling smirked before jerking his chin toward the room. I raised a brow at him in response.

"Do as you're told for once," he chuckled.

"Just this once," I mused before turning inside and closing the door. Blake was standing there, pure longing in his gaze. His slack jawed expression told me how much he wanted what we had. I really hoped this would help.

Please let this help.

I brought Blake to the couch before lighting the fire in the hearth. Blake's eyes widened.

"You're so good at controlling it," he murmured.

"Sterling worked with me a lot. Though he still says I use too much power."

Blake nodded slowly, eyes fixed on the fire.

"You've entered Stage Two, how's your training going?" I asked. I knew it would be tough for him to answer, but if we were going to make any progress tonight, I needed him to confront this. The root of their issues was tied to the variations in their affinities.

"Well you know, I don't really have anyone to train me. Sebastian, one of the Shamans, helped me on occasion when he was on duty in the training room. I have an issue with controlling my output too," He answered, attempting that careless charm he used to parade around when he was better at hiding his pain.

"Show me."

Blake held out his hand, opening and closing his fist, forehead crinkled in concentration. I wasn't sure what he was doing until I felt the small breeze. The fire flickered as the force of wind whipping around increased in strength.

"Air?" I asked, a bit shocked.

"It's the only one I can somewhat control," Blake said. I still found it a bit strange that he too had a double affinity. From what I knew, Executioner only had one. Was it possible for a fledgling to have more affinities than their Master? Was it due to his connection to Sterling? I mean, Sterling was technically his Grand Master, but I'm not sure if that really meant anything.

"And Earth?" I asked once the winds had calmed.

Blake's shoulders twitched, as if trying to hide.

"I can't," he whispered.

"Why not?" I pressed.

"I just–"

The door opened behind us, stealing our attention. We both knew who it was. But if I didn't before, Blake's reaction told me all I needed to piece it together.

Turning my head, I watched the two large men slowly enter the room. Sterling's presence ate up the space while Obediah's presence faded to nothing. The effect of each man was incredible, as if they amplified each other. It was this exact thing I wanted Blake and Obi to realize. Yes, Sterling and Obi were completely different, opposites even. But when they were together, it was undeniable how they complimented each other. Made each other stronger. Obi could blend into the darkness so much more easily with Sterling around because no matter what Sterling did, he commanded attention.

How could I make them see that that could be them, if they allowed themselves to coexist the way they were meant to?

Sterling led Obi to the chairs beside the couch. The urge to be close to Sterling, go sit in his lap and curl into his citrusy scent was hard to deny, but this wasn't about us.

I watched Blake. His shoulders hunched even further, teeth bit into his bottom lip like he was trying to hold in a scream. Obi wore his mask and gloves. His chin length wavy hair was tousled, but in an intentional way. His fingers twitched, but otherwise he remained composed. Easy to do when your face is obscured.

Sterling sat silently, looking at me, letting me lead.

Goddess, I wanted to touch him.

Clearing my throat, I focused my attention on Obi.

"Hello, Executioner," I greeted, giving him the same smile I gave Blake. The large man dipped his head in greeting. I waited, glancing at Blake from the corner of my eye. He was pointedly looking away.

I sighed, "Blake, aren't you going to greet your Master?"

Blake turned his head away like a petulant child.

"Blake," Sterling snapped. The warning was heavy in his tone. I glared at Sterling who raised an eyebrow in challenge, with a hint of amusement.

Asshole.

"Hi, Executioner," Blake mumbled.

He still called him Executioner. I mean, it could be because he didn't know if Sterling and I were privy to his actual name, but something told me that wasn't the case. He didn't know his real name. I'd even wager he didn't know what he looked like behind the mask.

"Hello," Obi responded in the softest, quietest voice I had ever heard.

Blake's head shot up, mouth gaping as he looked at Obi. "You spoke to me...you haven't spoken to me in weeks..."

Obi's head tilted downward, causing his hair to fall forward.

"I didn't ask you here to have dinner," I said to Obi. That was what Sterling told me he told him was the plan for the night. The man's head rose and though I could not see them through the filmy white sockets of the mask, I knew he was staring at me. "I want to help you both with your bond."

Obi immediately stood, panic practically oozing from his aura.

"Obi, please?"

Obediah's shoulders stiffened as both Sterling and Blake sat up.

"*Beau*," Sterling hissed in fury. My stomach dropped and my chest tightened, reacting to his anger, but I refused to back down.

"Trust me," I said to my Master. Sterling's lip curled, but he sat back in his chair. The rage still consumed the bond, making it difficult to think clearly, but I didn't ask him to shield it. I wanted to feel everything from him.

His eyes were fixed on me, emerald gaze like a raging storm. I tried my best to ignore it.

"Obi, can you take off your mask?" I asked.

Sterling's hands tightened on the armrests of the chair, wood groaning in protest.

Obediah looked at Sterling. When the Elder Vampire didn't say anything, he reached for the ties to his mask. Blake inhaled sharply as the mask fell away, revealing thick dark brows, sad brown eyes, a long and graceful nose, with soft looking bow sculpted lips. Obi slowly returned to his seat and looked down at his gloved hands.

Blake stared at him, awed and speechless.

"You are Vampire and fledgling, Master and mentee. If you can't bare every part of yourselves to each other, that bond will never get stronger."

"You didn't need to go this far," Sterling bit out.

"I did. You're worried that Blake can't be trusted with Obi's identity, but you're wrong. And even if you aren't, it won't matter. Blake won't survive long enough to tell anyone," I told them matter of factly.

A cold silence swept through the room as the implications of that dawned on them.

"What are you saying?" Blake whispered.

I looked at my brother fledgling with a sad smile. "You know just as well as I do, that you would not have survived the night. Not starved of blood, food, and the bond. Your body would have rejected the Change. But that's what you wanted after all, right?"

Obi let out a strangled noise. Without his mask, he could no longer hide his expressions and that only exposed the utter fear and heartbreak.

"Look at him," I whispered to Blake, who stared at Obi. "He *cares*."

"Why now? Why does it take *this*?" Blake gestured around us. "How come any time I've tried to get close to you, you shut me out and run away?" Blake's voice grew louder with each question, angrier. Anger wasn't exactly what I had in mind for this, but if it was what he was feeling, Obi needed to know. They needed to share how they felt with each other.

I watched as Obi retreated into himself, sinking into that stillness as if it would make him disappear.

"Obi, you have to talk to him...Or else you'll lose him. Don't you want things to get better? Don't you want to stop hurting? *Tell* him," I urged, hoping that I hadn't grossly miscalculated and that he hadn't completely given up.

"I...wish not to frighten you," Obi responded quietly. Barely above a whisper. "You were...so afraid that night."

"Who wouldn't be? I woke up in a dark room with no memories and a creepy man in a mask standing over me!"

Obi flinched.

He started to backtrack. I could tell as the sadness in his eyes slowly died, becoming empty, devoid of everything.

Not good.

"But you're not afraid of him now, right Blake?" I prompted, needing them to keep pushing through these hurdles. If we could get past the hard parts, they'll have a chance.

Blake didn't say anything.

"You told me you wanted to get close to him," I said firmly.

"I never–" Blake started.

"Yes. You did. You said that he didn't let you drink from him, touch him, talk to him. You said he was always leaving. You spoke as if these things *bothered* you. They did, because it wouldn't allow you to get close and you had to rely on the rumors about him to get to know him. Rumors that you *knew* did not represent him well. Be honest, Blake."

"Fine! Yes! That's what I wanted, what I *want!*" He threw his hands up exasperated. Then he whirled on Obi. "That's what I want. But you keep pushing me away. Why do you treat me like you want nothing to do with me? Why even turn me?"

That was a question I only had half an answer to. I would be lying if I said I wasn't interested in how Obi would respond. If he *did* respond.

"I was called to change you," Obi murmured.

"Called to? Someone told you to change me?" Blake demanded.

Obi hesitated before giving a small nod.

"Did you even *want* me as your fledgling? Or was all of this because you were told to?" Blake's words were heated, but I could see the desperation in his eyes. He wanted Obi to prove him wrong. Tell him he was wanted, *chosen* by him.

But Obi didn't say anything.

Blake deflated, sliding back into the couch, staring at the raging fire in the hearth with a defeated look.

"You turn my world upside down, chain me to you, and you don't even want me," Blake said numbly, eyes still fixed on the fire.

"That was not my intention," Obi finally said.

"What then? What do you want from me?"

"I wanted you to..."Obi stopped, swallowing hard. His gloved hands twitched, like he was aching to put his mask back on. To hide. To run.

Say it, Obi. Tell him. He needs to know. You *need to trust him or things will never change.*

"You wanted me to what?" Blake pushed, but there was no heat or warmth in his words. They were cold, detached, as he slowly fell deeper into the conclusions drawn in his own mind.

"I wanted you to save me," Obi whispered.

Yes.

Blake came alive again, thrown at this new revelation...*declaration* of Obi's feelings.

"Save you?" Blake repeated, staring at Obi again, who finally found the strength to look Blake in the eyes.

"Yes."

They stared at each other for a long time. I glanced at Sterling to figure out what he thought. But he wasn't looking at them, he was staring at me. His expression was unreadable, the bond shut tight. I hated when he did that.

I glared at him. His expression didn't change. He didn't even blink, just turned his head to the others. The dismissal hurt. The blatant displeasure curled in my chest, shot spikes in my veins.

Why couldn't he see what I could? This was *helping*. They were making *progress*.

The pair continued to stare at each other, with wonder and curiosity like a timid child, budding between them. I'd show Sterling that the risk was worth it. They just needed one last push.

"Blake," I said softly, breaking the spell they seemed to be under.

"You told me you couldn't control your Earth power. If you'll trust me, I can show you how to ground yourself, how you can find that control." I switched my gaze from Blake to Obi. "Obi, I need you to trust me too. I need you to both trust and understand that this will work."

I had no proof that it would, but something compelled me to try. It was like a voice in my head guiding me. My instincts took charge and I let them.

"Take your gloves off," I told Obi, who reluctantly removed them, revealing long pale fingers.

"Give me your hands," I commanded, holding mine out to each of them. They each grasped mine, but the hesitation and caution was clear in both of their eyes. "Trust me," I said again, then took their hands and intertwined them together.

Blake immediately tried to jerk away, but I forced their hands together with my own.

"I can't! I can't! I don't want to feel it!" Blake protested, squirming, trying desperately to break my hold but he was so weak after starving himself, it was hardly any effort to keep his hand there. Obi just stared at him, sadness in his gaze. But he didn't pull away, when he so easily could.

"You can and you will," I told him sternly. "Release the Earth. Let it out and let it go. It will make *sense*, Blake."

Blake screamed incoherently, still thrashing. I felt what he did. The coldness coming off of Obi. The darkness, the death, it was uncomfortable and he wasn't even releasing his power.

I turned to Obi, "Release your power, Obi."

Obi frowned, looking at Blake, then their clasped hands, unsure. "Trust that it will make sense," I said again, hoping that he wouldn't turn back.

Obi took a deep breath before letting it out slowly. As he exhaled, I could feel his hand grow even colder, feel the life seep out of the air around us.

Blake screamed even louder, "No! No!"

"Let it out, Blake," I snapped. "Or we will *both* die."

He was crying now. It was getting harder to hold on, but

determination kept me steady in my grip. Even though my head swam and dizziness started to settle in.

"Beau," Sterling warned, a hint of worry in his voice.

At Sterling's voice, I could feel Obi starting to pull back, reigning his death back in. "Don't you dare stop, Obediah. Keep releasing it," I growled, not meaning to be aggressive, but I was fighting hard to keep the moving parts in order while feeling my life drain from me.

"You will both die," Obi warned cautiously.

"No. Blake won't let that happen." I turned to Blake who had stopped screaming and now sobbed pitifully. "Will you, Blake?"

The fledgling took several shuddering breaths, understanding that I would not let go unless he did it. Slowly, I could feel it. Tentative. Unsure. But so full of warmth and life. I could smell the fresh churned dirt, feel the blades of grass, hug the vines that danced around my body in phantom sensations.

"That's it, Blake," I coaxed, as it chased away the coolness from Obi.

And Obi was completely mesmerized. He stared at Blake like he was watching a god be born. There was worship and utter adoration in that stare. His lip trembled as blood tears slowly descended along his prominent cheekbones, down to his sharp chin.

"It doesn't feel so bad now, does it?" I asked Blake, who was staring at Obi with that same awestruck expression. Carefully, I released them. Their hands still remained clasped as mine drifted away, but the sudden loss of their power left me drained. My vision blurred and I fell back onto the couch, unable to keep myself sitting up.

"They're going to be okay," I whispered.

Strong arms lifted me from behind with little effort. Sterling carried me to the bed, leaving the other two alone by the fire.

My Master bit his wrist and let the droplets of blood fall into my mouth. I lapped it up greedily, feeling the strength returning.

When a good portion of my energy was restored, I let my gaze return to the pair by the couch. Obi was standing, gloves on, mask in place. In his arms was an unconscious Blake who most likely expended too much power.

Obi was staring down at the man in his arms and though his mask was on his face, I knew there would be a hopeful expression behind it.

He looked at me briefly, giving a nod of thanks before turning and leaving as silently as he came.

When we were alone, I sat up on the bed and stared at Sterling.

"I'm ready," I told him with a sigh.

"Ready for what?" He asked, but his tone was distracted. Distant.

"For your lecture. For you to scold me. Tell me I was reckless...yadda yadda."

Sterling stared at me for a moment before shaking his head.

"No lecture."

I frowned. "Really?"

"Really."

"But...you were furious at me. Are you...not mad?" I felt the rage. He was *definitely* pissed.

"Not anymore."

Then he smiled at me.

What the fuck?

"You were right," he continued.

I laughed, the sound a little hysterical.

"I'm sorry, *what?*"

Sterling rolled his eyes at me, but the smile was still plastered on his face.

"You were right, Beau. I don't know how you knew what to

do, but I'm grateful. I saw the change in them. They're going to be okay now."

"To be honest...I was faking it. I had no idea what the hell I was doing or saying. That was the embodiment of...'winging it'. None of the research I'd done backed up my actions."

Sterling laughed, leaning over to kiss my forehead.

"Well, it worked. So thank you."

I shrugged nonchalantly, but curled up close, relishing in the praise.

They'll be okay and that's what matters the most.

12

NEW ARRIVALS

"What did you do?" Kyle asked as we sat in the dining hall for our daily 'lunch' date. Blake was suddenly glued to Obi's side, and Kyle noticed the change. Blake regarded Obi with a look of reverence, as though he were the most precious thing in the world, and Kyle immediately started hounding me about my involvement in the change. Since Alexander had left earlier, he had taken it upon himself to get some answers.

"I told you, I didn't really do much. They just hadn't given each other a proper chance. They are meant for each other, the perfect balance. They see that now," I said, sipping the glass of warm blood. It wasn't Sterling's and didn't taste nearly as good, but he insisted that I start drinking it. I swear, the first time I nearly hurled. It's bad enough not being able to drink it from the source, but slurping it up like it was a damn cup of orange juice made the experience even worse.

But I did what I was told. Even if I fucking hated it. It was worth it to hear him call me a 'good boy' in that teasing low timber. Don't get me wrong, I didn't suddenly become okay with the power dynamic and the condescension that came with those words, but it was like an ongoing joke between us. On the outside, everyone saw a fledgling totally besotted with their Master, being the picture of obedience. The reality was far from it. I challenged Sterling every step of the way, sometimes for no good reason other than to condition myself to push through the physical discomfort of disobeying him.

I was no one's slave.

Besides, Sterling liked it. It kept him on his toes. Our bond became more stable now that he viewed us on equal grounds. He won't admit it, but I knew he didn't view fledglings as equals. Not because he's some pretentious asshole–even though he could be on occasion–but because of the way the hierarchy worked. It was like a child and parent rather than partners. That's how it's always been and that's how all Vampires and fledglings alike, view their bonds. The strong ones...the *true* partners...they knew. Just because something had been ingrained into society, didn't make it right, something he's started to grasp.

As much as everyone avoided admitting it, that's what set Asher and Cadence apart from the rest. Stasia's bond with them was strong because they viewed the twins as equals. It was obvious in the way Stasia spoke to them, behaved around them. If my senses didn't know any better, I would have thought that they were full blown Vampires at this point.

"What Stage are Asher and Cadence in?" I asked, cutting Kyle off mid rant about something I admit, I was not paying attention to. Most likely Blake, he seemed to be fixated on that whole situation. Though I think the only reason he kept talking about it was because Alexander wasn't there to bring it up himself. He was usually the gossip of the pair.

"Why do you want to know?" Kyle asked suspiciously.

I raised a brow at him.

He sighed. "Stage Two still, I believe. But I think they might be close to Stage Three. It's been a few years since they were brought here."

"Why do you say that?"

Kyle shrugged, before digging back into his food. "Just a hunch."

Before I could question any further, the dining hall doors opened and a quiet hush fell over the room.

Dozens of Vampires and fledglings poured into the hall, occupying the several empty tables. I didn't recognize any of them.

"Who are they?" I whispered to Kyle.

My friend had gone tense and still, eyes marking all the new faces, clearly assessing for any threats. It was amazing how the easy going blonde went from all dimples and smiles to the dangerous Knight faction Warrior in less than a second.

"The visiting Coven houses. Here for tomorrow's celebration." There was steel in his tone. It was scary, but the tense atmosphere wasn't special to our table. There seemed to be unease radiating from the rest of Athen's Coven.

"Is it always like this when a Coven visits?" I asked.

"No," Kyle said and didn't elaborate.

What changed?

Wanting to ease some of the tension, I asked Kyle, "What faction are the twins in?"

Kyle frowned, "Elites. It's why they are rarely at the Coven house. Shouldn't you already know that?"

"Why would I?"

"You *are* in the Elites, aren't you?"

I looked down at my glass, "I haven't chosen a faction yet. I was going to see Julia a little later and ask her about it."

"You probably won't be able to. Last I heard, she collapsed last night. The third Elder whisked her away before anyone could figure out what happened and won't let anyone see her.

Rumor has it, she's finally entering Stage Four and completed the transition," Kyle answered, finishing up the last of his food.

"Why now?" I asked before choking down more of the blood. It would taste even worse if I let it get too cold.

"Samhain probably. This close? Everyone's power is a little amplified. I wouldn't be surprised if *you* change tomorrow."

I coughed, choking as the blood went down the wrong.

"What makes you say that?" I wheezed, patting my chest to keep the fluids moving.

Kyle gave me a 'look'.

"Right, dumb question."

I glanced around again, at the new faces. Something felt off. Wrong. But I couldn't pinpoint it. They weren't doing anything wrong or suspicious. They grabbed some food, sat down, ate or drank, socialized, just like the rest of us, nothing out of the ordinary. So why did it feel like a boulder sitting in my gut?

I tried not to think about it, grateful when Kyle asked me a question.

"So...what's it like living off of only blood?"

I pursed my lips in contemplation while swirling the dark red contents around in my glass. "Weird. I have no urge to eat regular food, but the habit is still there, if that makes sense."

Kyle nodded, staring at the glass with curiosity.

"It's strange to see someone go through all the Stages so fast," he murmured.

"It's never happened before?" I asked.

Kyle shook his head. "You and Blake are the only ones that I know of who have gone through the Stages in a matter of weeks rather than years."

"But Blake is still in Stage Two," I pointed out.

"Neither Hale nor Joel think he will be for much longer, especially now that he's feeding again. He'll probably enter Stage Three tomorrow."

Does Lilith really not have control over it? Does she truly not know when we'll change or why?

But what reason would she have to lie?

As I opened my mouth to ask Kyle about his experience during Stage One into Stage Two, my chest tugged and the door to the dining hall opened again.

Sterling and Hale walked with purpose to our table. All around, I saw heads bow to my Master, paying respect to the first Elder. He didn't acknowledge them or even look in their directions. Those eyes were only for me.

When he was close enough, I stood. His hand came to caress my neck affectionately. Distantly, I heard Hale whisper, "Done eating, love?"

Sterling looked at the table to my half empty glass. There was a silent order in his eyes. I sighed, took the glass and chugged the rest of it before setting it down on the table.

"Good boy," he whispered. I rolled my eyes, but smiled. "We have a meeting to attend."

I frowned. When he said 'we', it didn't seem like he was talking about Hale and himself.

With one commanding jerk of his chin he led us out, Hale and Kyle followed as we left the dining hall in a brisk walk, making our way to one of the large conference rooms. I could taste the tension rolling off of him and knew that now was not the time for questions.

Something was up and I prayed he would tell me about it later tonight. Or else I'll find out for myself and no one liked when I did that.

The conference room was much like the others, hidden behind dark wood double doors. Inside, there was a long round wooden table with several chairs surrounding it. At one head, there was a throne-like chair, gilded in gold with a massive back and covered in deep purple velvet. Opposite of that, at the other head, was a chair similar in style but less grand. I didn't need anyone to tell me which was Lilith's and which was Nexus's.

The room was illuminated by flickering candles in the wall sconces. There were a few seats along the surrounding walls and nearly all of them were full with Vampires and a few fledglings. Two of which were Asher and Cadence.

At the table, near the purple chair, sat Stasia. Marcelle was not present which made me think there might be some merit to rumors Kyle told me. Filling some of the other seats at the table were unfamiliar faces. Vampires. Powerful ones.

A Frenchman in his late forties, early fifties sat primly. His dark hair was peppered with gray and he had a goddess damned Van Dyke beard. His mustache was perfectly twirled at the tips. His face was twisted up like he smelled something sour.

If Frollo had a brother...

Beside him was a younger Indian woman, dressed in a dark red formal duster. She looked like she was ready to step on to a runway rather than sit in for a meeting. Next to her was an older Japanese man, with a tailored suit that probably cost more money than this entire building. His face was unreadable, but there was a grace in which he held himself that spoke more than his expression ever could.

Across from him was another woman, but I couldn't discern her features as she was covered head to toe in a black niqab and matching loose-fitting abaya. Her eyes were large, all-seeing. They sparkled a light honey-brown, full of warmth and maternal affection.

Beside her was a dark skinned woman with a shaved head and dark brown eyes. Silver lined her eyes, matching the several piercings that adorned her ears. While the others were dressed in some form of formal wear, she was all casual in a worn dark leather jacket, black cropped tank top, and dark jeans.

They must be the High Priests and High Priestesses from the

visiting Coven houses. Don't know if they even noticed how much they stood out. I could tell from a first glance that they were...*other*. Blending in must not be a priority for them.

Sterling led me to one of the seats along the wall. I glanced around for Kyle and Hale but it didn't look like they followed us inside, probably standing guard outside the door.

With another affectionate brush to my neck and a small smile, Sterling left me to go sit in the chair directly to the right of the purple throne.

I took my own seat, noting that the young man sitting beside me didn't look up or even acknowledge our presence.

Rude.

The urge to look around was strong, but I wasn't entirely sure of the etiquette in this situation. These people didn't seem like they played by the same rules and I didn't want to do anything that might reflect poorly on Sterling.

Vampire politics. *Total bullshit.*

Instead, I kept my eyes on Sterling. His face was smoothed into that cold, calm, unshakeable mask. Upon my stare, his eyes found mine. While his expression didn't falter, I could feel a wave of warmth and affection flood through the bond. It lit me up, like a small flame bursting into a roaring fire within my core.

I shifted in my seat, fighting and failing to keep a smile off my face. The corner of Sterling's lip twitched before he looked away.

Everyone stood, thoroughly distracting me. I hesitantly followed suit as the double doors opened. Nexus stepped in, dressed in white. His long waves were pulled back into a loose braid. On his arm, was the Mother of All. Lilith was stunning in a dark red gown, loose flowing and elegant. I noted the intention of that style, keeping the focus away from her stomach. Her braids were formed into a crown with dark red jewels and live red roses intertwined throughout.

Nexus led her to the purple throne before moving to take the other.

As Lilith sat, we all followed.

"Greetings, my children." She smiled as she spoke, looking around the room happily.

"Greetings, Mother," everyone recited unanimously with a respectful bow of their heads. It was a bit freaky, but I joined in anyway. Wouldn't do me any good if I offended someone.

"My children don't often visit their Mother," Lilith tsked, speaking to no one in particular, but the sneer on her face was meant for everyone.

Like scolded children, some looked down at their hands or toward the wall. Anywhere but at her.

"Apologies, Mother. The recent uprisings have made it quite difficult to find the appropriate time to," the Frenchman said. If I was honest, I expected him to have an accent but he sounded as American as I did.

"Carlisle," Mother chided, turning her glowing red gaze to the Frenchman. Though she only said his name, her tone alone spoke volumes.

So that was Carlisle...fitting I guess. There was something... *slimy* about him. It doesn't come as a surprise that he'd been overstepping his position and causing a stir.

"There haven't been any...*uprisings* near your Coven house, unless there is something you'd like to share?" Stasia taunted. Carlisle's eyes tightened slightly, but it was such a small movement that it took concentration and full attention to catch it.

"You should use my title in this setting, Elder," Carlisle replied, levelly, unaffected even though the accusatory implication had definitely ruffled a few of his feathers.

"Apologies, High Priest," Stasia mocked. Carlisle's nostrils flared. He didn't entertain the encounter any further. Stasia leaned back in their chair with a satisfied smirk.

Lilith sighed.

"How many new children have you brought for me this Samhain?" she asked before turning her gaze back to Carlisle. "Carlisle?"

"Seven, Mother," he answered.

"Kawana?"

"Three, Mother," the woman in the niqab responded with a voice that was deep and soothing.

"Yaeyem?"

"Four," fancy suit replied.

"Duaa?" Lilith asked, focusing her gaze on the woman with a shaved head.

"Eight, Mother," she responded.

"And Ninetta?"

"Six, Mother," replied the woman in the red duster.

So that was Ninetta? The other one mentioned to have been riling up the Vampires and challenging Lilith? I mean, Carlisle looked like trouble, so I'm not surprised by his involvement. Ninetta on the other hand, she seemed kind, loyal, trustworthy... *normal*. I never would have suspected.

I guess years of practice can do that. She had to be ancient. She had this aura about her...they all did. No matter how modern their clothing and speech were, their auras exposed everything. Maybe that was a Vampire thing.

"What a bountiful harvest," Lilith clapped. "With our fourteen, that makes forty-two new Vampires. This celebration will be grand."

"Indeed, my love," Nexus cooed, looking equally pleased.

They went on to discuss the logistics of the rituals to take place and I easily lost focus. While everyone was distracted by the conversation, I took the time to study the room. There were about seven Vampires and ten fledglings, sitting along the walls as I was, excluding the twins and myself.

I studied the rude guy who sat beside me. Took in his curly dark hair, pale blue eyes, lean physique, and strong chin with a tiny dimple. There was a small tattoo peeking from behind his collar, creeping along his neck. The design was stark against his pale skin. So black it seemed to eat up the light in an unnatural way. Several jagged lines connected in a ring linked with another. It felt symbolic. Like a bond or...contract.

After an intentional grunt to get his attention, I held out my hand to him. "I'm Beau. Fledgling of the First Elder, Sterling."

He didn't even look at my outstretched hand, but smiled. "I know who you are," he mused. As I was about to press him for his name, he stood suddenly. Everyone did.

I rose to my feet watching as everyone began shuffling out of the room.

"I hope you survive, Beau," the man said before giving a small nod and walking off...right to Carlisle's side.

Survive?

Was he talking about the change? Did he know I was close to transitioning fully?

Staring after him confused, I didn't notice Stasia approach.

Fighting not to startle, I hurried to bow my head in respect.

"Third Elder," I greeted.

Stasia smiled, and it was quite unnerving. Even more so when it dropped from their face, suddenly serious. They leaned in close, lips just brushing my ear before whispering, "Don't drink the blood on the night of Samhain."

I frowned, opening my mouth to ask what they were talking about, but they had disappeared. As did the twins.

Figures.

Don't drink the blood...Stasia definitely knew more than they were letting on. It was frustrating. All these hints but no concrete answers. Was it helpful to be this cryptic? Or did the universe just enjoy watching me pander around without a damn clue?

"Let's go," Sterling said as he approached. We were the last two in the room and I hadn't even noticed. Too caught up in the fact that I still don't know what the fuck was going on.

As we walked down the hall, back to our rooms, the excitement that had previously been buzzing around the Coven house had died. In its place was a slightly uneasy energy, heavy with tension.

"I have a bad feeling about Samhain," I murmured to Sterling. The Elder sighed, glancing around the hall and taking in the obvious discomfort with the visiting Covens.

"Me too, Beau. Me too."

When we reached our door, Obi was standing there. Waiting.

Sterling frowned.

The large man pointed at me, "Lilith wishes to see him."

My brow furrowed as I looked back and forth between him and Sterling, then pointed at myself like an idiot. "Me?"

Obi nodded.

Sterling made a move to turn back down the hall, no doubt leading us to Lilith's rooms but Obi's voice stopped him.

"Alone."

Sterling bristled visibly. It was the first time I'd seen him slip up in his composure while in front of others.

The hurt sang through the bond. I grabbed his hand and squeezed it.

"We must go," Obi pushed.

Executioner led the way down the hall.

I gave Sterling's hand one last squeeze before I followed behind Obi while he watched us go. The pain intensified with each step, I staggered under the weight of it. Sterling clearly noticed because the bond shut and I could feel nothing from him.

I turned to glare at him, because he knew I *hated* when he did that, but he was gone. The door closed firmly behind him.

I sighed. I'll deal with him later.

For now, curiosity got the best of me. Why me? Why alone? Sterling had always been there when I saw Lilith and it was usually because the business she had was with the First Elder, not his fledgling.

I knew better than to ask Obi. It was hard enough to get him to speak normally, he definitely wasn't going to volunteer any sort of insight into the situation.

So like a good little fledgling, I followed him. Letting him lead me down the darkened halls, through Lilith's quarters, to a tiny room that I had seen once before.

Sitting on the ledge, by the window, Lilith waited, still dressed in her formal gown from earlier. The moon illuminated her features, making her look just that much more otherworldly.

"Thank you, Obediah," she said, not looking at us.

Obi bowed his head before turning to leave.

A part of me panicked. I didn't want to be left alone with her. What if I said or did something wrong? I didn't want to offend or disrespect her in any way.

"Relax child, come sit with me," she smiled at me, with bright white teeth. Her arms opened. Compelled, I stepped toward her, sitting between her legs as she wrapped her arms around my middle and rested her chin on my head, just as I had before in this very spot.

Of course, Obi and Sterling weren't fucking two feet away this time.

Even pressed against her, I couldn't feel her stomach. At

least, it didn't protrude any more than average from what I could tell. It was odd...was there truly a child?

When she didn't say anything, just hugged me in silence, I grew antsy, unsure of whether or not I should speak.

Was I in trouble? I don't remember doing anything to warrant her wrath. To be honest, she didn't seem very wrathful right now. If anything, she seemed sad.

"I've been waiting for you," she said.

I sputtered in panic, "I'm sorry, Mother. I came as soon as I found out you wanted to see me."

She laughed, "Hush child, that's not what I meant." She stroked my hair. "I've been waiting for a fledgling like you to be born."

I paused in my panic, frozen and confused.

"You are special," she continued. "Special because I *made* you special."

"Special?" I asked.

"You have done what every fledgling is capable of but never has the courage to do. You challenge your Maker."

I stiffened.

"I see you. Fighting the compulsion every day. You have a strong sense of self. A demand for freedom. Perhaps it is because you've had so little of it in your last human life. It is refreshing."

I stayed quiet, not really sure what to say. *Was I really being praised for being a pain in Sterling's ass?*

"You'll transition tomorrow and it will not be pretty. You may hurt. You may remember things. I cannot protect you from that and neither can Sterling."

Joy. More pain.

"You have lived many lives over the millenia. It is a cycle that I have ended, and for that I am sorry. It was selfish of me. But I knew you would be good for him. That he needed you, especially when I am gone."

"So you can control the call? Who is chosen to be a Vampire?" I asked, not completely forgetting the whole reincarnation thing. I would definitely be asking for more clarification on *that* little detail.

"Sometimes. Only for a certain few. I do not do it often. I try not to. It goes against nature. But with you...I had to. There was no one else I could trust with this. With her."

"Her, as in the new Mother." It wasn't a question.

Lilith hummed an affirmative note.

"Does everyone get reincarnated?"

"No. Only those worthy of it."

"Why me?"

"You are what some call a lightworker or Earth angel. You guide others, help them, heal them, a bright light in times of darkness, full of compassion and love."

I didn't feel like any of those things. I wasn't particularly helpful to others. At least, I didn't think so.

But then I thought about Blake and Obi. Maybe she was onto something.

"There is much darkness in this world and it only grows. I did not want to leave, not when it is like this, but I felt it coming, the end of my cycle. I made the decision to change you, bond you to Sterling and now I must face the consequences. But I trust you with my first and with my predecessor. You will guide her to light and protect her from darkness."

"You took away my choice," I told her, feeling just a little bit bold with the anger that bubbled from the realization that yet another person has taken my will away. "You value my sense of self and demand for freedom, but that's the very thing you've taken away from me."

"I know. I am sorry."

Her apology only made me angrier. I pulled away from her, turning to look her in the eye.

"That was incredibly *selfish*," I hissed.

Lilith met my gaze head on, "I know."

And the part that pissed me off the most? I wasn't actually angry at her. Angry at the situation? Yes. But there was this inherent part of me that understood why she did it. A part that actually *wanted* to help.

Fuck!

"Does Sterling know?" I asked.

She shook her head. "No one does."

"If you value him so much, why do you keep pushing him away? It hurts him."

Lilith gently rubbed her chest, as if it hurt. She felt it, what she did to him, I *knew* she did. So why?

"Sterling...he is precious to me. He is my first, and with the first, you always make mistakes. I held him too tight and now he will suffer the most when I am gone. I am trying to right my wrongs. He will hurt now, but the more he detaches from the situation the easier it will be for him to move on. If I continued to hold him close, he would not survive my end. Please...I am asking you to save them."

I stared at her, long and hard. I didn't see the Mother of All Vampires, the First. I just saw a Mother. Exhausted and desperate.

My heart ached.

I nodded. Maybe *too* easily. I didn't ask nearly enough questions.

Her smile was gentle, warm.

"Thank you," she whispered.

And we sat there, as the weight of the Moon sat heavily on our shoulders.

13

SAMHAIN

"I heard you the first seven times," I grumbled, tugging on my boots and lacing them tight.

"And I'll say it another seven times so you know that I'm serious. If at any point, you feel something off, see something suspicious, you don't investigate or even ignore it, you run. Run even if I'm not with you, I promise I'll find you. Wherever you go, I *will* find you. You have to keep your guard up, use discernment, and protect yourself," Sterling lectured again.

Ever since the weirdness of last night and when I told him about Stasia's warning, he'd been even more on edge, if that was even possible.

I didn't say anything about my meeting with Lilith, though I knew he was curious.

I understood his concern, truly I did, but we still weren't certain anything bad *would* happen. Of course, this contradicts my instincts, I *knew* that, but...I didn't want to jump the gun, and *he* shouldn't either. It would alert others to something being up.

The constant fretting was a bit overkill. I let him though, because I could feel through the bond how apprehensive he was. Especially since his duties would force him to be away from me for the majority of the night.

I'd be careful. I promised him, and I'll keep that promise the best I could.

The giant was still towering over me as I finished lacing my boots. His thick arms crossed over his broad chest and head bowed as he stared down at me. The skin between his dark brows were pinched.

I stood, reaching up to smooth the wrinkled skin with my thumbs. Hate to admit that I had to go on my very tip toes just to reach.

"I'll be fine, Sterling. I *promise*."

His jaw clenched in frustration. There was something else bugging him, it was the only explanation for this level of worry. "What is it?" I pushed, needing to understand, to reassure him.

"I brought you here, *changed* you, because I wanted to keep you safe. I wanted you to be happy and not worry about danger. You have already been through *so much,* it's not fair to you."

He didn't know that the choice to change me had not really been his own. This would have happened whether he wanted it to or not, because *Lilith* wanted it to. I wasn't going to tell him, there was no need. Not when he anguished this much. Besides, it didn't matter, what's done is done.

I smiled at him, "It's not your fault and you know it. I'm grateful, Sterling. Grateful that you changed me, that I have a second chance and nothing will get in the way of that. Not even some super creepy Vampires."

Sterling's lip quirked. It was the closest thing to a smile I was going to get while he was like this. I kissed his shoulder and stepped away.

His hand latched onto my wrist before I could go far. I stopped and looked back at him.

"Keep these on you," he said, handing me three small vials filled with a dark red liquid.

I nodded, taking them from him and tucking them in the inner pocket of my red cloak.

He brushed my neck, kissed my forehead, and slipped into his own cloak. We pulled up our hoods before leaving the room and entering the fray.

People were everywhere, all dressed in the same red cloaks. Autumn decorations covered the halls leading to the opulent salon where most of the people congregated. In the center, right before the dais where Lilith's throne sat, was a huge pile of wood.

Tiny unlit candles were laid out in a five pointed star, the wood pile at its center. The roof of the salon had been pulled back to reveal the night sky sprinkled with stars. I didn't even know the roof had that function, but it made sense, the smoke from the bonfire had to go somewhere.

Lilith sat on her throne, dressed in a gold jeweled cloak. The large billowing hood cast a shadow on her face, only allowing her red painted lips and tiny delicate chin to be visible.

Beside her in a white cloak with the hood pulled back was Nexus. All the Vampires and fledglings alike took their turns greeting Mother. They bowed at her dais, offering a few drops of blood in the large wooden bowl at her feet.

There were a few fledglings, though, that stepped past the bowl and knelt directly at Lilith's feet. Each time, she raised one long slim leg, offering her ankle, and the fledgling would take a bite. I wanted to ask Sterling about the significance, but we weren't allowed to speak during the celebration.

"The dead don't speak," Sterling had told me. "And this night is about honoring the half of us that is dead."

Searching for some familiar faces amongst the crowd, I

spotted Blake and Obi in a dark corner. They were close, but carefully looking away from each other.

From my understanding, they were doing better and nurturing the bond, so why act like strangers now?

Unless they were trying to cover the fact that they were bonded. As the Executioner, Obi has made many enemies, even within the Coven. It was why he wore a mask and his identity was the biggest kept secret. Hence, calling him "Executioner" and not Obediah. While everyone in the Athens Coven knew that they were bonded as Vampire and fledgling, it was unlikely anyone outside the Coven did. So they would feign indifference while our guests were here.

Best to avoid them then rather than risk a potential slip up and reveal something they were clearly working hard to hide.

Instead, I looked for Kyle. Sterling told me earlier that Hale wouldn't be participating in the celebration due to being on guard duty, which meant Kyle would be alone. If something was going on, it would be safer to stick together.

I couldn't find him, even as Sterling and I made our way through the throngs of people–who silently greeted each other with light caresses–towards Lilith.

Focusing my attention on the ritual, I followed Sterling, kneeling at Lilith's feet. She raised her ankle first to Sterling who gently caressed her skin, planting three soft kisses to her ankle before biting down for a quick sip. When he finished, I was startled to see her shift her ankle to me. Sterling warned me I would be drinking from her, but I guessed a part of me still didn't believe it.

With wide eyes, I looked to Sterling, who gave a small nod.

As gingerly as I could, I grasped her ankle, taking note of the various smears of blood and wounds unhealed, glistening in the flickering light. She should have healed immediately after each bite. It was a sign of her weakening and I couldn't be the only one who had noticed.

Carefully, I placed my lips on her warmth, trying to find a spot that had not already been bitten. It was like the fire and water within me surged. Power swelled and I had yet to even taste her. Lowering my fangs, I pierced her flesh. The moment her blood touched my tongue, the world around me erupted.

Metaphorically, of course.

Just a sip and I felt invincible. The well of power in me was endless. I wanted to scream. I wanted to feed. I wanted to *fuck*. The sensations were as overwhelming as they were incredible.

If Sterling hadn't touched my arm in a silent warning, I would have embarrassed myself in front of everyone.

Bowing deeply, I backed away. My vision was suddenly crystal clear. My heart thudded in my chest, threatening to push past the confines of my skin and bones. My cock thickened as the blood hastened through my veins.

A soft moan left my lips.

Fuck.

I grabbed Sterling, unable to stop myself. My hand went straight for the promise between his legs. His cock was hard, straining against the confines of his pants.

He needed me like I needed him.

Desperate, I tried unbuttoning his pants, right there in the middle of the damn salon. But Sterling was quick, grabbing my hands, planting several kisses along my knuckles, before giving a firm shake of his head.

I whined, but he muffled the sound with his lips to mine. It wasn't intended to insight the heat that roared within me. It was a warning to be silent and behave. But how could I when the power racing through me threatened to rip its way out of my veins?

Sterling grabbed my hand in his, taking control, and led us

to a fairly secluded corner where one cloaked figure seemed to be waiting. With each step, Sterling drew on my hand with one finger. It took a moment to realize he was writing a message. I focused, trying to fight past the desires and heat, deciphering his words.

Danger. Baby. Run.

That sobered me up, real quick. I tried to keep the fear and shock off my face, plastering on the neutral expression I had practiced. As we approached, the cloaked figure lifted their head.

Kyle.

Sterling pulled me to stand by Kyle's side before reminding me with a finger to his lips to remain silent. He kissed my forehead before heading to the center of the salon.

Kyle flashed me a smile before turning back to the ritual. I couldn't focus, not with Sterling's warning. My eyes tracked from left to right, trying to spot anything out of the ordinary, but I didn't see anyone or anything suspicious. Everyone was transfixed by the ritual.

Sterling, Nexus, Obi, and Duaa had made their way to the center of the salon. Each stood at a point of the star, holding one tall, white, unlit candle.

Lilith stood and with a grace only she could manage, walked to the remaining point of the star. Behind her, Stasia had lifted the giant bowl of blood that almost everyone there had contributed to. With them was Asher and Cadence, holding a bowl of water each. One by one, they approached fledglings and Vampires alike. They each cleansed their hands in the bowl of water before dipping one finger in the bowl of blood, sucking the dark red liquid off their finger.

Don't drink the blood on the night of Samhain.

As Stasia and the twins neared us, I tugged Kyle back, to hide behind one of the pillars we stood in front of, but Kyle shot me a surprised and slightly annoyed look before stepping up to the bowl and continuing with the ritual. I sighed, remaining hidden...or so I thought.

Stasia's eyes met mine, clearly seeing me, but they continued on their way to the next person. It was that same fledgling from before, the one with weird tattoo. Instead of dipping a finger into the bowl, he extended his wrist and cut deep. More than a few drops fell into the bowl before he pulled back and licked his wound. Stasia continued on.

Still, my eyes trailed the bowl of blood, dark and ominous. Something about it, its scent, felt familiar. I had seen everyone contribute, to make it full this very night, and yet, it looked...old. Too dark, too handled. How hadn't anyone noticed?

When everyone had taken the offering, Stasia returned the bowl to Lilith, who lifted the bowl to her lips and gulped the remaining blood down. I watched in horror as it splattered all over her golden cloak, staining her mouth, her chin, and her entire front in red.

With the bowl emptied, she tossed it into the pile of wood and made her way east around the pentagram lighting all the candles for each element.

When Lilith returned to her spot at the remaining point, the candles on the ground blazed and the bonfire crackled to life. Roaring as the elements danced around it. I could feel them, hear them, smell them, as they whipped and twirled. All of our human selves, returning to us tonight. Celebrating. It was as beautiful as it was chaotic.

That feeling before the energy that seemed to hum as I drank Lilith's blood was now buzzing all around the room. Crackling and uncontrollable. *Raw power.*

Slowly, cloaks were shed, bodies were joined, and the mating portion of the ritual had begun.

Lilith watched as everyone joined with one another. Naked

bodies twisting and gyrating, giving life back to those we've lost. It was as hypnotic as it was jarring.

I didn't see Sterling, Stasia or Obi anywhere, having faded into the chaos while I was bewitched by Lilith. I didn't even spot the twins amongst the hoards of writhing bodies.

Almost leaving my hiding spot to look for them, I hesitated, noticing how everyone seemed to twitch and convulse and fuck and feed. I mean, this was my first time experiencing Samhain with Vampires, but this didn't feel right. Something in my gut warned that this was *not* the normal ritual.

Their movements were jerky, rough, desperate...*frenzied*. I looked at Kyle who had collapsed with a Vampire from another Coven. As their clothes fell away, their tongues entwined in a heated dance. But his eyes, the pupil and sclera were all consumed by an inky blackness.

This is the stuff horror movies are made of.

My eyes snagged on movement behind them. Nexus helped Lilith up the dais before she stopped. Her face contorted in pain as her hands flew to her stomach. Nexus, concerned, leaned down to whisper in her ear before the two turned back around and headed out of the salon, toward their rooms.

I looked around to see if anyone noticed, but it was like everyone was caught in some sort of trance.

Everyone except me...

Why wasn't I lost to this frenzy?

The blood.

Fuck! I had to find Sterling. The blood must have been spiked or something. It was happening, they were making their move.

Fuck, fuck, fuck!

The moment I stepped from behind the pillar, a cloaked figure stepped in front of me. I paused, cautious. When they pulled their hood back, I realized it wasn't another Vampire. I couldn't even sense the tell-tale signs of a fledgling.

Human?

He was tall, broad shouldered, and solid in build. His skin was a warm medium brown and his hair a forest of skinny dreads falling down to his shoulders. His eyes were a deep dark brown, big and round. Mournful. *Lucid.* As unaffected by the spell everyone was under as I was.

And so familiar...

"Who–"

"Jamal."

I stiffened, eyes narrowed as I studied the stranger. How did he know that name?

"Who are you?" I demanded.

The man glanced up before swearing under his breath. "You shouldn't *be* here. You weren't supposed to *be* here. They *warned you*." Frantically, he made a grab for me.

Instinctively, I pulled back, but he caught my arm in an iron grasp. And...I couldn't break free.

How the hell?

The man tried pulling me again until suddenly he stopped, face shooting up toward the exposed sky. Peering up at the darkness, I noticed several tiny black spheres raining from the opening above.

Curious, I watched as they fell, trying to figure out what they were. I barely felt the body slam into me because when the first one hit the ground, the world exploded.

14

CHAOS

The chaos was tangible. Every scream and panicked thought pelted against me as I stood in the rubble. Frozen. My head hurt, my eyes stung, but I couldn't erase the vision from my head. The gore. The death.

She warned me that it may happen. Naively, I believed I had nothing to worry about because this was a part of me long forgotten. But how could I forget what was literally carved into my soul? I had *sold* my soul.

No.

She had *taken* it.

The screaming. It blurred in and out, like my head being shoved under the water again and again but not even the release of death would relinquish me. I was stuck in this never ending nightmare.

How many lives have I lived?

How many times have I rebelled and others paid the price?

How many deaths were my fault?

"Beau!"

The screams turned to numbness before deafening me with the reality that it was all coming apart again.

I didn't want to remember. I didn't want to be a part of this cycle again, a pawn in a game I never wanted to play.

Suddenly, Blake was there, his face coming into focus, filling my vision and shielding me from all of the rubble, the chaos.

"Beau! We need to go!"

I couldn't speak, could barely *see* him as his face morphed into one I was promised to forget.

"Anthony?" I whispered.

He didn't hear me. *Couldn't.* Because he was dead. He was dead. *Anthony was dead.*

I could see it so clearly. His head at an odd angle in the middle of the circle as everyone cheered. His murderer standing above him, hollow-eyed and lost, covered in blood and filth like we all were. Slaves. They bled us, they fucked us, they made us fight to the death for their own entertainment.

So many times, I tried to close my eyes, block out the never ending death. So many times, I tried to resist, to fight them, to help the others that were so far gone they teetered on the edge. And *so* many times, I made it all worse.

So many fucking bodies.

The only one who ever gave me hope was Anthony.

Anthony, who tried so hard to protect me when we were taken. The one who taught me how to cope, taught me what he could remember from school because he wanted me to be able to adapt once we escaped, because he was *so sure* we would. The one with a love for history and the reason I knew as much as I did because even surrounded by suffering and death, he still managed to find a reason to smile.

Anthony...He was dead and they fucking *cheered*. Celebrated.

Monsters. All of them were monsters.

And it was my fault. It was *my* fight, but he took my place, because I didn't keep my head down, because I tried to *save* someone else. Now he's dead and so was everyone else.

Their bodies burned.

It was all my fault.

"Beau, *please!* Come on!" Blake was back. His eyes wide with panic. I watched the trails of blood and dust streak his face.

"Blake?" I whispered. My voice was too hoarse to make any real noise, like I had been screaming. Maybe I had been. It was all I could hear anymore.

But that name...it seemed wrong. It wasn't *Blake*. There was another, but I couldn't remember anymore. It had faded along with the sense of discovery. A piece of the puzzle finally slotted in place had been ripped out and tossed away until I was left confused again.

I wasn't allowed to remember.

"Where did he go?" I heard myself murmur. There was someone else...

"Who are you talking about?" Blake hissed.

Without truly processing what was happening, Blake yanked me to my feet and started to run. I stumbled after him, gazing around. The bodies, the screaming, the blood, the chaos. It's like I was floating in another reality. None of this was real.

Where was Sterling?

"Sterling?" I whispered. Tugging on the bond, I felt nothing.

Fear gripped my throat and squeezed.

I can't feel him. I can't *feel* him.

"Sterling! Where is Sterling?" I glanced around frantically, the smoke and fire doing little to aid me in my pursuit of my Master. Why can't I feel him?

I tried to pull from Blake's grip but the adrenaline must have made him stronger because his hold on me was firm and unbreakable. He wouldn't let me go.

"I need to find him!" I protested.

"We need to get out of here. If he survived then he will find you, but until then, we need to go. Now," Blake hissed before tugging me behind a fallen pillar. The salon was hardly recognizable anymore. After the first explosions, it was hard to tell if the Coven house was still standing. The smoke was everywhere.

As we crouched, a few hooded figures passed by, blurs of movement. Searching. What were they looking for?

The baby.

Shit.

"We can't leave yet," I whispered to Blake, watching the figures, but sticking to the shadows. I kept the flames around us, willing myself not to use too much power, like Sterling taught me. I was careful to make sure they did not harm Blake, but kept where we hid secure. As they passed us by, not noticing our hiding spot, I started to creep forward until Blake tugged me back.

"Are you insane? We need to *leave*," he hissed.

"No, they're after the baby. We can't let them get to the new Mother."

Blake frowned, not understanding. That was fine. He didn't need to know the details, it was probably better for him in the long run. But I would need his help if we were to pull this off.

"Follow me," I whispered, before sinking into a crouch and creeping along the rubble, remaining in the deepest shadows and wielding the flames to aid in creating more where there were none. Darkness can only be created with light.

We ducked and dodged, weaving through the debris and darkness, edging closer to the main hall where Lilith's rooms were. The smoke was thick, not being a full Vampire, I couldn't hold my breath as long. It grew difficult to go further without being affected by smoke inhalation. But thankfully, Blake had mastered enough of his air and earth affinities to maneuver less smoke and more oxygen in our direction. I was impressed with his level of finesse.

Things grew trickier when we neared the entrance. Several cloaks were surrounding the door, darting in with purpose.

Combat wasn't something I had much experience in after beginning my transition. It was saved for those who pledged to the Knights faction. I'd seen them practicing at times, but always from a distance and never for long. A part of me feared fighting the cloaks. They were Vampires. I couldn't possibly stand a chance against them. But Sterling was counting on me, fear wouldn't hinder my mission.

"Don't burn out," I ordered Blake before moving. Stealth killing a Vampire shouldn't have been possible, but one thing I did pick up on wasn't from training or even from my Master, but from observing Obediah. How someone so large and imposing could reduce his presence to nothing, achieved by utter stillness.

As we slipped through the doors and each cloak sensed us, we were on them. Relentlessly murdering. Burning them from the inside out, stealing their oxygen until they choked on the nothingness, manipulating the water in their blood–much harder to do than I originally imagined–and taking them down with a speed we shouldn't have been able to possess. All of them taken by surprise, they didn't have the time to process how to fight back before they were dead. Though, the real reason we were successful wasn't just because we had taken them by surprise, but because they were untrained. They were nothing like our Knight faction. Children playing war.

Stepping over the bodies, we made our way to the commotion. There were several of the black cloaks facing off two Vampires I knew well.

My chest deflated with relief as I laid eyes on that familiar gray hair. Sterling stood with Hale, breathing heavily. Blood was smeared on his face, but I couldn't tell if it was his. And even though he stood not even fifty feet away, I could not feel him through the bond.

Was he blocking me again?

If I couldn't sense him, did that mean he couldn't sense me? Did he know I was there?

I knew there would be no outward acknowledgement, there is no way he would draw attention to us. Pulling Blake along with me, we ducked behind one of the pillars before anyone could spot us. From our hiding spot along the wall, I had a better view of the battle.

High Priest Carlisle faced off with Sterling. Seven cloaked Vampires behind the male, waiting for his order to strike. Despite being outnumbered, Sterling and Hale could handle it, right?

But no. Hale wasn't moving. Though he was barely standing, I could see the deep wounds that covered his body. He wouldn't die from them, but it left him vulnerable, open for attack that could well and truly kill him.

They need help.

I glanced at the slim opening that, timed right, would allow us to slip past the guards to where Lilith usually slept. There was no guarantee that that's where she'd be, but from the way Sterling and Hale were guarding it, it had to be there.

I couldn't leave them though, not when Hale was so injured. As powerful as Sterling was, he couldn't take them all down alone. I didn't know how powerful Carlisle was, but the title High Priest couldn't have gone to someone who was too weak to defend their Coven.

What should I do?

"Go. I'll stay," Blake whispered.

I had forgotten he was beside me. He must have noticed the

indecision on my face. Bless him for knowing what I needed without having context.

"Are you sure?" I whispered back. He was only just now gaining his strength after all that happened with Obi. There was a high risk of him burning out.

Blake nodded before darting out. I watched as he took down two of the Vampires before anyone realized he was there.

With the group distracted by Blake's attack, I ran for the doorway. I had to be quick. I couldn't stop. But I also couldn't help watching Sterling, if even only for a moment. His eyes darted toward me briefly before swiftly returning to the fight at hand. I slipped by them into the familiar darkened halls turning into that small room where Lilith found her comfort.

I didn't know what I'd find in there or what to expect. I shouldn't have been shocked to see the room occupied, I mean that was the whole reason I came there in the first place. Only, Lilith wasn't there. Instead, the floor was littered with bodies, one of which belonged to High Priestess Ninetta. Another?

Obi.

He was propped against the ledge where Lilith usually sat. In his massive arms, caged and protected, was a small wriggling bundle who surprisingly remained silent.

Rushing to Obi's side, I glanced over, noting the injuries. Sticking out from his chest was a beautifully ornate blade.

A *silver* blade.

He was still alive, just barely. I could see the slight rise and fall of his chest, but he was out cold. Even unconscious, he was still protecting the baby. His dedication was admirable.

I shouldn't remove the blade, it might do more harm than good, but with the baby squirming, I was afraid she might fall, or worse, jostle the blade lodged in his chest making his injury worse. As I reached for the bundle, Obi suddenly gasped. One hand reached for his throat as the veins in his neck bulged.

"Executioner? What's wrong?" I panicked, but he continued to gasp and wheeze.

From behind, I heard a wet *squelch* before Obi sagged back into unconsciousness. I whipped around.

Cadence.

She yanked her blade from Ninetta's chest, wiping it clean on the High Priestess's cloak. Those ice blue eyes met mine.

"Make sure your enemy is *dead* before letting your guard down," she scolded, coming over to us.

I tensed, unsure if she could be trusted. I mean, she did just murder the enemy but that didn't automatically mean she was on our side.

Cadence kneeled beside me, in front of Obi. She took one look at the blade before yanking it out. It happened so fast, I didn't have the time to react. In mere moments, she had pulled the baby from Obi's arms, handed her to me, and was feeding Obi from a slit she made in her arm. Obi, even in a state of unconsciousness, had latched on and sucked deep. After a little while, Cadence pulled her arm away and Obi slumped over. The wound in his chest stopped spewing blood, but the rate of his healing was still much too slow.

"That won't do much. He needs Lilith's blood," she said, searching him over. The blood of his Creator, it would heal the most dire of injuries. Except Lilith wasn't his maker, not that Cadence would know that.

Passing Cadence the baby, I reached for one of the vials Sterling had given me, kept safe in my cloak pocket. Removing the small stopper, I poured it into Obi's mouth after prying it open. Massaging his throat until he swallowed it all, I watched as the wound closed. Breathing a sigh of relief, I took the baby back from Cadence, who was staring at me suspiciously.

"You have vials of Lilith's blood?" she asked.

Keeping my expression neutral, I adjusted the new Mother to a more comfortable position in my arms.

"From Sterling. The blood of my grand sire is more potent than that of my sire," I lied. I didn't know if that was true or not, but from the way people reacted from having Lilith's blood, I'd say it was a believable lie.

Cadence stared for a few beats longer before turning back to Obi. "You really are favored. Like Master like fledgling, I suppose."

Before I could respond, Cadence stood, lifting Obi over her shoulder with ease. It was an incredible sight, witnessing her tiny, barely five foot frame, hoist all six feet five inches of Obi over her shoulder like a sack of potatoes. His form completely dwarfed hers.

"Come on, we have to get out of here before reinforcements show up."

I glanced at the door. Sterling was still out there. And Blake and Hale. I couldn't just *leave* them. What if they needed help?

"We don't have time to waste. Your Master is already aware of the plan. He's going to meet us, but we have to move. Our priority right now is getting *her* out of here," Cadence pushed, jerking her chin at the bundle in my arms.

I looked down at the baby, so impossibly small, with blotchy red spots all over her light brown wrinkled skin. Her dark hair was plastered to her head, still covered in blood and other viscous fluids.

He told me to find her and run, no matter what. He'd find me. He promised.

With a nod, I got to my feet and followed Cadence out. We didn't go back out the way we originally came in. Instead, Cadence took us through another door which led into narrow dark halls. It made me wonder if the sentient house was helping us escape.

I brushed the walls as we walked, feeling it warm up and pulse under my touch.

Thank you.

And just like that, we were out. The night air was brisk, still courting that autumn chill.

We ran around the building until we reached a small gate in the back. After hustling down the street, which was thankfully empty despite it being what humans called Halloween, we turned down an alleyway where a black SUV was parked. The driver's door opened and Asher hopped out. He opened the backseat door and helped slide Obi in. I slid in after him.

There was a carseat for the baby, so I strapped her in. They had been prepared for this.

Cadence hurried to the passenger's seat as Asher climbed back in the driver's seat. We pulled out and headed for the highway.

"Where are we going?" I asked, glancing around as the building and cars blurred past us.

"Safe house," Cadence said.

"What about the others?"

What about Sterling?

"They'll catch up. They know where to meet us," she answered.

I tried to let that calm me. With a tentative brush, I felt for the bond that connected Sterling and I.

Nothing.

Damn it! I can't tell if anything is wrong or if he's still blocking me. If he–no *when* he meets up with us, he is going to *hear* it.

I glanced at Obi, who's breathing was a little ragged. I pushed open his shirt and saw that the wound was starting to close but the healing process was still a bit sluggish. I reached in for another one of my vials, feeding him the blood and watching as it kick started the healing process. When a little color returned to his skin, I let out a sigh of relief.

Cadence watched me from the rearview mirror. I didn't meet her suspicious gaze. That was a can of worms I refuse to open.

We drove for about an hour and a half before we reached our destination in the downtown area of Atlanta. Asher pulled into a lot that connected to an apartment building. Thankfully, the parking lot didn't have any of the humans dressed up in ridiculous costumes, wandering about. We'd passed throngs of them on the way in.

Obi was still out cold and had to be carried to what looked like a basement apartment. It was spacious and updated. But even more surprising were the few people waiting for us.

"Beau!" Alexander ran toward me, enveloping me in a hug. I was careful to shield the new Mother from being squished. "I'm so glad you're okay."

"Yeah, you too. I'm glad you weren't around for all the chaos."

Alexander frowned. Joel came up beside him. "Is it just you four?" he glanced at the baby. "Five?"

I nodded.

"The others will be meeting us here shortly," Cadence said, laying Obi down on one of the couches.

Like clockwork, the door opened. Judas walked in, supporting a stumbling Kyle.

Thank goodness he was safe. I had lost him in the explosion and if I'm honest, I thought he was dead.

Alexander rushed to help him. The fledgling seemed dazed and confused, but he wasn't still in that trance like before.

The new Mother began squirming again. I rocked her in my arms until she settled. It was strange. The entire time she hadn't made a noise, only wiggled on occasion. Guess supernatural babies didn't have the same tendencies as human ones.

"Kyle!" Alexander gasped.

My head whipped up. Kyle had collapsed and was seizing. Blood trickled from his nose as his eyes rolled to the back of his head.

"What's wrong with him?" I asked, rushing over to them.

"Back up!" Cadence barked. She pushed by us and with a quick and efficient chop, knocked Kyle unconscious.

"What's *wrong* with you?" Alexander cried. "Why'd you do that?"

"He was going to die if I didn't," Cadence replied unbothered. Alexander didn't look like he believed that one bit.

Asher squeezed past them both, picked up Kyle's limp form, and carried him down the hall disappearing behind one of the multiple doors lining the way.

"You didn't have to be so rough," Alexander hissed, before storming off in the direction Asher had disappeared.

Cadence rolled her eyes before pulling out her cellphone and going to what looked like a kitchen to take a call.

It'd been a while since I had seen a cellphone. I didn't even think about owning one. Anyone I'd possibly call was always in the same building so there was never a need. Now that Sterling and I had been separated...and Blake, a phone would have made me feel better. I could call him and talk to him, know for certain that he's alright. *They* were alright.

I looked at Joel who was staring warily at Jude. Jude looked worse for wear. As if he too had been fighting for his life. I hadn't seen him at the Coven house, but that didn't mean he wasn't there. Or maybe it wasn't an isolated incident?

Before I could ask if the two Vampires knew anything, the front door opened again.

I knew. I knew without looking.

Sterling.

He walked in looking exhausted, still smeared in blood.

Stasia and Blake followed closely behind him. The moment Blake caught sight of Obi lying unconscious on the couch, he gasped. Obi's name caught in his throat. Even panicked as he was, he didn't slip. Still keeping Obi's identity a secret.

Blake rushed to tend to his Master while I marched up angrily to mine.

"Stop *shielding*," I hissed at him. He sighed.

"I'm only trying to–"

"I don't *care*. Drop the shield, *now*." The command burned its way out of my throat. I could feel my mind and body screaming at me.

Must submit.

Must obey Master.

Submit to Master.

Obey.

Obey.

Obey.

I didn't care though. Not when I'd been scared for hours, not knowing what had happened to him, if he lived or died.

The bond flooded with Sterling. His aches. His exhaustion. His anxiety. His affection. I could feel every bruise, every cut and scrape like it was my own.

"*Never,* do that to me again."

"Beau–"

"*Never*, Sterling. Promise me," I glared up at him. He stared right back, green eyes blazing, expression solemn.

"I can't do that."

I swore and turned away from him. How could he not understand how I felt? How it killed me every time he did it?

"It *hurts*, Sterling."

His arms wrapped around my waist from behind as his chin rested on the top of my head.

"And it'd hurt a lot more if I had kept the bond open," he murmured, planting a kiss on my neck.

Doubtful.

"Are you two done? Cuz we have shit to discuss," Stasia drawled.

Their usually neat blonde hair was ruffled. Their clothes were torn and they looked a little worse for wear despite the haughty look on their face.

They need to feed.

I don't know how I knew that, but there was some innate instinct that could sense it. That saw them as competition. That saw them as a threat to my hunting grounds. I ignored the feeling and Stasia together, turning back to Sterling.

"Are you okay?" I whispered, still angry, but mostly worried. He did not make it here unscathed.

"I'm fine," Sterling replied, eyes softening as he looked down at me.

I glanced around and noticed that we were missing a person.

"Where's Hale?"

Sterling's expression tightened and jaw clenched before he gave a slight shake of his head.

Oh no.

Kyle was going to be devastated. Which meant that seizure...

Fuck.

"Will Kyle be okay?" I asked, but Sterling didn't answer.

The silence said enough.

My chest ached.

Sterling inhaled deeply before glancing at the bundle in my arms. He smiled at the quiet infant, gently brushing the dark wisps of her hair.

"Lilm," he breathed.

"Is that her name?" I asked. I'd been calling her the new

Mother in my head this whole time. It would be nice to have an actual name for her.

Sterling nodded.

It should have been weird. Her name was so close to Lilith's. It made it that much more real that Lilith was being replaced. But surprisingly...it fit.

"Yes, yes. The baby is *wonderful*. But we *really* need to talk about what happens next," Stasia snapped.

"They're right," Joel said softly.

We all made our way to the remaining couches, careful not to disturb Obi and Blake.

Sterling spoke first. "They're calling themselves the 'Devout'. Carlisle managed to escape with a few of them. All the others are dead, either by our hands or suicide. Nexus stayed behind to help the surviving Coven members."

"And the High Priestess?" Joel asked.

Sterling shook his head. "Couldn't find her. I'm hoping once Executioner wakes up, we'll have a bit more insight. He was the last to see her."

"You don't think she's...?" Blake started, joining the conversation.

"We would have felt it," Sterling said. The 'we' being him and Stasia.

"What about Marcelle and Julia?" I asked.

"They made it out safely. Like Joel and Alexander, they had a special assignment that kept them away from the celebration tonight."

"Does the High Consort know? About the baby?" Joel asked, figuring out that it couldn't possibly be mine.

Sterling shook his head again. "If he finds out about her now after all that's happened, he'd never let the baby out of his sight and that'd make him a target. We need him. He's the only one who can lead the Coven while Lilith is gone."

My stomach tightened. While I understood the reasoning behind it, it still felt wrong to keep her a secret from him. She was his daughter too, after all.

"So now what?" Jude asked, speaking for the first time.

"We need to regroup. Heal. We'll hide out here until we regain our full strength and have more information on the situation," Stasia said. "Besides, it's still Samhain. The fun's not over yet." They smirked at me before getting up and disappearing down the hall.

The fun's not over yet.

What the hell did that mean?

I looked at Sterling, but he was heaving Obi into his arms and carrying him down the hall. I blinked at his retreating form, then looked at Blake.

"I'll take her," he said with a smile. He held his arms out for her. I gave the bundle to him reluctantly. Why did it seem like everyone knew something I didn't?

Blake seemed to notice my confusion when he said, "There's still a chance you'll change."

Right.

I'd forgotten about that. I'd likely become a Vampire tonight.

As if the night hadn't been crazy enough.

STAGE FOUR

15

THE VAMPIRE AWAKENS

Apparently there were five rooms in this massive apartment, chosen in preparation for this very night. I could tell it was newly furnished, some of the items still had their tags attached.

We'd all separated into rooms. Stasia with the twins, Obi and Blake, Joel and Alexander had taken Kyle, and Judas had a room to himself, while Sterling and I shared one. I noticed there was a small crib in the corner of our room which meant Lilm would likely stay with us.

Tonight? The crib remained empty.

Sterling toweled off his hair as he sat down on the king sized bed. I watched him warily. Not wary *of* him, but of what happened next.

"Do you...think it'll actually happen tonight?" I asked cautiously.

Sterling glanced up at me, the wound on his face hadn't closed which told me he needed to feed. He probably used up a lot of his strength and overdid it by using his affinity. All to keep everyone safe.

"The probability is high, but there is no guarantee," Sterling said softly. The wet tendrils of his darkened gray hair were plastered to his head. He slicked it back a few times. I watched with hunger, but still unable to shake the worry.

"What does it feel like?" I asked, coming to sit next to him.

Sterling pondered for a moment before answering. "I don't remember, exactly. I think, it happens gradually. Senses get sharper. Your body gets stronger, then blood lust. But it's been so long, I don't know if that's entirely accurate."

Blood lust.

How could I feed off of him when he could barely stand on his own? He was depleted. He needed to heal and I didn't want to be the reason it took any longer. Who cares if his injuries were minor? They weren't to me.

"Beau," Sterling said softly, a gentle warning in his voice. "I can feel you worrying. You don't need to, I'll take care of you."

"That's just it! You *can't* take care of me. Not right now. I need to be the one to take care of you, you need to feed."

"I'll be fine–"

"Sterling please. I have been so worried about you. I can't take from you. Not now."

Sterling's jaw clenched. "And how exactly were you planning on feeding? You need it."

It didn't have to be Sterling. I just needed to feed, right? There were several others here that could help me.

The mere idea of it made my stomach churn.

"I'll ask one of the others," I determined resolutely. Sterling scoffed.

"You hate drinking from others."

"I'll do it if it means giving you the time to heal."

"Beau, you are blowing this out of proportion. It's not that big of a deal," he chided.

Maybe it wasn't. Maybe I was overreacting, but I didn't care. As I stared at him, exhaustion evident in the purple bruises under his eyes and the cut across his cheek that *still* hadn't healed, I couldn't bring myself to take a single drop.

"I'll be back," I told him.

"Beau," he called out again, exasperated, but I was already out the door.

I couldn't go to Blake or Obi. Obi was too injured and would need Blake's blood. Joel and Alexander had to care for Kyle. I couldn't weaken either of them. Judas wouldn't be caught dead sharing blood with me. Besides, the man was depleted himself.

There was only one person it could be.

...Or three.

Stasia had two fledglings and despite everything, neither one of them were depleted, intentional I'd wager. Stasia would only need to feed from one to regain their strength and quench their thirst. But would they let me?

I knocked on their door, heart pounding in my chest. I may have been nervous, but I didn't let it show. A neutral mask was plastered on my face as soon as the door opened.

Asher ate up the doorway with his impressive frame. His shirt was off, revealing a myriad of swirling tattoos covering his bulging pectorals. He watched me with cool blue eyes. Not menacing. Not anything. Just blank.

"I need to speak to the Third Elder," I told him.

There was a soft noise from within the room before Asher stepped aside, allowing me in. The room was large with an even larger bed in the middle. I guess Stasia was the one who found this place because there is no way a bed that large wasn't planned for. The rest of us would have made do, but something told me Stasia didn't know the meaning of it.

The Third Elder was sprawled on the bed, a soft looking blue sheet covering their waist, exposing their lean muscled stomach and chest. My eyes couldn't help but linger on their pink nipples and long pale throat. I looked away only to find a completely nude Cadence curled into their side.

It was obvious they had just fed, or fucked, or both. My timing was perfect then.

"Third Elder," I greeted, bowing my head in respect. Those gray eyes watched me curiously before they sat up and grinned.

"Baby vamp, what can I do for you?" they purred.

Inhaling deeply before letting out a long exhale, I raised my head and met their gaze. "I need your help."

Stasia hummed in amusement. I could feel Asher moving behind me. The door shut with a soft click.

Was this a good idea?

As Stasia watched me, like a predator hunting their prey, it was starting to look like a really bad one.

"I need *all* of your help," I clarified, looking at all of them, nearly jumping when I realized how close Asher was standing behind me.

They circled me like vultures. Cornering me. Not literally but the intention was there with the charged air between us all.

"What is it?" Stasia prompted with a raised ash blonde brow.

Clearing my throat, I spit it out. "My Master has been greatly exhausted and depleted. I do not wish to take any more from him until he has recovered. As you know, I'll need to...feed. If any of you would be able and willing to...*assist* me with that, I would be grateful."

There. I said it.

Cadence looked disgusted. Asher remained unfazed. But Stasia...was grinning like the Cheshire cat.

Definitely not a good idea.

Letting my instincts finally take over, I turned to flee the room, but nearly slammed into Asher's massive chest. He blocked the door.

And smiled.

Oh fuck. Bad idea! Bad *fucking* idea!

"We can't have you *starving* now can we?" Stasia purred.

They were so close now. I hadn't heard them move, but suddenly, they were there. All of their nakedness pressed against me from behind. Their lips had brushed my neck with each word. I felt the wet curl of their tongue brush my skin. Tasting.

My cock stirred.

No. Bad cock. Stay *down*.

I knew this would happen eventually. Everyone had warned me about it; that soon it wouldn't be just Sterling. Sterling *himself* had told me.

We are creatures of sensation and gratification.

It felt wrong and right at the same time. I was so fucking conflicted.

"I will help you. As a favor to your...*Master.*"

With those words, Stasia moved, knowing that I likely wouldn't be the one to initiate. Their arms wrapped around my waist. I could feel their hard cock press against me through my pants.

"Help me, darling?" Stasia purred.

Darling?

Asher moved, tugging my cloak from my shoulders. It dropped to the floor, as Stasia made work of unbuttoning my shirt.

"I-I only need to feed!" I protested, trying to pull away from them, but there was nowhere for me to go.

Shit.

"We'll help you feed. All your needs," Stasia whispered, pulling off my shirt. I stiffened at the sudden exposure. Asher moved to the waistband of my pants, but didn't pull them down. Over my shoulder both fledgling and Master kissed. So close. I could hear every exhale, every slide of tongue, every scrape of teeth.

There was no hiding it now. I was hard.

So hard it hurt.

I watched them with pure lust. Eating up every moment, like I was there with them. I could feel their tongues colliding with my own. It reminded me of that first night. With Kyle and Alexander as they rode their Masters. I could taste their pleasure, feel their orgasm like it was my own.

When someone's hand–Stasia or Asher, I don't know who–cupped me through the thin fabric of my pants, I groaned, falling back against Stasia.

"That's right, baby vamp. Let us *feed* you," Stasia cooed.

I was being led back to the bed. I hadn't realized until the softness of the sheets had caressed my skin. The warmth of their bodies surrounded me. I felt hot and tingly. My fangs dropped slightly, not completely unsheathed, nicking my bottom lip as my pants rolled from my hips and a mouth sucked on my exposed nipple. Back arching, cock throbbing, I let myself fade into the sensations.

It didn't matter that this was fucking Stasia and Asher of all people. The only thing that mattered was the pleasure.

I wanted it.

I wanted them.

I wanted *everything*.

Pure want raged through me like a fever. Unrelenting and vicious. I craved their touch. Their bodies.

As Stasia's cock slid against my thigh, hips gyrating to create friction, I sighed, blissfully, needing more.

My mouth watered as Asher tugged off his own pants, thick cock red and pulsing as it bobbed like a threat. The veins bulged as the broad tip glistened with the smear of precum.

No one compared to Sterling of course. But I would be blind

not to appreciate the glorious beauty before me at this very moment.

Stop thinking.

Just *feel.*

"So responsive," Stasia murmured, nibbling lightly on my nipple again. I hissed at the slight pain of their fangs scraping the sensitive bud. And I don't know, maybe I'm a masochist, but that little flash of pain made my dick twitch.

"Look at him, Darling. Isn't he just the most delicious thing you've ever feasted upon?" Stasia prompted. Asher hummed, lips traveling down my stomach, planting heated kisses in his wake.

I tried not to squirm under their ministrations, but my hips lurched forward of their own accord, thrusting my hard cock in the air. I ached.

My lips parted, fangs fully dropped. So good. So damn *good*.

Asher's hot, wet tongue slid along the tip of my dick before his warm mouth encircled it completely. I choked, the moan caught between Stasia's lips as they kissed me with fervor.

I wanted them so badly. I wanted to touch. I wanted to fuck. I wanted to feed.

I was *starving*.

My fangs throbbed in sync with my cock as Asher slid down the length taking me deep in his throat. I stroked the soft brush of his hair while cupping Stasia's dick in my other. They were warm and velvety smooth. The delicate veins pulsed as my fingertips brushed them. I squeezed them in my fist.

Stasia's soft moan fanned against my face. It was surprisingly gentle, I didn't expect it.

"Beautiful," Stasia hummed, licking a stripe up my cheek. Those gray eyes peered down at me. "Absolutely beautiful. Right, Sterling?"

My head whipped up. In the corner of the room, leaning

against the wall near the door, Sterling stood there. Shirtless. Watching us with heated green eyes. The burning lust in that gaze sent the fire in me roaring. I hadn't even heard him come in.

"Master," I whimpered.

Touch me, Sterling. I need you.

"Oh no you don't. He's here to watch. Watch you bloom," Stasia chuckled. A keening whine left my throat, making everyone laugh.

It wasn't meant to be funny.

It was *meant* to be *desperate*.

"Stunning," Sterling praised and my dick twitched, precum dripping from my wet tip. Asher licked it up before devouring me whole again.

Stasia tweaked my nipples, kissing my throat, squeezing my ass. All of it was too much. I felt like I was running straight for the sun. They were burning me up.

As the heat grew, I could feel Sterling there. Right through the bond, sucking the fire away, keeping me from coming.

"Need more," I whispered. Asher released me, sitting up on the bed while Stasia straddled my waist. They rolled their hips seductively. Our cocks rubbed together in the most delicious way.

Slick, wet, hard, and hot.

Stasia leaned forward until their dazzling face was all I could see. They didn't kiss me, though their lips were mere millimeters from mine. Instead their face was twisted up and their mouth opened as they silently moaned. It took me a moment to realize Asher was leaned over too, face stuffed between Stasia's spread ass cheeks. I panted beneath them, their neck outstretched. Delicate. Vulnerable.

Hungry.

The tip of my tongue trailed a line from their collarbone up their throat until I reached their chin where my tongue curled back into my mouth, savoring the sweet taste of their skin. I wanted more. I wanted everything beneath it.

Stasia pulled back suddenly, a wicked grin on their thin lips. Something tugged from inside me. I hadn't even realized Asher had been prepping me until suddenly, at once, Stasia slid themselves on my dick while Asher sheathed himself inside me.

My dick spurted, painting Stasia's insides with ropes of cum. Not a sound escaped my lips. It was too much, but it felt so fucking good.

I needed more.

Neither waited for me to catch my breath or for me to adjust. They moved in sync, rocking their hips, drowning me in pleasure. I was so sensitive after releasing, I didn't think it was possible for me to recover that fast, but suddenly Sterling was there. In my face. His green eyes ate up my vision. So close. So fucking close.

"I need it, Master."

"You don't get to feed on them. Not this time," he whispered huskily. And with one hand pinning my arms down, the other dug into Stasia's hair, tugging their head back and exposing the pale white unblemished skin of their neck. Both of them watched me. Green and gray, molten and passionate.

And then Sterling struck, his fangs buried into Stasia's neck, blood dripping down the corner of his mouth and the middle of Stasia's chest. Stasia screamed in pleasure, still riding me with enthusiasm. Their dick erupted as cum splattered against my chest.

Sterling drank deeply, I could see the tent in his loose pants. I wanted to touch. I wanted to fuck, but then Asher hit that spot, that *sweet* spot inside me. I saw stars. My flaccid dick plumped right back up.

I moaned and mewled, toes curling, hips thrashing. The

bastards were teasing me.

"Fuck!" I screamed.

My throat was burning.

I could hear my heart pounding in my chest, the blood that rushed in my veins, *their* veins. Goosebumps covered my arms as the hair on the back of my neck stood at attention. It was like the world had exploded into a kaleidoscope of sensation.

And I was fucking starving.

Sterling pulled back from Stasia who fell back into Asher's chest. Asher, who thrusted into me so hard both Stasia and my hips lurched off the bed. Sweat coated his skin as he pumped into me, blue eyes sparkling.

Asher watched me over Stasia's shoulder, licking the dripping blood from their neck with deliberate slowness.

I shivered, body aching until with a few more thrusts, Asher was groaning, clutching Stasia tight while he filled me with his load.

I felt the warm wetness inside, and as he slid out, so did it. A steady stream, trickling out of my gaping hole.

My dick twitched again.

"Sterling," I begged. The burning in my throat grew hotter. Uncomfortable to the point that it nearly overshadowed the pleasure.

Sterling leaned over me again, lips brushing mine as we shared a sweet kiss glazed with Stasia's blood. He pulled back with a smirk and tilted his head, exposing his neck. The wound on his cheek had healed. The bruises under his eyes were gone, and his cheeks were flushed with lust.

I struck.

My fangs buried deep in his neck, tasting the clove and citrus blood that made me cum all over again.

I drank and drank, coming again and again. Faster than I should have been able to.

My eyes flew open and I could see with so much clarity. The wisps of gray hair danced across my vision. Past them, I could see Stasia bending Cadence over on one of the chairs, fucking her as Asher fucked them.

I spread my thighs, inviting Sterling in.

Now was the time for *us*.

Sterling peeled back his pants, releasing his aching cock. It was covered in sticky fluid which meant he must have came in them earlier. It was hot. I could feel it smearing along my leg as he adjusted himself, not even bothering to take the pants off completely. He thrusted inside me, not needing to stretch me. I was ready for him.

This felt right. Felt perfect. My aching cock twitched again as another orgasm overcame me at once. Sterling's cum joined Asher's as he emptied himself inside me. That was all it took, becoming one with each other.

I released his neck, licking my lips as the last drops of his blood slid down my throat. Falling into the sheets, sated, I nestled into their warmth.

My head was spinning. I felt light and floaty. Sterling fell on top of me, chest heaving as he fought to catch his breath. The others were still fucking, still moaning. I could hear the wet slaps of flesh, the quiet keening, and furious sucking as they brought each other to completion. I hummed, enjoying the sounds.

If I wasn't completely spent, I would totally want to go again. It was an odd change of pace for me.

When Sterling finally calmed, he slid his pants up, grabbed my clothes, covered me in my cloak and scooped me into his arms. With a nod in Stasia's direction, he carried me back to our room.

He pulled the cloak off and set me on one of the lounge chairs in the corner of the room. I couldn't even move, my body felt boneless. So, I sat there, waiting silently until he returned, floating on a high, completely mesmerized by my heightened senses.

The feeling of a wet cloth was soothing against my overheated skin as he carefully cleaned me off, then himself. Tossing the rag in a corner with our soiled clothes, he carried me to the bed. I let him, falling against him like a rag doll as he slid in behind me, spooning me.

"Sleep," he commanded.

In seconds, I was out cold.

༄

I THOUGHT IT WAS OVER.

That I'd gone through the worst of it. Well, that was a *goddamn lie*. The fire returned to me with vengeance at some point through the night. I rose from the bed like a blood sucking demon. Full on Dracula.

I hated myself for attacking Sterling when he slept, but it was like my body was on autopilot. I threw myself at him, scrambling to straddle his hips, trying to fit his soft dick inside me.

Obviously it didn't work. The rational part of my brain *knew* it wouldn't. But unfortunately, that's not what was in control right now. There was a monster underneath my skin and it wanted one thing more than life itself–to ravish Sterling.

I ground my hips and thrust my cock between his pecs, mewling at the friction. He woke slowly, bleary eyed. It took two seconds before they cleared and he was awake and alert. He sat up, holding my hips, but keeping me straddling him.

I whined, unable to produce actual words with my throbbing fangs in the way. My throat burned again, so much it was hard to swallow. I couldn't retract my fangs. I couldn't stop my hips from rutting against him. He smiled at me.

"How naughty you are," he whispered. "Needy."

Yes. Yes. I *needed*.

His cock grew gloriously hard. I didn't care about prep. I impaled myself on him. But that initial discomfort without it was nothing like the parched feeling in my throat.

How could I possibly be starving, *still*?

I fed not too long ago. I don't know how long we slept, but it didn't feel like more than a couple hours. So why?

Why did I need more so badly?

"I've got you," Sterling cooed, easing my head down until my lips were flush against his neck. I rocked my hips, riding him as my fangs pierced his neck. His blood gushed into my mouth, flooding with that taste that was so uniquely Sterling. No one's blood could compare.

Well...maybe Lilith's...but no one *else's* blood could compare.

I drank him long and drank him deep. Each pull quenched a little bit more of that need deep inside me. Sterling's fingers dug into my sides as he kissed my collarbone, guiding himself in and out of me with sensual, drowsy slowness.

It was hard and fast before. Now? It was slow and passionate. Sterling always knew exactly what I needed.

I pulled back, feeling full, licking the remnants of his blood from my fangs. Hugging his neck, I moaned, loving the way he completely stretched me. Loving how the head of him caught on the rim of me with every slow drag.

I loved it. I loved everything about it.

I loved everything about *him*.

"I love you so fucking much," I cried, unable to contain the swell of affection that clogged up my chest.

Sterling's thrusts stuttered for a moment, but quickly continued.

Too caught up in the moment, I didn't realize he didn't say it back.

16

ONLY JUST BEGUN

I felt *amazing*.
The next "morning", I woke bright eyed and full of energy. The same could not be said for Sterling though. He was passed out, covered in healing bites and fading hickies. If I could still see them now, there must have been a million of them. I watched him, lying on his stomach, with his arms tucked around his pillow.

The poor man had only gotten to sleep about an hour ago. Feeling more than a little guilty, I got up, careful not to wake him, to leave him to his rest.

I headed for the shower, noting how each step I took felt light. I was in tune with my body, hyper aware of every limb in a way I hadn't been before.

The bright lights hurt my eyes. Now I knew why the Coven House was only lit with candles. Actual lighting was excruciating. I showered in complete darkness, the fluorescents of the light too much for me. Surely, this would calm? I can't imagine the other Vampires just living like this.

Other Vampires...I was *one* of them. *I was a Vampire.*

Strange to think that my life had changed so spectacularly in the span of a month. I've made a new life, had a new mission, gained an affinity for two of the four elements, fought and survived an invasion, fell in love...

Love.

I froze, my hand stuck on the doorknob of our room, returning from my shower. The memories of last night pouring in with detail I had let myself forget.

I love you so fucking much.

Why did I say that? Did I even mean it or was it just a moment of passion? Was it the sensations of the bond? The process of the Change?

Sterling's smiling face flashed into my mind and with it, my chest ached and stomach fluttered in that annoying way that told me I sure as hell meant it.

He hadn't said it back though.

Had my confession made things awkward or would he pretend it never happened? Would he draw the conclusion I had, that it was all a heat of the moment thing? That I didn't actually mean it?

Would that be worse?

I sighed, opening the door. There was no use hiding. We still had so much that needed to get done.

Sterling was still sleeping, so I dressed quickly and quietly, not wanting to disturb him. For more reasons now than before.

When I was dressed, I slipped back out of the room, down the hall to Blake and Obi. I knocked softly. Blake answered almost immediately, blocking my view of the room. He glanced around the hall before, letting me in and securing the door behind him.

His caution made sense when I saw Obi sitting up on the bed, baby in his arms, mask lying on the table. The Vampire looked up at me, gaze soft. It was almost like he was smiling, but his expression hadn't changed.

"You are...Vampire," he murmured.

Blake grinned at me, dimples puncturing his cheeks. "I'm happy for you!"

I smiled at them both.

"What's it like?" Blake asked, leading me to one of the lounge chairs while he sat beside Obi on the bed.

"Strange," I answered. "But also the same? I feel complete, like I'm no longer stumbling behind someone else's lead, yet the hierarchy is still there? I know it doesn't make sense. I don't know how else to describe it though."

"I guess I'll know when it happens for me," Blake shrugged. "I entered Stage Three last night. Seems the moon was in full power."

I congratulated him, then watched Obi stare down at Lilm. Wonder and awe in his gaze. He was completely transfixed by the baby. To be expected though. With someone so close to death, the miracle of life must be fascinating to him.

"It must have been rough, taking care of Obi, Lilm, and entering Stage Three."

Blake shrugged again. He didn't look tired or anything. If anything, he was glowing. It was a nice change from his previous condition. I was really worried.

"Has she fed?" I asked, jerking my chin at the baby.

Blake nodded. "We didn't know if she needed blood or formula so we gave her a mix of both. She took it well. Quietest baby I've ever seen. Has not made a sound, even when things got loud."

"Loud?" I frowned.

Blake gave me a knowing look. "The walls are thinner than you think."

I blushed furiously. Their room was right across the hall from Stasia and the twins. No doubt everyone heard us.

"No shame. Though, I do not know if I would have been able to do anything of the sort with those three," Blake shivered.

"It was actually really good," I admitted. Blake's face scrunched up in disgust. I grinned at him. "Don't knock it til you try it."

"Never," Blake said, mimicking gagging.

I rolled my eyes at his dramatics. When there was a knock on the door, I tensed. It was an involuntary reaction, I certainly didn't mean to, but after last night...

Blake raised a brow at me, then the door. He had obviously noted my reaction.

"It's Sterling," I said softly, schooling my features into blank pleasantness.

I wasn't fooling him or anyone for that matter. I knew that. If anything, it was for my own benefit. Knowing what I did and the insecurities that followed, I didn't want to wear the hurt on my face. Besides, I meant it, we have more important things to deal with right now. Making a big deal out of this would be selfish.

I shut down the bond. Almost immediately, the knocking became banging. Blake made a move toward the door, but I stopped him, going to it instead. Cracking the door a little out of respect to Obi, I looked out at Sterling. Looked up, is more like it. His towering frame completely dominated the hallway.

After checking that no one else was around, I opened the door wide enough for him to slip past before shutting it again. I lingered by the door, too afraid to turn around. With a deep shaky breath, I steeled my resolve, checking that the wall on our bond was in place and my expression was masked, I turned, smiling.

The smile may have been overkill, but it wasn't *for* them. It was for me. If I faked it long enough, maybe it would start to feel real after a while. Or just until we got through this hell when I could properly address it.

Sterling was staring holes into me. I pretended not to notice. When a tiny nudge tested the bond, I strengthened my wall.

Nope. That was not going to work on me. Deal with it. Maybe now he'll understand what it feels like and how much it sucked to be locked out.

But his reasons for doing it and mine were completely different. He had good reason, I was just being selfish.

No.

I wasn't. Because I am trying to make sure that my own personal issues don't get in the way of what we need to do. Like figuring out who is gunning for Lilith and the baby, or where Lilith was, or what we're supposed to do now. That took priority. Those were the issues that affected more than just me and my feelings.

I couldn't be selfish. Not now.

I brushed by Sterling and kneeled in front of Obi who was rocking Lilm gently, eyes wide as saucers. It was kind of adorable.

I peeked over the lip of the blanket and saw big red eyes staring back at me. There was an intelligence, awareness, that shouldn't have been there, not after only a day of life.

She's a born Vampire. She clearly can't be compared to human babies. Her temperament alone spoke volumes.

"Has she cried at all?" I asked Obi. He shook his head, still completely mesmerized.

"He's been like that for the past four hours. He won't put her down," Blake said ruefully. His smile was fond though, as he gazed at his Master. It was truly heartwarming to see them that way, after they had been through so much. It was completely different from the way it was before. In such a short time, their bond had solidified. They'd be a strong pairing. Equals.

I stood, not bothering to take Lilm from Obi. He was clearly enjoying holding her.

"Obi." Sterling's voice was soft. It tugged at my chest even with our bond closed. I fought all the urges and instinctual demands to touch and beg, instead keeping my distance. It was getting easier now, as a full-fledged Vampire. "When you went to get Lilm, did you see Lilith?"

Obi stopped looking at the baby, his sad eyes full of something, but I couldn't decipher the look. However, Sterling seemed to know. It was like a second conversation happening and he only spoke aloud for Blake and I's benefit.

"Yes."

"Were you there for the birth?"

Obi nodded. "I...helped."

"Do you know where Lilith went?" Sterling pressed.

Obi shook his head. "I was fighting. She told me to protect the baby. I was stabbed in the chest with silver. I fell unconscious after that."

Sterling's jaw clenched. I knew it wasn't anger or frustration toward Obi, but more so at the dead end. Obi was the last person with Lilith before she disappeared. If he didn't know where she went, how would we find her? He was our only lead.

"Someone couldn't have taken her, right?" I asked. But why would they leave the baby if that was their objective?

"She's the Mother of All, surely she's too powerful to be held hostage?" Blake said in disbelief. I was inclined to believe him, but I remembered that look. The pain on her face. Something happened that night, while everyone was frenzied with lust. Something in the blood.

"She had just given birth, that's bound to weaken her, if even a little. But that little bit might have been an opportunity. Especially if her focus was keeping Lilm safe," I pointed out.

I mean that was the logical explanation right? She wouldn't abandon us. She isn't dead. So she was taken.

"It's a possibility," Sterling admitted.

"We need to find out who could have possibly taken her, because something tells me it wasn't Carlisle."

"Couldn't have been. He might have escaped, but he was definitely too injured to manage it."

"There was someone..." I started, then hesitated, unsure if I should be sharing this information. But if there was anyone I could trust the most, they were here in this room. Clearing my throat, I tried again. "Before the explosions. I was a bit confused with all that was going on, everyone had seemed drugged, but there was someone there. Someone else who wasn't affected by whatever spell everyone was under. He looked familiar, but I don't remember ever meeting him before. He kept calling me Jamal."

Sterling visibly stiffened.

I don't know why, but I kept the second half of my story to myself. I didn't share that the only reason I was still alive was because they had saved me. Shielded me from the explosion.

"Jamal?" Blake asked, confused. Sterling and Obi were staring at each other. It hadn't even occurred to me that Obi might have known me as a human too.

"It was my name...as a human," I explained to Blake.

Blake blinked, wide-eyed, like the concept completely threw him. I wouldn't be surprised if the thought never crossed his mind. Most of the fledglings lost interest in their human lives, too entranced by the newness of their Vampire one. What was the point of looking back, right? Not me. I was different.

And I was really starting to hate that I was.

"Beau."

Snapping out of my head, I stared at my maker. I noticed they were all staring at me. Clearing my throat again uncomfortably, I continued, leaving out several details.

"He said that I shouldn't be there and he grabbed me. I

resisted but...he was strong. After the explosions went off, I didn't see him again."

"Why do you think that's connected to Lilith?" Blake asked.

"It was odd. He wasn't a Vampire, that much I could tell, but he had more strength than a typical human should. A normal human's hold would have been easy enough to break, but I struggled. And at Stage Three, that shouldn't have been possible. I don't know who or...*what* he was, but there might be other players involved," I said.

The group was quiet.

Sterling and Obi shared a look again, but this time, it was a silent conversation. Something they didn't want Blake or I to know.

Weren't we past this?

Taking the baby from Obi's arms, ignoring the look of disappointment, I slipped by Sterling and headed to the living area. Lilm squirmed a little, then turned and rested her cheek against my chest, slowly drifting to sleep.

I nearly bumped into Stasia who took one leering look at me and grinned. "Vampirism suits you." Their tone couldn't be mistaken for anything other than flirting.

I don't know why they were so fascinated by me. I showed no outwardly impressive traits. Maybe they could sense what Lilith did?

But as I stared at them, I knew they didn't know. They couldn't possibly know what Lilith did, who I was before, the lives I've lived...but they could sense it and that was enough apparently.

"Let me know if you ever want a sip," They purred before passing by me. Not once did they glance at the baby nestled in my arms.

Aversion to children? I wouldn't put it past them. They seemed like the type, but that wasn't any of my business.

Honestly, it surprised me they even had the patience for fledglings. Made me wonder how old the twins were.

Then it occurred to me. Before Stasia was completely gone, I turned and called out to them.

"Third Elder?"

Stasia paused, then slowly turned to face me, a questioning brow rose. Glancing around to make sure no one was lurking about, I approached them.

"Did you know me? Before I was changed, I mean," I asked.

Stasia pursed their lips before looking me up and down with deliberate slowness. Not so much to check me out but to assess me for...something. Obviously they were contemplating, but I couldn't figure out what.

When I had apparently passed their test, they folded their arms smoothly across their chest.

"Normally, I'd tell you that's information better left in the past," they stepped in close, lips brushing my ear, "But you looked so sexy when you came all over yourself last night, I can't help but want to reward you."

I could feel my face heat, thankful for my darker complexion, knowing it wouldn't show too much. Stasia only grinned, but created distance between us once more.

"I was not around when you were turned, as you may already know. Before I went on my *private* mission, I had heard about you. Vaguely. Sterling had felt the calling when checking out one of the slave rings. One of the most brutal we've seen in a while. At least, that's what one of my sources said. Why Sterling keeps changing everyone he finds at these places, I'll never understand, but who can fight the calling I suppose? Slaves are always so *traumatized,* it hardly seems like any fun."

Stasia paused, tapping their lip thoughtfully. Those pale eyes slid to mine, glinting dangerously. "Perhaps it's a fetish," they said with a cruel smirk before turning on their heels and walking away.

I let him go, fighting hard not to bristle at their last comment. It's what they wanted. To rile me up.

But they had given me valuable information whether they knew it or not. Knowing Stasia though, they knew what they were doing. Everything they did was meticulously planned.

Taking Lilm back to the living room that was thankfully empty, I sat down, rocking her gently.

Stasia mentioned Sterling changing everyone he finds at slave rings. Were they implying that they knew Obi was changed by Sterling? And that he was from a slave ring too? Or were there more like me? Was I not the first that Sterling had made?

Did he lie to me?

And this idea of fetishization hadn't been completely new. Stasia mentioned it to get a rise out of me, I'm sure, but there was still a tiny part of me that doubted. That wondered if maybe Sterling's intentions weren't that far off. I knew Lilth's role in the matter and that these feelings were groundless...but I couldn't shake them.

Maybe that was because he kept so much from me. It was hard to trust someone completely when they hold so much close to their chest. And honestly it wouldn't be that big of a deal, everyone was entitled to their secrets, but it affected me and the rest of the Coven. I think on that front, telling *me*, his fucking fledgling, would be a no brainer. Even worse, a lot of the secrets seemed related to me in some way.

How much more was Sterling hiding? How many more times am I going to get disappointed because he put his trust in someone else after continuing to pledge to me how important our bond was?

Actions weren't matching words and I hated that the most.

Glancing down at Lilm, it made me wonder how we were

going to truly care for her. Did Sterling know more about her than he was letting on?

If we were to raise her, him and I, we should at least know the basics on how to properly care for her.

Would she age at a normal rate? Years didn't seem to affect Lilith in the same way. Would that apply to her daughter? Or will Nexus's genes play a role in that?

Was it okay to feed her blood and formula? She was a born Vampire. It'd make sense that she only fed on blood. But who knows if that's truly the case. Feeding her both seemed like the safest bet, but what if it was stunting her growth and we just didn't know it? How long would she eat both? What happened when she grew to be a child? How would we be able to tamper the hunger of a creature so powerful and so impulsive? What were the limits of her power? How much of Lilith was in her?

Were we well and truly ready for this?

I'm not so sure.

17

KEEP A SECRET

"You're upset with me."

Sterling watched with keen eyes as I pointedly ignored him, cleaning up after changing Lilm's diaper. It was strange, seeing a diaper filled with blood and other unmentionables. The first time it happened, Blake and I panicked for a good hour, trying to figure out if she had her period or not. We didn't know how her body matured.

Maybe she aged quickly?

Did Vampire females even *get* their periods?

We tried asking Cadence but she rolled her eyes and walked away.

When Stasia made the determination that it was likely due to her diet, we relaxed. One day at a time, we learned more and more about her. About babies in general and took turns caring for her. Though she mostly spent her time with me in our room. It'd been a week since we got here and most of the group had fully healed. Now a restlessness settled in the air as we waited for news.

Tensions were running high, so it's understandable why he chose *now* to confront me.

"Are you seriously going to ignore me?" Sterling sighed, folding his arms across his chest and leaning against the wall. Not once did he even offer to help. Though in his defense, I'm not sure I wouldn't have bitten his head off.

Yes. I was angry. I had a lot of reasons to be angry. But why the hell should I be the only one coughing up information?

Putting Lilm down in her crib, I gently brushed the thick curls back on her head, watching as her jewel red eyes began to close.

She was getting older quickly. But it was still hard to grasp the rate in which she was growing.

"Beau!"

I turned to him sharply, fangs bared. "Quiet!"

The familiar pang of regret and urge to beg for forgiveness curled in my stomach like a lead weight determined to bring me down. Determined to make me grovel. It could not because *I would not*. And each time, it got just a bit easier to ignore.

"Yes, Sterling. I am upset with you."

As I moved to walk past him, out of the room, he grabbed my arm. I expected it. There was no way he was just going to let this go, but I had still hoped he wouldn't do it when I just put Lilm to sleep.

"Why are you acting like this?" Sterling asked.

"Why?" I laughed humorlessly. *"Why?* Because I am very tired of all the secrets, Sterling. And every time I trust you, you give me another reason not to. It is all *quite* confusing."

Sterling frowned as if he didn't know what I was talking about.

Okay, so we're going to play dumb? Lovely.

"I don't understand. Are you mad about that night?"

I stiffened. We both knew which night he was referring to. Though neither of us had spoken of it, it was even more infuriating that he knew. He knew how I felt and remained indifferent.

It was fine if he didn't feel the same way. It hurt, yes. But at this point? I'm so used to being hurt, it would only be another day in this very long existence.

"So you think I'm throwing a hissy fit because you didn't say you love me?" I asked, calmly.

Sterling rose an infuriating dark brow.

"Truly?"

Sterling nodded.

I inhaled slowly, letting my eyes close, then let it out with a smooth exhale. "Lilith is gone, Sterling. And here we are, left with her child. Forced to not only raise and protect a creature we do not comprehend, but guide her so that she might bring the next generation. This task was given to you and me. The small group here are the only ones who know. We are all we have left in this bond. Yet you still find it pertinent to hide things from me."

Sterling's eyes tightened and nostrils flared.

"You do not understand what's at stake–"

"I would if you *fucking told me*," I hissed. "You have a lot of nerve, going near feral because Lilith trusted Stasia and kept you in the dark about her cycle ending. Now you're gonna sit here and tell me I don't know what's at stake? Mistakes are supposed to be learned from, not repeated. The Coven is literally in shambles right now, the least you could do is tell me what's happening."

I fixed him with a cold glare, challenging him, despite everything in my being screaming to submit.

"Beau, I don't know much more than you. I'm–"

"Who is he, Sterling?" I interrupted, getting right to the point since he was *so* determined to miss it.

The pinched gaze on my Master's face should have invoked fear in me, as it did to anyone who breathed in his direction. But I knew better. There was no one who knew him as intimately as

I did.

"Who. Is. He?"

Sterling's jaw clenched.

I laughed again. "And that's exactly what I mean. You not only keep things from me that might help us gain some footing after this massacre, but you keep things that are directly connected to me. *Me.* Your *only* fledgling."

I watched him, before leaning close. "Or am I?"

Sterling said nothing and this time, he let me walk away.

Maybe I was too angry. Maybe he didn't deserve being treated that cruelly. But he had to know how serious this was. He had to know that it's *not* okay. I understood that he had a lot of pressure on him and that everyone was looking to him to figure out what to do next, but he wouldn't have to do it alone if he would just *let me in*. I'm sick of him making decisions for me under the guise of protecting me. It wasn't right.

Frustrated, I went to the living area, because where else was I going to go? I was trapped down here in this tiny fucking space where I couldn't even storm off properly. Well at least I started to, until I saw Judas sitting there, watching the news.

Can't go back to my room and can't go to the living room. Being in this cramped apartment with so many people was really starting to grate on my nerves. I knew how necessary it was, but it didn't mean the circumstances didn't suck.

Deciding to stay, I made my way to one of the unoccupied couches, scanning the breaking news on the bottom. Surely there would be mention of the Atlanta Coven House going up in flames. Did the human media catch wind that Lilith was missing? Or was this all old news?

It could be a good and bad thing if they did. One that would broadcast to everyone, especially the humans, that we were weak without our leader. On the other hand, it could divert attention away from the situation, allowing us the freedom to search without dealing with the media.

But there was nothing.

"Has there been any mention of what happened?" I asked, forgetting that Judas made me uncomfortable from his unexplainable hatred towards me. Surprising me, Judas actually answered.

"No. It's strange. There hasn't been any mention of it all week. It's like it never happened."

"How is that possible? No one noticed a giant building burning in the middle of Athens? The home of the first Vampire? You'd think that would be all over."

Judas leaned forward, fingers laced together as he rested his chin on them and braced his elbows on his knees. The couch barely creaked with his movement.

"Unless someone is covering it up."

I'd assumed Nexus would be the first to speak, set the narrative. But if he hadn't appeared to the media…did something happen to him?

A knock sounded on the front door.

Both of us froze, head snapping in that direction with speed and attention only Vampires could achieve.

No one was supposed to know where we were, and everyone who knew our location was already here.

We moved in sync, easing across the floorboards, not making a sound. We each took a side, framing the front door before I gestured to him that I would take a peek. Looking into the peep hole, I scanned the surroundings.

Surprised, I pulled back, and glanced at Judas.

"Duaa," I mouthed.

A look of relief crossed over his features. He relaxed his position, straightening before reaching for the locks.

Not sure why we bothered locking the doors. If a Vampire

wanted to get in, they would. The door would hardly be a hindrance.

But I supposed Vampires weren't our only enemies.

When Judas opened the door, Duaa stepped inside. We both bowed our heads in respect to the High Priestess.

"Where are the Elders?" She asked.

"Here," Sterling said, appearing from thin air. He stepped from the walkway and guided Duaa to the couches. One by one, the others came filing into the small space, taking any available seat they could. All except Kyle, but we hadn't seen much of him this past week. He wouldn't leave the room, let alone bed. Alexander and Joel advised us to give him space to grieve, so we've been respecting that request. My heart ached for him though.

Judas lowered the volume on the TV, all of our attention on the High Priestess. A part of me was glad she was alright. I hadn't seen her the night of Samhain after the explosion, but I had no doubt that she was caught in the fray.

"Any news?" Sterling asked, getting straight to the point.

Oh so he *could* actually get to the point?

Funny.

"How are you doing, Duaa? Glad you *survived*. Oh! I'm alright, thanks for asking!" Duaa retorted, fixing Sterling with an expectant look. Sterling just blinked at her.

She rolled her eyes in response. I liked her already.

"Nexus has taken control of the Coven and they're working on repairs now. Kawana stayed to assist. The place was in shambles. It was the only reason I was able to get in and out without detection."

Sterling frowned. "Where were the guards?"

Duaa shrugged, "A lot of people were lost. He hardly has the manpower to defend the Coven, go after the Devout and search for Lilith. It's quite literally a madhouse."

"How many did we lose?" I asked.

Duaa sighed sadly. "I didn't get a full headcount, but a lot. We lost many fledglings. Be it from the explosion, falling debris, silver to the heart, or the fire. They are strong, but still close to their human selves. What wouldn't kill a Vampire, would certainly kill them. I was able to get a few pictures."

I leaned forward as she pulled out her phone, passing it around. When it came to me, I flicked through them, noting how many dead bodies there were. She was right, we had lost too many.

Subtly, I tried scanning through them to see if any of the bodies resembled that man I saw. The one who called me by my human name. Instead, I came across something more interesting.

There were a few close up shots of one body in particular. It was different from the others, the cause of death not similar to the ones surrounding it. They were covered in bluish bruises and sores. Their skin was taut and withered like a mummy.

The most shocking? I recognized them. If it wasn't for their features that had been severely distorted, it was definitely by the tattoo on their neck.

"I know this one," I said, handing the phone back to Duaa. She glanced at it, then her eyes darted back to me.

"How?" she asked.

"I spoke with him the day before Samhain. He was one of Carlisle's fledglings."

"What did he say?" Judas pushed.

"That he hoped I survived. I thought something was off about it, but I assumed he just meant the Change. It wasn't a secret that I was likely to transition," I answered.

"Why you?" Alexander asked. It wasn't said in malice, but curiosity. He didn't know much. No one really did, but it made me question whether it was a good idea to share. I didn't want to be like Sterling and hold valuable information close to my chest, but what could I really tell them?

"I'm really starting to wonder the same thing," I muttered.

In both instances, with the fledgling and the unknown man, they both alluded to the fact that I wasn't to be involved in the massacre.

Stasia said something similar, if I remember correctly. Could they be related?

Why wasn't I supposed to be there?

And what did Stasia know?

I tried not to glance at them, but I was now suspicious of them. They were too much of an anomaly. It was hard to gauge what side they played for. Lilith seemed to trust them, but Sterling didn't. And of those two, who did *I* trust?

I sighed. Soon my brain was going to explode from it all. I'd much rather go back to being oblivious and fighting with my desire to learn about my human life. Things were much simpler then.

But that's not true at all. I wouldn't have been able to stand it...the ignorance. It would have driven me crazy. It's better that I know because this puzzle wasn't going to solve itself.

"How did you recognize them? They're in pretty rough condition," Joel asked, glancing at the phone over Duaa's shoulder.

"That tattoo on their neck. I saw it before, and thought it was strange."

They stared at it a bit longer, before filing it away for further investigation.

"Carlisle still hasn't returned to his Coven. We have a few eyes out there," Duaa said, putting her phone back into the pocket of her worn leather jacket.

"Likely hiding out at one of the slave rings. He's probably still in the general area. I can't imagine with his injuries he would have been able to travel far. Especially without being spotted," Sterling added.

"We still don't know anything about who is pulling the strings. What's the purpose of the slave rings, because it can't just be to sway public opinion of Lilith. That would be like putting a cast on a papercut. Too ostentatious and less effective in the long term. And that baby? Why are we keeping her a secret? It seems like the cause of it all," Duaa muttered.

"And why is her cycle ending now?" Sterling added quietly.

"What?" Duaa hissed incredulously. She stared at Sterling, demanding in her gaze and tense stance.

Sterling sighed. "Lilith's cycle is ending. It's why we have the baby, it's why we must protect her at all costs. She is the daughter of Lilith and the new Mother of Vampires."

Duaa swore.

"This information cannot leave this room. Not even Nexus knows and it has to stay that way," Stasia added.

"Why?" Joel asked.

"Because if Nexus finds out, he's not going to want to leave her side, it'll make him a target. It's safer if he doesn't know. We need him to handle the outward facing issues with the Coven. We can't have his attention divided," Sterling explained.

"And we promised Lilith it would stay a secret from him. She didn't want him to know. There are too many unknown factors surrounding this. We don't even know where Lilith is. Last thing we should do is go against her plans when we have no idea what's at stake," I added.

The room fell into silence.

"We will protect her...until she is of age," Executioner added. His voice was a quiet whisper in the room, but I had no doubt that every single person heard him.

"Hiding out here isn't going to help. We need to be more proactive," Joel said and I couldn't help but agree. Yes, it was important to keep Lilm safe and away from danger, but we couldn't keep our forces divided like this. We had to maintain a united front and patch up the cracks left behind with the massacre. Nexus needed us.

"Joel's right. We can't leave Nexus defenseless. He likely thinks we're all dead. He has no one else there to provide leadership support. It isn't fair for us to leave that all on him," I added.

Sterling's face was pensive, likely running through possible moves we could make. His lip twitched when he finally decided on one.

"We'll split up. One group will scope out Ninetta's territory. There is bound to be some chaos there now that their leader is dead. It's the perfect time to obtain information. Another group will go and provide support to Nexus, help make sure that the Coven house is properly fortified. The rest will stay here, to protect Lilm."

There were murmurs of agreement. Duaa straightened.

"I'll return in three days, hopefully with more information."

Sterling nodded, then turned to Joel. The group began to discuss the logistics. While they were distracted, I followed Duaa to the door under the guise of walking her out. When we were a little bit away from the others, I pitched my voice low.

"High Priestess–"

"Just Duaa, young one," she said with a smile. "I take it you have something you want to ask me?"

I nodded.

"Among the bodies that you saw...were there any humans? In particular one with short dreads, about my height, dark brown eyes, scar on his temple?" I couldn't shake the anxiety in my gut as I pictured the man who saved my life with perfect detail.

Duaa frowned, pursing her lips as she contemplated. Waiting with baited breath until she shook her head.

"I don't think so, but it's possible they could have been one of the unrecognizable ones," she said softly.

My chest tightened. An unfamiliar pain rolled through me, as foreign as the stranger was to me.

Why did hearing that upset me so much? It's not like I knew him. He was likely the enemy. I shouldn't care if he was dead. If anything I should be happy about it.

But...I couldn't.

Was it because he saved me?

Or was it because his death would have been entirely my fault?

With a clenched jaw, I nodded to Duaa. "Thank you."

She patted my shoulder. "I'll be on the lookout and let you know if I find out more about your mystery human."

I nodded my thanks and closed the door behind her. Staring at the handle, I fought to compose myself.

If I let it show, the others would grow suspicious. I didn't want Sterling getting involved, he'd try to block me from finding anything more out.

"Keeping secrets, are we?"

I flinched, turning to see Stasia leaning against the wall by the corner of the hall. A casual smile on their face.

"I was only trying to get more information since you Elders like to hold that close to your chests," I bit out, no longer concerned with showing respect.

I was tired. Tired of playing the games. This aspect of Vampirism? I wasn't cut out for it. It unnecessarily complicates things, holds us back from making any real progress. But that's not something they would understand.

After all, secrets are what they keep best.

"You're going to get hurt if you keep sniffing around things that you have no business with," Stasia warned darkly, their pale eyes glinting.

I stared back.

"Yeah, well, it seems like an inevitability at this point. I'd rather make progress than hide behind politics. Now if you'll excuse me," I said harshly, stepping past them.

"Those who play with fire, will always get burned," Stasia whispered as I passed them by.

Good thing I had an affinity for fire then, huh?

18

BETTER LEFT IN THE DARK

I could hear them. The screams, like a distant cry for help. Some of them were. Calling out, begging, hoping, praying.

But in the end, they all died. Except me.

In those hazy blurs of laughter and childlike wonder, I saw those faces again. Still unidentifiable to me, from their overexposed features blotting out everything that could help me remember who they are...*were*.

One in particular stood out, a child. I laughed with him, played with him, cried with him, as we huddled together in the closet. Two bodies just feet away, slowly bleeding out. A siren's call of death easing them to the other side.

Then there were the whispers. The platitudes. The "stay calm Jamal, don't make a sound". All of the small games of name that country and accent impersonations all in order to keep me from losing it. Promises that when we got out, we would travel the world.

Keep your eyes open, Jamal. If you let them close, they'll never open again.

Run, Jamal! Run!

A subtle waft of frankincense curled in my nostrils forcing me to remember the scent fondly with a sense of nostalgia that should have been lost the moment Sterling's blood entered my body.

And at the end of the tunnel, a dark and damp place, full of fear and hopelessness, violence...I saw a body. Twisted neck and broken limbs.

Through my own haze of pain and despair, one voice drowned out all the others. One face that broke through the terrifying trance, dispelling the clouds like a beacon of possibilities.

"I can save you, Jamal. But you have to want this...Do you want this?"

Sterling.

"Do you want to live?"

I woke with a gasp, the blood pounding in my skull, drowning out all of my thoughts. My chest heaved as I panted, wiping away the sweat that beaded along my hairline. Tiny little bumps decorated the skin on my arms and I could feel the hairs rising at attention.

Feeling eyes on me, I glanced at the crib.

Peering over the edge was a set of large glowing red orbs. There was a steady awareness that did not belong to the small frame that held it. Small, yet, impossible.

That couldn't be...Lilm?

Her head full of wild curls that had certainly not been there a few hours prior and a face of delicate rounded features that looked so similar to Lilith, was all the confirmation that I needed.

Unblinking, she watched him in the darkness for a few moments longer before calmly lying back down in the crib, turning over and going to sleep.

Why do I get the feeling she had something to do with my

dreams? I mean, that's not entirely out there, right? She was a magical creature. Daughter of the first Vampire, she was bound to have powers beyond our comprehension. Especially with her clearly accelerated growth rate.

The others were definitely going to freak out when they saw her. It was hard not to.

Needing to wash the sweat that had dried on my skin, I got up and stretched before heading to the shower. Though not before glancing over at the crib.

The diaper Lilm had been wearing was now straining against her much larger frame.

We'd need to get her some new ones, bigger clothes too. Thankfully she wasn't wearing any before the growth spurt. I can't imagine how terribly that could have gone.

The shower was much needed, a temperature cooler than I typically set. I needed the chill to cool me down. My racing heart had heated my skin to a point of discomfort. Panic was never a good idea when tensions were this high. If I panicked, I lost control, and that's the last thing we needed right now.

After the discussion yesterday, it was agreed that Blake, Obi, Kyle, and I would stay to guard Lilm while Judas, Joel, Alexander, and a few of Duaa's trusted would scope out Ninetta's territory.

There was bound to be some disarray since their High Priestess was dead. And from what I knew, the other Covens didn't have Elders or Consorts to take their place if anything happened. That privilege belonged to Lilith alone. Besides, none of them were strong enough to maintain the power required to forge and keep those bonds.

Stasia, the twins, and Sterling would make their way back to the Coven house. I was angry at first, but Sterling wouldn't hear any of it. He was dead set on keeping me away from the fray. It seemed like whoever it was that had known me as a human, worried Sterling enough to keep me away from everything. Whatever significance I had, wasn't worth the risk according to him.

Just thinking about it made the rage in my gut roil. Bubbling with heat, I clenched my jaw, willing the cool spray to calm me. But it continued to burn. Each droplet of water that hit my skin fizzled into smoke as the fire within me fought to escape.

Deep breaths.
In and out.

There was no use getting worked up about it, I couldn't change his mind. Not while I was angry. It would only make him shut down. I knew that much.

I shut the water off when I was able to feel the cool temperature again. Drying off and putting on some fresh clothes, I was about to head back to my room, but Cadence was leaning against the door, judgment on her face while she looked me up and down.

"Can I help you?" I asked, not snarkily, just genuinely confused as to her sudden appearance. "Are you looking for Sterling?"

With a hip cocked, she pursed her lips, icy blue eyes narrowed. "No, I'm here for you, baby vamp."

I snorted. It made sense for Stasia to call me that, they've been a full-fledged Vampire for four hundred years. But to hear that from a fledgling? Laughable.

The message was clear though. She held no respect for me. I had known that from the beginning, it didn't bother me, so I didn't waste my time getting riled up like she clearly expected me to.

I raised a brow at her. "Well?"

She stood straight, approaching me. Her tiny frame was a lot less intimidating when she was this close and I towered over her, but it would stupid to let my guard down. She was dangerous.

Her biggest advantage was people making the mistake of underestimating her. I didn't.

"I don't like you," she started.

"Noted," I drawled, then made a move to walk around her. She stopped me with her next words.

"But I understand why my Master likes you."

I stopped, frowning. I mean, it was clear that Stasia had some weird interest in me. Why? I had no idea.

She had my attention and knew it. It was evident in the tiny smirk that quirked the corner of her lips.

"Care to share?" I pressed when she didn't say anything further.

"You have been teetering on the edge from the moment you were changed. There are two sides to your future. One, the part of you hellbent on putting others before yourself in an attempt to heal what they are not strong enough to do on their own. The other? Letting your emotions dictate your actions out of selfishness."

I frowned, but waited patiently for her to continue. Those two didn't seem mutually exclusive.

"My Master sees themself in you. Your inability to pick a side speaks to them personally. For many years before my brother and I were called to their side, Master had been forced to make sacrifice after sacrifice for others. Obligated to put others first at risk of themselves and their own well-being."

"So, what? You want me to stop putting others first?" I questioned. If this was what made Stasia so interested in me, they're going to be disappointed. I couldn't turn my back on anyone. I wasn't built that way.

But aren't I turning my back on Sterling?

Cadence's eyes glinted. "No. I'm saying you need to stop letting your desire for helping others consume you, but also not let your own emotions cloud your judgment when making decisions for others. My Master was meant to strike the balance between the two and ended up falling hard on the side of selflessness because they could not fight their need to protect others. They deserve it after the years of servitude at the cost of their conscience. You were not meant to make the same mistake. If you don't find the balance, you'll end up dead in the long run."

Hard to imagine with the way Stasia was viewed within the eyes of the Coven that they were acting on selflessness, but that was pretty much the same as Obi. No one knew the depth of his character. They simply assumed and feared. Would it not be the same with Stasia? Who knew what they were actually instructed to do or the motives behind their actions? They were trusted with information and assignments that not even Sterling was privy to. It wouldn't be that farfetched.

"Why are you telling me this?" I asked.

"Logic lives longer," she replied, then added with a casual shrug of her thin shoulder, "And you're pathetic. It's hard to watch."

I rolled my eyes at her retreating form. As unpleasant as she was, there were valid points in what she said.

I had been teetering. It was as if one moment I was all for giving my all to this new life, then the next, I was questioning everything. I couldn't figure out if Sterling was my everything or an enemy. And I *had* been letting my emotions cloud my judgment, when it came to Sterling at least.

Have I been too hard on him? Have I not been viewing his actions from an objective standpoint? If I could do it with Obediah and Stasia, I should be able to do it with my own Master, right?

Besides, leaving things the way they are, with tensions running as high as they were, could only result in sloppy mistakes. We couldn't afford mistakes, not this late in the game.

Sighing, I sought out my Master.

The bond between us, a solid rope of gold with a near palpable hold, hummed as I finally released the block I'd been keeping in place. Tugging, I followed the hint of anxiety and shock to Blake and Obi's room.

Knocking on the door gently, I waited for someone to answer it. Expecting Blake, though I should have known it would be Sterling who answered. Especially after I opened the bond. His expression was unreadable, guarded as he stared down at me.

"Can we talk?" I asked, meeting his gaze levelly. I made sure my emotions were calm, letting that be the only thing to filter through the bond. If I willed it with enough conviction, I could make it true.

I *was* calm...for the most part.

Sterling nodded, before murmuring something over his shoulder. He stepped into the hall, closing the door firmly behind him. We walked back the short distance to our own room in silence.

He didn't even glance at the crib, where Lilm rested. It made me wonder if he had noticed the sudden change in her appearance.

He sat on the edge of the bed while I remained standing. I didn't trust myself to sit beside him. A part of me was still angry. Angry at all the secrets and lack of trust, but I was willing to listen now, to come to a solution. I could do that standing.

"If we don't hash things out now, this tension will put not only us in danger, but those around us and I'm not willing to have that on my conscience. We need to be in sync now more than ever," I started.

Sterling's shoulders dropped. I couldn't tell if that was relief or defeat. It was hard to see with his face and emotions as neutral as they were. So I continued.

"I won't apologize for getting upset. It would be dishonest, but I am willing to listen if you explain to me the reason. The reason you keep things from me, is it because you don't think I can handle it?"

I gestured to him, allowing him the floor to speak.

He stared at me, green eyes burning with something I was still unable to identify. Then he took a deep breath, releasing it in a slow and gentle wash of sweetness.

"It's not that I don't think you can handle it, but that you shouldn't *have* to," he replied quietly. My eye twitched, but I fought not to say anything. I said I would listen and I meant it.

"I just...I want to protect you. I was the same when I was a fledgling, demanding to know what I had forgotten. Lilith warned me. Told me again and again that the life I left behind was best kept in the past. I didn't listen. Eventually, she caved."

I waited in eager silence. This was more than he had ever given me before. I knew nothing about *his* past either. As a Vampire or a human.

"I was changed on the battlefield. Lilith found me in a sea of my dead comrades on the brink. She didn't ask if I wanted to live, but she seemed to just *know*. While I'd been fighting in the war, famine and the plague had torn through my village. My father had fallen ill. In order to afford the doctors and medicines, my younger sister tried going to the market with her wooden carvings. She was a spectacular artist, but many wouldn't acknowledge her since she was a woman. No one bought her carvings, but they did offer to buy her body. So she sold herself. Not long after, she stopped coming home. A few villagers found her body in the woods. Without the income from my sister, my mother could no longer afford the doctors and my father inevitably died. While my mother didn't end up catching the plague, she was kicked off the land and forced to live as a beggar. It did not take long for grief and poor circumstances to claim her life as well. Six months was all it took for my entire family to be stolen from this world."

Without realizing it, I had made my way to the bed, sitting beside the stricken Vampire who tried to harden himself to the emotions that still threatened to bring him back to that difficult time.

"As a direct progeny of Lilith, our transitions are much longer. Every Elder endured six months of the Frenzy. It was during that time that I lost my family. It was hard for me to grasp back then. I grew depressed because I thought I could have prevented it. Could have saved them. It ate at me, until I stopped feeding. I nearly died from the Change rejecting me due to starvation. It wasn't until Lilith explained to me that they would have died regardless. Had she not changed me, I would have died on that battlefield. It would not stop the plague from claiming my father, or my sister from being murdered, or my mother from being thrown out on the streets. There is *nothing* I could have done. And knowing that, only made things worse for me. It's a weight that I still carry and there is not one day that I don't wish I had just *listened* and accepted that my past was lost with my memories."

I waited, wondering if he was finished speaking. It was a lot to process and things made a lot more sense. *Six months*...three days was *already* excruciating, I could not imagine enduring six months of that torture.

"So...when you changed Obi?" I started. He seemed to pick up where my question was going.

"Obi is powerful. He's special in a way that no one else would come close. But his power comes with consequences. His mind is fragile. A prolonged period of that mental warfare would break him. It is why Lilith had me change him in her stead. Despite the call being for her, she was not entirely confident he would survive the Change and during the Frenzy the Maker must be strong enough to deny the need of their fledgling. Lilith did not think she could deny Obediah when she needed to. He has a past much like ours, best *left* in the past. It breaks something in us when we are reunited with our pasts. And I've been trying to shield you from that pain."

"I understand where you are coming from and I understand your desire, but Sterling, I am not you nor am I Obediah. Even my origin is different from either of yours. I don't blame you for trying to protect me from this, but it will come to find me no matter what. Quite literally in my case. Wouldn't it be better for me to have a moment to process the pain rather than be blindsided? I'd be stronger for it."

Sterling ran his hands through his hair. Something he did when he was feeling strong emotions. I grabbed his knee, asking for his attention. He gazed at me, pain and indecision burning in his eyes.

"I have lived many lives, Sterling. You didn't feel called to me because of the fates. Lilith chose me for you. Pain and loss are not the same to me."

Sterling's brow furrowed. I pushed the truth of my words through the bond. Everything I felt when Lilith had revealed my origin to me many nights ago.

Sterling's breath left him in a rush as he fought to process the new information. I could see the wheels turning as he stared at the floor. The puzzle pieces were slotting together.

"That is my truth that I have kept from you. I cannot remember all my lives, but I feel them. I am no stranger to the despair of life."

I didn't quite know where the words came from but I could feel it in my gut, they were true and I meant every one.

Reaching up to stroke his cheek, I turned his gaze back to me.

"I've told you my truth, will you tell me yours now?" I asked. "Will you promise me like I promise you to stop keeping secrets from each other? To trust each other with the entire truth?"

Sterling's jaw clenched, but his gaze never broke from mine. I could read every possibility running its course behind his eyes as he weighed his options. Then finally resolve.

"I promise," he vowed.

I nodded, then grabbed his hand and squeezed.

"Who was he, Sterling? Who was that man to me?"

Sterling's hand squeezed mine back. Then in a quiet voice he finally told me what I'd been suspecting this whole time.

"Anthony...your brother."

19

IT'S OKAY TO LET GO

It would be incredibly hypocritical of me if I lost it right now.

But the confirmation rattled me to my core. A chill settled deep in my bones as shock made its home in my soul.

It wasn't as if I hadn't heard the name before. With it, every memory that edged its way into my new reality of moments forgotten. And I *suspected,* I mean, all signs led to this, but...

It doesn't make sense. Anthony was dead, Sterling said so himself. And I *remember.* That mangled corpse in the middle of the ring. The cheers. The *blood.* I remember his death and the agony that came with witnessing it.

"He's dead, Sterling. Even you said so," I murmured to him.

"I know. I saw the body. But I cannot think of anyone else who would fit that description. There is a high chance that I am wrong, it could be a coincidence, but..."

"But coincidences are only for those in denial," I finished for him. "What happened that night, Sterling, when you found me?"

"There were reports of some activity and the possible location of another slave ring in the New Orleans area. Normally, one of the neighboring Covens would handle it, but the amount of incidents leaked by the media had their hands full and Ninetta couldn't be trusted. I stepped in as a favor for Stasia. When we got there, all of the slaves had been murdered and the ones in charge had not left a trace. This case was different though. Typically, they would burn the bodies to hide the evidence, but they didn't. It's how I was able to identify your brother among the fallen. I recognized him from a case several years prior. One of many where families were murdered and the children went missing. But then, when we swept the building, I found you in one of the lower levels, by yourself, badly injured and on the brink. At first, I was confused, you had lost so much blood, I thought you were dead. You *should* have been dead. But there you were, clinging to life, and then I felt the call."

I could remember after that. Him kneeling over me with a gentle concern on his handsome face. And I remember him asking me if I wanted to live.

Why was *my* life so important? Lilith, Carlisle's fledgling, Stasia, Anthony...enemies and allies alike were all interested in keeping me alive.

It had to be for a reason, why else would this Anthony look alike–because I *refuse* to believe it's actually him–be sent to me? Maybe this is something we could use to our advantage.

"I need to go with you to find Nexus."

Sterling frowned, not understanding the correlation with this new declaration and the night I'd been turned.

"It's too dangerous, Beau–"

"I don't think it will be for me. Think about it, all of them want me alive for whatever reason. Anthony is proof of that. Maybe I can get some information out of them. If they are still lingering in the area, which they most likely are, I can find out what happened to Lilith. Or maybe even who is behind it all."

Sterling sighed. "I can't just let you go into danger like that. If they want you, they could *take* you. Letting you go there would be knowingly putting you in danger. What kind of Master would I be?"

"It's not about you. It's not even about me. It's about finding Lilith and putting an end to all of this. You have to realize the opportunity we have here," I pushed. "Besides, I'm not a fledgling anymore. I'm not fragile." And I meant it. I felt the strength in me now. I wasn't helpless.

He was wavering, I could see it in his eyes. He knew I was right. After spending so long without any answers and constantly being one step behind, all the lives lost, it would be selfish not to use this advantage because of me.

"Fine. But you stay with me."

I released the breath I hadn't realized I was holding.

"I mean it, Beau. You don't leave my side. Not even for a second," he leveled me with a solemn look. I nodded eagerly.

Then, he tugged me into his arms, face burying into my curls.

"I missed you so much," he murmured. I breathe in his lemon and clove scent, missing him just as much. The distance between us hurt, even through my anger. But I wasn't willing to cave just because I missed him. We never would have gotten to this point, this level of trust if I had just let it go.

A cooing noise interrupted the moment. Both of our heads turned to the crib where glowing red eyes watched us through the slates.

Sterling swore softly, then rushed to the crib. Lifting her out of the crib, Sterling examined Lilm.

"She's grown ridiculously fast overnight."

I joined him, tickling her toes, making her squirm.

"Yeah, we'll have to tell Blake and Obi to make sure that they track her growth rate," I added.

Was this how fast Lilith developed? Did she even start as an infant or did she just appear into existence full grown? There has to be some sort of history on it, right?

"Do you know Lilith's origins?" I asked Sterling, who held Lilm in his arms with the care and consideration that suited a seasoned father. Or in this case, brother.

"No. It is not something she ever discussed with me or the others. Most of our history was lost due to the Change induced amnesia."

"It makes me wonder if she started out like this," I said, gesturing to Lilm. Sterling smiled down at the garbling toddler.

"No, I think Lilm is one of a kind."

"She's going to need some new clothes and diapers. We'll have to accommodate her accelerated growth."

"I'll send Judas. I don't want to risk any tracking through any delivery services or nosey humans," Sterling responded, laying Lilm back down in her crib where she snuggled with her blanket and promptly fell back asleep.

With a gentle kiss to my forehead, Sterling was out the door. As he disappeared into Judas's room, I headed over to Alexander and Joel's room. I wanted to check in on Kyle. It had been awhile since I last saw him, wanting to give him the space he needed to cope with losing his Master. If that was even possible.

Could one ever get over losing their Maker? Especially if they had no one else who relied on them? No other reason for living on?

When I knocked on the door, Alexander answered. He looked tired and worried. To be expected.

After stepping inside, I noticed Joel wasn't present. It was just him and Kyle. Kyle who was a immobile heap on the bed. He didn't move at my arrival. It was hard to tell if he was even breathing.

Alexander went and laid beside him, hugging the male who

seemed more zombie than fledgling. Broken, glazed over, and unseeing. There was no one home.

It was heartbreaking.

I joined them on the bed, hugging Kyle's other side. His body was cool and thin, even through the blanket he was wrapped up in. It made me worry all the more.

He hadn't left the bed since he got here a week ago. Pretty sure he hasn't fed or ate real food either. He was slowly withering away and there was nothing we could do to stop it. Fate had plans for Kyle and we could only wait and watch.

The silence was stifling. I could see the pain in Alexander's eyes as he gazed down at his friend, gently stroking his blonde waves from his pale and gaunt face. No longer glowing with that California tan. No longer full of life and mischief.

He wasn't even a person anymore. Just an empty husk, waiting for the end. Holding on by a tiny thread.

"I can't anymore."

Alexander and I both froze. Not just as the croaking voice we hadn't heard in a week. But the words that echoed in the room like a bomb.

Alexander's lip trembled as he stared at his fledgling brother in horror. The two of them had been changed around the same time. They'd been together for years, a much closer fledgling bond than I had developed with either of them. They really were like brothers. And the pain those words must have brought Alexander was unimaginable.

Tears welled in his eyes and he didn't fight them. They made their way down his cheeks until they reached the tip of his chin. One drop, then two, splattered on the fabric of the blanket, staining it red.

"Kyle, you can't give up. Hale wouldn't *want* you to give up. You can still fight. Still find a reason–"

I laid a hand on Alexander's shoulder, forcing his attention on me and shook my head. While I understood that he was in pain, it would be selfish to put that on Kyle.

Besides...Kyle was already gone. He had died that night, right along with his Master. There was nothing holding him here.

I pulled Kyle's hand in mine, staring into those unseeing depths, searching for that tiny sliver that was still holding on.

"It's okay, Kyle. You can let go now. Be with your Master," I told him gently.

With that last spark, that last bit of him, he managed a grateful smile.

And then...he was gone.

Alexander sobbed hysterically, his face a mess of bloody tears. I blinked back my own, needing to be strong for him. For both of them.

Pulling Alexander into my arms, we cradled Kyle's body.

"He'll be okay now," I promised, stroking Alexander's hair as he sobbed into my chest, fingers digging into my arms as he desperately mourned our fledgling brother.

He knew. He knew just as I did that the pain would never go away. Kyle would never stop agonizing over the loss, and no one should suffer that way. There was no point to him continuing on.

Sometimes...it was okay to let go.

20

LILM

The earth was hot against my skin, tiny particles of sand scraping against me.

The sand seemed to glow, illuminating the world despite the darkness. Like the moon had taken earth's place. Gone from the sky, but alive beneath my bare feet.

Where am I should have been the first question in my head, but I was oddly at peace in this strange world. I felt the comfort and safety of it. There was even a hint of familiarity.

For as far as the eye could see, there was nothing but pale sand...and a tree. One singular tree in the midst of the nothingness. In full bloom with white apples, ripe for picking, hanging from every branch.

I approached it, feeling called, then I knew why.

Kneeling beneath the tree, dressed in white, was Lilith with Lilm in her arms.

One could almost mistake them for a normal mother and child. Hearing the soft coos of a mother to her giggling baby was familiar in a way I had not imagined. Like somewhere in the crevices of my existence, I had been there. That happy giggling child in my mother's arms. A mother I could not remember, but somehow could always feel. Her soft breath, warm embrace, and gentle voice.

Yet the image before me was something vastly different. The two before me were not just mother and child, they were an incomplete trio waiting for their third. The Mother and the Maiden. But where was the Crone?

When I was close enough, Lilith smiled and said, "I'm afraid I've left you in a rather difficult predicament."

Well, what else was new?

"Is it really you or is this some sort of weird hallucination?" I asked, kneeling in front of the two.

"Yes, my child. It is really me."

"Where are you? Like in the real world?" I asked, not wasting a moment. If we could locate her, get a lead somehow, maybe we'd be able to rescue her before going to Nexus.

"I do not know. I have been unable to move, use my power, or communicate since I've been taken. But now that Lilm is older," she smiled down at the docile toddler who bore such a striking resemblance to her, it was like she was duplicated then shrunken down. "I have been able to use her as a bridge."

"You're still alive then?"

"Yes," she replied softly, the smile dimming. "But barely. I am being held prisoner and I cannot identify my captor. The blood...it is tainted."

Of course it wouldn't be that easy. I sighed.

"How come you appeared to me and not one of your Elders? Like Sterling?" I asked. It was odd considering they were the ones in charge. She had to know that in her absence they would step up. Certainly not me, a newbie Vampire, 'baby vamp' as Stasia liked to call me. I was virtually useless to her. Unless it was to relay information, which it seemed like she didn't have any to provide.

"My children cannot enter this place. No one can except those who are...*other*. As we are."

She looked back up at me then. Lilm followed her line of sight. Having them both stare at me, in sync, unblinking, was more than a little eerie.

"I am being punished by the fates, it seems," she continued.

Frowning, I waited for her to elaborate. She did not. As I opened my mouth to question her about it, she held up one palm to stop me.

"We do not have much time together. I grow weaker by the second." Her gaze sharpened and expression became imploring. "Listen to me, Beau. They want my power. The power of the First. And *you* are the key to ending all of this. But I cannot use you. I cannot damn my children."

I opened my mouth again, but she stopped me.

"When the time comes, you must kill me."

"Lilith–"

"You *must*." She shuddered, seeming weary. "Until then, I will continue to give everything to her."

The two gazed at each other before they turned their eyes on me. And in one blink, they were gone.

I gasped, jolting up out of the bed. My eyes immediately went to the crib.

Lilm was peering over the edge again, eyes locked on me. With a calmness and awareness that did not match her age, she laid back down and went to sleep.

It made sense now, it wasn't just Lilm. Lilith was in there too...somehow. Was the power she was receiving from Lilith causing her accelerated growth?

With Lilm back asleep, I got up out of bed, stretching before heading out of the room in search of Sterling. Maybe he would have better luck deciphering the messages Lilith left me. And even if he couldn't, I'm sure he'd want to know at the very least that Lilith was still alive.

I found him talking to Stasia and the twins, more than likely discussing their plans on how they were going to make it back into the Coven house.

"I think it would be in our best interest to enter through the front as we normally would. Any form of cowering would send a message to those who are lurking that what happened on Samhain had shaken us. What we need now more than ever is to show that we are not shaken. *Nexus* needs that," Sterling told the group.

Stasia shook their head. "If we barge in, we lose the element of surprise. Who knows who might slip up and get sloppy if they think we are still gone? That Nexus is weak? This would be the prime opportunity for them to strike. Is it not what we would do if the positions were reversed?"

Sterling pursed his lips, contemplative. I could see the benefits of both approaches. Neither were wrong, it was just difficult to determine which was the best option.

"Why not do both?" I asked, coming up beside Sterling. "Who is to say that showcasing we are alive won't draw out Carlisle? Or even better, the one pulling his strings? I think we should assess the situation there first, undetected, before announcing our arrival. That way we'd know what impact we'd have and which is the best course of action. We may even be able to sniff out some of the lingering Devout, I doubt they've gone far."

"He has a point," Cadence said, surprising me. "And we can't trust anyone from the Coven, we don't know if there are any moles."

They all came to an agreement to follow my plan. We'd head out tomorrow while Judas, Joel, and Alexander would head for Ninetta's territory tonight. It was the furthest out and they would need the head start to warn us if anything was amiss.

Duaa and her Coven would be surveilling Carlisle's Coven house, the ones that hadn't attended Samhain in Athens.

We weren't going to wait around anymore. We were healed up and ready to fight back. They wouldn't get away with this.

And tomorrow, we'd set things straight.

~

When dusk crept upon the horizon, painting the world in a purple and blue haze, the group prepared to leave. As Sterling and Stasia packed the car and ran over a couple of finer details with the twins, I headed to Obi and Blake's room. Lilm's things had already been moved.

"Be safe," Blake told me, eyes tight with worry.

I shrugged, "As safe as I can be." Glancing over his shoulder at Obi holding Lilm gently, gazing at her with that same adoring expression, I added, "It's not really me that's in danger."

We hugged before Sterling called for me. Sterling and Obi exchanged a look before Obi gave a small nod, right before we headed out the door.

The final sinking rays of sun stung a little, but it wasn't anything too painful. Despite the higher tolerance, Sterling still tugged my hood up protectively. I let him. There were few things he would have to get used to now that I was a full fledged Vampire, but protecting me in that sense, in that minor way, I wouldn't take from him.

As I slid into the truck, a different one than before which means Judas and the others must have taken it, I was a little disappointed when Asher slid in beside me. Sterling had climbed into the driver's seat, Stasia occupying the passengers. So the backseat was left to the twins and I.

It was a tight fit, with Asher's massive size. The ride was long and awkward, with the silence. I tried to distract myself by staring outside of the window, watching the cars pass by on the highway, the trees towering above on either side when we slipped outside of the city.

As the familiar streets near the Coven house came into view, a tightness spread in my gut, clenching with a sense of foreboding. We didn't park close, instead choosing to hide the car on a side street a few blocks away.

"Cadence, my love, do a sweep before we head out," Stasia told the smaller fledgling. Without a moment of hesitation, she slid out of the car and disappeared into the night.

"It's quiet," Sterling remarked.

Stasia hummed, "No reporters or any lingering humans. It's as if they can't see the decrepit state of the building."

"Lilith's magic?" Asher asked.

"Or the Coven house itself. It is sentient after all," I added.

"Either way, that means we have to stay alert. This could be a visual illusion which means there could be other things hidden from our senses," Sterling said.

"Cadence will not let anything escape her senses," Stasia hummed, looking at their nails nonchalantly. I rolled my eyes. Let's hope that's true.

As if summoned, Cadence knocked on the door, but didn't get in. Taking that as a sign for us to move out, we all got out of the car and joined her.

"The security is light. I didn't see anyone patrolling the outer perimeter and there are only four guards stationed near the entrances. We could easily slip by in one of the side entrances," she told us once we had all gathered.

Sterling sighed exasperatedly. "They have to know that they are vulnerable like that. Any one of the Devout could scope out the security just as easily as we did. They're sitting ducks like this."

"Well what else is Nexus supposed to do? We've lost too many."

"This is where we call in help from the other Covens."

"Sure, and potentially invite more of the Devout right in. We don't know which Covens are loyal and which are traitors. You can't possibly think it stops with Ninetta and Carlisle?"

"Of course not," Sterling scoffed. "But there are those who have proven their loyalty. Verene and Boris are the closest and easily could have sent reinforcements. Boris especially, since his Coven is large."

"Well, why don't you tell Nexus that then?" Stasia sneered.

Sterling pinched the bridge of his nose in annoyance before deciding to ignore Stasia. Turning to me, green eyes solemn, he leaned close, brushing my neck affectionately, the bond between us humming.

"Stay close and alert. Do *not* let your curiosity get the best of you. I mean it, Beau."

I nodded. Placing a kiss on my forehead, he turned to the others.

"Let's go."

We moved quickly and efficiently, embracing the shadows that hid our forms. Despite not having worked with them before, we all were in sync that embodied trust and practice moving as a unit. None of which we had.

Maybe having an orgy served the same purpose.

As Cadence told us, the guards were sparse, making it easy to slip in. The familiar halls greeted me, relieving me, providing me with comfort I didn't know was missing. But the air felt stale. Wrong. Had I not been there, I would not have believed the events that occurred on Samhain.

There was no damage.

Nothing. No bodies, no debris, nothing at all to prove that there had been several bombs that took the lives of many of our Coven members. It was business as usual.

For the most part at least. I could hear the heartbeats of several within the walls of the house, but none roamed the halls. Most stayed confined to their rooms. Understandable really, who would want to go roaming about after all that has happened. Still, it was a bit unnerving.

Aside from the occasional person wandering the hall, the place was deserted. And the air. I couldn't get over it.

"Stasia, you and the twins scope out the place. Beau and I will locate Nexus."

Stasia and the twins moved without another word, disappearing so fast, it was as if they had never been there to begin with.

"Stay close," Sterling told me again before making his way down the halls.

The further we moved, the more that stillness tried to choke me. Settling deep in my gut, clenching, growing heavier with each step.

Apprehension forced sweat to bead my brow. My heart that had slowed once I had transitioned, now beat furiously.

"Sterling, I don't feel good about this," I whispered.

My hand reached out along the dark wooden walls that had thrummed with life whenever I brushed it. I expected the warmth, the throbbing, the acknowledgement that always greeted me before.

Nothing.

Cold. Devoid of the sentient being that lingered in the walls.

Terrified, I placed both palms on the walls, searching for that little beat. Anything to tell me it wasn't gone, that the house hadn't been destroyed with the acts of the Devout.

None.

Nothing rose to greet me. There was no life there.

"Sterling," I said again, voice shaking.

No response.

I whipped around, but the hall was empty. Empty...and different. This wasn't the same hall I was walking down with Sterling. I didn't recognize it at all.

Shit.

I groped at the bond, tugging to let Sterling know I needed him but it was as if the end of that rope was held by a void. I pulled and pulled and pulled, but it didn't bring me any closer to my Master.

The fuck?

It wasn't like the bond was gone or shielded. Something else was happening. I just couldn't figure it out.

Sterling was going to be pissed when he realized I wasn't with him. He was going to scold me for wandering off. But I swear I hadn't. I stopped to touch the wall for a second.

How did I get here then?

"Jamal."

I whipped around the other side of the hall, hearing the familiar voice.

A figure stood at the end of the hall, shrouded in shadows. The sconces on the walls had gone out where he stood. But something about them seemed so familiar.

They took a few steps forward, I eased a few back.

Once the glow of the sconces that were still lit hit their face, I recognized them from before. The one who saved me during Samhain.

But no...that wasn't all.

"Who are you?" I demanded, rallying my power just in case.

They took another step closer. Dreads pulled back and big brown eyes so full of concern and worry.

"You don't remember? It's me, Jamal. Anthony."

Anthony. Sterling said he was dead. I *saw* him die.

Flashes of faceless voice, with a faint hint of frankincense. The blurry or overexposed smiles suddenly came back with clarity.

All of them with Anthony.

It really was my older brother.

21

ANTHONY

I stumbled back a few more steps, grabbing the wall for support, suppressing the urge to pull my hand away at the cool wrongness that greeted me with the touch.

"You're dead. I *saw* you die."

Anthony moved toward me. "I promise you, it's really me. I don't have time to explain, I have to get you out of here."

I raised my hand, a wall of fire separating us in the hall. I watched him with suspicion. "Not until you tell me how you're alive. If that's even really you."

Anthony sighed. With a squeeze of his fist, the fire snuffed out. I blinked in surprise, staring at the space where the fire once was, then back up at him. He raised an eyebrow in challenge. My chest clenched.

Something about that small mannerism felt so *nostalgic*. Like I had seen that before, several times. I had vague memories of trying to do it myself and getting frustrated while he teased me and rubbed it in my face that he could do it easily.

God, I *knew* him. I *had* to know him. But was it real? Were my memories playing tricks on me? They were so scattered and frenzied, I couldn't tell anything anymore.

My temples throbbed.

"Listen, we don't have time for this. If *he* finds out you're here, he's going to try to hurt you," Anthony pleaded, stepping forward again.

I sneered at him. "Well whoever *he* is, he's made it pretty clear that he wants me alive. Even his flunkies keep telling me so," I gave him a pointed look.

Anthony looked exasperated, yet another expression that seemed so familiar. One I had seen and incited many many times. Was it so far-fetched to believe it was really him? That he was actually alive?

A vision of him lying in a pool of blood, head at an odd angle, mangled body a victim of the slave rings we were forced to survive a majority of our life, hit me full force.

There was no way he survived that.

So who was this imposter?

"He doesn't have to kill you to hurt you. You should know that by now, Jamal."

"Beau."

Anthony frowned.

"Don't call me Jamal. My name is Beau."

Anthony smirked, arms folded across his chest. "Is it now?"

I glared at him. He had the audacity to laugh, full bodied and familiar. Whoever he was, he was doing a splendid job fucking with my head.

"How am I supposed to trust you? In case you've forgotten, I watched you die. There is no way you survived that fight. So who are you? How do I know you're not working with the enemy trying to trick me? You've already separated me from my Master."

Anthony scoffed. "Slave to the white man again? Have you learned nothing from our ancestors?"

Fury boiled in my gut, raging hot and wild. It wasn't him I

was mad at, but the topic had been a point of contention between Sterling and I, it was like poking at a still healing wound. It hurt.

Taking a deep breath, I calmed myself. Sterling may be my Master, but we both served Lilith.

"More like a slave to a black woman."

Anthony contemplated for a moment, then shrugged. "Then I guess we're the same in that aspect." He settled those big brown eyes on me with a gravity that knocked the jokes and games right out of the room. "I was never here for them. My priority is you. Always has been, always will be. The moment you closed your eyes, I would be the one to force them back open again."

I frowned, the words coming back to me.

If you close your eyes, you'll never open them again.
Don't let them close, Jamal. Look at me. We'll be okay.

It was him. I remember now. The voice that followed me, that kept pushing me forward. It was him, it had always been him. As a child and as a man. All until he died. And then I followed after.

Difference was, I woke up again. Anthony wasn't as lucky.

Or was he?

Blinking at him, tears, threatening to blur my vision, I fought back all of the emotion that came crashing to the forefront. I wasn't going to let this shake me. I couldn't let him in. Not if this wasn't real.

But damn did I want it to be.

"How long have you been following me?" I asked him. Clearing my throat a few times when the words wouldn't leave my throat.

"Like I said, the moment you closed your eyes. I've been waiting here the whole time. I'm bound here, it was the price I had to pay to be with you."

"The one who bound you, are they here?" I asked.

Anthony swallowed noisily, seeming uncomfortable with the question, but he nodded once.

"Who is it?" I pressed. If it was the one we were after and I could get that information to Sterling, he might be able to destroy them. We could save Lilith.

"They aren't your enemy, Jamal–er–Beau."

How could Lilith not have known that there was someone literally living here in secret? Especially since Anthony had apparently been here for weeks. No one noticed? Then again, Lilith had mentioned something about blindspots in her perception and that someone was taking advantage of it. If she was pregnant before I had been changed, it would make sense that she hadn't been as focused on the happenings in the Coven house. I had barely seen her when I arrived here.

A shudder quaked the building, vibrated the walls, and jostled us. Immediately on alert, I surveyed the walls and ceiling, searching for danger. Was there a fight happening? Was Sterling okay?

Anthony grabbed me and yanked me down the hall. I didn't even fight as he led me away. The faster we ran through the halls, the more stifling the wrongness grew. Glancing behind me as we turned a corner, I noticed the walls had caved in on themselves, melting and molding, eating up the distance like it would swallow us whole. I pushed on faster.

Hall after hall, we raced, until just at the end of a long one we saw a door. Anthony pushed us on faster. Just as he reached to open it, he froze, his whole body going stiff, and eyes wide.

"Anthony?" I yelled, reaching to shake him, but he was quicker, grabbing me by the shoulders.

"I have to go now, I used too much of my reserves in this form. Listen to me Beau, this is her last apology to you. I'm sorry I couldn't be with you longer, but I'm happy you're alive. We'll be looking out for you, always have and always will. We love you."

We?

Before I could even process the words, he yanked the door open and pushed me inside.

Right before the door closed, I saw him standing there, the halls a swirling, devouring monster behind him, smiling. Then he faded away as if he never existed and the door slammed shut.

What?

I tried reaching for the door, but it blinked out of existence.

"Seriously? Now you want to start?" I growled at the house, but there was no response. *Fantastic.*

Turning around slowly, I took in my surroundings. It was a large room, dark and damp, not one that fit in with the rest of the house's aesthetic. Tall pillars and high arches framed the room, leading down dark halls, like some scary decrepit basement.

None of that mattered though, not when I saw the shallow pool of blood in the center of the room.

And right in the middle of the pool, as still as a corpse, was Lilith.

Her skin was ashen, cheeks gaunt, eyes closed, but there was still a subtle rise and fall of her chest. She wasn't dead.

But just barely alive.

It shouldn't have shocked me. I knew this already. She told me herself the state that she was in, but something about seeing it robbed me of all the air in my lungs. I fought to breathe again. To not panic.

Glancing around, there didn't seem to be anyone lingering. At least, I had thought that at first, but deep in the shadows were...bodies. Piles and piles of dead human corpses. None had decomposed, their deaths fresh. Most of them were children, scrappy and disheveled...and so fucking familiar.

They were *slaves*.

Blood trickled from their corpses down the grooves in the ground all leading to the pool where Lilith lay.

Carefully, I edged a little closer, not daring to spark any flames in case that alerted someone to my presence.

The closer I got, the more my stomach dropped. I could see tiny little tubes attached to her arms, steadily feeding her blood. It must have been what was keeping her alive. But why couldn't she wake up?

"Beautiful, isn't she?" a familiar voice said from the darkness. I flinched, eyes darting around to locate the voice.

Stepping out from the shrouds of darkness stood a figure I knew all too well.

Nexus.

22

FATHER OF ALL

"Surprised? You really shouldn't be."

I watched Nexus circle the other side of Lilith. Kind and compassionate Nexus. Surely, he wasn't...he *couldn't* be...?

He was so devoted to her, anyone could see it clear in his eyes. He adored her, there was no faking that. So why?

It didn't matter, I had to get to Lilith. If Nexus was my enemy, so be it.

Eyeing the distance between me and the pool, discerning whether or not I could make it there before Nexus, I made a quick decision. Darting forward, I reached for her, nearly stepping in the tainted streams of blood flowing into the pool.

"Ah ah ah, that blood is the only thing keeping her alive. You wouldn't want to do anything that might upset your Master, would you?" Nexus tsked with a hint of amusement.

I froze, hand still outstretched as if I might reach out to her still. But what if I ended up killing her...what would that do to Sterling? He would be devastated. Not to mention that if there really was a battle taking place, he would need all of his attention on that. If what Kyle went through was any sort of example of how he may react at the death of his Creator, I couldn't risk it.

Straightening and smoothing out my expression into something like casual boredom, I examined my nails, taking a different approach. "I guess I can understand why you're doing this. Forever trapped in her shadow, never powerful enough to do anything about it. Do you hate her or something?"

Nexus's nostril flared incredulously. "Hate her? I *love* her."

Excuse me, what?

I frowned, "So why are you doing this?" The curiosity was real now. Not going to lie, I fully expected the stereotypical 'I want to rule the world, so I'll sleep my way to the top while slowly planning their demise' crap. If that wasn't the case, then what the fuck? And if *this* is how he showed he loved someone, I'd hate to see what he'd do to someone he disliked.

Just the thought made me shudder. Must be a Pisces, that whole crime of passion thing was strong with this one.

"Lilith is a *goddess*," he purred, eyes wide with adoration. "She is all that is *good* and *compassionate*. And it is my love's greatest *weakness!*" The last sentence came out as a snarling hiss. "She must not be tainted by the needs of the Vampire world. She must remain good, it is why I will do it for her. I will drown in blood if only to keep hers clean."

The way he stared at her now, clouded with mania, the fucker was *unhinged*.

Sweat beaded his brow as he gazed down at his lover with sadness and longing in his eyes. Like he *actually* meant it. Maybe he did, in his own twisted way, which made it all that much more terrifying.

"So, what? You plan on taking over her Coven?" I asked him, stalling him. If I could keep him talking, I may be able to figure out a way to get Lilith out of this. There was no one here to help me, I had to finesse this on my own.

Admittedly, not one of my strengths.

"My ambitions aren't so unimpressive," Nexus sneered, shooting me a harsh look before returning a tender gaze to his unconscious beloved. "I do not wish to be just High Priest. I will be Father of All."

He looked up and smiled at me. "And you have what I need to make that possible."

I tensed. "You know."

Nexus tossed back his head and laughed, the silky tresses of his ash colored hair jostled with the movement. "Of course I *knew*. It's fairly difficult to hide a pregnancy, but that did not stop my beloved from trying. She may not have shown physically, but it's hard to hide with blood."

If Nexus was the one pulling the strings this whole time then it was obvious he knew. No wonder we were always a few steps behind. Sending Carlisle and Ninetta to retrieve the baby was a calculated move. He'd been sitting here comfy, watching all of us lose our fucking minds.

He *knew*.

If killing Lilm stops the transfer of power and the title from Lilith, then killing Lilith meant the transfer would instantly be made to Lilm.

When the time comes, you must kill me.

This is what she meant. I'm sure of it. What a load of fucking bullshit. Thanks a lot, Lilith, for putting me in literally the *worst* fucking position. Save everyone and kill her so that Nexus couldn't steal her power and reek Goddess only knew what kind of havoc on the world, or destroy the one person my Master loved the most? There are literally *no* right answers here. Either way I'm fucked.

"I can see you piecing it together. Much quicker on the uptake than your Master, I must say," Nexus mused, watching me casually as his words sank in.

Sterling hadn't been given the information I had because he couldn't make this call. He literally wouldn't be able to. It wasn't his fault that he didn't figure it out.

"Though I must say," Nexuss eyes narrowed, fangs elongated with such unbridled hate, "He has been an enormous *thorn* in my side these past few decades."

Growling, I reached deep, trying to tug at the bond. I pulled and pulled, but nothing. It was still that same oddly endless sensation as before.

"You won't be able to reach him. Not in here. Not while he's preoccupied." Nexus grinned maliciously, blue eyes dimming with ill intent. "If he loses his concentration, he just might lose his life. Foolish of you to split up your forces I might add."

I snarled at him. *How the fuck did he know...?*

"I have eyes everywhere."

From the corner over Nexus's shoulder, I see a figure almost materialize from the darkness. Stepping forward, I could see his face clearly and snarled in rage.

Fucking Judas.

"Goddamn *snake*, I *knew* you couldn't be trusted," I hissed.

The cold gray eyes didn't even budge. No reaction, nothing but pure unadulterated loathing in those eyes. All directed at me.

"Aw, don't be like that. You are brothers of blood after all," Nexus chuckled.

I frowned, not understanding the phrasing.

"You didn't really think you were Sterling's first fledgling did you?" Nexus purred, completely amused by my reaction to this revelation.

I knew it. I fucking *knew* it, but Judas? Seriously? His reaction towards me finally made sense now. Especially when we first met. He not only seemed to hate me on sight, but hated the relationship I had with Sterling even more.

"A secret Sterling kept even from his precious Mother. An unsanctioned Change. Poor Judas was a victim of Sterling's selfishness, cursed to live on the outskirts, looking in but never a part with a one sided bond. Then you came along and stole *everything* from him," Nexus narrated like some melodramatic movie scene.

"Oh fuck off!"

I was not going to sit here and let this turn into some terrible cliché. Odds weren't looking good, two against one now. It'd be even harder to get Lilith out of here.

But was that really the right thing to do?

Sterling would never forgive me if I killed her. I knew him. Our bond...it wasn't strong enough to protect me from him. It wasn't like theirs. In time, maybe, but not yet, not this soon. If he knew I was the reason she died, he'd probably kill me.

He'd kill me.

"And since you've let the lion in your den, the baby is left unprotected. Only a matter of time before she's dead and the power reverts back to Lilith," Nexus goes on.

"You would kill your own daughter?"

"I would kill my daughter and my beloved if that was the right thing to do," Nexus growled, no longer soft featured and amused. No, that was a beast behind a pretty smile. Something dangerous.

I smirked at them.

"You'll be waiting for a while then," I said, then turned to Judas. "You didn't really think we'd just leave her there? Not even *I* know where she is."

Sterling and I didn't feel comfortable leaving Blake and Obi alone with Lilm without proper protection and worried that they might be discovered because of us. So we told them to find another place to hide and not to tell anyone, not even us.

They were the perfect people to raise Lilm. Sterling and I

would get everything under control here and make sure it would be ready for her return.

We were trusting each other. Them for taking care of Lilm, and us for taking care of things here. We'd build a new environment to welcome Lilm too. I had hoped that that instruction and welcome would include Lilith, but...my choices are lessening by the minute.

There was only one real choice.

Forgive me, Sterling.

I raced for Lilith's body, catching the two by surprise. Spears of water came at me with blinding speed, embedding itself in my thigh and shoulder, forcing me to stumble just out of reach.

Two could play that game.

Sending the heat raging within me toward the pool, I burned the tubes connected to Lilith, feeding her the blood from the pool. Immediately her body began to seize.

Now that I'm wounded, I can't go near that tainted blood, who knows how it will incapacitate me. Grabbing a vial from my stash, I tipped it back and relished in the cool sweetness of Sterling's blood. I could feel it work through my system. The wounds themselves were not fatal, so the extra boost accelerated the rate at which it healed. I could feel the sting as they closed, just as Nexus threw more, face twisted in anger.

I rolled and dodged, trying to edge closer. When Lilith was just in my grasp, Nexus growled ferociously, the sound biting the walls and echoing in my ears. He was so close to her. *Too* close.

Would I make it?

I watched in horror as Nexus reached her first, but just as his hand moved to grab her, his eyes widened and body jerked. A trail of red dripped from the corner of his mouth as a matching pool blossomed on his shirt, right above his heart.

A faint protrusion poked the fabric, disappearing only as

Nexus's body fell forward into the pool splashing the toxic blood everywhere. I jumped back to avoid it.

Behind him, hand poised with a bloody heart in his fist, was Judas. That cold hatred he had directed toward me was now pointedly fixed on Nexus's still form.

"I would *never* betray my Master," Judas hissed at the corpse angrily.

When his eyes rose to meet mine, there was none of that hatred there. Only solemn sadness.

Oh...so he wasn't a traitor...*whoops.*

That's not enough to kill him though...

"Judas!" I shouted, tossing my silver blade to him as Nexus's body began to twitch. Judas caught the blade with ease before sinking it into the heart with a wet squelch. The excess blood still trying to pump through the arteries squirted on the ground with a wet splash before it finally went still.

For good this time.

We stared at each other in stunned silence. It certainly wasn't the turn out I was expecting to happen, but I guess it made sense.

Betrayal was an infection. When it got too deep, spread too far, sometimes you won't notice the signs.

Nexus died because he was too cocky. It was that cockiness that made him sloppy and was the only reason why we survived tonight.

Tugging Lilith out of the pool, I kneeled on the floor beside her.

Judas approached, kneeling on the other side of her, blade in hand. I stared at it, then at him.

"Is there really no other way?" He asked, voice heavy with emotion.

I looked down at Lilith.

"No," I said softly. "He's going to feel it and it's going to hurt." Not just him, but we'd feel it too. Through the bond.

I wasn't sure how strong Judas felt the bond with Sterling, but if it was enough to betray Nexus, then I'm almost certain it's strong enough for this to be just as terrifying and heartbreaking to him as it would be for me.

A shame, we didn't have a chance to really know one another. He could have been family, someone to talk to about Sterling and what it meant to be bound to him. We could have shared our own bond. Yet another future stolen from me.

Judas looked at Lilith then me, holding the blade out. "Together?"

I inhaled shakily, eyes blurring as my chest twisted.

Fuck, Sterling. I'm so fucking sorry.

"He's going to kill us," I whispered, choking back on a sob. Knowing that this would be the end. Without us and without her, Sterling wouldn't have anything else to live for. I wouldn't be able to do what Lilith created me to do.

Wrapping my hand around Judas's on the hilt of the blade, I gave him a sad smile.

"Together."

Then we shoved the blade into Lilith's heart.

23

HYPOCRISY

There was no way to prepare for the world ending, the excruciating pain that overwhelmed us. Maybe the world really *was* ending. Fuck if I knew.

But the moment it happened, the moment it was done, the entire building shook. Deep trembles rocked the ground, dust and small debris rained from the ceilings. The house screamed and moaned.

Or maybe that was us.

I don't know. I couldn't feel anything but the soul crushing loss and debilitating agony that pierced me straight in the chest, burning through bond like a forest fire.

But I took.

And Judas took.

And together we siphoned until the act became impossible to maintain. Still we tried. Because we would do that for him.

For Sterling.

The world around us was as uncertain as our futures. Spinning and pulling, collapsing and exploding. Doors appeared and disappeared, the room changed again and again like we were being sucked into room after room. The chaos of it made my stomach turn, but there was nothing I could do, not while the pain still rocked through me.

My head throbbed.

I could feel Judas's hand still in mine. No longer holding the blade but each other like we were the last tethers to reality. The moment we let go, we'd be sucked into the vortex that is the Mother of All.

And then...it all went silent.

No more churning, no more screaming.

And we were no longer alone.

We'd been transported somewhere, hard to tell where from the utter destruction that littered the place. Bodies were everywhere, like a battle fought and lost.

But none of that mattered. As if bringing us together in one final wish, Stasia and the twins were suddenly there. Looking worse for wear. Bleeding, clothes ripped and dirtied. Both held Stasia's near limp form between them as they gazed at Lilith's corpse, tears of blood streaking their face. Shock had wiped all charming grins and sarcastic smirks from their face leaving only the desolation of losing a Master.

And then there was Sterling.

My breath caught in my chest as I watched the heartbroken devastation encase his features. It spilled from his pores, through the bond, and dipped his shoulders until there was nothing but defeat left.

No...not defeat.

Rage.

The one that bore no boundaries, no reason.

The kind that would *kill*.

I looked at Judas fearfully, but resigned to my fate. We chose this. *I* chose this. And this would be my punishment. I'd accept it.

No matter what.

As Sterling began to stalk forward, I gripped Judas's hand tightly. When he squeezed back, he gave me a small smile.

"Take care of him."

No.

"Judas–"

He leapt for me, silver blade in hand, but there was no malice on his face. Instead, there were tears in his eyes as he stared down at me.

Resignation.

Take care of him.

He couldn't possibly expect me to do this. He couldn't take the blame, to leave this burden to him.

It was all for Sterling.

Judas knew as well as I did, if we died, Sterling would die with us.

Just as Judas mimed bringing the bloodied blade down on me, Sterling was on him.

I heard it, a sickening snap of bone with a wet pop of tendon and tissue mixed with viscous fluid, then felt it as a rush of sticky red heat drenched my face, slipping down my throat like mint and smoke. I could see nothing but red.

A dull thud hit the ground beside my head.

I blinked past the red, turned to the side and nearly screamed in horror as Judas's head stared back at me, detached from his body.

Two brothers gone. One lost to the memories of a new life started and the other, gone before I'd ever gotten to know him.

Turning my head to my Master in terror, I watched as the large man trembled. Tears freely streaming down his cheeks in an endless waterfall of red. Judas's heart cradled in his hands as he sobbed, then devoured. Each bite killing a part of him that he had left in his fledgling.

Dead by his hands.

Fuck. I hated this. I fucking *hated this!*

Now what? I'm supposed to keep it to myself? Let the blame fall on Judas? He dies while I get to live on with our Master? That's so fucked up!

But if I don't, Sterling will lose it. We couldn't afford for our last standing leader to lose all composure, the Coven needed him. *Lilm* needed him. None of the other Elders could take over after all of this chaos and bloodshed until Lilm was of age.

After Sterling finished eating Judas's heart, still sobbing, he cradled Lilith's body in his arms, sobbing into her neck like a child who had lost their mother. I scooted close, wrapping his shaking form in my arms, letting my own tears out freely.

Stasia stared for a few moments longer before wiping their face clean of emotion. Softly, they whispered, "I've done my part. I'm leaving the rest to you." As they left, the twins followed.

I doubted I'd ever see them again.

I guess I understood now...why Vampires keep their secrets. I hated them for it before. But now I've become one of them. In the end, I'm just a hypocrite.

Still, I'd keep this secret, until my last breath.

EPILOGUE

FOUR YEARS LATER

The hall was dark, buzzing with excitement as whispers crept from the shadows and danced along the walls.

It was that time of year again. Preparations for the Samhain celebration were in full force. Fledglings and Vampires alike darted around, gathered supplies, gossiped and giggled. It was the first one in a while that allowed for outside Covens to visit and the house was in a frenzy over it.

But this celebration was special in more than one way.

"Excuse me, First Elder, the room is ready," a young fledgling, still in Stage One, approached with a starry eyed look on their face.

It was strange, having that directed at me. Fairly certain I'd never get used to it. Or the title for the matter. Especially when it came from Vampires much older than me and a part of this Coven way longer than I had been.

None of that mattered though. Things were going to change soon.

I nodded at the fledgling before carrying on down the hall. Casually, my fingers brushed the smooth surface of the wooden slated walls, newly built after the destruction those few years ago.

I remembered when it flooded with warmth at my touch. The life that seemed to rush and swell with each day spent here, and the being who lived within it.

A soft pulse made me hesitate. I paused, glancing at the wood for a long moment.

A sad smile ghosted my lips before I wiped it clean, moments before entering the salon.

Feeling the tug at that special, glowing cord, I followed the trail to the center of the salon. A new dais had been erected with a blood red and black throne upon it. Sitting there, looking regal as ever, was a man who did not know how to *relax*.

I strolled up to the throne and casually sank down on his lap.

Green eyes bore into me and a thick dark brow rose in amusement. Stroking back the long gray tresses, I stared down at my Master with a smile.

"All work and no play, huh?" I mused.

Sterling grinned at me.

"There is much to do."

With a roll of my eyes, I bent forward to place my lips on his, sliding my tongue along the petal soft swell of his bottom lip.

"Even *you* need a break," I whispered. "Let me help you relieve some of that stress."

"Beau," Sterling groaned, but I was already crawling between his legs. Massaging his muscular thighs through the thin nylon of his pants, it took little to release his cock from the confines, using only my mouth.

The thick length of him swelled before my eyes, standing

proud, veins throbbing. My fangs descended as I watched him. Then with a devious smirk, I ignored his dick, nuzzling the crook of his thigh where it met his pelvis. Moving my hands up his thighs to the waist of his pants, I tugged them down. He raised his hips to help me.

When they were low enough and his naked skin was exposed to me, I found that spot again and nuzzled my nose there.

Flicking my gaze up to meet his, I trailed the tip of my tongue along his skin right above his femoral artery. A shuddering sigh left his lips as he tilted his head back.

I struck, sinking my fangs deep. Spicy, citrusy blood flooded my mouth and it was like all the stars had aligned. My eyes fluttered closed as I savored the taste of his blood. Rich and powerful. Heady. Warm. *Perfect*.

It was everything. Just like him.

Sterling groaned, hands flying to my head as his hips undulated. The thick cock I had ignored strained and bobbed, slapping my cheek with every involuntary jerk of Sterling's hips.

Pulling back, I licked the squirting blood, watching as the wound sealed before retracting my fangs and putting my mouth on something else.

Sterling's cock sank deep down my throat. I relaxed around the length of him, humming so he could feel the vibrations.

"You goddamn incubus," he hissed, hand fisting my hair as he held my head down for a few moments. Upon my release, I pulled off with a gasp and chuckle, catching my breath, then sealing my lips back over his crown.

I sucked and licked until his balls tightened and cock jerked.

"Fuck!" he moaned as cum flooded my mouth.

I swallowed, barely tasting it. Tucking him neatly back in his pants, I watched as he sank into the seat, near boneless.

"Better?" I grinned.

His eyes cracked open a little to stare at me before he laughed.

"You're dangerous."

"I know," I sang, before standing. "They'll be arriving soon."

"Already here!" a familiar voice called. I turned and saw three figures approaching. Ones I hadn't seen in *ages*.

I ran to the one who spoke, wrapping him in a hug. Light brown skin flushed in response, with eyes a startling amber–much different from the hazel I remembered–cheeks still dimpled, and...bright red hair.

That's new.

I stepped back to look at him. "Vampirism looks good on you, Blake."

Blake smiled widely, fangs fully extended as if to show off.

Behind him, ever the stone statue, stood Obi, mask and gloves firmly in place. That sadness that always seemed to shroud him, wasn't gone, but had lessened considerably.

I always knew they would be good for each other, they just needed to learn how to be.

Standing beside Obi was a smaller cloaked figure, aout five feet two inches with a dark red mask in place.

I bowed deeply.

Behind me I sensed Sterling approach. It was as if my own personal sensor was attuned to his heat, allowing me to feel it with great clarity.

He stared at the figure for a long while.

Everyone waited in silence, before finally, he sank into a deep bow.

The figure pulled their hood back and removed the mask. Staring back with big red jeweled eyes, a barely tamed mane of coils, and a face so similar to Lilith's it would be difficult not to mistake the two.

I smiled at her.

"Welcome home, Lilm."

The End.

BEAUTY AND THE BEAST

Obediah, Blake, Lilm, Stasia, and the twins will return in *Beauty and the Beast*. Coming soon...

ACKNOWLEDGMENTS

Putting this book together wasn't a solo gig, so I wanted to give a massive shout out to the people who helped make this possible!

Huge thank you to my readers on Patreon, Wattpad, and Tapas who enjoyed the story in its raw, unedited form.

To my family and friends who always provided endless support and lifted me up when my insecurities almost got the best of me during the publishing process, y'all are real ones.

A SUPER special thank you to my beta readers! Dango and Fosterkitten, thank you so much for all your help and being able to work within my crazy deadlines, catching details that slipped through the cracks. And Aurora...your help was *invaluable*. Thank you so so much for all your suggestions and commentary. You guys are all the *best*!

And of course, thank you to my amazing Patrons whose support made this a reality.

Phoenix Tier Patrons:
ALStoffregen
Cialysse
C S
Dawn
Hollie Scrivener
Isis1331
Nicola Honey
Nora Ranke
Oliver
VikaVex

ALSO BY N. A. MOORE

The Consorts (Chronicles of Astoria #1)

The Black Curse (Chronicles of Astoria #2) - Coming 2024

Heat (Heat #1)

Rut (Heat #2) - Coming Soon

Sick & Twisted: A Novella

ABOUT THE AUTHOR

N. A. Moore was born and raised in New Jersey. She began her creative journey early in life, reading whenever she could or filling up notebooks with fantastical stories. She started posting her stories online in 2008. She works as an artist and candle maker under the name The Awkward Bean with her kitty assistant, Icarus. She has an unhealthy obsession with coffee, anime, and Minecraft. You can visit her at her website: www.theawkwardbean.com or any social media!

- patreon.com/namoore
- instagram.com/author_namoore
- goodreads.com/firelipz
- facebook.com/AuthorN.A.Moore
- bookbub.com/profile/n-a-moore
- tiktok.com/@theawkwardbean
- youtube.com/@theawkwardbean
- x.com/author_namoore

N. A. MOORE

THE
CONSORTS
SECOND EDITION

THE CONSORTS - FIRST CHAPTER

AT THE AGE OF FOURTEEN, Killian Innis was brought before an Incubus and a Succubus. Both were tall and imposing, bare of all but thin white robes.

High King Ellis Innis of Astoria watched his son with an attendant by his side. He asked his child, voice careful but expectant, "Which of the two calls to you?"

Killian knew his father referred to his *Haise*, a feeding of lust and sexual energy that all S-Level Incubi and the rare few Succubi endure. It was the curse of their species that few were forced to bear.

As beautiful as both were, Killian found something alluring about the lean muscled Incubus with tawny skin and squared features. He ogled the male's impressive frame and intoxicating scent, feeling his chest tug him toward the Incubus. The prince stood with a crown too big and lips parted in wonder. His *choice* had been made.

"Ah, the Incubus, very well," the High King said simply, then gestured to the attendant who began writing. Killian had no idea that this choice would define his future, having been more concerned with the frivolous desires of a child.

The choice determined the pool of suitors he would choose from to be his Consorts. High King Ellis and the five females that made up his Consorts played a part in raising all four of their children. Jessa, the first impregnated and the High King's Rank One, was the High Queen Consort and Killian's mother.

It was incredibly important for the Royal family to reproduce as quickly and plentifully as possible. They were an example to be followed. A task that proved to be more of a burden than an honor.

Succession in Astoria was a competition of sorts. A tradition shared across all species...who could supply the heir first. It did not matter if the current heir was the carrier or the breeder. It was the responsibility of the chosen Consorts to plant or accept the seed that would bring about the next ruler.

But most species were allowed one Consort, two at most. Only Incubi and Succubi were allotted five based on the Astorian hierarchy put into place by the first rulers of Ancient Astoria. It kept the Incubi numbers inexhaustible and limited the repopulation of other royal lines.

None were able to compete against the strength and power of the Incubi race. Some tried, but most learned to adjust.

The Gods above, in their sacred home amongst the Clouds, willed it so. They watched, but did not interfere, showing their blessing. Incubi would not have been built for success had it not been the plan of the divine. They were *chosen*.

As firstborn, it was Killian's duty to maintain order after his father stepped down, as well as continue the line of ruling. From the moment he was born, he became sacred. His body and his virtue were of the highest value and to compromise them in any way was treason. He understood why, purity being of the utmost importance when aiming to please the Gods, but it still left him isolated. There were many things he could not take part in because of the risks, while his siblings could do as they pleased.

It had been that way for twenty-three years, six moon cycles, and fourteen days.

At times, Killian wished he hadn't been born first or that he was a normal Incubus. Sure, S-Level Incubi were revered as precious and special–those who experienced the *Haise* were the purest of their kind–but he didn't care about that. He wanted to be free like his siblings, making his own choices and not dealing with the complications that made up his biology.

As if ruling an entire Realm wasn't terrifying enough.

"Are you ready to be dressed, Your Highness?" a voice called from beyond the grand door of the bath. Killian moaned as a thick heat wrapped around his body like an embrace he never had. It would be the last time he bathed alone.

"I will be out in a short moment," Killian called in the soft, even tone he always maintained.

He climbed out of the bath slowly, letting the steam kiss his flushed lavender skin. The bright maroon curls he had inherited from his mother, swayed with the weight of the water pouring, clinging to his skin with an aggressive grip.

After drying himself with a fluffy towel from the heating rack, he slipped into a silky red robe bearing his family's crest of four horns wrapped in vines. Not his first choice in fashion, but he would not complain. He *never* complained.

When he opened the door, Ethel and Kara, his attendants, were waiting for him. They had his clothes ready once they ushered him back to his room. It was a special occasion which meant the outfit was incredibly intricate.

Killian pulled on his sheer white undergarments, which made a mockery of his claim to purity even if the latter was true, and white shorts made of soft silk. Kara helped fasten the skirt while piling layers of gold and rubies, only serving to weigh him down.

The attendants slipped him into a tight white sleeveless vest that exposed his upper hips before attaching a long white mesh cape to his shoulders, three gold armbands on his biceps and forearm, before a crown was gingerly placed on his head. He remained unfazed as they tugged his tail through the opening in the back. After being handled this way his entire life, he'd hardly noticed the slight violation.

Though he wore it with pride, Killian had to admit, this was the most revealing and daring outfit he had ever adorned. His stomach filled with agitated little flutters at the knowledge of anyone other than his attendants seeing him this way. Exposed as he was, it suggested that he was finally reaching a new point in his life where this was acceptable. It was the first step toward that tiny sliver of freedom he so desperately craved.

The attendants stepped back and smiled in approval at their work. A firm knock interrupted their admiration.

"Come in," Killian called.

A servant poked her head in, informing them that it was time for the official announcement.

Nervousness settled in Killian's gut. Was he ready for this? Truly?

He had never been around other Incubi aside from his brothers and father. Once his attraction to Incubi had been declared, the ones that worked in the palace were forbidden to come anywhere near him. No exceptions. He only ever had Succubi as his servants or attendants. The unknown terrified him.

"Don't be frightened, this is a joyous moment in your life, Your Highness. One that you have been eagerly waiting for," Ethel said sweetly to the quivering prince. She was older, with short gray hair and pale blue skin. Killian adored her. When he was younger, she would sneak him pastries before dinner and always told the most amazing stories before bed. She was closer to him than his own mothers, and he had five.

"I am worried they may not find me appealing. I do not wish to force anyone to be my Consort if they do not have feelings for me," Killian admitted. Worry shone raw in his red jeweled eyes.

"Nonsense! You are kind, gentle, intelligent, and absolutely beautiful. There are none who would not fall to your feet. Do not fret," Ethel insisted, her smile even wider than before. It did not go unnoticed that the traits she emphasized were not ones he wanted to be defined by. Artificial and shallow, how could that possibly bear the fruit of love?

Even so, Killian let himself be reassured by her words. The tightness in his chest eased and the clenching in his gut became less intense. He let out a soft breath before smiling at the older Succubus, finally ready to meet his Potentials.

As they made their way to the main hall, Killian's heart began to thump rapidly again. He doubted anything could be said to make him calm down at this point. He could hear nothing over the blood rushing in his ears.

Killian didn't know if he was ready. What if he couldn't decide? What if he didn't like any of them?

What if...they didn't love him back?

When they finally approached the tall double doors that led to the main hall, Killian was close to fainting.

"You'll be fine," Ethel whispered as the trumpet blared and the doors opened.

Killian couldn't hear the attendant announce his arrival over the blood rushing in his ears from his overactive heart. Instead, he relied on his other senses, hoping they'd guide him through what was sure to be a disaster of his own making.

The High King stood before his throne with High Queen Jessa. Killian's siblings and Consort mothers were standing a little off to the side, whispering to each other. He didn't want to look, but his eyes couldn't help drifting over to the line of Incubi, at attention with their legs slightly spread, wings exposed, and hands clasped behind their backs. All twenty-five males waiting for his perusal.

Each one wore a small black loincloth showcasing their sculpted physiques. While looks were important to some degree, the real intention was a display of their strength and physical capabilities.

Not that the outward appearance told all, Killian thought to himself. Traditions were as strange as they were performative. Something he had learned to grin and bear early on in life.

He averted his gaze, careful not to make any impolite noises. Though as if she could sense his discomfort and real risk of embarrassing himself, Lisa, his third and least friendly attendant, shot him a warning glare as they proceeded forward.

Killian and his attendants bowed respectfully as the High King came to greet him. High King Ellis looked as regal as ever, with his long chocolate brown waves plaited down his back, and body draped in the magnificent reds and whites he favored. His gray eyes sparkled with pride and excitement. So much so that one might mistake this for *his* Consort ceremony.

"Father," Killian said softly.

"Killian, you are breathtaking. A spitting image of your mother at our ranking ceremony. The rubies were a nice touch, eh?" He said, winking at Ethel.

Ethel nodded in agreement. "Yes indeed, Your Majesty."

No matter how old, High King Ellis could charm the pants off anyone he set his sights on. It was a dangerous skill that Killian had hoped he would one day acquire, and yet, he managed to fall short once again.

"Come, meet your Potentials. If you see one you do not like, they will be discarded at once," High King Ellis announced, voice boisterous and commanding, reverberating off the vast walls and echoing in the tense silence.

Killian's heart hammered behind his chest with the sincere hope that he wouldn't throw up. That would make for one awkward first impression and Lisa would quite actually murder him.

Guided by the High King, they turned toward the line of Potentials.

Each one was huge; tall and incredibly muscular. The shortest of them towered over Killian by at least a foot. Their faces were void of emotion as they looked forward and not at the royals as was instructed.

Prince Killian was to inspect them, not the other way around.

The King put his hand on Killian's back, gently leading them to the front of the line, to begin the inspection.

As they approached each Potential, the High King ordered the Incubi to state their name and region. It was important for the High King's Consorts to be diverse in background, preferring each chosen to be from a different region.

Of course, there was no way in his frazzled state that Killian would remember the information presented, but it would give him a little insight. What he didn't know could always be asked of his attendants.

As they progressed down the line, Killian found himself surprised at the experience. He expected to be attracted to them all, but some held the same interest as his kin, completely platonic. Was it supposed to be that way?

His inexperience in the matter made him uncomfortable, but he worked hard not to let it show. Wiping all but a pleasantly blank expression from his face, favoring none over the other.

High King Ellis, on the other hand, enjoyed himself a little too much. He was open with his interest and blatant perusal. It couldn't be easy remaining calm under such an intimidating inspection, but the males all managed. That alone was impressive.

"Go on Killian, see what you're working with," High King Ellis encouraged. Killian fought not to react at his father's audacity. It shouldn't have come as a surprise, High King Ellis had always been...*eccentric*.

The High King stepped up to a Potential with bright green skin and hair like spun gold, tied tightly in a ponytail, bound with a worn red ribbon. He looked at the Potential intensely before grabbing their genitals through the cloth, giving them a quick squeeze, then pulled the material away to peek.

A collective gasp of surprise came from the servants and attendants watching while Killian's mothers all giggled knowingly. To Killian's surprise, the Potential didn't even flinch. There was no outward change to his stance, expression, or demeanor.

The King turned to his son with a wide grin.

"This one's packin'." He jerked his thumb at the Potential he just groped before ordering, "Name and region."

"Drek Leon of Gemp, Your Majesty," the Potential replied in a low, even tone that made Killian shiver. The sensation foreign.

"I like him, keep this one," High King Ellis laughed before continuing down the line of suitors.

Killian vaguely heard High Queen Jessa scold him. "This is *Killian's* ceremony, not yours, Ellis."

Killian blushed but kept his head high as he passed the Potential.

Drek snuck a glance at him, bright green eyes twinkling. Then he smirked, causing Killian to blush even harder. The damn blush always gave him away. Lisa was going to give him an earful after this.

They walked slowly down the line until Killian found

himself transfixed by a Potential with onyx skin. He hadn't realized he stopped in front of him, admiring the Incubus. Something about him fascinated the young prince, either his solid black eyes or the four pointed horns protruding from his forehead.

Most Incubi and Succubi had two. Stronger ones leaned more toward three. The exceptionally powerful had four, like the royal bloodline. Very few had strength that matched the royal family, less than twenty total. To think this Incubus was one of them...

The Potential's face was carved like the gem his skin resembled, with a sharp jawline, elegantly slanted deep-set eyes, a wild mane of long black hair, and sinfully full lips. His ears were pointed–another sign of power–and his body was incredible. He oozed authority and dominance. Killian was left in awe.

"Found one you like?" High King Ellis mused, then addressed the Potential, "Name and region."

"Rem Brangwen of Tenebris, Your Majesty."

His voice was a deep baritone that nearly coaxed a soft moan from Killian's lips. He hadn't realized his eyes had fluttered shut until they popped open again and he was staring into pitch-black depths. The Potential had him locked in his gaze; he was unable to tear himself away.

The High King smiled knowingly. "Why don't you touch him, Killian?"

Killian knew his father would keep pushing until he did it at least once. If there were ever a male he wanted to touch, it was the one before him.

Killian swore his father enjoyed making him uncomfortable.

With a deep breath, Killian stepped up to the Potential, heart sputtering. He didn't have it in him to be as daring as his father, but he did tentatively place a hand on the Potential's chest.

The skin beneath his palm was warm and soft. There were raised symbols pressed in his chest. They danced around his left pectoral and trailed their way down his bicep. Killian brushed his fingertips over the marks, feeling every rise and dip, embedding it into his memory.

This close, Killian could smell him. It was an intoxicating scent like clove and myrrh. Killian shivered, involuntarily stepping even closer. His fingers grazed the Potential's impressive pectorals again when he noticed the left nipple was pierced with a silver hoop.

Killian wanted to touch it yet chose to hold himself back. Instead, his hand traveled south, down every ripple of abs. Killian could feel the Incubus' dark eyes boring into him unwaveringly. The gaze heated his skin wherever it landed, branding him through the fabric of his gaudy clothes.

"Your wings," Killian whispered a little breathlessly, unable to make his voice any louder in fear of what embarrassing noises might escape and the lectures that would follow.

The Potential immediately unfurled his wings. The spines were black like the rest of him, but the webbing was a dark red. Killian could see the tiny black veins, pulsing with blood as the sunlight tried and failed to pierce the wall of them.

The waves of power radiating off him were almost enough to call Killian's *Haise*.

Killian backed away from the Potential feeling dizzy and disoriented.

"Are you well, Prince Killian?" Ethel asked, appearing beside him.

"Y-yes, I am fine," he answered shakily, hating the slip of composure. It showed *weakness,* which would never be tolerable from a King.

"Rem, what is your combat specialty?" The King asked, continuing the assessment.

"I excel in all weaponry."

Killian shivered as he spoke again. The King's eyes widened, clearly impressed. Killian's Consorts would not just be his lovers; they would be his protectors, advisors, best friends, and his family. It was required for them to be highly skilled in combat.

"Lisa, take note of this one," High King Ellis commanded.

"Yes, Your Majesty," Lisa obeyed, writing on her parchment pad furiously.

"Come, Killian." His father pulled him away from the Potential. He followed reluctantly, fighting the instincts that begged him to stay, to touch.

Killian's eyes lingered on his black skin before they slid to the next male.

This one was the stark opposite of the previous, with bright white skin as vibrant as freshly fallen snow and long straight hair to match. His eyes were as black as the previous Potential's skin, completely consuming his sockets. He had two pointed black horns to match. His symmetrical features, small mouth, and elegantly sloped nose gave him a soft appearance that appealed to the prince.

"Name and region," the King said when he noticed Killian had stopped again.

"Faust Akili of Sapientae, Your Majesty," his voice kind and gentle like a soothing lullaby.

"Take note of this one too, Lisa."

"Yes, Your Majesty."

They continued down the line and found a couple more that fascinated Killian before they were all dismissed.

After briefly speaking to his parents, Killian retired to his rooms, until his siblings came bursting in, disrupting his peace as they sometimes did. The excitement over the ceremony and having them all together after such a long time fizzled in the air.

It was for those reasons alone that Killian didn't kick them out, instead, letting them take over his sitting room.

"Killian, you are so lucky! They were gorgeous! I wish I was heir," Gilra sighed dreamily as her eldest brother sat gracefully on the couch across from her, back straight, but unable to keep his composure completely intact. He nervously fiddled with the jewels in his ridiculously gaudy belt, only stopping when he looked up to address his sister.

"But then you'd never be able to sing at galas," Killian said with a gentle smile. His tone was sweet, conveying none of his underlying bitterness.

Gilra, the second youngest sibling, was born to their father's Rank Five. She had a Cloud given voice and frequently sang at banquets and galas in town. She made numerous friends and almost always had company over. Killian was rarely allowed near her.

"I like that Orion guy, he looks like he's good with a sword," Pierce said with a grin. "Pick him, brother, so I can spar with him."

Pierce was still in his training uniform, short white hair slicked back and blue eyes glowing with excitement. He was the youngest of the four siblings, born to their father's Rank Three. He was always with the warriors, training in combat. The King said it would most likely be Pierce who took over the mantle of Lieutenant or General of the Astorian Army.

"That Rem guy looked like he could take them all without breaking a sweat. If you want someone to spar with, little brother, that's the one," Ian pointed out, lounging comfortably on the chair, resting his arms casually along the back of it.

Killian was elated that Ian came home for this. Ian, the second oldest, right after Killian, born to their father's Rank Two, spent his days traveling the world, establishing relations with foreign Kingdoms, learning new languages and cultures. It was something Killian would never be able to do. Astoria was too large. He needed to be in Heltzig at the main palace. If there were ever an emergency in the fifteen regions, ambassadors needed to know where he would be. They came to him, not the other way around. A dominance tactic that only served to limit his freedom further.

Ian arrived last night from Tarr, crossing three seas to get here. Killian knew Ian's mother had a lot to do with it, but the gesture was still appreciated. He looked just like her with navy shoulder-length hair and bright green eyes.

"I think Rei has my heart already," Gilra giggled.

Pierce whacked her on the head.

"Keep your heart to yourself, idiot!"

Gilra pouted while the rest laughed.

"Who do you like, Killian?" Gilra asked. When three pairs of eyes fell on him, the laughter died from his lips. His mind immediately went to the black-skinned Incubus. Killian held in his shudder of pleasure just from the thought of that deep voice and soft skin.

"We already know the answer to that. You saw how long he stayed with that Rem guy. Only one he touched too. I was almost certain he would bust a *Haise* right then and there."

Killian glared at his youngest brother.

"You are so crude, Pierce!"

Pierce shrugged and grinned.

"I do not know what to think. This is the first time I have been around Incubi that I am not related to. It is...overwhelming."

"Well, whoever you don't pick, I'll take them," Gilra sang.

"I second that," Pierce piped up.

Killian rolled his eyes and laughed with them, but a part of him was annoyed. They always wanted what little he had when they had what Killian did not, the world at their feet.

They had billions to choose from for suitors, but they wanted his twenty-five.

He pushed the ugly thoughts away and continued to jest with his siblings until Lisa entered the room.

"Your Highnesses, it is time for dinner."

The siblings rose and headed for the dining hall. Killian sat next to the High King across from High Queen Jessa while the rest of his Consort mothers and siblings filled out other available seats.

Food was served immediately after seating.

"Killian, what did you think? Who was your favorite out of the males presented?" The High King asked as they all devoured their food.

"Well, we all know the answer to that. It was clearly the Incubi with skin as black as coal," Mae smirked.

Killian ducked his head and blushed furiously before uttering in a small voice, "Was it really that obvious?"

"Yes," everyone chorused.

Killian sighed, trying not to let his embarrassment show.

"There is nothing wrong with that. He looks strong, capable, intelligent; an excellent choice for a High Consort and even better for a King," High King Ellis said.

"I do not know what I want."

"It's okay, sweetheart. You take all the time you need to figure it out," High Queen Jessa said gently, regarding Killian with red eyes that mirrored his own.

After dinner, Killian had a few lessons with a history scholar before it was time to retire for the night.

"Did you want to take a bath before resting, Your Highness?" Lisa asked.

Killian knew some of the Potentials would be in there right now and while he may be required to wear his robes now when he bathed, he knew they were not. That was something he was not quite ready for.

"You can try all you want to avoid them, but now that they are here, it will be impossible to do so for long," Lisa tsked before leaving the prince to sleep. Killian collapsed in his bed, thoroughly exhausted.

Almost immediately he fell asleep, dreaming of waking up in someone's arms.

Heat
AN OMEGAVERSE COLLECTION

N.A. MOORE

HEAT - FIRST CHAPTER

BRAN

The Autumn wind began to chill. Still, so early in the season, the temperature change felt like a drop of ice in a warm drink. Sudden, though unnoticeable, before it gradually dulled the heat into a gentle coolness. The leaves were still young and green, hardly beginning that rapid decline to bright yellows and crispy browns.

It was moments before dusk. The sky was still brightened by the setting sun that was hardly visible over the horizon, painting the world in a beautiful red violet.

As mesmerizing as it was, Bran couldn't spare it more than a glance. His pacing had grown near violent as each minute ticked by.

Where is he?

It was almost eight. He was supposed to be here two hours ago!

Sweat trickled down the back of his neck despite the low temperature in the house. The fire was raging in the hearth and the fluffy brown rug before it looked inviting, but Bran knew his body would protest if he stayed still for too long.

Not with it so close.

The front door clicked, and Bran raced for it.

"Honey! I'm home!" Kain sang, as he juggled a bunch of shopping bags and shuffled inside. Bran stormed toward him, anger hot in his veins.

"Don't you *'honey'* me! Where have you *been?*" the Omega demanded, fury a live writhing beast inside him.

Kain sighed, clicking the door shut and setting the bags on the ground. His tall broad frame swallowed Bran whole as he scooped him up close, burying his nose in his hair. Bran sighed, feeling himself grow calm with Kain's scent.

"I wanted to make sure we had everything we needed. I already called out of work, so I'm yours for the week, okay?" Kain reassured softly, his deep honey voice sending tingles down the Omega's spine.

"I *need* you," Bran whimpered against his chest, nuzzling closer to his warmth, combating the heat that still blazed from within.

"I know, love of mine. I'm here," Kain murmured, rocking him gently.

They stayed like that for a few minutes until Bran's anger had completely receded and he was floating on a wave of bliss. He protested when Kain pulled away, but the Alpha kissed his forehead and said, "The ice cream will melt."

"Mint chip?" Bran asked softly.

Kain grinned down at him, his green eyes sparkling. "Of course."

Bran grinned back.

He bent down to scoop up the bags and disappeared into the kitchen. Bran could faintly hear the cabinets being opened and closed. He slowed his breathing before following the Alpha into the kitchen.

Kain barely glanced up as he finished putting everything away, keeping out a few materials and pulling out a plate, knife, and cutting board.

"Babe, why don't you go start the bath? I'll make the platter."

"Not hungry," Bran pouted, knowing he was being a brat. But he always lost his appetite around this time...well for food at least.

Kain frowned at him. "You know you need to eat. You need all your strength and energy. You don't want to burn out."

Bran continued to pout until Kain sighed and slid his arms around the Omega's waist, pressing their foreheads together. His green eyes filled Bran's entire vision. His medium brown skin shimmered in the faint glow of the house.

He was so beautiful.

His Alpha.

Kain kissed Bran's neck and the Omega moaned, pushing into him.

"Go start the bath, I'll be there in a minute," his low throaty voice commanded.

Bran pushed against him harder.

"Such a stubborn Omega," he growled playfully before pulling back and smacking Bran's ass. "Do as you're told."

Bran grinned wickedly, "Yes, Alpha."

He sashayed out of the kitchen to the master bathroom and started to fill the large jacuzzi tub. He put out a few scented candles around the bathroom and the bedroom to fill the space with pumpkin spice and apple cinnamon, some of his favorite scents for the season. Bran poured a few oils into the water as the tub filled. They were supposed to help with his hormone release. Keep him calm, or so the doctors liked to tell him.

The bath was nearly full by the time Kain swept in, closing

the door behind him, balancing a large plate full of meats and cheese cubes. He set it down on the small table that was set up near the bath.

"How long?" he asked.

"Ten, maybe twenty minutes," Bran said softly, admiring his strong and muscular frame. His five o'clock shadow was neatly shaped, matching his closely shaven head. His cheekbones were pronounced and his jaw sharp enough to cut glass.

The Omega stepped up close to him and brushed his fingers along his jaw, feeling the prickly hair scrape against his skin. He glared at him. "I thought you said you were going to shave."

Kain grinned sheepishly, rubbing his jaw.

"I like it too much," he said.

Bran's eyes narrowed into slits.

"Well, I *don't* like when it's scraping against my nether bits."

Kain came close and whispered, "I'll be careful."

Bran rolled his eyes, "Sure you will."

Kain laughed and the sound was magical.

His hands slid along Bran's sides before gently unknotting the belt to his robe. Ever so carefully pulling the fabric apart until the fluffy mass slipped off the Omega's shoulders and pooled on the ground at their feet. With his exposed body bare to Kain's gaze, Bran could feel the light kisses of his heat beginning to lick at his skin.

Kain's gaze traveled up and down his naked frame slowly. The Alpha's cock thickened in his trousers, bulging obscenely.

"Alpha mine, I've been waiting for you," Bran whispered.

Kain growled lowly.

With a smirk, the Omega backed away and dipped into the tub, loving the way the hot water hugged his body. Kain shed his clothes in record time, climbing in behind him before he could really appreciate the sight of his Alpha's naked body. But Bran felt it, pressed snuggly against his backside, just begging to be buried deep within him.

Bran purred, moving closer until his back was flush against Kain's chest.

The Alpha washed him slowly, tenderly. Occasionally slipping a piece of meat or cheese in the Omega's mouth. The platter was gone in record time. If Kain hadn't been the one feeding him, Bran never would have put anything in his stomach. His Alpha took such good care of him.

Bran settled against Kain, feeling his eyelids droop.

"Soon," Bran whispered, then turned his face until his cheek pressed against Kain's shoulder. "Do you think this time we'll...?" he couldn't finish that question. The anxiety curled in his gut, but his wonderful mate knew what he was trying to say. Kain *always* knew. They were two halves of a whole.

"We will have our family. Don't fret, Omega mine. Be patient."

They'd been trying for so long, Bran was starting to think there was something wrong with him. Kain didn't like when he doubted himself, but he couldn't help it. He wanted to give his Alpha a family. He wanted them to have a little one running around the house, causing a wreck so they could smother them with love. Bran wanted that so badly that it killed him inside when he thought he might not ever have it. That *Kain* would never have it, because of him.

Kain kissed the top of Bran's head and whispered sweet nothings in his ear. The Omega let himself be carried away by him, not even noticing when he pulled the Omega out of the bath and dried them both off. The heat was beginning.

Kain laid Bran on the bed gently and sat on the armchair across the room.

Bran frowned at him through the lust-filled haze.

"The doctor and psychiatrist both agreed to three knots a

day," Kain reminded him. "We don't want to push it, you could get sick again."

"Need you," the Omega mumbled.

"I know, Omega mine," Kain said softly but made no move toward him. Bran understood why, but it didn't make it any better. A part of him had hoped Kain wouldn't listen. That he would sense Bran's need and do it anyway, but that wasn't Kain. Especially after last time. The look on his Alpha's face when he woke up in the hospital would forever be imprinted in his mind. No...Kain wouldn't bend. Not about this.

Bran whimpered, starting to feel uncomfortable. His body heated and his limbs felt tight. He needed. He needed. He fucking *needed*.

His cock swelled against his thigh until it slowly stood at attention. He fought against touching it, knowing that once he did, he wouldn't be able to stop.

The Omega moaned, writhing on the sheets, feeling the slick slide out of him, wetting the bed slightly. Kain released a small wave of pheromones, coaxing his heat out. Bran mewled, toes curling, temperature rising.

He blindly reached under the pillow for the alpha dildo.

Kain was quick, hurrying over to snatch it from his hand, "Not yet, sweetheart. You're not ready, you'll hurt yourself."

Bran whined in protest, reaching for him, but he dodged and retreated to his chair.

"Need," Bran whimpered.

"I know, love. I know. Soon."

Bran knew Kain was only looking out for him, but it was frustrating being denied when he so desperately needed him. Bran wanted him to be as wild with lust as he was, but the doctor prescribed him Alpha suppressants so that he would be clear-headed during Bran's heat and better care for his needs.

Still, Bran couldn't stop the irrational thoughts from crowding his head.

He doesn't want me.

Why doesn't he want me?

Tears filled his eyes.

Bran fisted the sheets, clenching his teeth, unable to hold back the hot tears that spilled out of his eyes and ran down his cheeks in heated streaks. Kain's face crumpled.

"Baby, what's wrong?" he asked, concern clear in his voice.

"You don't want me," Bran cried.

"Bran, you know that's not true. I love you. Of course I want you."

"Then why won't you touch me? I need it, Kain. Please," the Omega begged. He rose on all fours and crawled across the bed toward Kain. Bran watched as his Alpha's hands clamped on the edge of the armchair, his eyes wide as another wave of pheromones crashed into the Omega. Bran cried out, slick gushing from his hole, dripping down his thigh.

"Bran, stay on the bed," Kain warned.

Bran made it to the edge, carefully sliding one leg to the ground until his foot was pressed against the cool hardwood floor.

Kain swore.

"Bran, don't make me get the chain. I really don't want to tie you up."

"Then don't. Breed me, Alpha," Bran hummed.

Kain gulped audibly, before shaking his head to clear it. When he set his gaze on the Omega again, his eyes were clear and serious.

"Bran, get on the bed. Now," Command leaked in his voice.

Bran's body reacted on its own, moving back on the bed, but his body prepared to be stuffed full. He leaned his face down into the pillows, spread his legs, and presented himself to Kain. Arching his back, just the way he knew Kain liked it.

Exposed and completely vulnerable, Bran knew that no matter what, he was safe with the one he loved. Kain would never harm him or take advantage. He loved him too much to do so.

Safe. Cared for. Treasured. Loved.

He was *everything* to Bran.

"Gods, Bran!" Kain hissed.

The Omega rolled his hips, wiggling side to side. Beckoning with every fiber of his being. Bran willed Kain to come enter him. Claim him. Breed him.

"Need," Bran whispered.

"Touch yourself, sweetheart. Let me see," Kain commanded. Voice so impressively low, it made every molecule in his body burn.

Bran slid a hand back, feeling along his flushed skin until his fingers were coated in the wetness of his slick. He brushed the rim of puckered flesh and gasped in pleasure. Those feather-light touches were always the most shocking, the most pleasurable to his sensitive skin.

"That's right Bran, slide yourself inside. Feel that wet warmth," Kain groaned from across the room.

Bran did as he was told, slipping a finger inside and moaning in contentment, but still slightly frustrated. It wasn't nearly enough. He needed to be stuffed, filled to the brim with his Alpha's love. Needed him like he needed the blood in his veins.

"Need," Bran moaned.

"Put another one in, love," Kain commanded.

Bran stuck another finger inside, hissing at the stretch.

"Not enough," the Omega cried. "Please, Kain. I can't take it!"

"It hasn't even been an hour, sweetheart," Bran heard him

say softly, but it sounded so far away. His blood was pounding in his head, rushing in his ears. It felt like the world was boiling.

Bran clenched his teeth and dealt with it.

He'd experienced heats for years now and knew what to expect. Having an Alpha to help him through it was even better, but it wasn't easy. All his thoughts were fuzzy and irrational. He said and did things that he normally would be appalled by, but nothing mattered. Nothing but being knotted and pregnant.

And Kain.

He was so perfect, so understanding, so *caring*. He always knew what to do, the best way to help Bran. The Omega was so lucky to have him as an Alpha.

Because of Kain, he got through it every time.

The first hours of the heat were always the worst. Bran knew that he wasn't at his limit, but the urge to call out his safe word was so hard to fight. The only thing stopping him was the thought of betraying Kain's trust in him. Bran couldn't abuse the safe word. So, he endured.

"How are you feeling, love?" Kain asked softly. It had been about seven hours since the heat started, and the third wave was starting to ebb away. Drenched in sweat, Bran clutched the damp bed sheets, in his palms. His eyes could barely stay open, he was so exhausted.

"Tired," Bran groaned.

Kain chuckled, his voice much closer. His hands brushed the sweaty hair from the Omega's cheek. As much as Bran wanted to, he was way too tired to even lean into it.

"Up you go," Kain said as he wrapped Bran's limp arms around his neck and hauled him to the bathroom where he proceeded to clean him up. He placed the Omega in his robe, so full of his scent, and rested Bran in his chair while he changed the sheets on the bed. When he picked the Omega back up and slid him under the new sheets, Bran sighed, curling into his chest.

"How long, baby?" Kain whispered, his arms tightening around Bran.

"A couple of hours, maybe," he mumbled.

"Get some sleep then."

"Knot me next time?" Bran asked, voice leaking with desperation.

"We'll see," he said.

Bran whimpered, but Kain hushed him and pulled him closer.

His intoxicating scent lulled Bran right to sleep.

∽

Bran got a few hours in before the next wave hit him, stronger than before. He shoved the alpha dildo inside, but it failed to ease any of the discomforts he felt.

"Need!" Bran screamed, reaching for Kain.

The Alpha's hands were gentle but firm, yanking Bran's face to him. "Use your safe words, Bran."

"Breed. Breed. Breed. Breed," Bran chanted.

"*Bran*. Safe words."

God, he felt like he was *dying*.

Tears blurred his eyes. "Need!"

"Sweetheart, look at me. Listen to me. Green or Red?"

It hurts. It *hurts*.

"*Red!* Red, red, red! Please, Kain! Red!" Bran sobbed, shaking.

Kain was swift, pulling the dildo out. His lips pushed against the Omega's neck, breath hot and sweet. "I'm sorry Omega mine, I know you're hurting."

"Kain, *please*."

His heated lips scorched a trail between Bran's shoulder blades and down his back until they were right where the Omega wanted them. That place he needed to be filled.

His tongue, his hot tongue, his amazing tongue.

"*Kain!*"

Slurp. Slurp. Slurp.

Bran's thighs were shaking and his back ached, but he sank deeper into that arch, presenting himself fully to his husband.

Kain moved, his body flush against Bran from behind. The pads of his fingers traced up the Omega's ribs until they brushed the sensitive tips of his nipples. Bran gasped at the sensation, rocking his hips back against him.

"Easy, love. Easy," he murmured against the Omega's neck.

"Need," Bran whispered.

"I know, baby."

And then he pushed inside. The blunt head of him stretching Bran's slick opening. It burned slightly, but the pressure, the *sensation* of being filled, being *bred* was better than anything in the world.

"Relax, sweetheart. Deep breaths," Kain cooed. Bran could hear the tension in his voice, the strain. His body was like a rubber band pulled tautly, still, he kept pushing in, slowly, keeping himself in control.

Bran's teeth clenched as he hissed, eyes screwed shut, nails raking the sheets.

"Talk to me, baby. Green or Red?"

"Green, baby, *green*. Keep going, don't stop!" Bran begged. Kain littered kisses on his neck, praising him, telling him how much he loved him and how happy he was to have him as a mate. He spoke promises about having a little one to cherish. He painted a picture for Bran until he was helplessly dreaming about the future.

Kain's thrusts were smooth and powerful. They had him drooling into the pillows. Bran met him for each one. Eager. Clenching his body around Kain's length. It was heaven.

"Fuck baby, I'm gonna knot," Kain whispered.

"Knot me, Kain. Breed me, Alpha mine."

Kain's hips snapped up sharply, nearly raising his own off the bed. Kain stayed there, pressed tightly to him. And then he felt it.

Felt it like the sun on his skin, like the breath in his lungs. Expanding, growing, molding him to his lover.

"Yes," Bran hissed.

This is what he needed.

Bran sighed in contentment as Kain's knot grew to its full form. And in a wave of heat, the Alpha released inside him. Coating his insides, owning him so completely. Enough to shatter him right there in climax.

Both of them were left panting. Bran purred in contentment.

Kain let out a breathless laugh. "Feeling better baby?"

"Much."

Made in the USA
Las Vegas, NV
05 February 2025